Edith Wharton and the Conversations of Literary Modernism

*To Dakin —
See what you helped get started?
Thanks!
Jennifer*

American Literature Readings in the 21st Century

Series Editor: Linda Wagner-Martin

American Literature Readings in the 21st Century publishes works by contemporary critics that help shape critical opinion regarding literature of the nineteenth and twentieth century in the United States.

Published by Palgrave Macmillan:

Freak Shows in Modern American Imagination: Constructing the Damaged Body from Willa Cather to Truman Capote
By Thomas Fahy

Arab American Literary Fictions, Cultures, and Politics
By Steven Salaita

Women & Race in Contemporary U.S. Writing: From Faulkner to Morrison
By Kelly Lynch Reames

American Political Poetry in the 21st Century
By Michael Dowdy

Science and Technology in the Age of Hawthorne, Melville, Twain, and James: Thinking and Writing Electricity
By Sam Halliday

F. Scott Fitzgerald's Racial Angles and the Business of Literary Greatness
By Michael Nowlin

Sex, Race, and Family in Contemporary American Short Stories
By Melissa Bostrom

Democracy in Contemporary U.S. Women's Poetry
By Nicky Marsh

James Merrill and W.H. Auden: Homosexuality and Poetic Influence
By Piotr K. Gwiazda

Contemporary U.S. Latino/a Literary Criticism
Edited by Lyn Di Iorio Sandín and Richard Perez

The Hero in Contemporary American Fiction: The Works of Saul Bellow and Don DeLillo
By Stephanie S. Halldorson

Race and Identity in Hemingway's Fiction
By Amy L. Strong

Edith Wharton and the Conversations of Literary Modernism
By Jennifer Haytock

Edith Wharton and the Conversations of Literary Modernism

Jennifer Haytock

EDITH WHARTON AND THE CONVERSATIONS OF LITERARY MODERNISM
Copyright © Jennifer Haytock, 2008.

Permissions:
Harry Ransom Humanities Research Center
The University of Texas at Austin

University of Nebraska Press, for reprinting a revised version of "Marriage and Modernism in Edith Wharton's *Twilight Sleep*"

All rights reserved. No part of this book may be used or reproduced in any manner whatsoever without written permission except in the case of brief quotations embodied in critical articles or reviews.

First published in 2008 by
PALGRAVE MACMILLAN™
175 Fifth Avenue, New York, N.Y. 10010 and
Houndmills, Basingstoke, Hampshire, England RG21 6XS
Companies and representatives throughout the world.

PALGRAVE MACMILLAN is the global academic imprint of the Palgrave Macmillan division of St. Martin's Press, LLC and of Palgrave Macmillan Ltd. Macmillan® is a registered trademark in the United States, United Kingdom and other countries. Palgrave is a registered trademark in the European Union and other countries.

ISBN-13: 978–0–230–60469–8
ISBN-10: 0–230–60469–2

Library of Congress Cataloging-in-Publication Data

Haytock, Jennifer Anne.
   Edith Wharton and the conversations of literary modernism / by Jennifer Haytock.
      p. cm.—(American literature readings in the 21st century)
   Includes bibliographical references.
   ISBN 0–230–60469–2
   1. Wharton, Edith, 1862–1937—Criticism and interpretation. 2. Wharton, Edith, 1862–1937—Political and social views. 3. Wharton, Edith, 1862–1937—Knowledge—Modernism (Literature) 4. Modernism (Literature)—United States. I. Title.

PS3545.H16Z6625 2008
813'.52—dc22
                                                                2007035675

A catalogue record for this book is available from the British Library.

Design by Newgen Imaging Systems (P) Ltd., Chennai, India.

First edition: May 2008

10 9 8 7 6 5 4 3 2 1

Printed in the United States of America.

*To
Benjamin Michael
and
Elizabeth Grace*

Contents

Acknowledgments   ix

Introduction   1

1 Troubling the Subjective: The Problem of Impressionism in *The Reef*   21

2 "Any Change May Mean Something": *Summer*, Sexuality, and Single Women   45

3 "Unmediated Bonding Between Men": The Accumulation of Men in the Short Stories   75

4 "A Sign of Pain's Triumph": War, Art, and Civilization   101

5 "The Readjustment of Personal Relations": Marriage, Modernism, and the Alienated Self   131

6 Antimodernism and Looking Pretty: Wharton's Artistic Practice   159

Afterword   181

Notes   185

Bibliography   193

Index   201

Acknowledgments

I wish to thank Kelly Reames, Elizabeth Jane Wall Hinds, Lara Kees, Amy Guptill, and RUSH (Rochester area United States History writing group) for their time in reading and commenting on this manuscript. I am grateful to The College at Brockport, The State University of New York, Colleen Donaldson, and United University Professions for facilitating and awarding me the Dr. Nuala McGann Drescher Leave. Special thanks to Dakin Dalpoas. As always, I owe much gratitude to Linda Wagner-Martin.

I am indebted to the Beinecke Rare Book and Manuscript Library at Yale University for assisting me with the Edith Wharton Collection. I also thank the Harry Ransom Humanities Research Center at the University of Texas at Austin for help with the Edith Wharton Collection and for permission to publish from her letters. Thanks to *Legacy: A Journal for American Women Writers*, in which an earlier version of chapter 5 first appeared, and to the Edith Wharton Society, at whose conference I presented a portion of this manuscript.

Introduction

Refashioning Wharton and Modernism

This study has two interrelated impulses: specifically, to expand the ways we view Edith Wharton and her writing and, more broadly, to rethink the way we discuss literary modernism. Although usually considered a feminist realist writer, Wharton and her oeuvre do not rest comfortably in those bounds. She was a curious woman, and that curiosity produced decades of sustained creative engagement with the world around her. Literary modernism historically excludes her, however, because the established definition of modernism has been built around a masculinist vision of art and the individual. I show that Wharton concerned herself closely with the ideas of modernism: the break from Victorianism, the impact of World War I on the individual and society, the isolated self, the possibilities and limitations of language, and the nature of the artist and the artist's role in society—it is on these last issues that she differs most from modern writers, and these differences are the source of her greater unease with the modernist movement. To facilitate my investigation, I have organized this book around a series of contested topics related to literary modernism, including the influences and implications of French Impressionist art, changing attitudes toward women in light of new perceptions about female sexuality, the interrogation of the mysteries of patriarchal power, the problem of a unified sense of culture in light of World War I, the subjective self in the intimacy of marriage, and the nature of the artist. As my title suggests, the issues of modernism demand debates: there are at least two sides to these questions, and by simply accepting a traditional definition of modernism, we lose important voices in what may be the most crucial conversation in twentieth-century aesthetics.

The categories of realist, sentimental, naturalist, and modern that literary scholars so prefer to use for late nineteenth- and early twentieth-century writers rarely fit the practice of the living, breathing artist. Thus I do not postulate that Wharton was or was not a modernist, but rather my project investigates the ways in which Wharton participated in some of the literary and cultural conversations of her time. Wharton was interested in women's lives and the forces that shaped them, including marriage, divorce, socially prescribed behavior, sexuality, money, and power. Women's experiences were not openly regarded as interesting or pressing by the authors and critics of the 1920s who initially defined the scope of modernism, yet as we look back on the twentieth century, the changes in women's lives that began around the turn of the twentieth century profoundly affected our ideas of work, family, sexual politics, and sexual identity. Wharton's position as a professional writer left her feeling unsexed at times,[1] but such floating gender identification allowed her greater scope. It also reinforced her experience of gender as created. If modernism, in its early narrow definition, did not recognize her literary contributions for their profound artistic and cultural value, we see now that those contributions are vital to our understanding of a changing world.

Wharton herself chose not to identify as a modernist writer. Late in life, she lamented the tendency of young writers to disregard old forms and established values in favor of radical experiments and a rigid adherence to "theory." I do not dispute that Wharton overtly rejected modernist forms, that modernist writers frequently (although not always) disavowed the past, or that the "amorality" Wharton saw in modern fiction existed. Rather, I argue that once we take a broader look at modernism we see Wharton's engagement with it—her "uneasy dialogue," as Amy Kaplan puts it (66). Literary debate over the beginning of modernism indicates clearly that the forces that thrust modernist literature to the forefront of the 1920s were at work well before that fruitful, tumultuous decade. Wharton lived through social, cultural, and political changes that affected the growth of modernism, reflected on artistic movements that led to modernism, and addressed influences on modernism in her own writing.

EDITH WHARTON'S MIDLIFE TURNING POINTS

Waiting for Ellen Olenska's train to arrive in Jersey City in the 1870s, Newland Archer of *The Age of Innocence* reflects on future possibilities for American life: "there were people who thought there would one day be a tunnel under the Hudson through which the trains of the Pennsylvania railway would run straight into New York. They were of the brotherhood of visionaries who likewise predicted the building of ships that would cross the Atlantic in five days, the invention of a flying machine, lighting by electricity, telephonic communication without wires, and other Arabian Night marvels" (284). Wharton wrote this passage in 1920, and with the benefit of hindsight, she described the technological developments that had altered her own world. Born in 1862, in the midst of the Civil War, dying in 1937, as the rumblings of World War II began to threaten across Europe, she witnessed some incredible events, from those that affected daily life, such as the bringing of electric light to streets and into homes, the invention and widespread use of the telephone, the creation of New York City's subway system, and the invention and increasingly ubiquitous presence of the automobile, to those that crashed an unsuspecting world, such as World War I and the Great Depression. Wharton lived through the years that saw the transformation of a rural, violently divided nation into what we consider the modern era, a world that we recognize today. Because she began her writing career later in life and often drew on earlier years in her life (particularly for the works for which she is most well known), it can be easy to forget how much change she saw—not only technological but also social, cultural, and literary.

Although she was born in New York, Edith Newbold Jones spent much of her childhood in Europe. In 1866, financial difficulties drove the Joneses overseas, where they could live more cheaply than they could in the United States. The family traveled across Europe, from Rome to Spain to Paris, where they stayed for two years. Abroad, Wharton learned to read as well as developed her faculty for languages and her absorption in the markers of culture and custom. In 1870, when the family was in Germany, she fell ill with typhoid and nearly died; she spent her recovery period reading. When Edith returned to New York in 1872 at the age of ten, she was so accustomed to European sights that she found the United States unbearable: in her unfinished and unpublished autobiographical fragment, *Life and I* (1932), she wrote that her first reaction to America was "*How ugly it is*" (19), claiming that this impression never went away and that she always felt "an exile in America" (20 emphasis in original).[2] Back in her native country, Edith found herself immersed in the confines of old New York, a wealthy, insular society that brooked no dissent and viewed artists as belonging to a lower class.[3] In her published autobiography, *A Backward Glance* (1934), Wharton describes the society in which she was raised as fiercely resistant to change and difference, although she also credits this community with "the concerted living up to long-established standards of honour and conduct, of education and manners" (5). Her biographers emphasize the limitations of old

New York. Shari Benstock, for example, in *No Gifts from Chance*, points out that "for American women of Edith's social class, education reined in rather than expanded their natural curiosity, cultivating in them a charming, but false, naïveté" (32). Due to her poor health and her parents' conventional fear that too much schooling was dangerous for girls, Edith did not receive a formal education but rather was let loose in "the kingdom of my father's library" (43). In *Life and I*, Wharton explains that her mother objected to novels, and until she was married, Wharton asked permission each time she wanted to read one. As a married woman, Wharton kept up a regular schedule of social obligations and ran her household like any other wealthy young matron. But she also preserved time for her writing, and in 1889, Edward Burlingame began printing her poems in *Scribner's* magazine. Ten years later, she published her first volume of short stories, *The Greater Inclination*.

Shaped by a society that restricted women and did not value artists, Wharton was not destined to live out her life in it or to be destroyed by it. After marrying Edward "Teddy" Wharton in 1885, designing and building her own house, The Mount, in Lenox, Massachusetts, and beginning a writing career, she escaped to Paris, where she experienced three crucial turning points in her life and in her writing: she had a passionate affair with William Morton Fullerton (1907–12), she divorced her husband (1913), and she saw firsthand the devastation of World War I (1914–18).

The affair with Fullerton, which Clare Colquitt calls "the most significant gamble Edith Wharton ever made" (79), has been much discussed by Wharton biographers and critics.[4] Wharton, then in her mid-forties, seems to have first experienced emotional and physical passion in this relationship. Wharton's letters to Fullerton show that with him she felt simultaneously the fullness of companionship and the terrible loneliness of knowing she cared for him more than he cared for her. In a later dated March 31 (no year given), Wharton insists on baring her soul to Fullerton even as she recognizes that he will eventually move on, if he has not already:

> No, I want you to know once for all what that feeling is—how grave & deep & tender—& how it has so illuminated my life & kindled my heart, that even now, with the certainty ahead of profound pain & a long, long abnegation, I give thanks, I rejoice, I exult in it, I would not exchange my lot for that of any other woman—except, dearest, alas! that of the woman who succeeds me in your heart...(Ransom Center)[5]

The letters also reveal her fear of her inadequacy as a lover, particularly in light of her awareness of his greater experience. In a heartbreaking letter, written in March 1908, she worries that her love and her expressions of it seem trite to him: "I'm so afraid that the treasures I long to unpack for you, that have come to me in magic ships from enchanted islands, are only, to you, the old familiar red calico & beads of the clever trader, who has had dealings in every latitude, & knows just what to carry in the hold to please the simple native—I'm so afraid of this, that often & often I stuff my shining treasures back into their box, lest I should see you smiling at them!" (Lewis and Lewis *Letters* 135). But the letter continues with a strong move of self-assertion on her part:

> Well! And if you do? It's *your* loss, after all! And if you can't come into the room without my feeling all over me a ripple of flame, & if, whenever you touch me, a heart beats under your touch, & if, when you hold me, & I don't speak, it's because all the words in me seem to have become throbbing pulses, & all my thoughts are a great golden blur—why should I be afraid of your smiling at me, when I can turn the beads & calico back into such beauty—? (emphasis in original)

Wharton shows her appreciation of her own talents—her ability to "turn the beads & calico back into such beauty." Indeed, Fullerton himself condescendingly but prophetically told her that she "would write better for this experience of loving" (162). Wharton's powerful novels *The Reef* (1912), *Summer* (1917), *The Age of Innocence* (1920), and *The Mother's Recompense* (1925) in particular prove him right, as each of these novels portrays the joys and sorrows of passion, elements strikingly absent from *The House of Mirth* (1905).

On the other hand, as Alan Gribben points out in his analysis of Wharton's letters to Fullerton, the relationship may have undermined Wharton's confidence in her writing ability and in language itself, as she came to realize "that her awesome writing skills were completely ineffectual at gaining what she wanted most" (18). Fullerton was incapable of fidelity, and the relationship seems to have had only a brief period of bliss before lapsing into on- and off-phases. Long silences from Fullerton anguished Wharton, and eventually the end she foresaw from the beginning arrived. The affair taught Wharton deep passion and painful, inevitable loss.

Wharton's divorce from her husband followed close on the heels of the end of the affair with Fullerton. Biographers suggest that although the two were never well matched (Teddy being more interested in sport and less in intellectual matters), for many years they were good companions. They both enjoyed setting up and decorating houses, travel, and an intense devotion to dogs. Teddy was proud of his wife's professional achievements, but he increasingly felt overshadowed by them and unwelcome among Wharton's circle of literary and artistic friends (Lewis 272–73). Just as her success began, around 1903, his physical and mental health started to deteriorate, and his behavior became erratic. In 1909 he embezzled money from his wife's earnings to support his mistress, and Wharton found it necessary to take her business affairs out of his hands—an insult that only worsened his mental health. In letters to Fullerton, Henry James, and others of her circle of friends, Wharton discusses Teddy's struggle with depression and her own suffering in his company. Although Wharton and Teddy were often apart, when he joined her in Paris he needed to be with her all the time, even wanting her to teach him French; "*Why?*" she wondered in a letter to Fullerton. His constant presence prevented her from writing and drove her nearly mad. On November 25, probably in 1910, she wrote to her friend John Hugh Smith: "If only my work were better it would be all I need! But my kind of half-talent isn't much use as an escape—at least more than temporarily. Still—there are lots & lots of other things, & it's not often that I drop into a stagnant back-water of indifference such as I'm in now. Come over soon & pull me out into mid-current" (Beinecke).[6] In a letter to Fullerton dated only "Saturday" but which seems to have been written in 1911, she says, "When I look around me, at my situation, I wonder sometimes why I don't 'lie howling'—or rather, I don't wonder, since you've set free in me such sources of light & laughter & renewal that nothing ever touches me—nothing!" (Ransom Center). Teddy once got better after she said she would leave him, a recovery that she found "grotesque." The situation with Teddy was immensely complicated, for his mental illness made him difficult to deal with and apparently drove him to uncharacteristic behavior, including sulking fits and temper tantrums. By 1912, "tears and recriminations had been the pattern of Teddy's behavior for more than two years," Benstock notes (262).

Wharton felt that divorce was necessary to her own health and her career and went ahead with it, although she pressed the suit in French courts in order to avoid the publicity an American divorce would entail. Writing to her friend Gaillard Lapsley about the settlement of her divorce, she reveals her relief: "I feel as if Pelions & Ossas had been lifted off me, & now at last know how tired I am!" (Lewis and Lewis *Letters* 289). She also writes that she is "still pinching" herself, as though the end of her marriage were too good to be true. Lewis suggests that Wharton "felt propelled out of her metaphorical prison" (339), as evidenced by her increased travel in the years immediately following the divorce. Nevertheless, as Cynthia Griffin Wolff argues, "nothing else she ever did...affected her with such deep and painfully contradictory feelings" (226). Her grief over the divorce, though less evident than her relief, stayed with her for years. In addition, as Benstock shows, Wharton felt anchorless her in new social position: "For her, marriage was the primary relationship between adults" (291). Though glad of her freedom, Wharton was not entirely comfortable with her role as a divorcée.

Not long after the divorce, Wharton's writing and plans were again thrown off track by Germany's invasion of Belgium. In the summer of 1914, she was preparing to move to a house in England and was working on a manuscript called *Literature*. When the war broke out, she returned to Paris, began the charity work that would occupy much of her time and energy for the next four years, and dropped *Literature*, never to return to it.[7] It was a contradictory and confusing time for Wharton. She lost friends in the war, yet she also experienced the excitement of trips to the front. On March 11, 1915, she wrote to Henry James that "once within the military zone *every* moment is interesting" (Lewis and Lewis *Letters* 351 emphasis in original). She adopted new forms of writing, in particular the pro-war propaganda that was condemned as a waste of her talents. Scholar Alan Price argues that the experience of writing propaganda was transformative for Wharton. For a woman so wedded to the distinction between private and public life and to the outward forms of social existence, propaganda and the "tremolo note" it required "initially stuck in Wharton's throat. Its obvious appeals to sentimentality and bathos struck her as inauthentic—it was making a private situation public" (Price xv). As Price notes, this inversion of private and public was what she so abhorred in the modern writing of James Joyce, D. H. Lawrence, and others. During the war, Wharton saw other situations in which the distinctions between private and public were inverted or eroded. On one of her trips to the front, for example, she visited a church that was being used as a hospital, only "it is not a hospital but a human stable. The poor devils sleep on straw, in queer little compartments made of plaited straw screens, in each of which compartments a dozen or so are crammed, in their trench clothes (no undressing possible)" (Lewis and Lewis *Letters* 352). In *Fighting France, from Dunkerque to Belfort* (1915), a collection of essays based on her visits bringing supplies to the front lines, she writes of homes whose outer walls have been blown away, exposing the intimate interiors for all to see. On a larger scale, Wharton viewed Germany as initiating a war of cultures in which not merely lives but an entire civilization was at stake. As a writer who relied on cultural structures in her work, "the idea of Germany imposing a master culture on France or England or Italy was not just a political and military invasion, it was an assault of the cultural gradations that made [her] art possible" (Price xiii). For Wharton, the war meant excitement, hard work, new opportunities in writing, and a threat to her valued way of life.

My focus on these three events in Wharton's life is almost a random extraction of events that might occur in any life, but their close clustering combined with Wharton's own sensitive, reflective, and intelligent nature created a powerful brew that combusted into her writing. These three experiences also brought her in close contact with issues that modern writers would take up. What is the nature of the self, that it can be shaped and controlled by society? What is the fate of women who break the rules that govern behavior? How can an individual communicate with another, and what happens when that communication fails? How does an individual cope with visions of devastation that belie the truths on which civilization is founded? In a literary marketplace profoundly affected by capitalism, what is the role of the artist and of art? Although Wharton's answers to these questions tended to differ from those of James Joyce, Virginia Woolf, Ernest Hemingway, and F. Scott Fitzgerald, to name but a few, it is her engagement with those questions that I investigate.

Wharton on the Left Bank

Wharton lived on the Left Bank in Paris during the years that modernism flourished there, when Paris was the center of the literary lives of Gertrude Stein, Joyce, Hemingway, Fitzgerald, Thornton Wilder, Djuna Barnes, and so many others. It was also the time and place of innovations in art: Pablo Picasso and Paul Cézanne frequented Stein's salon and mingled with the artists and intellectuals there. Yet Wharton was a generation or more older than most of those figures and had little or no contact with them. She never met Stein or Hemingway, and although she was admired by some of the new writers—Hemingway owned copies of *The House of Mirth*, *Ethan Frome*, and *The Age of Innocence*, among others, and Fitzgerald contrived to meet her twice and sent her a copy of *The Great Gatsby*—she was not sought out by them as a literary mentor, nor would she have welcomed the attentions of a new mob of scribbling writers. Even Stein, of an age with Wharton, was not a likely candidate for her acquaintance. As Robert A. Martin and Linda Wagner-Martin point out, "Stein's being both lesbian, openly running a lesbian household though of the most discrete kind, and Jewish, a people Wharton had already caricatured in *The House of Mirth*, would have been enough to distance Wharton from her.... Wharton did not like Stein's art, or her lifestyle, or her clothes, or her bluestocking education, or her notoriety—and she had probably not read any of her writing" (106). Happy though Wharton probably was with this state of affairs, it resulted in her exclusion from the circle of high modernists and the critical attention they drew and generated.

Despite not being part of the modernist literary circle in Paris, Wharton nevertheless admired and corresponded with writers long considered modernists. Her friendship with Henry James is well known and documented, although her admiration of him did not extend to his late work, which she found unreadable. She sent a copy of *Summer* to Joseph Conrad, who, as he wrote her on October 1, 1917, admired her "rhythms so very fine, distinct, and subtle" (Beinecke). Wharton greatly enjoyed Anita Loos' *Gentlemen Prefer Blondes* (1925), allowing herself to be quoted as calling it "*the* great American novel" (Lewis 468) and recommending it to her friends. On January 26, 1926, she wrote to John Hugh Smith: "I knew you were worthy of 'Blondes'! How I wish we could talk that masterpiece over!" (Beinecke). In the same letter, she reported that she had sent copies to her friends Royall and Elisina Tyler. Biographer Hermione Lee points out that Wharton's book orders in the 1920s "show her looking out for new interests," such as works by May Sinclair, Elizabeth Bowen, Katherine Mansfield, Somerset Maugham, Bertrand Russell, and Evelyn Waugh (616). Late in life, Wharton enjoyed the writing of H. G. Wells, and she and Aldous Huxley were friendly neighbors.

Despite living for most of her career in France, Wharton remained interested in and engaged with events and cultural developments in her native country. She read American newspapers and corresponded frequently with friends and family in the United States. As already noted, she continued to read American authors. She also showed an awareness of and sense of humor at the complexities of American culture. For example, with a December 17, 1923 letter to Lapsley, she enclosed a newspaper article titled "Foreign Peeps at American Firesides"; the author's point is that American films present Europeans with a distorted view of American domestic life. Wharton underlined: "There are no books and never any music on the piano. The chief household occupations are writing checks, answering telephones, reading hasty messages, and composing notes of marital farewell.... Both [husband and wife] take a motor to cross the street." Although not underlined, the following comment probably also amused her: "The telephone, neatly hidden in pillars or statue pedestals, is always answered by just the person for whom the call is intended—proof of the miraculous efficiency of our telephone system" (Beinecke). Wharton seems to have drawn on this article when writing *Twilight Sleep*, published in 1927; in a scene particularly telling about communication, Nona Manford answers the phone assuming her would-be lover has responded to her thoughts about him, crying, "It's you, darling?"—but the caller turns out to be her brother.

Wharton was to some degree scornful of modern culture, but she was also highly entertained by it. In a letter a few years later, written again to Lapsley on the unhappy occasion of being called to Paris to attend to Walter Berry's declining health, she pasted in headlines to amuse herself: "Rubber Furniture Vies with Blimp at Exhibition at Grand Palais," "Woman Swindled by Fake Egg Message," "Bobbed Hair Fad Makes Cows Happy" (Beinecke, January 2, 1927). When her novel *Twilight Sleep* was held at Customs in Italy because it was "'thought to be pornographic'!!!!!" Wharton remarked wryly to Lapsley, "Fame at last" (Beinecke, June 11, 1927). If Wharton did not feel popular culture was *her* culture, exactly, she did pay attention to it and enjoyed examining its nuances.

A Critical History of Edith Wharton

In 1871, William Dean Howells became the editor of *The Atlantic Monthly*, a position from which he found and encouraged young writers, particularly those of the school of realism that he, along with Henry James and Mark Twain, helped establish. He read Stephen Crane's manuscript of *Maggie: A Girl of the Streets*, which he then worked to get published—and thus served as midwife for the naturalist movement in American literature. On October 29, 1900, Howells, in a new partnership with Harper & Brothers, wrote Wharton to ask her for a book, preferably a novel: "if it happened to be a story of contemporary American life, with no hint of history in it—not of day before yesterday—that would be most to my mind" (Beinecke). She did not produce a book for him, instead setting to work on the historical Italian novel *The Valley of Decision* (1902). Her next novel, however, *The House of Mirth*, though not written for his press, met his criteria. The American literary world in which Wharton made her debut was dominated by the entrenched school of realists such as Howells, James, and Twain, by the newer naturalists such as Theodore Dreiser, Stephen Crane, Frank Norris, and Jack London, and by local colorists such as Sarah Orne Jewett, Mary Wilkins Freeman, Charles Chesnutt, and Kate Chopin.

This last group posed a problem for Wharton and also for her critics. In the late nineteenth and early twentieth centuries, local color was the place of the woman writer. Yet Wharton did not identify with many other female writers, nor did she want to be relegated to one "place" in literature. She was dismissive of the New England local colorists, such as Mary Wilkins Freeman and Sarah Orne Jewett, whose vision of small-town life she claimed to have written *Ethan Frome* to correct. Critic Donna Campbell points out that for Wharton, rejecting the label of local color was more than an aesthetic choice: "[she] realized that to be taken seriously in the 'man's game' that American literature was becoming, she would have to repudiate the local colorists thoroughly and unmistakably" (173). Wharton was also unable to find a connection with another woman writer whose career corresponded chronologically with her own: Willa Cather. In a letter to Gaillard Lapsley dated July 18, 1928, Wharton wrote, "The Lost Lady, with your note enclosed, came the day before yesterday, & agree with you in thinking the book much better than any other by the lady with the blurry name. But I find all her books blurry—like the name! She had a splendid *donnée* this time, but, oh, how much more she might have made of it! Nothing has any edge—"(Beinecke). Wharton regarded herself as a lone woman making her way in a male-dominated field.[8]

Critically, Wharton was long overshadowed by Henry James, the "psychological realist" to whom she supposedly played apprentice, though as a lesser "social realist." Certainly it was James who encouraged Wharton to "*Do New York!* The 1st-hand account is precious" (Lewis 127). More recent scholarship has recognized the James/Wharton relationship less as that of master and student and more of a dialogue between equals. Two landmark studies of Wharton established her as a writer worthy of attention in her own right. Cynthia Griffin Wolff's *A Feast of Words* (1977) examines the growth of the wealthy woman as artist, declaring that Wharton "paid life the ultimate compliment of becoming a profoundly anti-Romantic realist" (9). Elizabeth Ammons' *Edith Wharton's Argument with America* (1980) focuses on her critique of American society's treatment of women. "Wharton's argument is not simple," Ammons writes. "It begins in the 1890s uncertainly, develops during the years of the progressive movement into a highly sophisticated critique that fuses sociological, economic, psychological, and anthropological perspectives, reverses much of itself and grows conservative in the 1920s, and comes to rest in the early 1930s, mystically" (ix). In *The Social Construction of American Realism* (1988), Amy Kaplan firmly locates Wharton among the realists as a professional of her own merits. Wharton, Kaplan argues, was "an author who wrote at the intersection of the mass market of popular fiction, the tradition of women's literature, and a realistic movement which developed in an uneasy dialogue with twentieth-century modernism" (66).

In the 1980s and 1990s, Wharton drew the attention of feminist critics who found her observation of American cultural practices ripe ground for the study of women's lives. In 1982, Carol Wershoven published her study of "the female intruder" in Wharton's novels. The intruder, who is "at once more vital, braver, and more receptive to all of life than the society she must confront and challenge" (22), unsettles society's traditional values, including but not exclusive to those related to women. In *Edith Wharton's Letters from the Underground: Fictions of Women and Writing* (1990), Candace Waid similarly focuses on the unique woman in Wharton's work, the one who writes. Waid locates her study in Wharton's "self-conscious attention to writing and the conditions of art and a deeply ambivalent preoccupation with women and the conditions of female identity" (3–4). In *The Sexual Education of Edith Wharton* (1992), Gloria Erlich investigates Lucretia Jones's distance from her daughter, her refusal to satisfy Edith's questions about sexuality, and Wharton's subsequent lifelong quest for both mothering and knowledge of passion; these issues, Erlich argues, play out in Wharton's fiction. Kathy A. Fedorko's *Gender and the Gothic in the Fiction of Edith Wharton* (1995) contends that Wharton reinscribed the conventions of Gothic literature to explore gender roles. Fedorko interprets "Wharton's Gothic as an enactment of gender tension as well as an experiment in envisioning human beings who are comfortable with both gender selves" (xi). All of these approaches, and more, offer readers a clearer understanding of Wharton's imaginative and cultural concerns while providing greater insight to the conditions that shaped women's existence in the early part of the twentieth century.

Not uniquely, Wharton has been charged with creating a few masterpieces (often identified as *The House of Mirth*, *Ethan Frome*, *The Custom of the Country*, and *The Age of Innocence*) and a series of lesser works, largely her novels of the 1920s. Wolff finds the end of *The Age of Innocence* to have an "essential rightness" (342) that reflects Wharton's own peace with and longing for the era in which she was raised, and Wolff regards the later fiction as "not as strong as her earlier work" (343). Ammons suggests that Wharton's postwar novels "do not compare favorably with her earlier ones" (166): "Age, expatriation, and commercialism may explain part of what went wrong, relatively speaking, with Wharton's fiction about the twenties; but certainly another important factor...is the author's near obsession with the subject of motherhood" (168). In studying the later works, critics face challenges related to artistic merit as well as problems about literary placement.

It is clear from her letters and her critical writings that Wharton objected to the modernist movement. In particular, she bemoaned what she saw as its disregard of order and its abandonment of morality. Frederick Wegener, who has usefully compiled Wharton's uncollected essays on writing and art, argues that her insistence on form is tied to her social conservatism: "In one of several familiar gestures of critical reaction in her later work, Wharton links the disappearances of 'scruples' to the vogue of 'the new methods' in fiction, considering those methods not only symptomatic of a larger moral crisis or decline but somehow morally defective themselves." Wegener suggests that Wharton's real concern was not morality but rather her displeasure at increasing disruptions of the social order ("Form" 117). Penelope Vita-Finzi, in her study *Edith Wharton and the Art of Fiction* (1990), emphasizes Wharton's belief in tradition as the foundation of art and beauty: "Traditional society provided the structure that people—the artist as much as others—needed in order to function fully and progress" (2). Vita-Finzi also notes, however, that Wharton was not exclusively committed to an ideology of tradition and order: "her intellectual wish for rules and formulae to guide the writer could not override her intuitive knowledge of an inexplicable, subjective quality coming from an unknowable source within the individual artist" (2).

Literary scholars often examine Wharton's work outside of the context of the American expatriate and modernist movement—or, to put it another way, scholars of literary modernism frequently ignore Wharton's work. Although Benstock includes Wharton in her overview of the *Women of the Left Bank* (1986), other studies of women and modernism, such as *The Gender of Modernism: A Critical Anthology* (1990), edited by Bonnie Kime Scott, and *Modernism, Gender, and Culture: A Cultural Studies Approach* (1997), edited by Lisa Rado, do not mention her. One of the reasons for this critical oversight may be the extraordinary success Wharton achieved before the critical dates by which we tend to identify modernism: 1922, perhaps, with the publication of Joyce's *Ulysses* and T. S. Eliot's *The Waste Land*; or the years of World War I, which shocked the world and in the process altered the literary landscape forever; or the New York Armory Show of 1913; or the Ballet Russe performance of Igor Stravinsky's *The Rite of Spring* that same year—a production that Wharton actually attended.[9] Virginia Woolf suggested that a key change occurred even earlier, postulating in "Mr. Bennett and Mrs. Brown" that "in or about December, 1910, human character changed.... All human relations have shifted—those between masters and servants, husbands and wives, parents and children. And when human relations change there is at the same time a change in religion, conduct, politics, and literature" (96–97). Having begun her career prior to these apparently seminal moments, Wharton seemed outdated.

Other critics, however, have begun the investigation of Wharton's relationship to literary modernism and modern culture. Kathy Miller Hadley, for example, has examined innovations in Wharton's writing style. Hadley's study, *In the Interstices of the Tale* (1993), "considers Wharton's narrative strategies, including her pervasive use of irony, her attention to the often 'untold' women's stories, and her concern with her characters' psychological development." She examines novels that contain "narratives below the surfaces seen by the centers of consciousness, each of whom has compelling reasons for *not* seeing other people clearly" (4). In *Edith Wharton's Brave New Politics* (1994), Dale Bauer argues that Wharton's late novels must be read in light of their cultural context: "[Wharton's] argument with American culture may be targeted at topics now too specific to her time to make immediate sense, but her intervention into that culture's process of identification was precisely the issue at stake during her late career when she created characters who challenged the personal and psychological politics of the American century" (6). These novels "conduct cultural conversations," Bauer explains, "in addressing eugenics, the 'revolt of modern youth,' the rising tide of individualism, and the emerging Italian fascism and German nationalism" (xiv)—all phenomena that preclude the possibility of the "inner life" that Wharton so valued. Perhaps most important, Bauer argues that "merely dismissing Wharton as antimodernist, a label suggesting uninterest in politics, wrongly erases Wharton's profound concern for changing her culture, which may even surpass her concern with authorship" (4).

Interest in Wharton is currently at a peak. *The Age of Innocence* and *The House of Mirth* have both been made into Hollywood movies, in 1993 and 2000, respectively. Critical studies have also flourished in recent years, including Stephanie Lewis Thompson's *Influencing America's Tastes: Realism in the Works of Wharton, Cather, and Glasgow* (2002), Jennie Kassanoff's *Edith Wharton and the Politics of Race* (2004), Robin Peel's *Apart from Modernism: Edith Wharton, Politics, and Fiction Before World War I* (2005), Paul J. Ohler's *Edith Wharton's "Evolutionary Conception": Darwinian Allegory in Her Major Novels* (2006), Emily Orlando's *Edith Wharton and the Visual Arts* (2007), and Hermione Lee's new biography *Edith Wharton* (2007). Numerous articles on Wharton have also appeared. Wharton's appeal, as a look at the above titles suggests, comes from her long career and the wide range of subjects her writing addresses. Her oeuvre offers an access point for understanding American culture, including race and art, as indicated above, but also consumerism, drug addiction, and fashion. Kassanoff's monograph, for example, significantly acknowledges Wharton's conservatism as seen in her representations of class, race, and national identity. Many of these recent studies show an ongoing interest in placing Wharton in literary history; both Thompson and Peel insist on Wharton's antimodernism. I too address Wharton's interpretation of her culture, but I am more interested in revealing her engagement with modernism rather than her disavowal of it.

THE CRITICAL STATE OF MODERNISM

Part of the invisibility of the feminine, including women writers themselves, in modernism came from male authors' deep anxieties about the changing role of women and what it meant for masculinity. In *Sexchanges*, Volume II of their three-part landmark series *No Man's Land*, Sandra M. Gilbert and Susan Gubar argue that male writers of the 1920s felt emasculated by the horrors of World War I and threatened by women's new power: "Feeling themselves to be coerced by women, at the mercy of women, bedded down in the terrible house of women, male writers from Joyce and Moore to Lawrence, Eliot, and Hemingway must have felt that they had painfully to extract the truth of their gender's ancient dominance from an overwhelming chaos" (343). Similarly, Marianne DeKoven argues that "a closer look at Modernism through its complex deployments of gender reveals not only the centrality of femininity, but also, again, an irresolvable ambivalence toward radical cultural change at the heart of modernist form and innovation in the works of both male and female writers" (175).[10] Much of "traditional" or established modernism, she argues, appeared in response to the changes and anxieties that the New Woman—educated, career oriented, and more sexually free than her predecessors—provoked in the social fabric.

The nature of the literary marketplace of the 1920s also affected the labeling of authors, particularly for such a prolific and financially savvy writer such as Wharton. Male modernists have held a monopoly on who can be considered "modernist" because they were also frequently modernism's best critics; they wrote the definition of their own difference and supremacy. In *Modernism, Mass Culture, and Professionalism* (1993), Thomas Strychacz argues that both modernist literature and criticism found it necessary to define themselves in relation to mass culture, either in stark contrast or in continuity. Criticism and literature also found themselves in a symbiotic relationship, he explains, and without criticism "modernist writing could not otherwise have amassed the cultural authority it undoubtedly possesses" (6). Strychacz continues, "the formal strategies of modernism were conceived dialogically; modernism and mass culture, the authentic and the inauthentic, must be theorized together and situated within the authoritative discursive structures of American society" (7). In this model, Wharton falls into the category of mass culture; she was part of the inauthenticity that modernism was defined against. Her books sold briskly, even when not well received critically—a state of affairs that must have irritated those critics even as it annoyed Wharton herself, who was frustrated that the critics did not take her more seriously. In addition, Wharton's apparent old-fashionedness—perhaps due to the publication of *The Age of Innocence*, a study of New York set fifty years earlier, in 1920 and of the *Old New York* collection in 1924—made her negligible at the very time when "literariness" was being defined and enshrined in universities and the academic community.

Over the past twenty or thirty years, critics have altered their definition of modernism and the modernist canon to recognize the innovative work of authors other than Joyce, Hemingway, Fitzgerald, Eliot, Pound, and Faulkner. Benstock's *Women of the Left Bank*, for example, has done much to change the perception that modernism was dominated by male writers and by issues of importance only (or at least primarily) to men. Benstock opens up the literary definition of modernism to include "the issue of gender as an important (and all too often disregarded) element in defining the aesthetics and politics, the theory and practice, of what we now call Modernism" (4). Picking up where Benstock leaves off, Linda Wagner-Martin argues that until recently, critical understanding of modernism has limited what could be considered "modernist" and that "seldom in the canon of this literature are there novels about the fulfillment of family life, positive relationships among sisters or among mothers and children, same-sex friendships for women, or a woman's capacity to find satisfaction in life.... And frequently, in fiction that seemed to be about men and women in relationships, the author's focus was on the male character" (*Novel* 6). Wagner-Martin endorses a definition of modernism that emphasizes the breadth of the writing produced in the 1920s and 1930s and that explores a multitude of strategies by which authors "made it new," allowing us to look more closely at works not previously considered in the modernist canon. In doing so, we can see that modernist writers took new approaches to a wide variety of topics—including women's issues, women's roles, and women's experiences in relationships.

Following in the footsteps of these critics, I am using a definition of modernism that recognizes the impact of gender on such issues as a sense of fractured identity, feelings of isolation paradoxically combined with the inherent inextricability of the self from others, and the difficulty of relating experience in words. I also view modernism very much as a response to the cultural changes of the early twentieth century, including technological breakthroughs, new social patterns brought about by class mobility, women's increasing sexual and economic freedom, the expansion of advertising, consumerism, and leisure, developments in the field of anthropology, and more. Literary modernism is, like so many literary movements, the attempt on the page to capture and create the fluidity of life.

Edith Wharton and the Conversations of Literary Modernism

In this book, I examine Wharton's engagement with issues that influenced and grew out of modern literature. Chapter 1 explores Wharton's response to French Impressionist painting, which emphasized the sensations of the individual. Impressionism helped lead to a belief in the truth as an individual perceived it rather than in truth as an external constant, and Impressionist painters broke down boundaries of what could be considered proper subjects of art, in turn leading to investigations of sexuality and social class. Wharton takes on these topics in her

1912 novel *The Reef*. Through its narrative form, alternating between the view points of Anna Leath and George Darrow, *The Reef* explores whether (and if so, how) one person can know another and exposes the limitations under which human relationships operate. The mere existence of Sophy Viner, the young woman with whom Darrow has had an affair and who becomes the governess of Anna's child, explodes the old codes of women's behavior and categorization as well as interrupts traditional assumptions about class difference.

In chapter 2, I examine the issues of birth control and prostitution as they affect the reading of *Summer* (1917). Although set in the late nineteenth century, *Summer* appeared to an audience who were intensely engaged in public debates about female sexuality. Margaret Sanger's efforts had made the birth control movement public and widespread, and Progressive Era reforms had focused attention on the prevalence of prostitution. Both of these public debates affected contemporary understanding of Charity Royall's choices and highlighted the changes in femininity that were so central to modernist writers. Charity is not a New Woman, but her story signifies the difficulties that continued to plague women despite their apparent emancipation: the near impossibility of avoiding the consequences of sexual independence and the continued need for marriage as a means of financial support.

Chapter 3 discusses Wharton's fear of how power functions in a male-dominated world. The lone woman among a group of male friends, Wharton is often viewed as enjoying that position, but her stories reveal her anxiety about being easily removed from that group. In this chapter, I focus on her short stories; although men and masculinity are vital parts of her novels, in some of the short stories Wharton gives freer reign to her imaginings about the male world and about the possibilities and perils of, as Eve Kosofsky Sedgwick puts it, "unmediated male homosocial desire." I center the chapter on "A Bottle of Perrier," in which Wharton vividly renders her unease about how male power works and is transferred among men. In the story, a young man inadvertently but literally consumes and layers over himself the body of an older, more established man. Thus the power transfer between men happens directly, without even the mediation of women, much less with the possibility of their equal participation. In other stories, Wharton uses pairs of male narrators to tell the story, a technique that assumes and reestablishes male authority but also, in some stories, shows how masculine exclusivity can go wrong. For a woman writer during the first part of the twentieth century, anxieties about male power relate to authorship and authority, and for Wharton, they illuminate her fears of exclusion from the literary canon.

In chapter 4, I show Wharton's investigation of the impact of World War I on a society that believed itself civilized and of the relationship between war and art. World War I has long been considered one of the primary catalysts for modernism, for it seemed to destroy any reliance on truth, old codes, and civilization itself. Wharton, one of the few women writers allowed to visit the Western front, wrote a great deal about the war, including essays, short stories, propaganda, and novels. Wharton's war writing, however, has not earned her a place among the modernists, as it did for many male writers, largely because of her refusal to disavow the war. As Julie Olin-Ammentorp explains, "While Wharton eventually abandoned the capitalized Ideals of the pre-war period, she never sacrificed ideals with a lower-case 'i' for the anti-idealism and irony of other wartime writers" (9), a cardinal sin that caused her exclusion from Paul Fussell's foundational *The Great War and Modern Memory* (1975) and her being labeled as a "lady author" who dealt in sentimentality about the war by Stanley Cooperman in his classic study *World War I and the American Novel* (1967). In my chapter, I focus on her examination of the impact of war on the concepts of civilization and art and on her conclusion that Western civilization endured through far more than it was disrupted by the violence and chaos of war.

Chapter 5 returns to an investigation of human relationships, particularly marriage, in which Wharton sees inherently isolated individuals as misled by the myth of marital unity. In her oeuvre, Wharton's portrayal of marriage has at least two strands: first, the indictment of marriage as a business that reduces women to decorative objects, as shown in *The House of Mirth* and *The Custom of the Country*, and second, an investigation of whether marriage can accommodate two living, independent individuals. I examine the second strand here, focusing primarily on *Twilight Sleep* (1927). Using three centers of consciousness, Wharton illustrates how characters misread each other and unsettles any assumptions that characters can fully know each other. Divorce, a sign of the failure of relationships, also functions as a metaphor for the weakness of character's self-understanding as well.

In the last chapter, I examine Wharton's most explicit writing about modernism, her novels *Hudson River Bracketed* (1929) and *The Gods Arrive* (1932) as well as her *Writing of Fiction* (1925). In the last decade or so of her life, Wharton reacted strongly against the "new" methods and forms in writing fiction. In *The Writing of Fiction* and her uncollected critical essays, she explains her theories of writing, which she also worked out through her character Vance Weston, a burgeoning writer in *Hudson River Bracketed* and *The Gods Arrive*. These novels satirize the reigning myth of the male artist as superhuman and instead gesture toward a possibility of creativity based on the female experience.

CHAPTER 1

Troubling the Subjective: The Problem of Impressionism in *The Reef*

Modernism did not occur in literature alone; all the arts responded to social and cultural changes that affected artists' understanding of their world. Gertrude Stein's Paris salon attracted not only writers but painters such as Pablo Picasso, Henri Matisse, and Paul Cézanne. In Paris in the early twentieth century, artists of different mediums fed off each other, working with similar ideas and transferring them from one "canvas" to another. These "new" ideas can be traced back to, or at least through, earlier roots, one of which is French Impressionism in painting. The Impressionists ushered in an era of disruptions in art through their theories of subjectivity and their emphasis on the self, their choice of unorthodox subject matter, and their practice of leaving the canvas "unfinished." For writers, the possibilities of the subjective and the "unfinished" opened up literary texts to new forms. From Henry James to James Joyce to William Faulkner, authors found that the "impression" corresponded usefully to the psychological processes they hoped to capture in words. Ezra Pound's editing of T. S. Eliot's *The Waste Land* produced a poem without transitions that required readers to fill in the gaps for themselves. In just these few instances, the modernist interest in the individual appears: that is, writers regarded the individual as inherently alone and often alienated from society, even though that society may have played an essential role in shaping that individual. By requiring the reader to work with an "unfinished" text, authors attempted to replicate that feeling of alienation via the text.

Edith Wharton, on the other hand, was less convinced that writing, particularly the novel, was meant to perform this work. *The Reef* (1912), her experiment with the literary implications of French

Impressionism, conveys the isolation of the individual psyche while at the same time argues against the value of emphasizing that isolation. In this novel, Wharton draws on Impressionist painting both as a method of revealing her characters' states of mind and struggles with morality and as a metaphor for the increasing and problematic reliance of the individual on him- or herself to cope with desire. *The Reef* becomes about perception, reading, and interpretation, but even more particularly, the novel illuminates the failures of a way of looking that relies only on the individual to see and to interpret. Without an exterior frame of reference, such as religion or a rigid social code, individual characters must depend only on themselves to negotiate difficult moral and emotional dilemmas. As Anna Leath and George Darrow seek to build their relationship, each character struggles and founders in the sea of individual perception, each moment's quest for meaning swept away by the next moment of experience. Wharton believed that overvaluing the impression or feeling of the moment leaves an individual bereft of a unifying vision of the world that can keep him or her from floundering abysmally.

Wharton wrote *The Reef* in 1911, during the last stages of her passionate affair with Morton Fullerton. Her marriage to Teddy Wharton had never been sexually fulfilling and by this time was fraught with fights over money and struggles with Teddy's mental illness. Biographers agree that with Fullerton Wharton first experienced sexual pleasure as well as the emotional state of being in love, although they frequently wonder at Wharton's blind adoration of such an emotionally and intellectually weak man. Elizabeth Ammons, for example, suggests that Wharton's investment in the relationship was less emotional than experiential; that is, although Wharton was deeply disappointed by Fullerton's weaknesses, she had "by 1910 gotten what she wanted out of the liaison" and was able to examine herself, in particular "her own delusions" (89). Ammons made this argument, however, before Wharton's letters to Fullerton were discovered and made available to scholars.[1] These letters show a deeper emotional investment on Wharton's part than Ammons allows, but I agree that after the affair ended, Wharton was able to examine herself, Fullerton, and the relationship itself with a detached eye. Fullerton's infidelities and general inability to sustain a relationship with her overshadowed the exhilaration of the affair and eventually brought about its demise. Still, letters from Wharton to Fullerton sometimes express a deep pleasure in his company and appreciation for his perspective. In a letter from Augsburg, dated December 3, 1909, Wharton suggests the strength of their companionship:

> I wrote a message on this post-card, & then the message grew, & lengthened into a letter, for everything I see or hear seems to strike from me a spark that flies in your direction. How I've wanted you today, in this fantastically, absurdly picturesque place, which we have seen under a balmy blue sky & the brightest sunshine. At every turn I thought how we should feel it together, & how, for me, the sensation would be deepened & illuminated by your share in it—as a reflection is often infinitely more beautiful than the object it reflects! (Ransom Center)

Here Wharton indicates that sensations can be magnified by the presence of another person and that it is not one mind alone that makes the sensation into something more. Yet most of her letters reveal an increasing loneliness in the relationship, and her repetitive cries for a response from him are painful to read.

During the affair with Fullerton, Wharton seems to have written little other than short stories, poems, and journals. It was through Fullerton, though, that Wharton may have become acquainted with Impressionism; according to biographer R. W. B. Lewis, Wharton "had her first guided introduction" to the modern paintings of Degas, Manet, Corot, Renoir, and Whistler in 1908 at the home of her friend Jacques Emile Blanche, whom she first visited in the company of Fullerton (213). After the relationship's denouement, she wrote *The Reef* in only a few months, in contrast to the almost five years she needed for *The Custom of the Country*. The novel contains highly personal material, including a mature woman embarking on her first real sexual affair with an emotionally unreliable man. Biographer Hermione Lee calls *The Reef* "one of [Wharton's] most autobiographical novels, looking not at all like autobiography" (354). In this novel, Wharton was able to explore sexual relations and female sexuality as she had not done previously. Just as important as this new content is the new narrative form and the infusion of the text with a blurred, impressionist vision as two of the main characters negotiate the feelings and the complications that come with an adult love affair.

A Brief Overview of French Impressionism in Painting: Issues at Stake

Impressionism in painting began in France in the mid-1800s, although the term "Impressionist" specifically came into critical circulation after an exhibition in 1874. In the nineteenth century in France, art was largely controlled by the state, which ran the École des Beaux-Arts and sponsored the annual "Exhibition of Living Artists." Painters submitted their work for the exhibition, called the Salon, and a jury selected canvases for exhibition in the Palais des Champs-Élysées. Admission to the exhibition was cheap (and free on Sundays), so anyone who wanted to view the paintings could. Usually thousands of visitors a day attended the show. The state-sponsored art world tended to insist on conformity to its principles, including those of technique and subject selection. The art school did not even teach painting but rather held to the classical principles that valued drawing, perspective, and anatomy. Artists were left to learn about painting on their own.

Édouard Manet was one of the early challengers to the system: like many artists who would become known as Impressionists, he did not attend the École des Beaux-Arts. Instead, he apprenticed himself to the painter Thomas Couture, who encouraged his students to paint modern French life rather than the biblical, historical, and mythic scenes that were deemed acceptable by the state. Manet and other Impressionists often chose to paint everyday scenes, the pretty and the not-so-pretty, streetlife and contemporary—and hence often industrialized—landscapes. In his 1859 essay "The Painter of Modern Life," Charles Baudelaire, poet and friend to the Impressionists, formulated one definition of

> a rational and historical theory of beauty, in contrast to the academic theory of an unique and absolute beauty; to show that beauty is always and inevitably of a double composition, although the impression that it produces is single.... Beauty is made up of an eternal, invariable element, whose quantity it is excessively difficult to determine, and of a relative, circumstantial element, which will be, if you like, whether severally or all at once, the age, its fashions, its morals, its emotions. (3)

Impressionist painters, to varying degrees, held this belief about art, and their attention to the "circumstantial element"—the awareness of contemporary life—made their paintings fresh and controversial. Manet's first submission to the Salon was entitled *The Absinthe Drinker*, a painting that evoked the immoral and criminal aspect of street life and was rejected by the Salon jury in 1859. Manet's paintings broke with tradition not only in his choice of subjects but also in his technique, playing with colors and depth in such a way as to confuse perspective and, unlike most painters at the time, leaving his brush strokes visible on the canvas. The practice of smoothing the surface of a painting had been long established to remove the painter's presence. Manet's technique shocked and upset many viewers of his canvases, yet other painters were adapting this method as well.

Manet, though not without his own predecessors in art, such as his mentor Couture and the Spanish painter Diego Velázquez, became known as the "father of Impressionism." The painters who saw themselves as his successors, however, did not necessarily have much in common—with him or with each other. Claude Monet, Camille Pissarro, Pierre-Auguste Renoir, Paul Cézanne, Berthe Morisot, and others all had their unique styles; what united most of them was their rejection of the traditional strongholds of art in France. These artists joined together to hold their own exhibitions, eight of them between 1874 and 1886, and it was these exhibitions that established the legitimacy of their work.

Claude Monet inspired the label "Impressionism" by naming an 1873 painting *Impression, Sunrise*. Art historian Meyer Schapiro interprets Monet's choice as a claim to individual experience and understanding: "The painting expresses a perception and, while less fully descriptive than the usual picture, it has its own validity—a truth to an experience" (22). The value of personal experience was rooted in nineteenth-century Positivist philosophy, which held that

> an impression was subjective in two senses: it belonged to the consciousness of the individual who experienced it and hence was not an accurate account of the world. But more importantly, [Positivists] argued that an impression took a form unique to the individual having it: because every individual was made differently, and because every individual brought her or his personal stock of memories, associations, and feelings to what she or he saw. (Smith 21)

Nineteenth-century physiologists believed in the "sensation," an effect on the human senses by the world around them: "The '*sensation*' was the ground of a feeling in the receptive observer, an effect of that directly perceived whole on mood and sensibility" (Schapiro 24 emphasis in original).[2] The "sensation" is closely related to the "impression," and the terms are sometimes used interchangeably. At the same time, however, that Impressionists believed an impression or sensation was intensely personal in that it was created out of a unique consciousness, they also suggested that their paintings reflected "the primal impact nature made upon their senses, or the raw, unarticulated appearance things had when seen without prejudice" (21). Thus Impressionism at its foundations probes questions of the nature of the self: is there a self not shaped by "memories, associations and feelings"? Is it possible for the self to remove "prejudice" and access, if it exists, "the primal impact"?

The Impressionists rooted their art not only in subjectivity but also in the science of light, color, and sight. In this way, Impressionism fused objective science and personal responses; by examining the landscape, objects, or people before them objectively—by only looking and not applying the knowledge that identified what they saw as a "tree" or "man"—they could justify apparently inappropriate uses of color, like orange or red, in a painting of trees. As Schapiro explains, "When represented properly on the canvas, [notes of color] harmonized with the rest and contributed to the liveliness of the whole; they corresponded to their sensations in observing the trees in strong sunshine" (23). Lilla Cabot Perry, an American painter, recalled that Monet advised her to paint only in color patches, adding that "he wished he had been born blind and then had suddenly gained his sight so that he could have begun to paint in this way without knowing what the objects were that he saw before him" (quoted in Smith 27). Recording such patches, Monet and others believed, was the way to capture unmediated sensations (28).

Monet was so interested in the effect of nature on his senses that later in his career he produced series of paintings of a single landscape painted at different times of day, in diverse weather conditions, or at various times during the year. His insistence on personal expression had several deeper implications; as art historian Paul Smith explains, Monet believed that

> people should be free to determine themselves as much as possible, without outside interference or influence. To this extent, Monet's work of the 1860s and 70s represents and expresses the belief in individualism and self-determination that was fundamental to the ideology of the new bourgeoisie to which he belonged. But on a deeper level, Monet's art is more than a trivial celebration of the individual and spontaneity: his attachment to the ephemeral moment as the source of value in life implicitly involves a rejection of the idea that value is to be sought in some higher or metaphysical dimension—not just the Ideal, but the afterlife. (89)

Monet and his work emphasize that the individual is the highest authority, the last and only judge of the world around him.

As already noted, one of the radical aspects of Impressionism was its appropriation of new subject matter. The École des Beaux-Arts expected artists to depict scenes from religion, history, and mythology, valuing these subjects over the landscape, portrait, and still-life. Manet, Monet, Degas, Renoir, Cassatt, Morisot, and Pissarro chose to take as their subjects a range of scenes, objects, and people, at a time when the middle class was becoming more visible and more culturally valued and hence when the old social order was called into question:

> These sources were seen as abstractions associated often with deforming constraints and illusions in personal and social life, while the impression, with its component sensations, was viewed as a basic primitive experience, an occasion in which we are most sincere, responsive, and capable of grasping totalities as aesthetic values. The occasions of impression and sensation became for art and also for moral and social thought the experiences believed to be most progressive and emancipating in society and personal relations.... (Schapiro 45)

Impressionists painted people of the middle and lower classes, such as actors, dancers, bartenders, prostitutes, and beggars, rather than focusing their attention on the wealthy upper class. Manet's 1863 painting *Olympia*, a famous nude with her face boldly staring into that of the viewer, provoked "anger and uncertainty," according to T. J. Clark (131), for while nudes and even courtesans had an established place in the art world, Olympia was a prostitute of uncertain class origins. Clark argues that "the achievement of *Olympia*... is that it gives its female subject a particular sexuality as opposed to a general one" (132). That is, she appears not as a symbol but rather as a real person, and the painting, as Clark suggests, reminds the viewer that interacting with a prostitute meant negotiating the class structures that simultaneously divided and united prostitute and patron.[3]

A commonplace about Impressionist art is that such paintings draw attention to their own production: the brushstrokes left visible on the canvas, the heavily layered paint, the sketchy lines, the unfinished edges. These methods continually remind the viewer that a picture of an object is not the object. Clark, in an argument too detailed to be rendered here,[4] explores the implications of such techniques, and he concludes that Impressionist "painting put equivalence at a distance" (21). To understand much Impressionist art, the viewer—and even the painter—must stand far enough back for the pieces and fragments of color to cohere into a recognizable whole. The viewer—and painter—must work to achieve "meaning" from the painting. However intimate the subject, the painting itself forces the viewer to remain apart.

Neo-Impressionism, also known as pointillism, was developed by Georges Seurat in the 1880s and was regarded, disputedly, as an offshoot of Impressionism; neo-Impressionists used flecks of color that were combined not on the canvas but in the eye of the viewer. The viewer again must stand back from the painting but still does not ever achieve a unified impression from the painting. Norma Broude explains that Seurat derived his method from the scientific theory of Ogden Rood: "this phenomenon, known as 'luster,' is essentially an optical vibration that occurs optimally for the viewer of a Neo-Impressionist painting only at the correct viewing distance from the canvas: that distance at which the eye struggles toward but does not yet entirely achieve a completely synthesis of the separate spots of color" (139). For both forms of painting, the experience of the painter and the experience of the viewer, though not the same, are paramount—experience is both the form and content of the painting.

IMPRESSIONIST NARRATIVE IN *THE REEF*

In *The Reef*, Wharton examines the implications of placing such emphasis on individual experience. Wharton's use of art in her novels is well known,[5] but usually she includes paintings and portraits to offer insights into characters, such as the suggestion of Lily Bart's sexual availability through her tableau vivant and Undine Spragg's growing ability to make social distinctions. Critic Helen Killoran argues that in *The Reef*, "allusions 'cluster' into two broad general categories, the deliberately hazy perceptions of the neoimpressionists and the crystal sharp outlines of Greek art and literature" (28), with Darrow and Sophy associated with the sensual neo-Impressionism and Anna limited by classical reasoning. I suggest, however, that the novel does not rest easily on such divisions and that the role of Impressionism is far more pervasive and troubling. Wharton experiments with art by using Impressionism and neo-Impressionism as lenses for characters' view of the world and for illustrating the way they make decisions.

The Reef begins with the American George Darrow on the verge of crossing the English channel, on his way to France to reunite with the sweetheart of his youth, Anna Summers Leath. Years ago in New York, Anna turned away from Darrow because of his flirtation with another girl; Anna since married and has been widowed by Frasier Leath. Having met again in London, Darrow and Anna have resumed their courtship, but Anna's last-minute telegram, announcing an "unexpected obstacle," reaches Darrow on the pier and asks him to wait two weeks before coming to her home in France. At that moment, Darrow unexpectedly runs into Sophy Viner, a young woman who used to work as a companion in a house he once frequented. Annoyed with Anna's apparent whims, he travels with Sophy to Paris, where she hopes to begin a career on the stage. After a few days exploring the city together, the two embark on a ten-day affair. Eventually Darrow and Anna reconcile, and four months later he completes his journey to Givré. There he finds Sophy Viner employed as governess to Anna's daughter Effie and engaged to Anna's stepson Owen Leath. At the chateau, the four adults become entangled with the undertones of Darrow and Sophy's affair, eventually requiring Anna and Darrow to come to terms with his infidelity. Sophy gives up Owen and departs, while Anna, having lived a sheltered life, struggles to understand how such casual relationships can happen and at the same time wrestles with her own physical desire for Darrow. She eventually spends the night with him, an act that succeeds in opening her eyes to physical pleasure but that fails to remove her moral distaste for Darrow's casual use of Sophy or to restore her trust in him. Finally deciding that the best course of action is to renounce Darrow to Sophy, Anna searches for her in Paris, only to find that the girl has left for India.

The use of Impressionism and neo-Impressionism within the written text brings together ways of knowing: of visual perception with the interpretation of the word. The prevalence of the word "impression" in the novel draws attention to the novel's investigation of subjectivity. For example, the chance of Darrow and Anna's meeting in London as well as something in Anna's manner leaves Darrow with the "impression" (21) "that he was a being singled out and privileged" (20). References to Sophy's "impressionability" (45) occur repeatedly. Just as Monet used "Impression" in the title of his early works to convey the value of individual experience, the repetition of the term in the novel reinforces the subjectivity of each character's knowledge of the others and of him- or herself. The novel is full of ellipses that suggest the unfinished edges of an Impressionist painting—the elements not sketched in, the brushstrokes left for the viewer. The novel's structure, with alternating sections narrated from Darrow's then Anna's point of view, reiterates the problem of knowledge limited by individual experience.

George Darrow tends to perceive the world around him impressionistically, as if automatically translating his environment into Impressionist paintings. This habit suggests both his sensuality and his unwillingness to examine his surroundings too closely. He becomes the *flâneur*, the spectator of modern life. Many Impressionist paintings place the viewer in this position of spectator, gazing at the painting's subject. The *flâneur* is not just any spectator, however; he has a specific personality. Baudelaire describes him as "the passionate spectator... [who] set[s] up house in the heart of the multitude, amid the ebb and flow of movement, in the midst of the fugitive and the infinite. To be away from home and yet to feel oneself everywhere at home; to see the world, to be at the centre of the world, and yet to remain hidden from the world—such are a few of the slightest pleasures of those independent, passionate, impartial natures" (9). Smith explains that "*flâneurie* was a pose; it involved making a serious profession out of the casual occupation of looking" (14). In *The Reef*, Darrow takes on the pose, observing his surroundings and other people, particularly women, from this detached stance.

As he and Sophy wander through Paris, the reader may recognize that, through Darrow's eyes, the sights line themselves up as paintings by Monet, first perhaps *The Thames Below Westminster* (1871) and *Houses of Parliament* (c. 1900) and later perhaps *The Railroad Bridge, Argenteuil* (1873) and *The Railroad Bridge at Argenteuil* (1874):

> Regaining the river they walked on in the direction of Notre Dame, delayed now and again by the young man's irresistible tendency to linger over the bookstalls, and by his ever-fresh response to the shifting beauties of the scene. For two years his eyes had been subdued to the atmospheric effects of London, to the mysterious fusion of darkly-piled city and low-lying bituminous sky; and the transparency of the French air, which left the green gardens and silvery stones so classically clear yet so softly harmonized, struck him as having a kind of conscious intelligence. Every line of the architecture, every arch of the bridges, the very sweep of the strong bright river between them, while contributing to this effect, sent forth each a separate appeal to some sensitive memory; so that, for Darrow, a walk through the Paris streets was always like the unrolling of a vast tapestry from which countless stored fragrances were shaken out. (51)

By regarding the sights of Paris as "scenes" Darrow distances himself, becoming an audience member for a play or a viewer of a painting—the disentangled *flâneur*. Away from Paris in the gardens of Givré, Darrow continues to perceive the world as if it were an Impressionist painting: "The atmosphere was still and pale. The muffled sunlight gleamed like gold tissue through grey gauze, and the beech alleys tapered away to a blue haze blent of sky and forest. It was one of those elusive days when the familiar forms of things seem about to dissolve in a prismatic shimmer" (162). Darrow enjoys his surroundings but does not look too closely; he lets images blend and blur and in this manner is able to remain detached.

Similarly Darrow enjoys Sophy Viner as if she were a painting, admiring "her small nose, her clear tints, a kind of sketchy delicacy in her face, as though she had been brightly but lightly washed in with water-colour" (27). As a *flâneur*, an expressly male pose, Darrow asserts the power of the male spectator over the female object of his gaze and "indulge[s] in a fantasy that subjugates the woman to his desire" (Smith 60). Darrow's view of Sophy is perpetually diffused, leaving to the reader the responsibility to interpret Sophy's feelings, to ponder her understanding of her situation, and to worry over her future. When Darrow tires of her, his feelings again take the form of a painting: "the rain...had thrown the whole picture out of perspective, blotted out the mystery of the remoter planes and the enchantment of middle distance, and thrust into prominence every commonplace fact of the foreground" (81). Unlike Darrow's usual vision, however, here the details—the very details he has trained himself not to see—are emphasized rather than blurred. This jolt of realism into Darrow's perspective, brought on by the sordidness of the affair and his lack of real interest in Sophy, signals to him that it is time to end the relationship.

Darrow's pictorial view of Sophy has larger implications than his emotional removal from his own irresponsible behavior; his impressionistic view point is grounded in *his* experience of life, an experience that is distinctly masculine. He sees not only Sophy but also Anna as a painting: "She was reserved, she was shy even, was what the shallow and effusive would call 'cold.' She was like a picture so hung that it can be seen only at a certain angle: an angle known to no one but its possessor. The thought flattered his sense of possessorship..." (128 ellipses in original). By viewing Sophy and Anna as paintings, he removes their humanity; he transforms them into objects that may be hung in public museums or exhibitions—as Sophy aspires to be exposed on the stage or, by extension, in prostitution[6]—or reserved for private viewing—just as Fraser Leath, the art collector and Anna's first husband, has done to Anna. Darrow, after all, "like[s] his 'ladies' and their rivals to be equally unashamed of showing for exactly what they were" (38). When he rediscovers Sophy at Givré, he again objectifies her into a painting: "For the first time he saw in her again the sidelong grace that had charmed his eyes in Paris; but he saw it *now* as in a painted picture" (162). As the passages quoted above suggest, he has always seen her as "a painted picture," and the fact that he only recognizes the nature of his sight "now" underscores his previous lack of self-awareness and his current desire to capture or "frame" the affair as a means of distancing himself from any responsibility to her. Part of his defense of his behavior to Anna is his claim to a greater knowledge of "the world," but his view of the past and present themselves as objects suggests that he has not broken out of any social conventions and that he has no claim to special knowledge—simply a claim to knowledge of a different experience. He has experienced the world as a man, but his wider freedom does not equate to more valuable knowledge. His ability to lead either Sophy or Anna into greater knowledge of the world is truncated by his own reliance on convention and his emotional retreat from experience.

Further, Darrow absolves himself from any moral responsibility for his behavior or its repercussions. As he attempts to explain his affair with Sophy to Anna, Darrow offers a condescending explanation about the nature of the broader world. In this speech Darrow, consciously or not, draws on the techniques of neo-Impressionism:

> What I meant was that when you've lived a little longer you'll see what complex blunderers we all are: how we're struck blind sometimes, and mad sometimes—and then, when our sight and our senses come back, how we have to set to work, and build up, little by little, bit by bit, the precious things we'd smashed to atoms without knowing it. Life's just a perpetual piecing together of broken bits. (289)

Darrow argues that to be able to understand life, one must step back, just as one must step back from a neo-Impressionist painting to understand the whole picture. Standing too close to the picture frustrates the eyes, and one can only discern the pieces of color that make up the whole and not the whole itself. What Darrow fails to realize, or chooses to ignore, is that even when one stands at a distance the flecks of color, or "broken bits," still resist an easy harmony. As contemporary art critic Félix Fénéon wrote of Seurat's *Sunday Afternoon on the Island of La Grande Jatte*, "The atmosphere is transparent and singularly vibrant; the surface seems to flicker. Perhaps this sensation... can be explained by the theory of Dove: the retina, expecting distinct groups of light rays to act upon it, perceives in very rapid alternation both the disassociated colored elements and their resultant color" (quoted in Broude 139). While Darrow thinks standing far enough away from the painting of life will blur the "broken bits," Anna knows that one cannot stand far enough away for that to happen, even if one wants to. She continues to see the "disassociated colored elements," that is, the "dark" side of not only Darrow's life but also, she understands, that of men in general. She resists "a 'best'... that's made of someone else's worst" (289). Darrow's infidelity and, more important, his emotional indifference to Sophy will never be far from Anna's view of him or even Darrow's view of himself.

Throughout the novel, Anna struggles to experience a reality that since girlhood she has felt has been walled off from her. Anna was raised to be a proper young woman, so well trained that "envious mothers cite[d] her as a model of ladylike repression" (91). This repression created the veil that "had always hung between herself and life. It had been like the stage gauze which gives an illusive air of reality to the painted scene behind it, yet proves it, after all, to be no more than a painted scene" (90). Anna waits for the veil to rise, and she hopes that Darrow will evoke the passion in her that will lift it. Ammons uses the Sleeping Beauty myth to illustrate Anna's struggle and her disenchantment when the "prince" arrives (80–88). Darrow cannot remove her veil because he also views the world through one, the "prismatic shimmer" of regarding life from a distance, of resisting the "broken bits" that he wishes not to see. Both of these veils are presented negatively, since both characters are crippled by them: Anna dearly wishes to overcome her sexual ignorance, and Darrow's distance from life and especially from women prevents him from acting other than selfishly. These veils in fact are the same, a refusal to recognize female desire. As Ammons puts it, "fairy-tale visions of love and marriage imprison rather than liberate men and women" (61). Wharton's larger point, moreover, is that perception is socially and culturally formed—"[n]o one is born knowing, or believing in, the myth of Sleeping Beauty" as Ammons points out (88)—and in *The Reef* Impressionism and neo-Impressionism become metaphors for all limited perceptions.

Anna is more complicated in her artistic associations than the other characters—more a mix of emotion and reason. But, as with Sophy, we must remember through whose vision we are given these impressions: quite often it is that of George Darrow, who prefers simple classifications for women. He frequently associates Anna with classical images, such as the Grecian urn (41) and "an amazon in a frieze" (183). When readers first meet Anna, however, mediated not by Darrow but by an unknown third person narrator, she stands with the background of Givré behind her, the description of which evokes an Impressionist painting: "From the escutcheoned piers at the entrance of the court a level drive, also shaded by limes, extended to a white-barred gate beyond which an equally level avenue of grass, cut through a wood, dwindled to a bluegreen blur against a sky banked with still white slopes of cloud" (87). Here Anna seems objectively placed in an Impressionist painting, and even Darrow recognizes the harmony between Givré and Anna: "You look so made for each other!" (119). More important, she sees impressionistically, even early in the novel, before Darrow arrives and before she learns of Sophy's sexual experience: "Two brown blurs emerging from the farther end of the wood-vista gradually defined themselves as her step-son and an attendant game-keeper. They grew slowly upon the bluish background, with occasional delays and re-effacements" (100). When she and Darrow first wander the grounds together, they gaze "across the river at the slopes divided into blocks of green and fawn-colour, and at the chalk-tinted village lifting its squat church-tower and grey roofs against the precisely drawn lines of the landscape" (111–12). Here, Darrow's and Anna's gazes merge in their early delight at being together and in their freedom finally to feel passion for each other.

The use of Impressionism as the characters' visual lens, however, helps the reader understand the problems facing Anna and Darrow. Each time they get close to each other, they find themselves pushed farther away, just as standing too close to an Impressionist painting leaves one facing incoherency. The distance created by conversation is in fact taken for granted by Anna: she "was intensely aware that as soon as they began to talk more intimately they would feel that they knew each other less well" (110). Indeed, at this point their relationship rests largely on memory; they do not know each other very well any more, but they want to pretend that they do. Communication becomes a struggle for the lovers, as spoken words lose significance and the unspoken gains it. As Anna questions Darrow about Sophy's history in order to better understand the young woman who wishes to marry her stepson and into whose care she will be leaving her daughter when she and Darrow go abroad, Darrow realizes "it was not Anna's questions, or his answers to them, that he feared, but what might cry aloud in the intervals between them" (183)—what the unfinished corners of the canvas will convey. But what, exactly, might be cried aloud? If he does not fear Anna's questions or his own answers, which might lead to the revelation of his and Sophy's affair, he fears the gaps in communication that might reveal that intimacy between one soul and another is merely an illusion.

As tensions, described as "atmospheric disturbances" (159), mount and intrigue deepens at Givré, both Anna and Darrow—and perhaps Owen and Sophy, though we are given limited access to their thoughts and feelings—come to depend almost not at all on spoken words and instead try to interpret the behavior and manners of those around them. This process of interpretation, however, depends on absorbing too much external information and negotiating it emotionally rather than intellectually. After finding Sophy at Givré, Darrow drowns in his panic: "His sensations were too swift and swarming to be disentangled. He had an almost physical sense of struggling for air, of battling helplessly with material obstructions, as though the russet covert through which he trudged were the heart of a maleficent jungle..." (140 ellipses in original). Anna too is overwhelmed by the hidden knowledge and emotions flowing around her, and she, "habitually so aware of her own lack of penetration, her small skill in reading hidden motives and detecting secret signals" (231), finds that she must learn to interpret those "secret signals" as well as navigate the flood of them. Soon she too cannot help but feel that everywhere around her flash moments of communication and knowledge that she must catch and interpret. Becoming "suddenly endowed with the fatal gift of reading the secret sense of every seemingly spontaneous look and movement" (232) is a curse, even when it brings her actual knowledge. Learning of Darrow and Sophy's affair and even sleeping with Darrow herself does not bring Anna any clearer vision than she possessed before. If anything, her vision becomes more blurred. On one of the early days of Darrow's visit, the two walk through gardens where "chrysanthemums, russet, saffron and orange, glowed like the efflorescence of an enchanted forest" (118); later, as she prepares to send Darrow away, "her tears magnified everything she looked at, and the streaked petals of the carnations, their fringed edges and frail curled stamens, pressed upon her, huge and vivid" (311). The revelation of Darrow and Sophy's affair and Anna's inability to understand it leave her lost and confused.

The Moral Implications of the Impressionist Vision and the Solutions of the "Artist"

Ultimately the problem of Impressionistic interpretation that Wharton exposes in *The Reef* is not one of failure or inability to know. Anna and Darrow are overwhelmed by their impressions but that does not mean their impressions are wrong. It turns out, for example, that Darrow does understand Sophy well. His explanation to Anna of Sophy's state of mind in Paris rings true: "She had the excuse of her loneliness, her unhappiness—of miseries and humiliations that a woman like you can't even guess. She had nothing to look back to but indifference or unkindness—nothing to look forward to but anxiety" (269). More tellingly, Darrow discovers before Sophy does that Sophy still loves him. Trying to discourage Sophy from marrying Owen, Darrow bets that "certain signs meant what he thought they did" and tells her, "You'll be wretched if you marry a man you're not in love with" (194). At the time, Sophy dismisses Darrow's interpretation, but shortly afterward she indicates that she intends to break her engagement, revealing to Darrow that she is, after all, in love with him rather than with Owen (240). Similarly, Anna discovers Darrow and Sophy's affair based on their avoidance of each other's eyes, an almost superstitious guess on her part (232). Her guess is presented, however, as inevitable:

> As [Anna] looked back over the days since Darrow's first arrival at Givré she perceived that at no time had any one deliberately spoken, or anything been accidentally disclosed. The truth had come to light by the force of its irresistible pressure; and the perception gave her a startled sense of hidden powers, of a chaos of attractions and repulsions far beneath the ordered surfaces of intercourse. (322)

As she was finishing *The Reef*, Wharton wrote to Morton Fullerton asking for his thoughts on the later chapters: "I want your opinion about the chapter in which, between Darrow & Anna, the truth begins to come out. It's not conventional, but I believe it's true."[7] As she does throughout her career, Wharton posits a truth that convention might deny or that lives outside of convention. Wharton makes clear in *The Reef* that there is a truth to be known and indicates that whatever the means of knowing, the truth does exist. It is Anna's response to her predicament—not the problem itself, as the story of the love triangle goes back ages—that demonstrates a remarkably modern mindset, particularly in her author's ability and willingness to convey it.

At this point in the novel, the problem, especially for Anna, shifts from what can be known to, given what one knows, how one should behave. Each time Anna attempts to send Darrow away, she falters and allows him to stay, a cycle she cannot break. In a novel so centered on art, it is perhaps not surprising that Wharton's characters look for artist figures who may have the knowledge and authority to suggest guidelines for action. Miss Painter's name and role of confidant to Madame de Chantelle clearly place her as a possible guide for behavior. Though she is gently ridiculed by both Anna and Owen, she turns out to be not at all a ridiculous or tedious character; rather, her "arrival at Givré produced the same effect as the wind's hauling around to the north after days of languid weather" (198). Miss Painter herself is unremarkable, but she brings energy and even clarity to the people around her. Darrow decides that it is "her blank insensibility" and "the freshness of a simpler mental state" (200) that produce a comforting effect on others. Later, however, he realizes that she has a "gimlet gaze [that] might bore to the heart of any practical problem" (203). Upon Madame de Chantelle bemoaning that "You think it's perfectly simple to let Owen marry a girl we know nothing about?" Miss Painter astutely replies, "No; but I don't think it's perfectly simple to prevent him" (203). Her strategy to cope with Owen's unorthodox choice of a bride rests largely on a knowledge of human behavior—she predicts that even if Owen were to be separated from Sophy and quickly married off to someone "acceptable," he will eventually return to Sophy and end up committing adultery—and on a Christian responsibility to help others act morally.[8]

The second artist figure who appears as a guide for Anna is Sophy's sister. Although probably a prostitute, Mrs. Laura McTarvie-Birch identifies herself as an "artist" (332). Lying in bed with her "uncovered neck" (331), "thickly-ringed hand" (332), heavily powdered face, and powder-puff dog under the covers, Sophy's sister invokes other Impressionist paintings, ones of people on the edges of mainstream life, the grotesque and the forgotten. Yet Clark points out that in the mid-1860s "the features defining 'the prostitute' were losing whatever clarity they had once possessed, as the difference between the middle and the margin of the social order became blurred" (79). As noted earlier about Manet's *Olympia*, the mid-century French prostitute was becoming more visible and at the same time less clearly defined; art historian Hollis Clayson notes that economic changes in France increased the employment of single women, many of whom "were suspected of being prostitutes hiding behind the cover of an honest job" (113). In *The Reef*, the blurring of social differences shocks Anna as much as the news of Sophy's departure, for this change is one of the things that have puzzled her about Sophy since finding out about the affair. "What *is* she?" (268 emphasis in original) Anna wonders aloud to Darrow. Her understanding of the social structure does not allow for a woman to have affairs and retain Sophy's appearance of respectability and generous, attractive personality. Mrs. McTarvie-Birch offers one answer to Anna's question, but by the time Anna meets her, she has moved on to the question, "What am I?"[9] If Mrs. McTarvie-Birch is the answer to this question as well, then Anna must indeed be confused and even horrified at the blurring of "prostitute" and "lady."[10]

Sophy Viner herself emerges as the artist figure with the most to offer Anna. As we see through her relationship with Darrow, Sophy becomes identified as an Impressionist. Explaining her situation to Darrow early in the novel, "she had brushed in this outline of her career with light rapid strokes" (17). Darrow experiences Sophy as an "extraordinary conductor of sensation" (59); he finds the play *Oedipe* "airless and lifeless" (65) until he hears Sophy's comments on it at intermission: "Seen in this light, the play regained for Darrow its supreme and poignant reality.... [He was] content to receive his own sensations through the medium of hers" (67). This is what an artist does, particularly an artist as conceived by Impressionism: he or she uses his or her finely tuned senses to experience the world and then finds a way to let others share in the sensation. At first, Sophy seems to suggest pure reception of sensation, without analysis or work in translating that impression into an art form; after the play, Darrow finds her "evidently unused to analyzing her aesthetic emotions, and the tumultuous rush of the drama seemed to have left her in a state of panting wonder, as though it had been a storm or some other natural cataclysm" (67). This lack of analysis was one of the criticisms leveled against Impressionist artists. Broude explains that one of the controversies in the study of Impressionism rests on the role and work habits of the artist:

> Claude Monet...was an artist who—contrary to the later popular depiction of him as "only an eye," a spontaneous but essentially passive and impassive recorder of nature out-of-doors—did in fact paint upon occasion in the studio away from nature, was capable throughout his career of changing his mind and changing nature within his pictures for the sake of working out and balancing his compositions, and was equally capable of reflecting upon and endowing his work with intentional meaning. (13)

An examination of the text reveals that Sophy is equally capable of reflection and of conveying "intentional meaning."

As previously noted, the novel uses only Darrow and Anna as centers of consciousness, leaving Sophy's view largely unknown. Rebecca Blevins Faery calls her the unknown itself, the "submerged text," unreadable to both Anna and Darrow (87). I agree that Sophy embodies and lives the female sexuality hidden in both the text and the culture, but I also believe Wharton provides clues to her inner life.

Although the story of Darrow and Sophy's affair is told from Darrow's perspective, Darrow also seems to receive glimpses of how she views the world. When he realizes that Sophy is a former employee at a house that he used to visit, he "discover[s] suddenly that the blurred tapestry of Mrs. Murrett's background had all the while been alive and full of eyes. Now, with a pair of them looking into his, he was conscious of a queer reversal of perspective" (30). Such critical speculation is tricky, of course, because Darrow sees what he wants to see in Sophy, but in Paris he does offer an interpretation of the streets around them that differs from his own and that he attributes to Sophy. If Darrow regards the scenes of Paris as a series of Impressionist landscape paintings, Sophy, in contrast, seems to look at the city as if standing too close to a neo-Impressionist painting:

> She seemed hardly conscious of sensations of form and colour, of any imaginative suggestion, and the spectacle before them—always, in its scenic splendour, so moving to her companion—broke up, under her scrutiny, into a thousand minor points: the things in the shops, the types of character and manner of occupation shown in the passing faces, the street signs, the names of the hotels they passed, the motley brightness of the flower-carts, the identity of the churches and public buildings that caught her eye. (48)

The difference between Darrow and Sophy is evoked here not only by how they see—Darrow blurring the details, Sophy focusing on them—but also what they choose to see. Darrow sees sky, gardens, architecture, and river: these things belong to a rural, Victorian setting and to an outdated morality that would condemn Sophy without a second thought.

Sophy, in contrast, sees the vibrant modern consumer culture, "the pressure of human significance" (45), a tendency that aligns her with the class awareness of Impressionist painters. Clark points out that

> modern art in its first manifestations—in the painting of Manet above all—did not accept the boulevards as charming. It was more impressed with the queerness of those who used them—the prostitutes, the street singers, the men of the world leaning out of their windows, the beggars, the types with binoculars. It wanted to paint Haussmann's Paris as a place of pleasure, particularly for the eye, but in such a way as to suggest that the pleasures of seeing involved some sort of lack—a repression or alternatively a brazenness. (78)

Sophy is willing to look at and into the "queerness" of the city. Her attention to shops, faces, churches, and public buildings indicates an interest in modern, daily human life—a curiosity that Darrow does not share and that is too easily ignored in his philosophy. Sophy's perspective is associated with the paintings of prostitutes, beggars, and other "unsavory" people in the city by Manet (perhaps *The Absinthe Drinker* [1858–59], *The Old Musician* [1862], *The Street Singer* [1862], *Corner in a Café-Concert* [1877–79], and *A Bar at the Folies-Bergère* [1882]) and street paintings by Degas (*Women on a Café Terrace, Evening* [1877]). In a study of Impressionism, Robert L. Herbert discusses a painting by Manet that, although titled *The Railroad* (1873), foregrounds a nursemaid and child: "Humans mediate the view, which becomes more than a view: it is a way of experiencing the modern city" (28). Sophy's vision of the Paris streets has the potential to undermine Darrow's or at least to present beside his an equally truthful view of urban life. At one point, her view actually inserts itself into Darrow's; when he remembers their time in Paris, he recalls a "wan old waiter with the look of the castaway who has given up watching for a sail...It was odd how the waiter's face came back to him..." (246 ellipses in original). Darrow does not see such faces; it is Sophy who does. Sophy disrupts the expected interpretation of the world, and therefore she stands as an artist of powerful, even transformative vision.

Anna herself is initially positioned as an artist, but as the novel progresses, any abilities she might have in that direction deteriorate. In the Impressionist view, the artist needs dual talents: to receive sensations and then to mediate them through the canvas, or in Anna's case through words. When we first meet her, Anna behaves as an artist in relation to her surroundings, as she "[lets] the whole aspect of the place sink into her while she held herself open to its influence" (87). After an afternoon with Darrow, "for the first time everything in her, from head to foot, seemed to be feeling the same full current of sensation" (123). Like Sophy, she is an apt receiver of sensations. She also feels the desire to convey those sensations to another person. Early in their reunion, she questions Darrow about Owen's sighting of him with a woman in Paris. She does not, she says, want him to explain, but "it's only that I want you to have the whole of my feeling" (116). Like an Impressionist artist, she seeks to translate her sensation to an outside consciousness—she wants to be able to convey her feelings to an audience.

Anna's artistic abilities, however, gradually become limited to receiving sensations, not sharing them. She lacks the capacity to translate her feelings and sensations into words, perhaps because her upbringing offered her no words for this situation. Although it is easy to see that Wharton, as she frequently does, indicts old New York for its repression of individuals, I believe she also suggests a larger problem concerning language and its connection to emotion and experience. During one of their confrontations over Sophy, Anna and Darrow become "beings of different language who had forgotten the few words they had learned of each other's speech" (270). This particular situation is beyond Anna's ability to cope, but Wharton insinuates further that every individual has his or her own "speech." As Smith writes of the Positivist philosophy that informed Impressionism, impressions are unique "because every individual was made differently, and because every individual brought her or his personal stock of memories, associations, and feelings to what she or he saw" (21). Similarly, in *The Reef*, each character's language and ability to interpret are so bound up in their own experiences that their languages do not match. In this way, Wharton anticipates the modernist sense of isolation and alienation, brought to fruition by Joyce, Eliot, Hemingway, and others. For Wharton, differences in experience are rooted in a deeply gendered society. Anna cannot understand Darrow's explanation of the affair, although she is desperate to comprehend: "she was tormented by the desire to know more, to understand better, to feel herself less ignorant and inexpert in matters which made so much of the stuff of human experience. What did he mean by 'a moment's folly, a flash of madness'?" (269). In Anna's world, that of the wellbred, chaste woman, people do not act on sexual impulse, and she cannot understand the euphemistic language Darrow uses. She is hamstrung as an artist because she does not possess the experience that would give her the linguistic range that she needs to convey her ideas.

Sophy, in contrast to Darrow and Anna, when she chooses to speak speaks "simply." When she tells Anna "You found it out, that's all—I knew you would. In your place I should have guessed it sooner" (261), Anna feels no resentment at the girl's claim to keener insight. Instead, Anna recognizes Sophy's superior gifts: "Yes, the girl would have had divinations, promptings that she had not had! She felt half envious of such a sad precocity of wisdom." Sophy's vision, Anna believes, is better, both clearer and more moral, than hers, not only because Sophy seems to have sharper interpretive powers but also, and more importantly, because Sophy has the strength to stand by a decision once she makes it, with none of Anna's wavering. Sophy reveals herself to be generous in sacrificing her own happiness for Darrow and Anna's and in conspiring to prevent Owen from learning the truth and becoming more unhappy than he already is. Her nobility of spirit and strength of will lead Anna to seek her out when Anna can no longer trust herself to make her own decisions. She believes that if she tells Sophy she has renounced Darrow, she will be inspired to abide by her word: "'She's kept faith with herself and I haven't,' Anna mused; and the thought was a fresh incentive to action" (329).

Ultimately, however, the artists can offer Anna few if any answers. Christian morality, even tempered as it is by Miss Painter's practical mind, and the moral ambiguity of Mrs. McTarvie-Birch's sexual freedom both fail to answer Anna's need for a modern, secular code of behavior and the resolution to stick to it. Even Sophy's model of a personal code of honor has its flaws. After all, she must not trust herself to continue to stay away from Owen or Darrow if she feels she must ship herself off to India as companion to the dreadful Mrs. Murrett to avoid temptation. But that perhaps is the point: temptation—to seek love, to yield to sexual impulses, to settle for financial security—is strong, and relying on oneself and one's senses to do what is right, even what is best, for oneself, much less for others, will inevitably fail.

Conclusion

In *The Reef*, Wharton drew upon ideas put forth by the French Impressionist painters. Their interest in the streets, with their swath of everyday urban life and the mix of social and economic classes, in particular the presence of beggars, prostitutes, and other "misfits," paved the way for Sophy Viner, who interrupts and disrupts the class and value systems of Anna Leath. Sophy makes tangible what had always been present: the large number of people clinging to the outside of the wealthy upper class. Sophy's willingness to relinquish what Anna and Madame de Chantelle would consider her position in society to become an actress threatens the very importance of social position, and her unique and fresh look at life contrasts sharply with the traditional views held by Anna and Darrow. Her affair with Darrow marks her as a sexual being without placing her in the category of the "sexually available" woman. From Sophy and *The Reef* we can see a direct path to Charity Royall in *Summer* (1917), another sexually active but not promiscuous young woman.

The Reef may be Wharton's only work in which she engages so extensively with Impressionist painting, and she did not again experiment with such extremes in perspective and emphasis on subjectivity.

Her personal taste in art ran more toward the Baroque and Italian masters, the artists she saw as a child in Europe and whose work she admired in her travels in Italy. In her letters, she seems not to refer to any Impressionist paintings or artists, although she did invite a few Impressionists, including Claude Monet, to contribute to *The Book of the Homeless* (1916), one of her charity projects during World War I. Even in *French Ways and Their Meaning* (1919) Wharton does not mention Impressionism. And Wharton disowned *The Reef* in a letter to Bernard Berenson on November 23, 1912: "Anyhow, remember it's not *me*, though I thought it was when I was writing it—& that *next time* I'm going to do something worthwhile!!" (Lewis and Lewis *Letters* 284 emphasis in original). *The Reef* may reflect or offer insights into Wharton's distance from Impressionist painting; ultimately, according to the novel, Impressionism and its associated subjectivity fail those who view life this way. The problem of only conveying, in Schapiro's words, "truth to experience," Wharton suggests, is the danger of too many experiences, too little analysis of them, and no moral basis on which to act. After sleeping with Darrow, Anna tries to soothe her misgivings by deciding that "to feel was surely better than to judge" (299). Wharton, however, declares that the opposite is true: Anna and Darrow both lack outside anchors through which to judge, in particular a code of morality that would guide them, and they drown in the overwhelming crush of sensations.

The influence of Impressionism can be seen in the writings of the 1920s, particularly in the stream of consciousness experimental writing of Virginia Woolf, James Joyce, and William Faulkner. Stream of consciousness emphasizes the perceptions of the moment, although frequently such writing does not allow for much reflection on the part of the character; rather, the work of processing the "sensation" happens in the mind of the reader. *The Reef* approximates this technique, such as when Wharton leaves us to worry over Sophy because Darrow does not. But Wharton never removes the insistence that we *should* worry and that, like Anna, we must find a moral solution to the emotional tangle at Givré.

Of course, Impressionism was not the sole influence leading to stream of consciousness; William James' work in psychology greatly affected Gertrude Stein, for example. In *The Principles of Psychology*, as Jonathan Levin shows, "James frequently complains about how language gets in the way of pure experience. Because our minds typically latch onto what he calls the 'substantive parts' of the stream of thought—those parts represented by concepts, ideas, images, nouns—we typically neglect to 'see' the 'transitive parts' of the stream, the infinite variety of relations that the substantive parts bear to one another and the ongoing process of constituting and reconstitution those relations" (147). Further, Levin explains, "the mind works not by holding some number of discrete objects before the passive mirror of consciousness...but rather by actively or imaginatively projecting, vaguely and indistinctly, an entire metonymic network associated with the objects that in turn constitutes the 'feelings' that register in the mind" (148).

Wharton agreed with some of these ideas; after all, both Anna and Darrow struggling to communicate or receive communications outside language. But she had little regard for William James, the man or his work, once calling his ideas "psychological-pietistical juggling" (Lewis and Lewis *Letters* 101–2). Wharton was less concerned with the paring down of experience to its component parts than with understanding how the mind contended with the ultimate responsibility of translating those parts into comprehensible experience. In *The Reef*, Wharton portrays the struggle to make sense of the fragments of thought, memory, sight, and sound that the mind receives. Wharton also believed art demanded a moral sensibility.[11] While writers such as Stein, Hemingway, and Dos Passos found inspiration in the techniques of juxtaposition used in Cubism and poets such as William Carlos Williams and Wallace Stevens were interested in Dadaism, the work of Picasso and Matisse left her cold. Such art offended her sensibilities and her need for order, including her belief that individuals must have an ethical foundation to guide them in their actions.

CHAPTER 2

"Any Change May Mean Something": *Summer*, Sexuality, and Single Women

James Joyce's Molly Bloom ("yes") and T. S. Eliot's Lil ("It's them pills I took, to bring it off, she said" [line 160]) have been immortalized in the landscape of literary modernism; together, the two women represent aspects of women's lives that were foundational to modernism. Women were experiencing a new level of sexual freedom and were in greater control of their reproductive activity—yet, as both Molly and Lil demonstrate, even as women were seen to subvert tradition, they remained subject to the laws of the patriarchy. Early twentieth-century changes in attitudes toward women's freedom, sexuality, and economic opportunity unsettled foundational concepts, such as masculinity, race, and civilization itself. These new ways of thinking also posed a threat to women themselves.

The "problem" of female sexuality reverberated throughout the modernist sensibility. The loss of the Victorian ideal of true womanhood went hand in hand with the loss of the secure sense of identity that was already being questioned in the Victorian era. Modernist anxiety over the self, seen in James Joyce's Stephen Dedalus, T. S. Eliot's J. Alfred Prufrock, Ernest Hemingway's Jake Barnes, and William Faulkner's Quentin Compson, among others, resulted from the lack of a structured framework that imposed identity from the outside. In the Victorian era, women were perhaps the only remaining anchor: their sexual passivity defined an active, aggressive male sexuality; their preoccupation with the home permitted men's physical freedom; their supposed spiritual purity substituted for male laxity. When femininity changed, masculinity became unmoored. At the beginning of the twentieth century, growing urbanization changed what women could do. Jobs as factory workers, secretaries, telephone operators, and department store clerks gave women at least the illusion that they could support themselves economically. The spread of movie houses gave them a picture of other places, especially cities, they could live, and improvements in transportation allowed them to get there easily. The 1910s saw the beginning of Margaret Sanger's campaign for birth control and the Progressive Era's quest to stamp out prostitution. Historian Mark Thomas Connelly points out that the problem of prostitution was closely related to the issues of the New Woman:

> Many aspects of the prostitute's life-style, such as the practice of birth control, the smart and forward language, the aggressive manners, and the suggestive clothing, were also increasingly evident, albeit in less extreme form, in the behavior of large numbers of urban women who were not, even under the broadest definition, prostitutes. In this light, the prostitute was deplored not only because she violated the beliefs and assumptions of civilized morality but also, and perhaps more importantly, because her life-style, attitudes, and behavior were ominous signs of change in the feminine ideal, which would ultimately influence the behavior of all women. (47)

This was also, of course, the decade of World War I, an event that fueled (though it did not initiate) looser standards for female sexual behavior. Most important, perhaps, these changes gave women the idea of another life: they created women's desire for their lives to be more independent, more significant, more glamorous. This yearning caused a corresponding anxiety in a society that relied on the idea as well as the actuality of women being at home, submissive, domestic, and dependent.

In this chapter, I examine Edith Wharton's exploration of the changes that occurred in social attitudes toward women and women's sexuality, particularly in the decade leading up to the perceived debauchery of the Jazz Age. In this decade, Wharton continued her lifelong interest in women's lives with the novels *The Reef* (1912), *The Custom of the Country* (1913), and *Summer* (1917). This interest often centered on the conventions that bound women, not only forcing them to conform to patriarchal standards but often distancing them from their own bodily experiences. Those women who did not conform, like Sophy Viner, risked social and often physical exile and economic uncertainty. As society became more open to women like Sophy, Wharton both celebrated that change and feared its repercussions. As the 1910s passed, a sexually active, unmarried woman like Sophy Viner faced less risk of social disapproval, but she did not make much headway in securing her economic position. Wharton saw that, in fact, increased tolerance of active female sexuality could lead to correspondingly increased financial trouble and new disruptions in women's relationships with each other—as well as fail to remove the old difficulties in relationships with men. Here I focus particularly on *Summer* as a novel engaged with female sexuality and the surrounding issues of birth control and prostitution, and I argue that the radical vision of the novel comes less from Charity's growth into a sexual woman and more from Wharton's anger at the treatment of women as disposable objects of men's pleasure. I then examine how we can view Wharton's other single women in light of the legacy of Charity Royall.

In 1916, in the midst of World War I, Wharton took a break from her charity work, the war, and her war writing to produce *Summer*, the story of Charity Royall, a young woman living in a small New England town. Born on "the Mountain," a community of outlaws and alcoholics, Charity has been "brought down" to North Dormer by her guardian, lawyer Royall, and raised by him and his wife. A few years after Mrs. Royall dies, Charity fends off a sexual advance from a drunken Mr. Royall. He repents of his action and the next morning asks Charity to marry him, but Charity is disgusted and uses the incident to assert her power in the household. She later develops a relationship with a young man from "the city," a man of good family and money. At first, Charity and Lucius Harney's relationship is purely platonic, but after Harney takes Charity to the nearby town of Nettleton for a Fourth of July celebration, they begin a sexual affair. Mr. Royall interferes, and Harney offers to marry Charity after he attends to some concerns in the city. During Harney's absence, Charity discovers that he is engaged to someone else and releases him from his promise to marry her; she then finds out she is pregnant. Desperate, Charity sets out on a quest to find her mother on the Mountain, but she arrives just moments after her mother dies. Charity realizes that she cannot raise her child in the squalor in which she finds her mother's body, so she sets off again, only to be met by Mr. Royall, who takes her to Nettleton and marries her.

Part of the radical nature of *Summer* is its portrayal of Charity's growing awareness of her own sexual desire. Many critics read that awareness as central to the novel. Elizabeth Ammons, for example, praises Charity as Wharton's "most openly sexual" heroine (134). Rhonda Skillern argues that "the thing that makes [Charity's] desire different from that portrayed in most male-authored novels is that she manages to keep it apart from the cultural imagining of feminine desire. She does not expect their romance to last forever; she does not consider sex a reason for marriage; and ironically, after actually having sex, she is no longer ashamed of herself" (125). Dale Bauer claims that "Charity chooses mutual desire throughout" (48) as part of her formation of an individual identity. Carol Singley describes the novel as a "tribute to individual will and freedom in nature" that is also "checked by a sense of inevitability that impedes choice" (150). Indeed, the novel's evocation of a young woman's learning about her body and her sexual desire marks *Summer* as a uniquely powerful story.

Although the literary portrayal of Charity as a sensual and sexual woman is radical, her sexual activity itself is not an act of significant resistance to the patriarchal system in which she lives. Such a reading fails to account for the sheer number of young women in the novel who do the same. Most of the other girls who appear in the novel are sexually active; Charity's friend Ally Hawes seems to be the only girl who is not, and her chastity does not seem to be of much help to her. As she peers over Charity's shoulder into a mirror, Ally's face is described as "the ghost of wasted opportunities" (84). Aside from Ally, however, all the girls' lives are remarkably similar. Charity, as the town librarian, incurs the wrath of other local girls by refusing to allow them to use the library for their lovers' meetings: "I wouldn't let Bill Sollas from over the hill hang around here waiting for the youngest Targatt girl, because I know him...that's all...even if I don't know about books all I ought to," she tells Harney (31 ellipses in original). Standing outside Harney's window late one night, Charity decides against knocking because "she had suddenly understood what would happen if she went in. It was the thing that *did* happen between young men and girls, and that North Dormer snickered over on the sly. It was what Miss Hatchard was still ignorant of, but every girl of Charity's class knew about before she left school" (71 emphasis in original). Even on her way home from this vigil, Charity spots "two figures in the shade" (73), although she cannot clearly make them out. Ironically, it is probably one of these figures who reports on Charity's activities and begins the gossip about her romance. The courting community of North Dormer is sexually active, and Charity knows it.

The only real danger with premarital sexual activity is getting "caught"—that is, becoming pregnant. North Dormer girls Julia Hawes and Rose Coles both became pregnant out of wedlock, although their fates differ: Julia has an abortion and becomes a prostitute, and Rose becomes trapped in a marriage of necessity. Charity finds herself at a loss in trying to determine which situation is worse. On the one hand, "[she] had always suspected that the shunned Julia's fate might have its compensations" (71). Rose's life, on the other hand, clearly does not:

> Distinctly and pitilessly there rose before her the fate of the girl who married "to make things right." She had seen too many village love-stories end in that way. Poor Rose Coles's miserable marriage was of the number; and what good had come of it for her or for Halston Skeff? They had hated each other from the day the minister married them; and whenever old Mrs. Skeff had a fancy to humiliate her daughter-in-law she had only to say, "Who'd ever think the baby's only two? And for a seven months' child—ain't it a wonder what a size he is?" (160)

Facing the prospect of forcing Harney to marry her, Charity wonders, "was there no alternative but Julia's?" She realizes that her "individual adventure" is not so individual, and there are no individual endings for her. She faces the same choices as every other unwed pregnant girl before her.

The young women in the novel perpetually mirror each other, bending and refracting their images back and forth among themselves. As the novel opens, "a girl" (3) comes out of Mr. Royall's house; his name is given but hers is not, and the first girl's name that appears in the text is not Charity's but rather that of upper-class Annabel Balch (4), who, it turns out, is engaged to Lucius Harney. Julia Hawes pairs with Rose Coles as Charity's two models for the options of unwed pregnant women. Charity and Julia reflect each other as objects of Mr. Royall's lust. Wearing Annabel Balch's old shoes, which fit her "perfectly" (128), Charity temporarily replaces the other girl at the Old Home Week dance, even as Annabel's "sallow and pinched" face and her "worried expression" (137) mirror Charity's faint—suggesting that perhaps Annabel is pregnant as well. Charity learns later that Annabel does not dance at the party because "her dress didn't set right" (148). Even Annabel Balch and Julia Hawes, the good girl and the prostitute, are linked, as Ally Hawes sews for Annabel the same pattern that she once sewed for Julia (147). These two girls also bracket Charity's experience of Nettleton; when Charity and Harney arrive in town, she wonders "if, at this very moment, Annabel Balch, on the arm of as brilliant a young man, were threading her way through scenes as resplendent" (90). At the end of the evening, Charity is appalled at the appearance of Julia Hawes on her guardian's arm. Other pairings with unnamed girls from both the Mountain and the town indicate the universality of female experience. Charity recognizes her allegiance with the girl on the Mountain, who, when she learns Charity is Mary's daughter, comments, "Her too?" (170). The girl may be Charity's sister, and Charity imagines herself growing up on the Mountain with her mother and "turning into a fierce bewildered creature like the girl who had apostrophized her in such strange words" (178). After she is married, Charity spots a girl at the hotel where she and Mr. Royall are staying: "a girl with her hair puffed high smirked and nodded at a dapper drummer who was getting his key at the desk across the hall" (193). The girls of *Summer* are all interchangeable and are, in fact, interchanged.

The differences among the girls, if there are any, tend to be literally man made. Bauer argues that Charity suffers from a "narcissism of little differences, seeing herself as distinct from the other young women of North Dormer," a narcissism that ends only with the confirmation of her pregnancy (48–49). Yet much of Charity's sense of her own uniqueness is determined by the men in her life. Mr. Royall confers class status on her, and Harney's gaze makes her feel special and defines her.[1] The first time he gets a good look at her, in the musty old library, he stops in the middle of a sentence, and "the fact that, in discovering her, he lost the thread of his remark, did not escape her attention, and she looked down and smiled" (9). That night, when Charity recalls Harney's reaction to his first sight of her, she looks at herself in the mirror: "Her small face, usually so darkly pale, glowed like a rose in the faint orb of light, and under her rumpled hair her eyes seemed deeper and larger than by day. Perhaps after all it was a mistake to wish they were blue" (26). She is so enraptured with her vision of herself as Harney sees her that she even kisses her own reflection. As their relationship develops, Charity continues to see herself through Harney's eyes. Once she starts accompanying him about the county in his architectural quest, she becomes "absorbingly interesting to herself" (39), and when he tells her she is "different," she believes him and takes pride and pleasure in his assessment (44).

The incident of the blue brooch encapsulates how his gaze molds her definitions of beauty and alters even what Charity chooses to desire. After Charity points out the gold lily-of-the-valley brooch, Harney "suggests," "Don't you think the blue pin's better?" "Immediately she saw that the lily of the valley was mere trumpery.... She coloured at her want of discrimination" (91–92). She responds, "It's so lovely I guess I was afraid to look at it" (92). Through a simple "suggestion," Harney directs Charity's gaze and shapes her taste in a way she never notices, and she later remembers the two of them "choosing the blue brooch *together*" (157). In the same way, Harney controls what Charity wants from their relationship. As long as Harney chooses to treat her as a friend and "a girl of his own class" (88), the relationship remains platonic. He even possesses the power of restoring Charity's feelings of respectability and self-worth after Mr. Royall shames her by telling her people are talking about her and after he calls her a whore in front of a crowd. Harney's gaze—not Mr. Royall's, not the town's, not even Charity's own interpretation of a situation—reigns supreme because he is the mythic "city fellow" (42), with all the urban mysteries and superiorities.

When Harney's gaze changes, Charity's behavior changes. After they kiss on the Fourth of July, Harney finds Charity running away to the Mountain. As she explains her actions, "she became aware of a change in his face. He was no longer listening to her, he was only looking at her, with the passionate absorbed expression she had seen in his eyes after they had kissed on the stand at Nettleton. He was the new Harney again, the Harney abruptly revealed in that embrace, who seemed so penetrated with the joy of her presence that he was utterly careless of what she was thinking or feeling" (111–12). This look returns to Harney's face when they reach the deserted house and have sex for the first time (115). Up to this point, Wharton has described Charity's increasing sensuality through her communion with nature and her awareness of her desire for Harney as she admires his body through the window at night. Charity's desire forms independently of Harney's desire, but Charity does not act on her feelings until Harney's gaze turns her into a sexual object.[2] Despite Charity's refusal to regret the affair, even at the end of the novel, it is hard to view the story as one of a woman's desire when that desire is controlled by the male gaze. Even the symbolism of their first kiss taking place on Independence Day becomes ambivalent; has Charity been freed of Victorian sensibilities and is now open to the possibilities of her body, or has Harney been released by Mr. Royall's proclamation of Charity as a "whore" and can now treat her as such? The gaze with which he turns her into an object of sexual desire, "utterly careless of what she was thinking or feeling," does not announce her liberation.

That Harney controls Charity's sense of self is problematic enough, but he does not choose to limit his power to one woman. During the Old Home Week festivities, Charity glimpses Harney with Annabel Balch, and "in her pretty thin-lipped smile there lingered the reflection of something her neighbour had been whispering to her" (134). Charity recognizes Annabel's expression as "the same smile of mischievous complicity he had so often called to her own lips." The feeling of being special that Harney creates in Charity he creates again in Annabel, and, although Charity never realizes the full implications of this "same smile," she does feel "terror of the unknown" forces in Harney's life and "of her own powerlessness to contend with them." She recognizes this powerlessness as her ignorance and lack of sophistication; she does not recognize it as her womanhood. That is, although she feels that the refined and educated Annabel Balch is utterly different from her and is completely suited to be Harney's wife, she fails to understand that Annabel's class does not prevent her, too, from being defined by Harney's gaze. They are both women—interchangeable women—and similarly lack agency in the face of male desire.

Nonmarital sexuality and women's desire were not new in 1917, and Wharton certainly knew it. Her affair with Morton Fullerton, by the time of *Summer* many years behind her, had opened her eyes to the power of female desire and placed her in an ambivalent position in regard to nonmarital sexuality. Fullerton's lack of constancy, while painful to Wharton, had the effect of linking her with many other women. In a note dated simply "Thursday," she wrote, "I have been too sad, for too long, & something in my nature—some lack, I suppose—has left me starving for what other women seem at least once in their lives to know" (Ransom Center). Charity's affair, like Wharton's, ultimately becomes shared female experience as Wharton does learn what other women know. A more difficult issue for Wharton than simply expressing female desire is what happens after that desire is expressed and acted upon. Her letters to Fullerton show anger and frustration at his ability to remove himself from her and from their relationship seemingly at will. In one letter, dated only "Tuesday night" but probably written in 1910, Wharton insists that Fullerton acknowledge his emotional responsibility to her:

> What you wish, apparently, is to take of my life the inmost & uttermost that a woman—a woman like me—can give, for an hour, now & then, when it suits you; & when the hour is over, to leave me out of your mind & out of your life as a man leaves the companion who has accorded him a transient distraction. I think I am worth more than that, or worth, perhaps I had better say, something quite different.... Don't imagine that I expect to see you often, or even to hear from you regularly. I know that a relation like ours has its inevitable stages, & that *that* stage is past. [...] Poor human nature has only a limited number of signs by which to express itself—& these signs, in cases like ours, are almost always much the same! (Ransom Center)

She continues to explain that her friends are free to see her or not see her, "[b]ut I do ask something more of the man who asks to be more than my friend; & so must any woman who is proud enough to be worth loving...." In *Summer*, Wharton returns to the male lover's responsibility to his female companion—or, perhaps more specifically, to the male lover's tendency to deny such a responsibility. Wharton resented Fullerton because she felt emotionally disposable to him; in her fiction, Wharton portrays other issues surrounding men's freedom to discard women when it suits them.

Disposable women lurk throughout *Summer*, most prominently in the form of Julia Hawes, Charity's "fallen" alter ego. The name of Julia's partner in sexual transgression is never revealed, although Mr. Royall's later association with her raises suspicions in his direction. In any case, the man walks away from her pregnancy without consequences or exposure. It is Julia's fate that is relevant, public, and expected. Julia has become a disposable woman. Her path, significantly, passes through the hands of Dr. Merkle, the female abortionist in Nettleton. Julia might have had an abortion quietly and returned to North Dormer (although the drama of her experience—"she came as near as anything to dying" [85]—might have precluded a discreet abortion); she might not have gotten pregnant in the first place; or she might have married her sexual partner. As it is, Dr. Merkle stands at the gateway to female disposability. Dr. Merkle's "false hair, the false teeth, the false murderous smile" (153) have often been noted as a sign of false mothering. Dr. Merkle's name also associates her with "merkin," a term for false pubic hair and fake vaginas.[3] By offering abortions, Dr. Merkle transforms women into merkins, objects with which men can have sex and avoid biological implications. Julia's abortion does not lead to a better life for her but rather leaves her firmly in the category of women dependent on men's pleasure and removed from their responsibility and protection.

When Charity realizes that Dr. Merkle is offering her an abortion, she is startled by "the grave surprise of motherhood" (153), and she leaps to her feet in anger and tries to leave. She never considers aborting her child. Bauer argues that "Charity takes control of the sexual act in deciding to keep her child" (43). Along the same lines, I suggest that Charity insists on acknowledging the consequences, both biological and emotional, of a sexual relationship and restores the reproductive function of sex. Although she has been disposed of, she refuses to dispose of her child or even to dispose of Harney. She recovers the blue brooch at great cost so that her child can have a connection with its biological father. Like Charity but perhaps more radically, by the end of the novel Mr. Royall too accepts that sexual activity has biological consequences; he cannot treat women as sexual playthings that he can walk away from. Charity, in this case, substitutes for Julia Hawes, the woman he perhaps should have married.

SUMMER IN THE CONTEXT OF THE BIRTH CONTROL MOVEMENT

Although written in 1916 and published in 1917, *Summer* seems to take place earlier in the century or even in the late nineteenth century. The changes that occurred between 1900, just as Wharton was preparing to settle at The Mount in Lenox, Massachusetts, and was traveling about the New England countryside, and 1917 create tensions in the ways that the novel might be read and interpreted. Those decades saw rapid and extreme changes in expectations for women's behavior; the Victorian ideal of the pure woman who tended the home and family and had no sex drive imploded against the reality of the New Woman, who was educated, independent, and often sexually active. How we view Charity depends on how we understand the expectations for women. Similarly, we must acknowledge the line between literary conventions and historical reality. Vectors of present and past, literature and history, create a web of interpretations of Charity Royall.

Although most of the birth control technology we rely on today was developed in the twentieth century (latex condoms, birth control pills), people have always practiced birth control and abortion to limit the size of their families. In the nineteenth century in the United States, birth control became a political issue, and the widespread transmission of information about contraception was made illegal in 1873 by the Comstock law, which prevented the sending of obscene material through the postal system. Historian Linda Gordon shows that that same decade saw a "remarkable" alignment among disparate women's groups such as the "suffragists..., moral reformers (in causes such as temperance, social purity, church auxiliaries, and women's professional and service clubs), and members of small free-love groups" (55); their point of unity was the notion of "voluntary motherhood." These groups believed that more power for women "would help to reinforce the family, make the government more just and the economy less monopolistic, and provide moral leadership in private life" (57). Even as they worked for voluntary motherhood, however, these groups ironically opposed birth control as artificial and as allowing women too much sexual freedom. They wanted to maintain the connection between sexual intercourse and motherhood, for one thing, and for another, they associated artificial birth control with prostitutes. If married couples could legally avail themselves of contraception, so could other people (66). Gordon continues: "the fact that sexual intercourse often led to conception seemed also a guarantee that men would marry in the first place. In the nineteenth century, women needed marriage more than men. Lacking economic or social independence, women needed husbands for support and status" (66). Gordon points out, however, that the real radicalism of these groups came from "another, potentially explosive conceptual change: the reacceptance of female sexuality" (57). In 1865, for example, Dr. James Ashton published *The Book of Nature: Containing Information for Young People Who Think of Getting Married*, in which, along with providing detailed information about male and female anatomy and contraceptive methods, he describes the courting process as grounded in mutual sexual attraction (20). He also explains that women are capable not only of feeling pleasure in the sexual act but also of experiencing multiple orgasms (34). Thus in the nineteenth century, birth control was highly contentious even while women's sexual desire became more openly acknowledged.

Any discussion of the birth control movement in the United States must include eugenics. The belief that traits such as poverty, criminality, alcoholism, and licentiousness could be bred out of the population fueled the push for birth control. Upper-class white Anglo-Saxons feared they would be overwhelmed by the prodigious birth rates of poor immigrants from Eastern Europe. The connection between birth control and the creation of a better race of Americans was not broken until the Great Depression, when sudden widespread poverty cast doubt on the genetic basis of poverty, and World War II, when Hitler's plans for and method of producing a superior race were made known. In this chapter, however, I do not address eugenics, as Dale Bauer has persuasively explained Wharton's concern with eugenics and illustrated how *Summer* was a reaction to the eugenics movement. Bauer shows that Wharton learned about the eugenics debate through Morton Fullerton and his critique of the movement (30), and she reads *Summer* as Wharton's "ambivalent mixture of her reaction to studies of family heredity and her rejection of the doctrine of maternal culpability, which accompanied theories of racial and cultural degeneration" (31). By not discussing eugenics here, I am not dismissing its significance; rather, I want to place *Summer* within a larger history of birth control and sexual attitudes, and I refer the reader to Bauer's excellent *Edith Wharton's Brave New Politics* for a discussion of Wharton's concern about eugenics.

Viewed in the broader context of the nineteenth-century birth control movement, the culture of North Dormer is one where what happens is precisely what would be expected to happen: Charity and the other girls become sexually active without access to birth control. Although prudish attitudes toward women's sexuality seem to dominate, in practice the town is lenient about couples' behavior. As rural women, the North Dormer girls' knowledge of and access to birth control is extremely limited. Charity's birth control options would more likely be in the form of abortion rather than contraception; while in the nineteenth century, "the continuity between abortion and contraception was natural" (Gordon 31), women with money were more likely to know about and have access to contraception while poor women tended to limit the size of their families through abortion (36). Dr. Merkle's casual approach to both Charity's pregnancy and the possibility of an abortion is callous but probably also reflects the reality of women's experience. Even her admonition of "The next time you'll know better'n to fret like this" (153) suggests that abortion is simply a fact of life for many women.

Charity's motherlessness and lack of role models for herself as a mother have been much commented upon.[4] Yet her motherlessness extends beyond the individual failures of her stepmother, her biological mother, and other mother figures in the novel; Wharton comments on a national culture of motherlessness that endangers all American women by refusing to inform them about contraceptive options. In her autobiography, the activist Margaret Sanger relates that during her trip to France for research into birth control methods and attitudes, she discovered that French women often learned about contraception from their mothers:

> When Bill Haywood began taking me into the homes of the syndicalists, I found perfect acceptance of family limitation and its relation to labor. "Have you just discovered this?" I asked each woman I met.
> "Oh, no, *Maman* told me."
> "Well, who told her?"
> "*Grandmère*, I suppose."
> The *Code Napoléon* had provided that daughters should inherit equally with sons and this, to the thrifty peasant mind, had indicated the desirability of fewer offspring. Nobody would marry a girl unless she had been instructed how to regulate the numbers of her household as well as the home itself. (*Autobiography* 104)[5]

Although it was not true that nineteenth-century American women knew nothing of contraception, Americans lived in a culture where such information had to be conveyed secretly or in code, if at all. In his study of birth control, *Eve's Herbs: A History of Contraception and Birth Control in the West*, John M. Riddle argues that although "knowledge of antifertility agents was eroded by centuries of laws, religious doctrine, social conventions, and witchcraft suppression," American women in the nineteenth century still managed to practice birth control because the capitalist marketplace provided the products that women no longer knew how to identify for themselves (234). For Charity, having a mother would not necessarily have provided knowledge of birth control since her substitute mothers, Mrs. Royall and Miss Hatchard, offer only veiled warnings about association with the opposite sex, not useful information. Her biological mother seems as ignorant of birth control as Charity. The real issue is a national one—a national "motherlessness" that prevents the explicit transmission of the knowledge to control reproduction.

Lucius Harney, however, would be likely to know about contraception. In her study of birth control, literature, and the law, Beth Widmaier Capo finds in Theodore Dreiser's *Jennie Gerhardt* (1911) an example of "the wealthy man with agency, while the female is a commodified object under the law," for Jennie's lover Lester Kane holds the knowledge that will prevent her from having children unless she and, more importantly, he want to (Capo 129). Although Harney's awareness of contraception is never explicitly stated, he fits into this category of the wealthy man with access to knowledge. He comes from the city, and his association with things French—choosing the French restaurant and speaking the language—hints at his knowledge. In nineteenth-century advertisements, "the denomination 'French' indicated a contraceptive device (a 'French letter' was a condom), while 'Portuguese' denoted an abortifacient" (Gordon 26). He may be unlikely to practice birth control, though, for in Charity he finds a girl already labeled a whore by her guardian and hence sexually available. A prostitute would be expected to know about contraception.

Although set in the late nineteenth century, *Summer* appeared to an early twentieth-century audience. The atmosphere surrounding birth control in America was very different by 1917. Despite our current popular sense of the 1920s as filled with sex and jazz, the break from Victorian standards for women happened earlier, as evidenced by bawdy vaudeville shows patronized by upper- and middle-class women starting around 1900 and by the Bohemian free love advocates centered in Greenwich Village in the 1910s. In contrast with the nineteenth-century birth control movement that was part of the ideal of "voluntary motherhood," birth control in the early twentieth century became linked with sexual indulgence (Gordon 128). Public awareness of contraception and its attendant issues was high, as Margaret Sanger had begun her extremely visible activism and publication on behalf of birth control. Her indictment in 1914 on obscenity charges for sending information about birth control through the mail attracted national attention, as did her founding of the National Birth Control League in 1915. In 1916 Sanger traveled across the country on a lecture tour, finding people eager for information even though many already possessed some knowledge of the topic. Sanger started a birth control clinic in Brooklyn in July of 1916 and was again arrested. By 1917, birth control was a national, public topic. And by 1917, the United States had entered World War I, putting thousands of young men in proximity to prostitutes and in need of condoms to prevent the transmission of venereal disease. The military did not distribute condoms to soldiers but rather practiced prophylaxis. General Order No. 6, issued by General Pershing, required prophylactic treatment for soldiers within hours of sexual intercourse and made infection with a venereal disease grounds for court-martial (Tone 101). Soldiers were, however, often made aware of condoms through informal routes.

It was into this national climate that *Summer* appeared. Charity Royall is a girl who needs information about and access to birth control. Charity's case is highly problematic, however, because she is not married. The vast majority of women who approached Sanger and other birth control advocates in the 1910s were married women who needed to keep their families small. In "What Every Girl Should Know" (1912), Sanger describes the "sexual impulse" as natural but not necessary to act on, and she explains that a girl should wait until she finds sexual desire united with "a freely conscious sympathy, a confidence and respect between her and her ideal" (45). Sanger does not explicitly advise that girls wait until marriage, but she does suggest that girls who act indiscriminately on their sexual impulses will be plagued by "social and economic forces" (44) and will end up as prostitutes. Nowhere in this tract does Sanger mention birth control. Charity's only chance of learning about birth control would be by word of mouth—and here, a conversation with Julia Hawes would have been helpful—or coming across an advertisement in a magazine or newspaper. As single women experienced more freedom in their sexual choices, American society was behind on informing them how to actually control their lives.

SUMMER AND THE AMBIGUITIES OF THE PROSTITUTE

Once pregnant, Charity faces her options, one of which is prostitution. Here Wharton seems to draw on a nineteenth-century understanding of prostitution, but the history of prostitution and the literary tradition of prostitution offer different and even opposing interpretations of Charity Royall and Julia Hawes. A long line of literary fallen women, from Susanna Rowson's Charlotte Temple, Thomas Hardy's Tess, to Stephen Crane's Maggie and Wharton's own Lily Bart, warns that one sexual misstep, or even the appearance of a misstep, will make a girl into a social outcast who falls down the economic ladder and ends up dead, often in a gutter. One such example of a literary prostitute appears in the form of Charity's mother, Mary Hyatt, whose body is compared to a "dead dog in a ditch" (171) and who is buried without a coffin. In her study of male-authored prostitutes, Laura Hapke explains that authors such as Stephen Crane, Harold Frederic, David Graham Phillips, and others viewed the prostitute as "a woman constantly threatened by entrapment, economic exploitation, and her own naiveté and vulnerability" (2), and these writers frequently depended on "the formulaic plot of the seduced innocent driven mad by city villainy" (3). A historical look at prostitution, however, reveals that "seduction" was rarely a reason given by women entering prostitution (Hobson 101). Nor was prostitution a one-way ticket to a depraved life. Historian Barbara Meil Hobson emphasizes that many prostitutes worked in the profession for only a few years:

> In assessing the meaning of prostitution in the course of a lifetime, it cannot be overemphasized that it was a temporary stage for nearly all who resorted to it. The age at which most prostitutes abandoned their trade was the age at which most women married. The decision to take up prostitution usually came a vulnerable point in a woman's life—a time when a daughter was seeking freedom from the restraints of home and several years before the age of marriage. For daughters of the working class, this period was often extended because their contribution to the family economy was vital. Thus, not only was prostitution a way for these young women to rebel against parental watchfulness over social and sexual morals, but it also meant freedom from familiar financial responsibilities—a way to live on their own and keep the income. (87)[6]

Women from rural families (as opposed to urban women and immigrant women) "viewed prostitution as the only way to escape boring and low-paid heavy work or as a means to support themselves or their children" (88).

The choice of a real (as opposed to literary) woman to become a prostitute must be viewed in light of women's economic opportunities. In the mid-nineteenth century, those opportunities were severely limited. A girl could earn more money working as a prostitute than in almost any other job, or she could supplement "honest" work through prostitution.[7] As one example of the difficulties for women in the marketplace, Hobson points to changes in the economy that made the cottage industry of hand-sewing one of "the most exploitative work environments for women," since employers had a vast supply of women with that skill (95). Julia Hawes, then, may be viewed in at least two ways: first, as a naïve girl who, like her literary predecessors, was seduced and will eventually succumb to disease, violence, and/or poverty; or second, as a bored young woman searching for a way out of the arduous and tedious life of her mother and sister. Wharton's description of Julia aligns her with the literary tradition of fallen women: "She had lost her freshness, and the paint under her eyes made her face seem thinner; but her lips had the same lovely curve, and the same cold mocking smile" (99). She is also described as "tipsy" (103) and hence associated with the vice of liquor as well as of sex. Even Julia's role as the town example of girls who "go wrong" marks her as a literary prostitute.

But other characters' attitudes toward Julia complicate our interpretation of her. She is humanized: Ally Hawes genuinely misses her sister. Charity's speculation that Julia's life has its "compensations" (71) suggests that Charity, who will never make enough money to leave North Dormer by working as a librarian two afternoons a week, understands the value of Julia's economic freedom, the frustrations of living under watchful small-town eyes, and the boredom from which Julia flees. Certainly Charity envies Julia's escape from North Dormer. Other evidence shows that Wharton did not accept the conventional view of prostitutes. In the same year that *Summer* was published appeared the novel *Susan Lenox* by David Graham Phillips. The title character chooses prostitution over her other options—marriage or factory work—and is rendered sympathetically by the author. She also survives prostitution and eventually leaves the profession. As Ammons shows, Wharton praised *Susan Lenox* for its honest portrayal of women's lives (153–55). Wharton's reaction to Phillips' book and her writing of *Summer* indicate that she wanted a real literature about women and their choices.

The contrasting literary and historical meanings of prostitution complicate our understanding of Charity's vision of a prostitute's life. She sees herself "earning its living and hers" by prostitution, giving the baby to someone else to raise, "hidden away somewhere where she could run in and kiss it, and bring it pretty things to wear" (179). Placed in a literary tradition, this imagined future seems unbearably naïve. Viewed historically, this vision is perhaps not so idealized. Hobson argues that the prostitute's "choice was reasonable in an irrational social universe: one in which social and economic conditions forced some women to earn a livelihood but fostered an ideology that denied them decent wages; one that censured only women in illicit sexuality but insisted that they were the weaker parties unable to protect themselves against male sexual advances; and one that idealized motherhood but did not provide social services for single women who had to raise children" (101).

One nineteenth-century response to prostitution was to "[envelope] the wayward personality in a blanket of domesticity" (Hobson 127). The 1870s saw a growth in women's reformatories that aimed to correct their inmates' impulses by teaching them domestic skills, "resocializing girls and women into the proper female roles of mother, helpmate for a husband, and moral custodian for society" (127). In *Summer*, Charity Royall's hands, though initially occupied in tatting lace (8), frequently sit empty in her lap while those of Ally Hawes work busily (146–47). Charity's laxity might be seen as a sign of her impending and actual sexual "delinquency." Mr. Royall assists her by agreeing to pay Verena Marsh to do the housework. Whether he knows it or not, by letting Charity off the domestic hook, Mr. Royall, in the Victorian view, helps Charity along toward sexual promiscuity—perhaps lending further credence to Charity's later assertion that he wants her "to be like those other girls...So's 't he wouldn't have to go out" (114). Ironically, however, becoming sexually active actually increases Charity's domestic impulses: the deserted house where she meets Harney is "furnished in primitive camping fashion...with an earthenware jar holding a bunch of asters...and in one corner was a mattress with a Mexican blanket over it" (122). Her housekeeping is basic, sensual, and exotic, reflecting its roots in an active sexual impulse and its corresponding threat to the established sexual order.

Charity is situated on the cusp of changing standards, and her sexual activity would have resonated differently with readers in 1917 than if she had appeared before a Victorian audience. As Gordon shows, prostitution dropped during the 1910s, and she argues that at least part of the reason for the change came from more women becoming sexually active outside of marriage:

> The basis for the decline in prostitution between 1910 and 1920 was not the conversion of men to purity; it was the conversion of women to "indulgence".... Though men and women were both becoming more likely to have nonmarital sex, the change for women was proportionally greater. Most significant, men were more likely to have sex with women they would later marry, thus making virginity a less universal requirement for a marriage partner, while the men's rate of intercourse with women other than future spouses remained almost stationary. (136)

In *Summer*, Mr. Royall finds himself struggling to reconcile the old standards with both Charity's and his own behavior. Even if Mr. Royall had not designated Charity a "whore," he still is the one to point out a reality about women's sexual freedom: "And you know why you ain't asked her to marry you, and why you don't mean to. It's because you hadn't need to" (141). He might also be referring to Harney's failure to reward Charity financially as opposed to matrimonially. That is, Harney has no need either to marry or pay Charity because she is willing to sleep with him for free. This does not make Charity a prostitute, but it does fulfill Victorian fears that men will not marry if they have no sexual incentive. Although Mr. Royall hypocritically denounces both Charity's and Harney's behavior, he at least has the grace to reconsider his own activity with prostitutes.

Despite the increasing nonmarital sexual activity of women after 1900, historical records up to the 1920s show the tendency of law enforcement and social agencies to fail to differentiate between women who had sex outside of marriage and women who charged money for sexual favors. A twenty-first century reader of the histories of women prosecuted for prostitution, lewdness, and disorderly conduct would wonder at the lumping together of professional prostitutes and women engaging in casual sex, even with their fiancés. Connelly points out that a worldview that failed to distinguish kinds of female nonmarital sexual activity resulted in a limited language; there were literally no words other than "prostitute" to label women who were sexually active outside of marriage (19). Charity's question—"Was there no alternative but Julia's?" (or Anna Leath's of Sophy Viner, in *The Reef*—"What *is* she?")—becomes a basic linguistic quandary. Describing the widespread paranoia about sexual licentiousness as a threat to national security during World War I, Hobson documents cases of the arrest of women appearing on the streets at night around army bases. These women were almost exclusively of the lower class, however—indicating that women like F. Scott Fitzgerald's Daisy Buchanan, Zelda Fitzgerald's Alabama Beggs, and even Zelda Sayre herself were free to associate with military men without legal consequences. Poor women were subject to prosecution and persecution, including forced medical examinations, for the same behavior Daisy, Alabama, and Zelda engaged in freely. Thus Charity Royall, who does not charge Lucius Harney for sex and is even embarrassed that he might think she pressured him into buying her the blue pin, would have been considered in the same category as a prostitute—a fact Mr. Royall makes clear.

Another effect of nonmarital sexuality for women had less to do with society's reaction to them than with the isolation it created. The increased sexual activity among unmarried couples in the 1910s had the effect of weakening bonds among women. Gordon comments:

> we notice that the sexual revolution was not a general loosening of sexual taboos but only of those on nonmarital heterosexual activity. Indeed, so specifically heterosexual was this change that it tended to intensify taboos on homosexual activity and did much to break patterns of emotional dependence and intensity among women. Greater freedom of emotional and sexual expression with men made women view their time spent with women friends as somehow childish in comparison, or at least less sophisticated and less adventurous. (131)

In *Summer*, part of Charity Royall's pleasure in her relationship with Lucius Harney comes from the way it sets her apart from other girls, and her friendship with Ally Hawes, though apparently never very intimate, becomes even less so with the consummation of the affair. Ally, hoping to live vicariously through Charity's adventures, produces the opposite effect by sewing Charity's dresses for the Nettleton Fourth of July and Old Home Week celebrations. Charity shuts Ally out, refusing to tell her tales of Nettleton (106) and snatching Harney's letter from Ally's hands without satisfying the other girl's curiosity (156). Heterosexual relationships seem to isolate all the girls of North Dormer. Other town girls resent Charity when Mr. Royall pulls strings to get her the librarianship, but, as already noted, they also begrudge her for her refusal to let them use the library for trysts with their suitors. Charity's lack of female friends leaves her even more vulnerable when she becomes pregnant. Even though the girls' experiences are so similar, each one ends up negotiating her difficulties on her own.

SUMMER AND THE LITERATURE OF WHITE SLAVERY

Summer would have resonated with readers of the decade who were familiar with the literature of the "white slavery" scare. White slavery tracts flooded the marketplace from about 1909 until 1914, even though a 1910 investigation by the Rockefeller Commission found no evidence of white slavery itself.[8] These narratives followed a standard plot: a young woman from the country leaves her home for the city, where, by methods ranging from an offer of marriage to being drugged in an alley, she is taken off to a brothel and forced to work as a prostitute. These stories were driven by several national anxieties, including unease over the increased number of unmarried women leaving their rural homes and entering the city workforce, fears about the growing immigrant population in the United States (many of the procurers and pimps of the tales were foreigners), and worry over the consolidation of economic power in corporate conglomerations. *Summer* is not a white slave narrative, and there is no evidence Wharton even knew about the genre. But the novel appeared among a readership that *did* know about white slavery, and each of the concerns driving the white slavery scare alters the interpretation of the role of women and female sexuality in *Summer*.

Charity's desire to leave North Dormer for the city is vague but persistent. She does not know what city life is like or what exactly she wants from it; she simply wants something more than the small town can offer. The only thing she does explicitly want is to escape the suffocating closeness of the community. Historically, the desire to leave small towns was at the root of the prevailing national anxiety over women's sexuality. The rise in number of young women living in the city provoked concern that core national values of small towns and rural life were being eroded. Connelly links "the country girl" to the myth of pastoral purity at the heart of American identity (122). The girl who left her country home threatened the belief that the country life was the ideal life, and, in response, white slavery tracts insisted that girls stay home. By practically forcing Charity to marry him, Mr. Royall follows the demands of the white slavery narrative to keep country girls safe in the country. Indeed, his Old Home Week speech, ostensibly directed at "the young *men* who are perhaps planning even now to leave these quiet hills" (132), ends up having the most impact on Charity.

One of the conventions of the white slave narrative was its insistence on a secret network or conspiracy run by immigrants; in the literature, girls who fell into the hands of foreign white slavers became part of a system of prostitution and its attendant evils. Connelly suggests that "the preoccupation with the violation of beautiful native American country girls by alien white slavers might be seen as a projection of native American's deepest sexual fear: immigrant males possessing the daughters of the land while their men stand unable to help or protect" (118). By 1917, those fears were mingled with war atrocity stories—tales of barbaric Germans raping Belgian women and cutting off the hands and feet of Belgian children. Wharton, living in Paris and working among Belgian refugees, heard atrocity stories firsthand. In a letter to Sara Norton, dated September 2, 1914, Wharton wrote: "The 'atrocities' one hears of *are true*" (Lewis and Lewis *Letters* 335 emphasis in original). Biographer Shari Benstock recounts atrocity stories Wharton heard, including that of "Mme Marguerite M.," who was held prisoner by the Germans in inhumane conditions, watched her daughter die, and heard her sister being raped (*No Gifts* 323). Wharton's readers would have heard those stories as part of the British and American propaganda machine (though many of the stories were made up by the British to incite American wrath). Dr. Merkle's apparent foreignness, as evidenced by her slight accent, thus signifies her role as procuress in the world of prostitution, and her offer to find Charity a job as a companion in Boston (154) hints strongly of other traps used to capture unwary country girls. Her behavior too would arouse readers' suspicions: Dr. Merkle "leaned her firm shoulders against the door as she spoke, like a grim gaoler making terms with her captive" (154). The danger Dr. Merkle represents is more than financial; she threatens Charity's freedom and, by extension, the integrity of the nation.

In her study of white slave narratives, Margit Stange de-emphasizes the literal fear of foreigners by pointing out that many white slavers took the form of the all-American boy-next-door (87). She argues that rather than exuding anxiety about immigration, the narratives reveal a different horror that also undermines traditional American values, the corporate trust: "White slavery's rendering of an economy in which organized operatives monopolize all the raw wealth, manage all the transactions, saturate and control the market, and put all the profits into their own pockets, provided the public with a version of the trust as an unequivocal evil—a version they could symbolically defeat and reform" (85). Stange connects white slavery and corporate trusts by reading white slave narratives as perversions of the exchange of women. In a white slave narrative, a family is robbed of its "own" women by white slavers, who, by forcing the girl to engage in sexual activity, wring all exchange value out of her, value that should belong to the family (80–84). This, of course, is the cultural problem with incest: a family group must designate some of its women as off limits so that those women must be exchanged with another family group, forming bonds among men. In *Summer*, Mr. Royall refuses to circulate his one remaining woman, but since she is already pregnant by someone outside the family group, his failure to exchange Charity does him no reproductive damage. Rather, he is incorporating, or "putting all the profits into [his] own pockets." Charity's child will bear his name and be regarded as his.

White slavery tales end either with the death of the enslaved girl or with her rescue. In *Summer*, Mr. Royall becomes Charity's rescuer by marrying her and by giving her the money to remove herself from Dr. Merkle's power entirely. Connelly notes, however, that white slave literature depicts the "slaves" as girls, emphasizing their innocence and childlike qualities even in characters who are as old as eighteen (126). Charity's increasing passivity toward the end of the novel aligns her with white slave victims. As if she were a child, Mr. Royall tells her what she really wants: "You want to be took home and took care of" (186). Charity follows him through Nettleton to the minister "as passively as a tired child" (188). Her behavior makes Mr. Royall's role as rescuer ambiguous;[9] he becomes *both* rescuer and white slaver, leading Charity home to the "red house" as a procurer would lead a girl to a house in the red-light district. Many white slave narratives focus on "girls who disappear,"[10] and at the end of the novel, one feels that Charity has disappeared. Her personality is wiped out by her fatigue and despair at her lack of options, and her final entrance into the red house sinisterly suggests that she will never again emerge.

Single Women, Urban Lives

Charity Royall's romance and its consequences play themselves out in a rural setting, under the watchful eyes of her small-town neighbors. Her forays into the larger town of Nettleton indicate an increased danger for young women in the city, who may have greater knowledge of the ways of life but are also at greater risk from its dangers. Dr. Merkle's veiled threat to send Charity to Boston reminds readers, if not Charity, of the nightmare of "white slavery." Wharton's fiction is full of single women in the city who must negotiate changing social and sexual mores on their own. Lily Bart, Nettie Struther, Lilla Gates, Anne Clephane, Nona Manford, and Halo Spear form a line of characters, spanning almost thirty years, who demonstrate Wharton's ongoing interest in the opportunities and limitations of single women in the city.

Even before World War I, single urban women excited a need for increased control over female sexuality. The particular focus was on working women: "In 1870, 1.9 million women were employed; in 1890, 4 million. By 1910 that number had doubled" (Gordon 135). These women often lived in groups with other single women—out from under the watchful eyes of parents, neighbors, churches, and schools (Gordon 136). They were thus free for and had the privacy for sexual encounters if they so chose. Gordon also suggests, however, that many of these women were underpaid and had to spend most of their earnings on housing and on appropriate clothing for their jobs, leaving them with not enough money for food: "Even without overspending, many independent women workers had to count on being taken out to dinner several nights a week in order to make ends meet" (136). Connelly, calling the amount of money a working woman could command "disgracefully substandard," quotes the U.S. Senate's 1911 report on working conditions for women in concluding that "the large proportion of working women were paid wages 'inadequate to supply a reasonable standard of living for women dependent upon their own earnings for support'" (31). Although, as Connelly shows, economic privation may not have driven women to prostitution, it did leave them vulnerable. Of course, Edith Wharton's single women, for the most part, are not workers. Many of them do live with their families. But circumstances often leave them negotiating the marriage market on their own, and they become embroiled with the larger cultural fears concerning single women. Wharton, who tended not to focus on the plight of poor and working women, shows that a woman does not have to be poor to be vulnerable.

The House of Mirth was published in 1905, right in the midst of the influx of single women into the urban workforce, and the story of Lily Bart illustrates anxieties about working women. Orphaned, Lily is left with only her aunt to care for her, and Mrs. Peniston demonstrates little interest in securing her niece's future in a financially advantageous marriage or in regulating Lily's behavior. Lily makes her own decisions about where she will go and whom she will see. Thus the first half of the book mirrors the second half; the losses of her aunt and of her inheritance only illuminate Lily's earlier position. She is a free agent in the marriage market. But without her aunt's protection and without money, Lily's life gets worse. By refusing to live with Gertie and taking her own room in a boarding house, Lily leaves herself open to charges of sexual promiscuity; even without the taint of Gus Trenor over her, Lily would be perceived as a prostitute. The other characters' appalled reactions to her living situation stem from not only horror at Lily's poverty but also at the sexual implications of her living on her own.

Lily's social and economic descent opens a window into the lives of single women without Lily's initial advantages. As a worker in a milliner's shop, Lily becomes acquainted with the entanglement of finances with sexual activity for women of the lower class. The casual chatter of her fellow-workers demonstrates a familiarity with men that hints at male expectations of female sexual returns in exchange for money spent: "I *told* her he'd never look at her again; and he didn't. I wouldn't have, either—I think she acted real mean to him. He took her to the Arion Ball, and had a hack for her both ways" (384–85 emphasis in original). This working girl's refusal to allow her date sexual access repeats Lily's rejection of Gus Trenor after he gives her money—and Lily is never "looked at" again, by Gus or his society. Nettie Struther explains her "fall" to Lily: "Work-girls aren't looked after the way you are, and they don't always know how to look after themselves" (425–26). Nettie is wrong, of course, in that Lily is not looked after even in the aristocratic hothouse world to which she was born, but the working woman faces more opportunities and pressures to put her in the way of "trouble."

Lily is trapped by the same labels that determine Charity's fate, and with less cause. Living worlds apart, geographically and economically, the women are judged on the same basis and fall into the same category. Not until the 1920s did psychologists and reformers attempt to differentiate among kinds of women's sexual behavior. The sociologist W. I. Thomas published *The Unadjusted Girl* in 1923, in an attempt to understand (and perhaps fix) the reasons why girls were behaving so differently from their forebears. He concludes:

> Thus fifty years ago we recognized, roughly speaking, two types of women, the one completely good and the other completely bad,—what we now call the old-fashioned girl and the girl who had sinned and been outlawed. At present we have several intermediate types,—the occasional prostitute, the charity girl, the demi-virgin, the equivocal flapper, and in addition girls with new but social behavior norms who have adapted themselves to all kinds of work. (230–31)

Rather sympathetically, Thomas suggests that the roots of the new behavior of women are cultural and contextual: "It is the release of important social energies which could not find expression under the norms of the past. Any general movement away from social standards implies that these standards are no longer adequate" (231). In her 1920s fiction, Wharton often attempted to decipher the new standards for women. She frequently concluded, as Melanie Dawson points out in her article on Wharton's young women in the 1920s, that such women end up "disappointments—collapsing, choosing safety, and embodying stasis" (90). In other words, despite a culture that celebrates individual expression and success, they get married.

In *The Mother's Recompense* (1925), Kate Clephane returns to New York and to the daughter she abandoned twenty years ago when she left her husband for another man. The novel examines Kate's moral and emotional dilemma as she realizes that her daughter Anne is in love with and intends to marry a man Kate herself had an affair with years ago. Kate's emotional journey is the story, but the novel offers a glimpse of Wharton's vision of single women in "the Babylonian New York" (29) of the 1920s, the era of parties, jazz, and flappers. For young women of this era—especially wealthy women of the families of old New York—"fallen-ness" is no longer the concern it was for Lily Bart. Anne's friend Nollie Tresselton has been divorced and remarried to no social outcry, and even Kate's niece Lilla Gates— also divorced but much wilder than Nollie or Anne—safely winds her way into a satisfactory marriage. Unlike girls in *The House of Mirth*, these characters, including and especially Anne, do not rely on their mothers to find them husbands. They assist each other in their romances and roam the city spaces freely for their assignations, out from under their parents' eyes—as, Kate believes, Lilla Gates does when she meets Chris Fenno in the park.

Lilla poses a number of problems, for her family, for Kate, and for the reader. She is a flapper who prefers "noises that don't mean anything" (55) and enjoys "going somewhere else in order to do exactly the same thing" (81). Her parents are anxious about her future, and Kate cannot understand the family support Lilla receives: "No one explained Lilla—every one seemed to take her for granted" (73). Although Kate believes that Lilla "as a symptom" could be "enlightening" (74), Lilla actually offers contradictory clues for Kate. She displays attributes that in earlier fiction would identify her clearly as a prostitute. The traits that make her a "modern" young woman would, a generation earlier, have marked her as a fallen woman: "She stood leaning against the piano, sipping the cock-tail some one had handed her, her head thrown back, and the light from a shaded lamp striking up at her columnar throat and the green glitter of earrings, which suggested to Kate Clephane the poisonous antennae of some giant insect" (79). Her drinking and her physicality stand out; her description as a "giant insect" links her with the trope of the dangerous prostitute who lures in and sucks dry unsuspecting young men. Her "sulky, contemptuous gaze" (78) links her to *Summer*'s "mocking" Julia Hawes. Lilla has "dyed hair, dyed lashes, drugged eyes and unintelligible dialect" (50), characteristics that link her with Sophy Viner's sister in *The Reef.* Even after she marries, Lilla does not tone down her appearance but rather emerges with "a bolder dash of peroxide in her hair" (181). Lilla, as a "symptom," thus gives no real information about the connections among a woman's appearance, her virtue, and her fate.

Kate Clephane takes comfort in the thought that her daughter is no Lilla. Anne seems to stand apart from "the new girls" in her simple, almost masculine taste in decorating her rooms (33) and in her "archaic" decision to observe mourning for her grandmother, however attenuated that mourning may have become since Kate's youth (60). Yet Kate's insistence on Anne's difference from Lilla is undermined by hints that the two girls are fundamentally not so dissimilar, as suggested by their physical closeness at a party in Anne's new studio (79). The studio itself is a marker of Anne's independence, which she waits until after her grandmother's death to establish because old Mrs. Clephane protested: "She thought paint so messy—and then how could she have got up all those stairs?" (77). The elder Mrs. Clephane objects to the studio because it is a space she cannot monitor. The studio, out of the house and away from any supervisory eyes, allows for romantic meetings. Lilla demands a latch-key, although she does not get one (79–80), and Kate later discovers Anne and Chris there. Just as Lilla's marriage comes about through the help of Nollie and Anne, Anne and Chris's relationship relies on Lilla as a go-between. Both young women do not expect or want their parents' help in arranging their marriages, as Anne makes abundantly clear.

Perhaps the most disturbing aspect of the connection between Anne and Lilla does not seem to occur to Kate. Kate briefly considers telling Lilla about the relationship between Chris and herself as a way to stop Anne and Chris's wedding, but she realizes that Lilla would not regard the mother's relationship a barrier to the daughter's marriage. She imagines Lilla's response: "Why, what on earth's all the fuss about? Don't that sort of thing happen all the time?" (192). Kate knows that "that sort of thing" does happen: "she had known such cases;... but that she and Anne should ever figure as one of them was beyond human imagining." Until the end of the novel, Kate believes that if Anne were to learn the truth she would turn from Chris, as well as from her mother. Kate never considers that if Anne were to find out, she might react as Lilla would and choose to marry Chris anyway. This, perhaps, is the true Gorgon lurking in modern relationships at which Kate cannot look—and this horror is the real if unconscious reason Kate cannot tell Anne about her relationship with Chris.

Kate consults a minister about the problem, and he returns a Howellsian answer about not causing "sterile pain" (212). But times have changed since Howells, girls know more than they used to, and Kate's not telling in effect protects only herself. Kate, deep in the denial that aligns her with mothers who decline to tell their daughters about sex before they marry, has failed to arm her daughter with the knowledge she will need to make informed choices about her life. Wharton knew about such withholding of information: her own mother refused to tell her daughter about sexual relationships. In her unfinished autobiography *Life and I*, written in 1932, Wharton recalls her mother's refusal to tell her about sexuality, even on her wedding day. She reflects on her enforced ignorance: "I record this brief conversation, because the training of which it was the beautiful & logical conclusion did more than anything else to falsify & misdirect my whole life...And, since, in the end, it did neither, it only strengthened the conclusion that one is what one is, & that education may delay but cannot deflect one's growth. Only, what possibilities of tragedy may lie in the delay!" (35 ellipses in original). Kate's choice to withhold information from her daughter may only "delay growth" and clearly leaves open "possibilities of tragedy." In a stroke of artistic brilliance, Wharton does not write a scene in which, after the marriage takes place, Anne discovers her mother and her husband's past; it is enough that the possibility of discovery will lurk forever over Anne's head.

Whether Anne and Chris's marriage is really the horror Kate believes it to be is an open question. The generational isolation in which the girls of "Babylonian New York" make their decisions is, for Wharton, clearly a troublesome matter. On the one hand, as Anne says, "we've all got to buy our own experience" (186), and Wharton, despite the pain of some of her personal life, probably agreed with Anne. Yet a reader of *The Mother's Recompense* cannot feel wholly comfortable with the Fenno marriage. Kate's unique position as the prodigal and hence powerless mother only magnifies the impotency of any mother's position in the new New York; after all, Kate has no *less* power than Lilla's mother in managing her daughter's love life.

Daughters have claimed their independence to navigate the city and its romantic possibilities as best they can, and even if the advice of mothers fails to protect daughters from unhappy marriages (as was Wharton's experience—and probably for the reason Anne herself claims: "You don't know me either, mother!" [152]), Anne might have at the least been allowed to make an informed choice for herself.

Another problem that *The Mother's Recompense* ponders is that of a society that allows a woman's desire to run rampant but only toward men and marriage. Despite Anne's early claim that "I shall never marry" (67), Kate does not believe her for a moment. Should she be forced to choose, Kate believes, Anne "would not hesitate to sacrifice her mother" for her lover (197). Kate feels vulnerable to a culture that values romantic love and sexual desire over family love and loyalty. Marriage is still the only role for a woman, and with the new freedom of expression for women's desire, the limitations of marriage are more dangerous. Anne's desire, not Chris's, fuels the romance; Chris goes away twice, only to be dragged back by Anne's passion for him. Anne's will, which both Kate and Chris acknowledge, overpowers any interference, even that which might be made in her best interests. This is a double bind: surely Wharton would not advocate returning to a system where parents dictated a child's marriage partner, yet she does not consider the new freedoms an improvement—at least not as long as they are based solely on women's sexual desire. What if Kate had taken seriously her daughter's declaration that she would never marry? Anne has an art studio, but no one to believe that she might actually make something of it.

Conclusion

In her later novels, Wharton continued to investigate the ramifications of single women and their romances in the city. Her next novel, *Twilight Sleep* (1927), struggles with the casualness with which young women like Lita Wyant decide to end a marriage and portrays the easy opportunities even a single woman has for adultery. Halo Spear, of *Hudson River Bracketed* (1929) and *The Gods Arrive* (1932), experiences an incompatible marriage and an out-of-wedlock affair. Tellingly, what she most wants in the beginning is a place of her own in the city: "Ah, how she envied the girls of her age who had their own cars, who led their own lives, sometimes even had their own bachelor flats in New York!" (104). These women are discussed in chapters 5 and 6, but I wish to note how frequently Wharton returns to topic of the single woman. Although some of these characters are repetitive (Lilla Gates and Lita Wyant, for example, have much in common), as a series they chart the changing attitudes and anxieties about single women—as well as the attitudes that do not change. Fundamentally, Wharton's women fall into two categories, although not those of chaste or fallen; they are either poor or financially secure, and it is this distinction that decides their fate. Lily Bart, Sophy Viner, and Charity Royall struggle because of the link between their poverty and their sexual status. Anne Clephane, Lilla Gates, Lita Wyant, Nona Manford, and Halo Spear evade disaster not because they make smart or safe romantic choices but rather because they have access to money.

One might wonder to what degree getting pregnant really dictates Charity Royall's future. Gordon demonstrates that despite the increase in availability of birth control mechanisms, the presence of women in the workplace, and receiving the vote, women's position in society had changed very little by 1930: "What seems odd, in fact, is that so many feminists of sexual liberation persuasion had somehow imagined that the assertion of female sexuality could erase deeply rooted male supremacy in the culture and in the economy" (163). Bauer makes the same point, as demonstrated by *Summer*: "Without an attendant legal equality, sexual freedom lands women right back under phallocratic law" (46). Even if phallocratic law permits Lilla Gates to make a successful marriage despite her past, that same law insists that Lilla and Anne Clephane must marry to have a meaningful life. Despite the freedoms of the New Woman and the flapper, Wharton suggests that women have few good choices. None of these women are encouraged to build a career for themselves; girls like Nettie Struther might work, but they cannot support themselves financially or emotionally. Wharton insists that the new freedoms offered to women of the 1910s and 1920s are simply window-dressing that hide the basic fact that women must marry.

CHAPTER 3

"Unmediated Bonding Between Men": The Accumulation of Men in the Short Stories

In her classic 1975 essay "The Traffic in Women," Gayle Rubin describes the dynamics through which power in a patriarchal society works. Bringing together the theories of Freud, Lacan, Engels, Marx, and Levi-Strauss, Rubin argues that patriarchy functions through socially created incest taboos that require family or tribal groups to exchange women for reproductive purposes and simultaneously forge bonds among those groups or, more specifically, among the men in those groups. Power travels through women but is never wielded by them. Edith Wharton, herself an avid scholar of anthropology, portrayed such a society in *The Age of Innocence* (1920), in which Newland Archer announces his engagement to May Welland earlier than planned for the express purpose of protecting May's cousin, the scandalous Ellen Olenska, through the backing of two old New York families. May is the glue that brings the Archer power, which in turn is linked through marriage to the even more formidable Van der Luyden family, into alliance with the Mingotts'. Women, though themselves powerless in the patriarchal structure, are the vehicles through which great power can be formed and used.

Eve Kosofsky Sedgwick, in her influential study of men's relationships in *Between Men*, also sees male power as configured through women. She theorizes male homosocial desire as a triangular structure, consisting of two men and a woman, in which "the bond that links the two [male] rivals is as intense and potent as the bond that links either of the rivals to the [female] beloved" (21). In the "normal" functioning of gender identities and sexual relationships, "there is a special relationship between male homosocial (*including* homosexual) desire and the structures for maintaining and transmitting patriarchal power" (25 emphasis in original). But Sedgwick also notes that the triangle can go wrong, that "unmediated bonding between men" can arise from an extraordinary devaluing of women (100). "Unmediated bonding between men" does not necessarily equate to homosexuality, but it does mean that homosocial desire is not channeled through women, as Western society usually dictates. This situation is one of Wharton's anxieties, revealed in some of her short stories: that women are not essential in men's alliances and, more important, that they are not necessary to the real functioning of society at all. Some of Wharton's short stories portray extreme cases of "unmediated bonding between men." Instead of the devaluation of women and their role in mediated men's relationships with each other, Wharton envisions the complete removal of actual women from men's relationships and the structures of power.

Wharton's fear may have biographical roots. As her career flourished, she surrounded herself with intelligent, literary men: Walter Berry, Henry James, Bernard Berenson, W. Morton Fullerton, Howard Sturgis, Gaillard Lapsley, Percy Lubbock, John Hugh Smith, and Robert Norton. As a professional writer in an era when such a career was extremely unusual for a woman (particularly a woman of Wharton's generation and class), Wharton frequently found herself out of place in traditional gender identities and dynamics. Most women, not having received the same education as men, could not offer Wharton the conversation she needed. In *A Backward Glance*, Wharton recalls the "mocking radiance" of days at the Mount with Berry, Bay Lodge, Lapsley, Norton, and Smith:

> these, with Henry James, if not by the actual frequency of their visits, yet from some secret quality of participation, had formed from the first the nucleus of what I have called the inner group. In this group an almost immediate sympathy had established itself between the various members, so that our common stock of allusions, cross-references, pleasantries was always increasing, and new waves of interest in the same book or picture, or any sort of dramatic event in life or letters, would simultaneously flood through our minds. (193)

Later, in Paris, Wharton corresponded with these men, traveled with them, and summoned some of them when she was feeling lonely. In the postwar years, Robert Norton, Gaillard Lapsley, and John Hugh Smith frequently spent Christmas with Wharton at her winter home in the south of France.

Despite accusations that she was not interested in women, Wharton did have close female friends. In *Edith Wharton's Women: Friends and*

Rivals, Susan Goodman emphasizes the importance of Wharton's friendship with Sara "Sally" Norton. Norton was the daughter of the distinguished Harvard professor Charles Eliot Norton, and she was intelligent and educated. Their friendship began in 1899, just as Wharton's literary career took off, and lasted until Norton died of cancer in 1922. The two women could and did discuss a range of issues, from their own health problems to Wharton's literary efforts. Goodman argues that the friendship "challenged assumptions that women's relationships had to be either unnatural or competitive" (47). A number of other women figured prominently in Wharton's life. Elisina Tyler was her right hand during the war, executing much of the day-to-day work of Wharton's charities; she traveled with Wharton, attended her during her illnesses, and was there when Wharton died. Mary "Minnie" Cadwalader Jones, Wharton's sister-in-law, was a regular correspondent, as was her daughter Beatrix Jones Farrand, with whom Wharton was fond of discussing gardening.[1] Scholar Mia Manzulli suggests that the Wharton/Farrand correspondence "created a shared space...where novelist and landscape gardener could achieve 'exquisite collaborations,' fruits of a rare partnership of creative equals" (36). Aunt and niece also shared the experience of being professional women in an economy where such women were a rarity. Margaret "Daisy" Terry Chandler, a childhood playmate, remained a friend for life, and Mary Berenson, wife of Bernard, also was a frequent correspondent.

Still, Wharton's male friends were a powerful force in her life, and this situation was not always comfortable. As the most famous of the group, Henry James and Wharton tended to dominate it, but even James could not compete with Wharton's power in the marketplace. As the only woman among apparently homosexual or asexual men, Wharton found some room to play with gender identity. Goodman suggests that the inner circle gave her "a secret sense of heterosexual superiority" (*Inner Circle* 26), an advantage she might not have been afforded among a different group of men. But the men in Wharton's inner circle did not necessarily grant her this superiority. Goodman indicates that they "viewed Wharton with affectionate skepticism" (26), and, though they were clearly fascinated by her, they did not need her as much as she needed them. According to Goodman, the men's fascination with her also allowed them distance from her: "'Knowing Edith,' was in some ways a kind of competitive sport that jocularly bound the men together" (23). As much as the men provided intellectual freedom and support for Wharton (in her later years, she would read aloud her works in progress to whichever of them happened to be with her), she could not entirely ignore her unique position among them as a woman. Goodman points out that "as the only woman in a group of men, Wharton could not escape the fact that she was an anomaly. The 'otherness' that was a source of pride was also a source of fear, another form of linguistic and spiritual exile" (112). Goodman also suggests that the group was not and could not have been as cohesive as Wharton remembered: "not unexpectedly, the refuge that Wharton found in an inner circle grew from her own imagination" (*Inner Circle* 8). It may not be surprising, then, that anxieties about this group and her own place in it found their way into Wharton's writing.

As a member of a group of men friends, even if the "group" was at least partially of her own imagination, she had an established place—a right to exist, even. If her place in that group was threatened, so was Wharton's identity. What if they did not need her at all? In this chapter, I investigate Wharton's subconscious fear that she could be eliminated from the group without consequence to the men and its larger implications. I start with "A Bottle of Perrier," written in 1926, the same year that she saw a "defection" by a member of her group, and then I examine some of her earlier stories. In 1926, Percy Lubbock announced his intention to marry Sybil Cutting, whose second marriage had been to another of Wharton's friends, Geoffrey Scott, and who before that had had an affair with Bernard Berenson, among others. Wharton believed Sybil to be a vapid, man-hungry type of woman that she herself despised—and envied. Goodman suggests that "Lubbock's defection substantiated the author's thesis that men naturally prefer a perfectly complected, childish woman to what Paul Bourget, using Wharton as a model, called 'the intellectual tomboy'" (30–31). When Scott married Sybil in 1918, Wharton wrote to Berenson that she expected never to see him again "except encircled by that well-meaning waste of unintelligence" (Lewis and Lewis *Letters* 403). When Lubbock later became involved with Sybil, Wharton complained about the relationship in letters to Gaillard Lapsley, John Hugh Smith, and Daisy Chandler, and part of her annoyance seems to have come from the removal of bachelors from her side. To Lapsley, she wrote: "This is the 3d of my friends she has annexed, & I see you & Robert going next, & then B. B. & finally even Walter—kicking & screaming!!!" (Lewis and Lewis *Letters* 487). Wharton never forgave Lubbock for marrying Sybil, and their friendship did not recover. Wharton was deeply hurt that Lubbock could so easily sacrifice her friendship.[2]

Wharton's short stories reveal her anxiety that power and knowledge occur outside and completely indifferent to the realm of women and, in particular, to the kind of woman she herself was. In *No Man's Land: The Place of the Woman Writer in the Twentieth Century: Vol. 1: The War of the Words*, Sandra M. Gilbert and Susan Gubar imagine the early twentieth-century literary marketplace as a pitched battle between the sexes for authority. Male modernist writers, threatened by women authors' increasing power in the public sphere, felt moved to insist on women's inability to create true art. Wharton, though commercially successful, is one of those women writers Gilbert and Gubar describe as "fighting for life"—an intellectual life and a life in which neither her writing ability nor her gender diminishes her. Her interest in masculinity is partly sympathetic; Lori Jirousek, in "Haunting Hysteria: Wharton, Freeman, and the Ghosts of Masculinity," argues that Wharton used her ghost stories to play out the tensions inherent in masculinity during the early part of the twentieth century. But her interest is also partly defensive, an attempt to understand the forces aligned against her. Several of her stories, both realistic and ghost stories, suggest a curiosity about and fear of what happens between men when women are not present, something Wharton could never know, even in the presence of her inner circle. True power, she feared, was male, mysterious, and utterly exclusive.

"A Bottle of Perrier": Masculine Authority as the Accumulation of Men

Wharton's anxiety about the elite male world from which she herself could be omitted culminated in the story "A Bottle of Perrier," written in 1926—after the deaths of many of the prominent men in her circle, including Henry James, Howard Sturgis, and Edgerton Winthrop. She drew on her experiences in North Africa, where she traveled in 1914 with Percy Lubbock and in 1917 with Walter Berry. The journeys struck her as forays into the unknown, a "magic land," as she wrote Morton Fullerton in 1914: "What amazes me is that beyond the *so* narrow thread of civilization along the coast, Europe has made no mark" (Lewis and Lewis *Letters* 315 emphasis in original). To Bernard Berenson, she described Algiers as "all effeminacy, obesity, obscenity or black savageness. But, oh, the dresses, the types, the ways of walking, sprawling, squatting—& the sun-sprinkled depths of the vaulted bazaars, & the white walls, the blue shadows, the tiled colonnades, the sudden fig-trees, the blacks carrying baskets of rose buds on their heads, & the little solemn pale children in the booths..." (318). She found North Africa similarly exotic on her second trip, writing Berenson about driving across the desert and arriving at a palace with a courtyard blooming with flowers, witnessing the ritual Sacrifice of the Sheep, and visiting with a sultan and his harem (Lewis and Lewis *Letters* 401–2). For Wharton, Africa was exotic and sensual and sexualized, the feminized black natives subordinate to the white imperialists and the many wives in service to their powerful husband.

For this reason, critics have focused on Wharton's role in and attitude toward European imperialism in Africa. In "Edith Wharton as Propagandist and Novelist" (1999), Judith Sensibar investigates the ways that *In Morocco*, Wharton's 1920 travelogue, overtly supports the imperialist myths and, through gaps and omissions, subverts the dominant ideology. Charlotte Rich, in "Fictions of Colonial Anxiety" (2004), examines two short stories set in North Africa, "The Seed of the Faith" and "A Bottle of Perrier," and concludes that "both stories reveal anxieties of the European colonizing perspective upon North Africa, depicting that region as a simultaneously fascinating yet frightening cultural and religious Other, imbued with destructive powers" (60). Wharton does not, I agree, seriously question the established attitudes toward Africa. Rather, in "A Bottle of Perrier," the colonized land becomes a setting in which to investigate the nature of white male power.

"A Bottle of Perrier" was first published as "A Bottle of Evian" in the *Saturday Evening Post*, March 27, 1926, and later collected in *Certain People* (1930). In the story, Medford, a young student of archaeology, travels to visit an older man, Henry Almodham, "a scholar and a misogynist," in his desert compound (*Selected Stories* 253). The two men had met only once previously, a year before. When he arrives, Medford finds his host absent, apparently having been called away by a local chief. Almodham's servant, an Englishman named Gosling, invites Medford to wait for Almodham's return. During the next few days, Medford enjoys the compound's hospitality, although he has trouble getting water to drink and to bathe in. Gosling is reluctant to serve him water, insisting that Medford must want wine, although Medford explains that a recent illness requires that he abstain. As the days pass, the water becomes increasingly foul. Medford grows closer to Gosling and learns the servant's story: he has desperately wished to visit England, but each year Almodham retracted his leave for one reason or another. After a week, Medford recognizes that he must depart; he is perplexed by his host's absence and comes to believe that Almodham has never left the compound but merely hidden himself in an unused compartment to avoid his guest. In a moment of frustration,

Medford tells Gosling that he knows Almodham can see him, at which point the servant breaks down. He confesses that he killed his master because Almodham rescinded his vacation for the twelfth time and that at that moment Medford arrived; lacking options, Gosling tossed the body into the well, the compound's only water supply. Thus in "A Bottle of Perrier," masculinity grotesquely accumulates in the body of the young successor to intellectual, social, and economic power.

The absent Almodham embodies a combination of authorities. Although his archaeological work has failed, he has taken over a "Crusades stronghold" (256), thus locating himself at the heart of religious, military, imperialist, and historical power. Rich explains: "The house is an emblem not only of the history of foreign domination that this territory has suffered, but also of the instability of cultural boundaries in this enigmatic landscape, suggesting the anxiety about maintaining the parameters of the (European) self that often underlies colonial discourse" (68). Almodham himself is absent and mythical; we hear stories about him but never meet him. Medford admires "Wise Almodham!" for escaping to the solitude and peace of the desert. His race, class, and supposed intellectual standing, enhanced by the remoteness that adds myth and mystery to what might otherwise be a prosaic personality, place him at the top of the male hierarchy. His power over and abuse of Gosling is one example of his authority, but just as important is his relationship with Medford, who is his intellectual heir—"a remarkable young man," he tells Gosling, "just my kind" (273). In this way, Almodham assumes the power of the father, choosing his successor while bypassing the necessity of a wife.

Although Medford admires Almodham, he also acknowledges the other's fallibility. He suspects Almodham's way of life stems more from falling victim to "a pose assumed in youth" rather than a true philosopher's respect for isolation. He also imagines that Almodham has escaped "an old wound, an old mortification, something which years ago had touched a vital part and left him writhing" (256). Probably jilted by a woman, Almodham has compensated by cutting women out of his life entirely. Medford further "detected an inertia, mental and moral" in his potential mentor (256–57). Knowing, or at least suspecting, these flaws, Medford nevertheless seeks Almodham out, suggesting that Medford too recognizes a kinship between the men. Indeed, Medford soon finds himself under the sway of "inertia"; he lingers on at the compound despite the absence of his host and spends his time indulging his every whim. Hunger, for instance, becomes "just the ghost of a pang, that might have been quieted by dried fruit and honey" (258). Medford does not, however, recognize that he might succumb to Almodham's other sins. For example, he makes the exact same promise to Gosling—that he will get his vacation in England—that Almodham has made and broken twelve times. Medford, probably like Almodham, may mean his promise, but there is nothing to keep a man of his social and economic standing from breaking a promise to a servant to suit his own convenience.

Despite Almodham's flaws and Medford's awareness of them, the younger man is nevertheless content to rest in the world Almodham rules. To Medford, the desert compound is an Eden: "the silence, the remoteness, the illimitable air! And in the heart of the wilderness green leafage, water, comfort—...a humane and welcoming habitation.... To anyone sick of Western fret and fever the very walls of this desert fortress exuded peace" (254). He feels removed from the confines of time: "There were no time measures in a place like this. The silly face of his watch told its daily tale to emptiness" (258). As Rich points out, feeling away from or out of time implies a removal from entire "Western conceptions of reality" (67). Yet, one wonders, what is the "Western fret and fever"—or the "Western conception of reality"—that a privileged young man like Medford is so anxious to escape? Perhaps, like Almodham, Medford seeks an escape from women, failed professional endeavors, or even a bustle of empty social engagements.

Despite these unsettling hints about Almodham's and Medford's characters and motives, the desert compound loses its sense of peace only when Medford starts to imagine that Almodham is still there. With the supposed presence of another upper class, educated white man, Medford feels the place to be "lonely, inhospitable, dangerous" (270). Finally grown suspicious at the long absence of his host, Medford begins to feel an "invisible watcher" monitoring his movements. He imagines the "gaze of his hidden watcher was jealously fixed on the red spark of his cigar" (271)—an overtly phallic reference, suggesting that Medford imagines that Almodham regards the younger man as a threat and by implication indicating that Medford sees himself as a threat to Almodham. Wharton suggests that for men, Western society is always "lonely, inhospitable, dangerous" in its demands on them, particularly in the competition for power, and in the way powerful men are constantly observed by their society. By this point in the story, Medford has shown his mettle by secretly negotiating with the Arab servants and threatening Gosling with his gun. He feels he has solved the mystery of Almodham's absence, and his satisfaction in his masculinity has made him, he imagines, a threat to the older man. Actually it is his knowledge, or his perceived knowledge, and not his wiles or physical bravery that ultimately establishes his authority. When he insists that Gosling admit that Almodham is still in the compound, Gosling takes the challenge as Medford's ability to perceive the supernatural and throws himself at Medford's feet. It turns out that Medford's "knowledge" of Almodham's whereabouts is correct if incomplete—yet it nevertheless produces the result of asserting Medford's supremacy in the other man's home.

In this story, the relationship between men is not facilitated by women. Only a few women, "chattering and exclaiming," appear in the story, in Medford's memory of his meeting with Almodham (256). Nevertheless, feminist critics have read the story as about gender identity and relationships. Carol Singley, for instance, sees the story as "an example *par excellence* of the female gothic narrative" ("Gothic Borrowings" 271) since the story positions both Medford, as a young man making his way up the ladder, and Gosling, the powerless servant, as feminine (282–83). She argues that these two men wind up "mothering" each other in a way that disrupts the traditional patriarchal power structure and class system (284–86). Singley's case is compelling, and the question she suggests that Wharton poses is fascinating and necessary: "What sort of life is possible without the familiar patterns of domination and control?" (287).

But Almodham's power has already transferred to Medford through the accumulation of masculinity via the consumption of the older man's body. That is, the transference of power between the men is made literal through Medford's drinking of the water in which Almodham's body rots. Medford absorbs the other man's body, using one male body to sustain another. Medford also bathes in this water, essentially layering another male body over his own, and he notes that "something sick and viscous, half smell, half substance, seemed to have clung to his skin since his morning bath" (268). He even breathes in Almodham's body. After sleeping by the well, he feels that "the sweetish foulish smell [from the well] clung to his face as it had after his bath" (271). Critic Jenni Dyman argues that "the literal scum of the well symbolizes a pervasive, clinging problem: patriarchal authority and elitist insensitivity passed from level to level in the hierarchy and from generation to generation" (123). This is how male power works: it is transferred, literally and culturally, from older men to younger men. The grotesque aspects of the transmission of power in the story signal Wharton's anger at the almost incestuous exclusivity of the domain of male power, and the "inertia" that both men feel indicates the extreme effort it would take to alter this system.

Medford enacts his assumption of Almodham's power in his high-handed treatment of Gosling. In conquering Gosling, who, as Rich points out, "effaces the distinctions between West and East so necessary to the maintenance of a Western sense of cultural superiority" (68), Medford brings Gosling back into the Western hierarchy, exorcises the "taint" of exoticism in the servant, and establishes himself as the new master. Though temporarily in limbo, Medford will fully assume his new powers once he moves back to the Western social realm.

Some readers question whether Gosling will permit Medford to return to the exterior world; in fear of having his crime revealed, Gosling may murder again. But I believe Gosling will let Medford go because he sees a difference between Medford and Almodham, even so slight a difference as Medford's apparently genuine promise to grant him his vacation in England. Justified or not, this belief in Medford's difference from Almodham stops Gosling from pushing Medford into the well (273). According to Wharton, differences among men, however minor, are encouraged and are necessary to the working of patriarchal power. As I argued in chapter 2, women run the risk of being interchangeable because they have no power. Men, on the other hand, have the potential and opportunity to be different from each other: they may have different jobs (lawyers, architects, engineers, archaeologists, painters, and others appear in Wharton's work), and they have chances to participate in a variety of experiences. Thus, men gather power as they accumulate—as they form networks and connections, from male body to male body.

Male Narrators and Masculine Authority

To a much greater extent than in her novels, in her short stories Wharton tended to focus on male characters and to use them as narrators. She used female first-person narrators only two times, in "The Lady's Maid's Bell" and "All Souls." ("The Looking Glass" is narrated by a woman within a third-person frame.) The rest of her short stories are told from an omniscient point of view or by a male first-person narrator. In her study of Wharton's short fiction, Barbara White points out that the use of a male narrator "increases the distance between the author and her material" (63). This distance lends the story credibility that a female narrator or author would not have, although at the same time it leaves the story open to question because of its limited perspective. In "Gender and First-Person Narration in Edith Wharton's Short Fiction," Elsa Nettels describes Wharton's typical male narrator:

> The male narrators, without exception, are equal or superior to the other characters in social position, and usually hold themselves superior in intelligence and accomplishment. The male narrators are cast from the same mold; all are bachelors with the means to gratify their cultivated tastes. They are connoisseurs and collectors of rare books of art.... Their vocations allow them abundant leisure but establish them in the ruling class.... They travel extensively, to Europe, Africa, Central America and the Far East. (247)

Nettels continues: "the male narrators, of their own choice, cultivate friendships with other men to the exclusion of other ties. Most of them have no romantic interest in women, for whom, at best they feel protective concern and liking, at worst, mistrust or contempt" (247). Nettels suggests a variety of reasons for Wharton's preference for male narrators: they are composites or reflections of her friends; they are socially acceptable and expected by her readers; they are part of literary tradition; and, in Wharton's view, the male narrator possesses the educated mind best able to "view a story as a whole" (Nettels 248–49). Still, it must have been profoundly disconcerting to Wharton that her own art placed her outside of itself, reminding her again and again that she was an interloper in the field of men's work.

Several times Wharton used a double male narrator technique, in which the story is told to the reader as one man tells it to a first-person male narrator. The stories with dual male narrators offer examples of how male power works—of how, as I stated above, it accumulates. Each member of the narrative pairing brings to the partnership his own authority, which comes from his education, his position in the economic market, his travels, and/or his social position. Because the men are not identical, their combined knowledge and experience result in overlapping authority. For example, two narrators may have similar educations but different professional experiences. The effect is a comprehension of the world that is frequently unassailable.

A clear example of this dynamic is the male narrative pairing in "The Long Run." Wharton published this story in 1912 in *The Atlantic Monthly* and later included it in her 1916 collection *Xingu and Other Stories*. The tale opens with the unnamed male narrator finding an old friend, Halston Merrick, at a dinner party; the two men had gone to school together but lost track of each other for twelve years. During the party, the narrator notices Merrick watching a particular woman, and a few days afterward, the two men meet for a private talk. At this point, Merrick reveals what is supposedly the heart of the story: he and the married Paulina Trant fell in love, and she, rejecting the clandestine necessities of an affair, offered to leave her husband. But Merrick refused to let her take the "risk," at the same time declining to stake his own life on a joint venture with her, and sent her back to her husband. Their subsequent lives become hollow and empty cages.

R. W. B. Lewis calls it a "brilliant and cruel story" (318), referring to the defeated love between Merrick and Paulina. My interest, however, is in the frame and in the relationship between the two men who share the story. Wharton devotes several pages to their friendship before she gets to Merrick's story, and in those pages, the narrator reveals Merrick's background and his own admiration for the other man. In his youth, Merrick has the potential to do great things; an experience abroad gives him "a fresh curiosity about public affairs at home, and the conviction that men of his kind should play a larger part in them" (*Selected Stories* 229). But he fails to win a state senate race, and he (like Nathaniel Hawthorne) loses a small government job due to a "change of party" and then publishes a book of poetry (230). The death of his father leaves him in charge of the family business, a post he does not want but to which he eventually resigns himself. His failure to do something bigger leaves the narrator "disposed to regret Merrick's drop to the level of the prosperous" (230). Immediately afterward, the narrator departs for China and then Africa, almost as if he could not bear to see his admired friend's acceptance of a mundane life.

The two men seem to share a bond that, at least from the narrator's perspective, defies the ordinary. Abroad, the narrator finds himself wishing, "in certain situations and at certain turns of thought, that Merrick were in reach, that I could tell this or that to Merrick. I had never, in the interval, found any one with just his quickness of perception and just his sureness of response" (230). Their friendship hints strongly of homosexuality, with their mutual interest in "curiosities and ardors a little outside the current tendencies" (229). They are "irresistibly" drawn together at the party (230), and instead of following the social obligation of seating himself next to a lady, the narrator chooses to remain next to Merrick. Further, the narrator, despite recognizing a strain in his conversation with Merrick, "felt a certain sense of well-being in the mere physical presence of my old friend. I liked looking at the way his dark hair waved away from the forehead, at the tautness of his dry brown cheek, the thoughtful backward tilt of his head, the way his brown eyes mused upon the scene through lowered lids" (231). This desire between the men stands out all the more given the narrator's apparent choice not to marry and Merrick's refusal to accept the woman he wants when she offers herself. The failure of Merrick's life may be the loss of Paulina or a fundamental inability to understand himself.

The desire between men, however, also reveals clues about the power structure of the society they live in. "Friendship" and "love" between men and women seem unreal to Merrick; he is passionate about Paulina as long as she remains safely unavailable as a married woman. The reality of her presence in his house shakes him out of his dreams, and he realizes he does not know what it is actually to be with her. Before he tells his story, he refers to her as both a "woman" and a "Muse": "Out of that very door they went—the two of 'em, on a rainy night like this: and one stopped and looked back, to see if I wasn't going to call her—and I didn't—and so they both went" (235). Merrick prefers that Paulina remain on her pedestal, and he decides not to chance her as a reality.

The relationship between Merrick and the narrator, however, can withstand reality because, both of them being men, they have the same or similar experiences on which to draw. Part of the narrator's comfort in sitting next to Merrick comes from their personal shared history and from the customs both men know: "All the past was in his way of looking and sitting" (231). Merrick only tells the narrator the story of Paulina because he "remember[s] what she was" (236). The telling of the story is a revelation of intimacies and an act of intimacy itself. We never hear the narrator's response to the story, whether he would have agreed with Merrick's refusal to run off with a married woman or would have declared Merrick a fool. Instead, the story ends with Merrick's description of his evenings with Paulina and her new husband and how afterward he "walk[s] back alone to [his] rooms...." (252 ellipses in original). Such an ending emphasizes that, despite any hints of homosexual desire, the telling of the story has not disrupted the social order in the least. It is the revelation of one socially accepted, powerful man to another; the story will remain between the two of them; and Merrick will continue to walk home alone. The dual narration adds authority and reinforces the finality of the current state of affairs. Each man's knowledge and experiences overlap with those of the other but also extend in separate directions, so there is strength and coverage in the telling of the story to the reader. The female author has almost disappeared from view.

WHEN MASCULINITY GOES WRONG, PART 1: THE DISRUPTION OF THE DUAL MALE NARRATORS

In "The Long Run" and similar stories narrated by two men, such as "The Confessional" (*Crucial Instances*, 1901), "The Verdict" (*The Hermit and the Wild Woman*, 1908), "The Daunt Diana" (*Tales of Men and Ghosts*, 1910), and "Coming Home" (*Xingu*, 1916), social and political structures are revealed but rarely openly challenged. In the stories I discuss in this section, Wharton does not use dual male narrators or even a male first-person narrator, but these stories demonstrate the principles on which the dual male narrative structure is based: men have power, they share that power among themselves, and women are excluded from the realms in which meaning happens. Wharton's story "The Bolted Door," first published in March of 1909 and collected in *Tales of Men and Ghosts* (1910), best illustrates these principles by portraying their negative; that is, the narrator of the story searches for his male partner, the man to whom he can tell his story and be accepted, and goes insane when he cannot find this partner. His madness is confirmed when he imagines that he finds his perfect listener in a girl.

The main character of "The Bolted Door," Hupert Granice, is a failed playwright who has lost the will to live. Because he physically recoils from any attempt to kill himself, he decides to confess to the murder of his wealthy cousin in the hopes that he will be given the death penalty. The murder occurred ten years ago and remains unsolved. Granice tells his story to a lawyer, a newspaper editor, the district attorney, an alienist, and a young reporter, but no one will believe him. He decides he needs to find someone who does not know him because he feels friendship and familiarity with his listeners cause them to reject his confession out of hand. Searching the city for the perfect listener, Granice unexpectedly finds a sympathetic face in a girl sitting on a bench. When he approaches her and begins to speak, she screams and runs from him. Granice is then locked up in a mental institution, although to him it is merely a place full of intelligent listeners.

Evelyn Fracasso found the title of her study *Edith Wharton's Prisoners of Consciousness* in "The Bolted Door": in his suffering over his wasted life and his listeners' refusal to believe his confession,

Granice feels himself a "prisoner of consciousness" (44). Having killed his cousin to relieve his material difficulties, he finds he still cannot make his life what he wants it to be. His mind has made of his life a hell: "In the long night-hours, when his brain seemed ablaze, he was visited by a sense of his fixed identity, of his irreducible, inexpugnable *selfness*, keener, more insidious, more unescapable, than any sensation he had ever known. He had not guessed that the mind was capable of such intricacies of self-realisation, of penetrating so deep into its own dark windings" (44–45 emphasis in original). He starts to experience his personality as a "viscous substance," much like the well scum in "A Bottle of Perrier"; he wakes "from his brief snatches of sleep with the feeling that something material was clinging to him, was on his hands and face, and in his throat" (45). Granice suffers from despair, feelings of failure, and isolation, and these emotions manifest themselves almost physically.

His quest for a listener is a search for companionship and self-justification, but it is also a bid for authority. He believes the repeated rejections of his plays over the past ten years have made him a laughingstock. His attempt to commit suicide by confessing to murder seems a roundabout road to the oblivion he seeks, but his physical inability to pull the trigger of his gun signals a bodily need for validation. That is, as I have shown in "A Bottle of Perrier," Wharton sees masculine authority literally embodied. Granice has assumed his current social and economic position by destroying the body of another man, a man described as physically repulsive. Granice calls his cousin, Joseph Lenman, "large, undifferentiated, inert" (18), "pale-fleshed" like his melons, "apathetic and motionless" (19), and "like a fat Turk in his seraglio" (20).[3] Lenman is monstrous in his refusal to be "worried" over the desperate living conditions of his relatives. In inheriting from him, Granice does not become materially selfish, but he does take on his cousin's egocentricity: he becomes so self-centered that he cannot live with himself. The "viscous personality" that clings to him is not his cousin's but his own. He wishes to shed his body and his consciousness; seeing workers in the street, he thinks: "Oh, to be one of them—any of them—to take his chance in any of their skins!" (45). But he immediately recognizes that "the iron circle of consciousness held them too: each one was hand-cuffed to his own detested ego" (45). The alienist's advice that he find an interest, "something to take you out of yourself" (58), seems simultaneously precisely what Granice needs as well as absurdly beside the point. Granice does need to break out of his mental prison, but to do so, he needs someone to acknowledge and validate his story.

His lawyer blithely comments that "confession is good for the soul" (14), but the essence of confession is that it be believed and that it result in forgiveness or punishment. Despite Granice's egoism, his desire "to find himself in another mind" (53) is not negligible. By refusing to believe Granice's story, all his listeners refuse to recognize him as a human being and, more important, as a man, and he is humiliated and frustrated by "the sense of being buried beneath deepening drafts of indifference" (60). Further, in the web of masculinity that Wharton portrays in other stories, Granice needs a listener who will believe him in order to secure his place in the patriarchal order. Disbelieved over and over, he faces the possibility that he will be "swept aside as an irresponsible dreamer" (60). In this light, it is interesting to consider where Wharton may have envisioned the reader. The young journalist's revelation, at the end of the story, that he believes Granice did commit the murder seems positioned to be a final "twist" to shock the reader, but I find no reason to doubt Granice's story at any point. The reader, who does not know Granice before he presents the story, is perhaps the unbiased "listener" he seeks—but since the reader might be male or female, the story threatens male authority by indicating that the gender of the "listener" is unimportant. Like the young reporter, however, the reader is powerless to grant Granice's wish: "*Do about it?* Why, what was I to do? I couldn't hang the poor devil, could I?" (69 emphasis in original). Ironically, it is the nature of the text that Granice will live forever entangled with his own personality.

Granice's frustration is made more pronounced by the fact that, within "The Bolted Door," examples of men establishing their relationships and their authority through conversation with each other abound. Lenman's dismissal of Granice's request for a loan on the grounds that Granice knows nothing about business is a humiliation that asserts Lenman's power. Other instances establish bonds: during the original investigation of Lenman's death, part of Granice's alibi for the murder hinged on the testimony of his friend the newspaper editor, Robert Denver, who frequently stopped by Granice's flat late at night to chat. Denver points out that this evidence is further supported by a conversation he had with another man, who saw Granice's shadow in his window before Denver got there (39). One of the reasons no one believes Granice's story now that he comes forward with his confession is that his innocence has already been established by the conversations of men of authority. When he attempts to break his own alibi, he must seek out the lower-class men who made the crime possible. To commit the murder, he needed a car, and he admits now that he had one. He stored it "in one of those no-questions-asked garages where they keep motors that are not for family use" (33). But in the ten years since the crime, the city has swallowed the evidence: the garage has been condemned and demolished, and anyone who lived in the neighborhood at the time has moved on. The men who could testify to Granice's guilt are lowest on the economic, social, and political ladders, and their knowledge has been swept away along with the men themselves.

Thus Granice continues to seek a listener, someone who will believe him, who will make him real to the exterior world, and who will then have the ability to bring about the consequences Granice desires. Telling his story calms him, but each listener's immediate skepticism brings back his feelings of alienation and increases his anxiety, for he fears the listener will have him committed to an insane asylum rather than arrested. Granice discovers that the masculine network now works against him, and he decides that he should find a stranger to listen because his friends are too prejudiced to be interested in the truth. And indeed they are prejudiced, though not necessarily in the way Granice thinks: the lawyer, newspaper editor, and district attorney—all prominent men of authority—will not act on Granice's story without evidence, partly, perhaps, out of friendship but also, quite justly, because lawyers and journalists require evidence on which to act. Without their belief, Granice's life becomes even more of a "stagnant backwater" (59), and he continues to try to establish the truth. He searches the streets for the face of the person who will be his believing listener, the other half of his narrative duality, and once he finds that person he imagines that the "spark" of belief will give him relief (63). To his astonishment, he thinks he finds his listener in a girl:

> Presently he passed a bench on which a girl sat alone, and something as definite as the twitch of a cord caused him to stop before her. He had never dreamed of telling his story to a girl, had hardly looked at the women's faces as they passed. His case was man's work: how could a woman help him? But this girl's face was extraordinary—quiet and wise as an evening sky. It suggested a hundred images of space, distance, mystery, like ships he had seen, as a boy, berthed by a familiar wharf, but with the breath of far seas and strange harbours in their shrouds...Certainly this girl would understand. (64 ellipses in original)

Granice should have stuck with his first instinct, for he barely introduces himself before she runs away screaming. Women, apparently, are barred from the magic circle of listeners partly because they would be ineffectual in men's business. The girl's reaction leads to Granice being committed to the insane asylum, not to his desired execution. Women also suffer from some inferiority that turns them away from a story before it can even be told. Masculine authority, which is the only authority, is built exclusively on relationships among men.

"Full Circle," another story in *Tales of Men and Ghosts*, also narrates what happens when male relationships become unbalanced, but instead of portraying weak bonds among men, it shows ties that have become too powerful. Geoffrey Betton, having achieved fame with a successful novel two years earlier, prepares for the publication of his second book. He expects a similar rush of praise and hoopla, including mountains of letters from eager readers, and to avoid having to read and answer the letters himself, he advertises for a secretary. He hires an old friend, Duncan Vyse, whose manuscript Betton had promised to get to a publisher years before but ultimately forgot about. Although the letters to Betton arrive as predicted, the "deluge" of them does not last, and many of them are unflattering. Betton's ego is damaged, and he resents having Vyse witness his failure. Betton begins writing letters to himself for Vyse to answer in order to keep up the pretense that his novel is well received. But Vyse suspects, so Betton stops. At the same time, Vyse's poverty makes him desperate to keep his job. The letters begin again, this time secretly written by Vyse in an effort to justify his wages. These letters are so interesting that Betton decides to answer them himself, so that a "full circle" of letter writing occurs between the two men.

The problems in this relationship derive from imbalances on each side. Betton is arrogant and self-centered, so when the letters first arrive he finds himself eager to read their praise and then to distance himself from their accusations of dullness. He is bothered by the book's lack of success "but not nearly as much as he minded Vyse's knowing it" (178). To be sure, his pride does not prevent him from later admitting to Vyse that he cares about his opinion. His arrogance, however, causes him to commit a much greater blunder: he fails to realize that the reason Vyse establishes a fake correspondence is neither to flatter Betton nor to revenge himself for his unpublished novel but simply to keep his job. For a novelist, Betton shows a spectacular collapse of the imagination in interpreting Vyse's motives. Vyse, for his part, carries the "deadly secret" of being "poor—unpardonably, irremediably poor" (170). He works two jobs but still owns only one set of clothes. He cannot walk away from Betton's arrogance; his fragile economic position requires him to submit to any indignity at Betton's hands in order to continue earning money.

These two are a far cry from Wharton's pairs of narrators, who enjoy a cigar and brandy over a good story. Betton and Vyse become so engrossed in the other's reaction to their joint situation that they become a closed loop of correspondence. Each man lives off the other as a succubus, Betton feeding his ego and Vyse his body. In fact, they almost become the same man, as Betton informs Vyse early on that Vyse will have to respond to Betton's letters as if he were Betton himself (164), and later Betton finds himself taking over Vyse's seat (187). The only women who play a part in their relationship are fictional: Betton invents two women correspondents, on one of whom Vyse develops a crush, and Vyse creates a girl from Florida, whom Betton falls for. Here, again, is Wharton's fear: that real women are not necessary in men's world, and that fictional women, no more than scraps of paper, will do just as well, if not better. After all, these fictional women are written by men.

A similar situation occurs in "His Father's Son," also published in *Tales of Men and Ghosts*, but here the implications of the closed male loop go one step further. Mason Grew's son Ronald, who is soon to marry an upper-class girl, comes into possession of a set of letters from his mother to a famous musician, and Ronald assumes the letters to be proof of his actual parentage. When he confronts his father with his "knowledge," Grew laughs. He himself composed the letters to pay homage to the great man, but he had his wife write them in the belief that the musician would be more likely to reply to a woman. The correspondence flourished, and it became one of the highlights of Grew's uneventful life. But it also created an offspring in the form of Ronald; Grew informs his son, "I'll tell you where the best of those letters is—it's in *you*" (99 emphasis in original). Ronald himself feels so, as he has no trouble imagining himself the son of a great artist, with his "love of music—my—all my feelings about life...and art..." (92 ellipses in original). Male authority has parthenogenetically reproduced itself.

In each of the stories discussed in this section, male authority has become so insulated that it damages the men who wield it. By exploring such extreme male relationships, Wharton exposes the dangers the system poses to men—but the stories do not suggest how including women is necessary or would produce better results. If women were to become socially and politically powerful enough to grant Granice's wish to be hanged, for example, or educated enough to participate in Betton and Vyse's closed loop of letters, the competitive and cold system of authority would simply reproduce with more members. Somehow, Wharton indicates, masculinity must fix itself, but, as the next section explains, the transference of power is so entangled, particularly among male bodies, that Wharton sees little hope for masculinity.

When Masculinity Goes Wrong, Part II: Devouring the Powerless

Grotesque as "A Bottle of Perrier" is, this story at least portrays power traveling in the "right" direction, from older men to younger men. But Wharton saw that the masculine system of authority has no built-in controls to ensure that power travels decorously from one generation to the next. In 1910, she wrote two ghost stories, "The Eyes" and "The Triumph of Night," that explore what happens when older men subvert this "natural" flow and not only refuse to share power with younger men but also seek to reabsorb power by sucking the life out of them, sometimes with fatal results.

In "The Eyes," one of Wharton's best-known ghost stories, a male narrator recounts an evening of storytelling at the home of an older friend, Andrew Culwin. The narrator and another young man, Phil Frenham, remain after the other guests have left to hear a ghost story from Culwin himself. And Culwin tells one: when he was a young man, he stayed with his aunt in her "damp Gothic villa" (250), ostensibly to write a book. The aunt "lends" him a cousin, Alice Nowell, to help with the manuscript, and Culwin becomes fascinated by the girl's boring niceness. He finds himself feeling that he ought to marry her, but the night after he proposes, he wakes to find a pair of eyes staring at him in the dark. He flees the house and moves to Europe. A few years later, Alice writes to ask him to look after her cousin, Gilbert Noyes, who has literary aspirations. Culwin finds the young man "beautiful" and "charming" (260), so he encourages Noyes even though his writing is bad. The night after Culwin lies to Noyes about his writing, the eyes reappear, and Culwin lives with them for months. Only when he tells his protégé that his writing is no good do the eyes disappear. At the conclusion of the story, Culwin confesses that he has not seen the eyes since his experience with Noyes, but he catches sight of himself in the mirror and, with Frenham and the narrator, sees the eyes in his own face.

This story is much commented upon by critics. Cynthia Griffin Wolff describes it as "the horror of self-discovery" (157). Kathy

Fedorko, in *Gender and the Gothic in the Fiction of Edith Wharton*, cites Culwin as an example of the "potential for cruel egoism in the writer's life" (58). The character of Culwin epitomizes the male effete that Wharton often criticized; R. W. B. Lewis finds the source for Culwin, "unshakably self-centered, cultivated but cold-spirited, witty but spiteful, and latently homosexual," in Morton Fullerton (288). Culwin's homosexual devouring of young men has more recently been recognized as not at all latent. Dyman, for example, notes that Culwin flees from Alice in a "homosexual panic" (52) in favor of a homosexual relationship with Noyes and later with Phil Frenham.

The structure of the story, however, is less well examined. It is one of the stories told by two male narrators, and what happens in the frame of the tale, before and after Culwin's story, reveals much about masculine relationships. White recognizes the importance of the frame as "a crucial part of the story and our sense of immediacy [is] increased by the fact that Phil Frenham and the narrator are not 'mere lookers-on' but involved participants." She does not, however, investigate the implications of the frame beyond acknowledging its effect of making the story "one of the few...that ends more vividly than it begins" (66). A closer look at the frame reveals that the narrator is deeply implicated in the power structure that allows Culwin to prey upon young men and that the narrating of ghost stories is part of a larger system that establishes the male order. The narrator indicates that the telling of ghost stories begins as a result of the atmosphere of Culwin's library, as if the man himself contrived to draw out the stories. The narrator concedes that ghost stories were an unusual topic for the group: "It surprised us all to find that we could muster such a show of supernatural impressions, for none of us, excepting Murchard himself and young Phil Frenham— whose story was the slightest of the lot—had the habit of sending our souls into the invisible" (243). Yet the telling of the stories functions as a point of pride among the members, and it turns into a contest to re-confirm station among individuals in the group. Such jockeying for position appears to be not at all unusual for the men. Culwin, the "wise old idol" (244), is not expected to participate. The narrator explains that Culwin, by virtue of his position in life as a "spectator," is not the "kind of man likely to be favoured with [ghostly] contacts" (244), yet he also seems exempt from the contest because his position at the top of the group is secure. "Young" Frenham, who the narrator admits has a good imagination, has his story deemed "the slightest of the lot," corresponding to his place at the bottom of the group's hierarchy.

The rest of the men, including the narrator, occupy a middle level of authority that depends on their slightly disrespectful attitude toward Culwin and on their complicity in keeping someone at the bottom. Various members of the group describe Culwin as "a bundle of sticks" and "a phosphorescent log" (244), and the narrator himself portrays Culwin as having "a small squat trunk, with the red blink of the eyes in a face like mottled bark" (245). The narrator continues with a description of Culwin that is not overly admiring: "He had always been possessed of a leisure which he had nursed and protected, instead of squandering it in vain activities. His carefully guarded hours had been devoted to the cultivation of a fine intelligence and a few judiciously chosen habits; and none of the disturbances common to human experience seemed to have crossed his sky" (245). The narrator also reveals that, given Culwin's insularity and self-coddling, the main reasons for the loyalty of his friends are equally his dinner table and his intellect, which offers "a forum, or some open meeting-place for the exchange of ideas: somewhat cold and draughty, but light, spacious and orderly" (245). In other words, Culwin provides a comfortable setting for other men to test their intellectual abilities and enjoy themselves, and he serves as a model for self-indulgent living.

Thus even before Culwin tells his tale, the narrator has revealed key aspects of the older man's nature, and further, he indicates the degree to which he and the others participate in Culwin's way of life. One of the men, referring to Phil Frenham as Culwin's latest "recruit," says that Culwin "liked 'em juicy" (246). The narrator concurs that in Frenham, Culwin "had a good subject for experimentation. The boy was really intelligent, and the soundness of his nature was like the pure paste under a fine glaze" (246). In his story, Culwin describes the mysterious eyes as "vampires with a taste for young flesh, they seemed so to gloat over the taste of a good conscience" (267). As is later revealed, the eyes are Culwin's own; he is the vampire feeding on "young flesh" and "a good conscience." But the narrator seems disturbingly interested in such a feeding: "the skill with which Culwin had contrived to stimulate [Frenham's] curiosities without robbing them of their bloom of awe seemed to me a sufficient answer to Murchard's ogreish metaphor" (246). While Culwin is the aesthetic dilettante who sucks the life out of young men, the narrator watches with admiration as he does it. Indeed, the story itself is an account of the narrator's participation, since when Culwin stops speaking, it is the narrator who must prompt Culwin for the final details. Frenham lies unmoving, sprawled across the table, as if drained of life by Culwin and the narrator jointly. Like the other stories discussed here, "The Eyes" reveals a cycle of men circulating power among themselves. The narrator's and Culwin's simultaneous recognition that "the eyes" are Culwin's own suggests a possible transition of power, particularly if Culwin has enough conscience left to crumble under the weight of his self-knowledge. By telling the story, the narrator assumes control of the older man's tale and sets himself up as the next authority figure, feeding off both the older and younger men.

First published in 1914 and later included in *Xingu*, "The Triumph of Night" is considered one of Wharton's lesser ghost stories. Yet when considered in light of "A Bottle of Perrier," the story becomes far more revealing about the nature of power and masculinity. In this story, George Faxon, having accepted a post as a secretary to a wealthy family living in the New England countryside, arrives at the train station, at night and in a snowstorm, to find that his employers have sent no one to meet him. Instead, he encounters young Frank Rainer, who takes Faxon to the home of his uncle, a wealthy and well-known businessman named John Lavington. Rainer suffers from tuberculosis, and, although a doctor has encouraged him to spend a year in the Southwest to recover, he has stayed on in New England on the advice of a second doctor. Accidently walking into a meeting with lawyers in Lavington's study, Faxon is asked to witness the signing of Rainer's will, and as he does, he looks up and sees a stranger standing behind Lavington, who gazes at Rainer with "pale hostility" (255). Over dinner, the figure reappears when the lawyers and Faxon encourage Rainer to leave for New Mexico after all. Faxon realizes this figure is a manifestation of Lavington's hidden feelings for his nephew, and, overcome with horror, he flees the house. Rainer, at the urging of his uncle, comes after him. He falls ill from exposure and dies, and his uncle, who was secretly about to go bankrupt, inherits his nephew's fortune.

This tale, like many of the others discussed in this chapter, revolves around pairs of men: the new young friends, Faxon and Rainer; the uncle and nephew; the two lawyers; Lavington and his ghostly double. This last pair opens the possibility of a networking among men in which both men are the same person. That is, Lavington's exterior face, which shines on his nephew with "untroubled benevolence" (255), is a necessary front or partner for his hidden self, manifested only for Faxon to see. This hidden self appears not on Faxon's command but at points of anxiety for Lavington, such as the signing of Rainer's will and the suggestion that Rainer head to New Mexico for his health (263). The double is usually read as Lavington's true self who needs his nephew to die in order to save his business, but it also seems that there is a real duality in Lavington, part of him that loves his nephew and part that is desperate to save himself. When Lavington agrees that New Mexico might be best for Rainer, the double changes: "The watcher behind the chair was no longer merely malevolent: he had grown suddenly, unutterably tired. His hatred seemed to well up out of the very depths of balked effort and thwarted hopes, and the fact made him more pitiable, and yet more dire" (264–65). Whether Lavington is merely divided by surface and exterior or actually feels conflicted about his plans for his nephew, he acts on his double's emotions, not the benevolent face but the hidden hatred, and sends Rainer out into the snow to his death. Thus the securing of his place at the top of the financial and social world rests on his consumption of not only his nephew but also of his better self.

Part of the Gothic horror of the story is Faxon's knowledge of Lavington's intentions and his failure to do anything about it. Faxon and Rainer are their own pair, equals in age if not in station in life. Faxon is attracted to Rainer, finding his voice "agreeable" and his "features to be in the pleasantest harmony with his voice" (243). He has a "smile of such sweetness that Faxon felt, as never before, what Nature can achieve when she deigns to match the face with the mind" (246). Faxon recognizes Rainer's physical weakness because of the "quivering nerves" that he himself possesses (243), and he feels such a bond with the other man that before they have known each other fifteen minutes, Faxon speaks to him out of "elder-brotherly concern" (247). Yet when real danger threatens his new friend, Faxon runs. He blames his lower-class status for preventing him from helping: "Any one of the others, thus enlightened, might have exposed the horror and defeated it; but *he*, the one weaponless and defenceless spectator, the one whom none of the others would believe or understand if he attempted to reveal what he knew—*he* alone had been singled out as the victim of this dreadful initiation!" (208–9 emphasis in original). As Faxon realizes, it may be because he is a stranger that he is able to see the double. But other of his thoughts suggest more sinister explanations. Faxon wonders, "What business was it of *his*, in God's name?" (208 emphasis in original). Faxon lives a struggling life, in which he is doomed to be "perpetually treading other people's stairs" (251), but he, like Lavington, is divided. He resents always being the stranger in the house, but he also finds refuge in it; as the outsider, he does not have to get involved. When Rainer most needs him, Faxon deserts him and only offers his assistance and protection when it is too late. His reluctance to go up against the wealthy and powerful makes him just one more pawn for Lavington to consume, but, by dividing his desires, Faxon has first consumed himself.

Conclusion

In her novels, Wharton frequently shows patterns of men replacing each other and accumulating power as they do so. Usually these men appear as a series of husbands: John Amherst replaces Bessie Westmore's first husband in *The Fruit of the Tree* (1907); a line of men replace each other as Undine Spragg's husband in *The Custom of the Country*, with Elmer Moffatt, the first husband, also becoming the fourth; Anderson Brant replaces John Campton as husband to Campton's wife in *A Son at the Front*; Dexter Manford replaces Arthur Wyant and almost replaces his stepson Jim Wyant in *Twilight Sleep*. Each of these husbands tends to be distinctly different than the previous one and usually more socially and economically powerful. Elmer Moffatt, for example, though both first and (presumably) last husband to Undine Spragg, is not the same Elmer Moffatt; that is, the first time he marries Undine he is working his way up, while the second time he has established himself socially and economically. He has also absorbed the bits he needs from Undine's previous husbands, including Raymond de Chelles' family tapestries and Ralph Marvell's son's affections. In the novels, however, Wharton includes women as part of the power transactions, for their biological necessity, if nothing else, cannot be ignored.

Her short stories allow greater room for suspicion. The ghost stories permit the exploration of sexual relationships, for example, in ways that Wharton could not develop in her more realistic novels. Similarly, the short stories offer a space for glimpses of life behind the scenes, as it were. Here Wharton could write her fear of women's superfluity, that men transmit power from one to another without the intervention or even knowledge of women. By writing stories that combine two male narrators, Wharton both participates in the consolidation of power within male groups and ambivalently exposes it, for after all there is a third narrator, Wharton herself, standing behind the men. Either the woman writer can co-opt the male voice and its power, or she is merely a puppet in a power structure too overwhelming for her. Wharton seems frequently to have been unsure which role she played, a position highly uncomfortable for a woman writer in a world of men.

CHAPTER 4

"A Sign of Pain's Triumph": War, Art, and Civilization

On June 28, 1914, Gavrilo Princip assassinated Austrian Archduke Franz Ferdinand and his wife Sophie, setting into motion a chain of events that led to the violent hostilities of World War I. By August, French, British, and German troops were mobilized and entrenched along what would be known as the Western Front, and Belgian and French refugees flooded into Paris. During the first Battle of the Marne, which took place between September 5 and 12, Allied forces stopped the German advance in France, but half a million soldiers died during that week. Machine guns and chemical weapons made the war unlike any other previous armed conflict, and the scale of human destruction was unprecedented. For many people, World War I was seen as a definite break in human history. Modern writers tended to regard the postwar world as a new era in which civilization would be redefined. Edith Wharton, however, though profoundly affected by the war, saw the war not as a break from the past but rather as part of the fabric of human civilization. War offered opportunities for her to explore questions about morality and individual experience. In this chapter, I examine her short story "Coming Home" as a meditation on disturbing questions about ethics during war and about the isolation of individuals through bodily pain. She continued to explore the issue of modernist isolation in her war novel *A Son at the Front* (1923), and in that novel she also delves into questions about the relationship of civilization and war. Wharton took the idea of World War I as the war to defend Western civilization seriously, and the novel lends itself to several manners of reading "civilization," including its homosocial foundations, its constructed realities, and the possibilities of its "progress." John Campton, a painter, offers insight into Wharton's perspective on the possibilities of art in times of violence and chaos: art, Wharton saw, could accommodate war.

Wharton's involvement in World War I is well documented. Alan Price details her activities during the war, particularly her charity work, in *The End of the Age of Innocence* (1996), and Julie Olin-Ammentorp comprehensively examines her war writings in *Edith Wharton's Writings from the Great War* (2004). Wharton was living in France when war broke out, and she quickly established sewing rooms in Paris for refugee and suddenly unemployed women to earn a little money to support themselves and their families. Her charity work both energized and drained her, and her health cycled through highs and lows during the war. She continued to write, producing a wide range of material including short stories, reportage, propaganda, the novels *Summer* (1917) and *The Marne* (1918), the nonfiction collections *Fighting France, from Dunkerque to Belfort* (1915) and *French Ways and their Meaning* (1919), and the edited volume *The Book of the Homeless* (1916). For her charity work and for her attempts to mobilize Americans in support of the war, the French government made her a Knight of the National Order of the Legion of Honor; the citation reads: "Since the beginning of the war she has won broad sympathy for the French cause through her speech, her articles and other publications; and she has been widely recognized for her charities and her devotion to humanitarian relief." The war was also a period of personal losses for Wharton, with the deaths of her friends Henry James, Edgerton Winthrop, and Anna Bahlmann (a servant of many years) in 1916 and the deaths of her young friend Ronald Simmons and her cousin Newbold Rhinelander, both in 1918.[1] The war captured her imagination long afterward, from *A Son at the Front*—begun during the war but not finished until 1923—to novels and stories that use the war as a backdrop, such as *The Mother's Recompense* (1925), *Twilight Sleep* (1927), and "Her Son" (1933).

Wharton's biographers and critics generally agree that she never seriously questioned the justness of the war or wavered in her loyalty to French and later American goals. Olin-Ammentorp charts Wharton's reaction to the war in stages: her initial fascination with and romanticization of the war, her adjustment to living and writing in war conditions balanced by a desire to escape, and finally her sense of the need to memorialize the war and its fallen soldiers and to consider how the war continued to affect life and art. Although none of these stages suggest Wharton was disillusioned with the ideals for which the war was fought (her experience with her charity work, however, did result in her disappointment at the continuing pettiness of human nature), some of Wharton's war writings raise significant questions about the effect of war on individuals and society, morality and human relationships. For

Wharton, World War I created new problems as well as illuminated previously submerged issues.

Some of the questions the war raised were quickly apparent to Wharton. In her early war story, "Coming Home," published in her 1916 collection *Xingu*, the frame narrator acknowledges the difficulties of telling or writing stories about the war. The story opens:

> The young men of our American Relief Corps are beginning to come back from the front with stories.
>
> There was no time to pick them up during the first months—the whole business was too wild and grim. The horror has not decreased, but nerves and sight are beginning to be disciplined to it. In the earlier days, moreover, such fragments of experience as one got were torn from their setting like bits of flesh scattered by shrapnel. Now things that seemed disjointed are beginning to link themselves together, and the broken bones of history are rising from the battle-fields. (*Xingu* 45)

The chaos, shock, and terror of the first months of war made storytelling impossible, the narrator tells us, using a simile that links destroyed bodies ("bits of flesh") to kernels of stories ("fragments of experience"). Wharton's imagery recreates for the reader the very horror the speaker and reader "now" are supposedly accustomed to, but the sentence that marks this transition graphically reminds us of what war does to bodies. By linking the body with narrative, flesh with word, Wharton lays out a fundamental connection between the physical and the cultural, a link I will explore throughout this chapter using the work of Elaine Scarry. In Wharton's passage, bits of flesh correspond to an explosion and devastation of meaning. Only after the war has been endured and survived for a certain amount of time can the mind begin to make sense of it and in doing so formulate a narrative—a story or a history. As Wharton describes it, meaning is literally resurrected, brought back to life from death and made more powerful for having been destroyed.

The unnamed frame narrator of "Coming Home" introduces H. Macy Greer, who relates the body of the tale. But the frame narrator takes care to inform us of Greer's limitations as a storyteller: he "speaks with the slovenly drawl of the new generation of Americans, dragging his words along like reluctant dogs on a string, and depriving his narrative of every shade of expression that intelligent intonation gives." His narrative abilities are redeemed, however, by his powers of observation: "his eyes see so much that they make one see even what his foggy voice obscures" (46). The problems of telling a war story, then, particularly for a home front participant (like a woman), are acknowledged and alleviated by the assertion of the power of this eye-witness. Wharton's technique affirms her own authority to tell a war story, since she was herself an eye-witness. She was one of the few civilians and fewer women permitted to travel to the front. Although Wharton was always hesitant to depend on her experiences as an observer to justify her authority on the war, many critics, including myself, consider the war witness to have legitimacy in speaking and writing about what he or she saw.[2]

After the opening frame, Greer narrates one of his experiences in the war. He drives a supply car about the lines, and at one stop, he meets an injured French lieutenant, Jean de Réchamp, who has had no word from his family since the war started. His family and his fiancée were in a small village when the war began, and he knows the Germans have occupied his town. Several months later, Greer and Jean meet again, and conditions have changed so as to allow them to try to get to Réchamp. On the drive, Jean reveals that in addition to his obvious concern about his family under enemy occupation, he is also worried about how his family are treating his fiancée, Yvonne Malo, since his parents and grandmother objected to the marriage. The two men drive across a desolate, destroyed landscape to find that Réchamp is safe and whole. The family attribute Yvonne's resourcefulness for saving them: according to Jean's grandmother, when the Germans arrived, Yvonne met them with a meal and entertained them by playing the piano, and the officers responded well to such civilized behavior, staying briefly and leaving a letter of protection when they left. The day after Jean and Greer's arrival, however, Yvonne encourages Greer to take Jean away quickly, and she contrives to avoid her fiancé's presence, indicating that she does not want Jean to hear about "horrors we were powerless to help" (87). It turns out that the infamous (fictional) Oberst von Scharlach, known for being the cruelest man in the German army, was the commanding officer during the occupation. Greer takes Yvonne's hint and gets Jean back on the road. As they return to Paris, they are asked to take a wounded German prisoner back to the base, but on the way, the car runs out of gas. Greer goes for fuel alone, and when he returns to the car, the German is dead. Only when they arrive at the base does Greer discover that the German soldier was Oberst von Scharlach himself.

The story is harsh in its unspoken secret: that Yvonne has saved the town and the family by sleeping with the German officer. Jean's grandmother believes Yvonne's music tamed the violent beast, but the girl's frantic insistence that Jean leave before he hears any rumors suggests that the truth is much darker. But here readers are left in a quandary: Jean's family and the neighbors were predisposed to believe Yvonne is an immoral woman because of her unconventional life in the city, her untraditional upbringing, and her inheritance. Before the war, Yvonne was a musician living on her own in Paris, and Jean's family fears her as "a young girl who chooses to live alone—probably prefers to live alone!" (59). To Jean, she is astonishing: "The girl who comes and goes as she pleases, reads what she likes, has opinions about what she reads, who talks, looks, behaves with the independence of a married woman—and yet has kept the Diana-freshness—think how she must have shaken up such a man's inherited view of things!" (59–60). Not only does Yvonne have a "questionable" life as an adult, she was raised by a guardian with a dissolute past. Jean's family objects to his marrying her, because, as his grandmother tells him, there are "[t]hings in the air...that blow about...[...] Why did Corvenaire leave her all that money—*why*?" (63 ellipses and emphasis in original). The present gossip that Yvonne fears Jean will hear may simply be an outgrowth of the old gossip. The clash between civilized and uncivilized takes an ironic turn: it may be that music did civilize the barbarian, but the neighbors, with their petty and low minds, choose to believe otherwise.

It is, however, more likely that Yvonne exchanged sexual favors for the safety of the town, and Jean clearly believes this scenario to be true. He is torn between horror at and gratitude for what she has done; he admits that "she's saved everything for me—my people and my house, and the ground we're standing on. And I worship it because she walks on it!" (88). Her sacrifice has made what she has saved even more sacred. And in her actions, Yvonne has placed women as legitimate actors in the theater of war. As critic Mary Carney argues, "Malo's sexual skill functions as weaponry to defend the household, yet her silence and alienation from her fiancé are signs that this sexual encounter constitutes a hidden, unspeakable war wound" (113). In saving everything, Yvonne has confused gender roles, and by refusing to reveal what happened, she assumes the masculine role of shielding her partner. She has unmanned him by protecting his family, and in order to balance the scales, Jean apparently resorts to cold-blooded murder of the man who dishonored his fiancée. Greer has no way of knowing if Jean murdered von Scharlach; in fact, he cannot see how Jean could have known the identity of the German officer they are transporting. Yet after the man dies and before they learn his identity, Greer feels that Jean "had somehow got back, in the night's interval, to a state of wholesome stolidity, while I, on the contrary, was tingling all over with exposed nerves" (95). Greer waits anxiously until they arrive at the base and he hands over the German's papers. When the name "Oberst Graf Beno von Scharlach" is announced, the death is pronounced "a haul" and "a good riddance" by officials and doctors (96). The story ends with Greer returning to where Jean is waiting, and the two men walk off "arm in arm" to look for breakfast (97).

The story is rife with moral problems. Is Yvonne excused for sleeping with the enemy in order to save her fiancé's family and home? Is Jean justified for murdering the enemy whom his fiancée appeased with sexual favors? And to what degree is Greer complicit, especially at the end when he fails to denounce Jean as a murderer? If war permits these acts to occur uncensored and perhaps even condoned, is there a civilization left worth fighting for? These questions seem answered by Jean's, Greer's, and even Yvonne's silent acceptance of their own and each other's actions. Yet Wharton does not openly describe the horrors at the heart of the story. Instead, she leaves them to the reader's imagination, and it follows that she leaves moral judgment to the readers as well. Greer's willingness to abandon his discomfort with what he assumes Jean has done may not sit well with readers—particularly Americans in 1916, the very readers that Wharton attempted to sway with her war propaganda. Characters who respond to atrocity with atrocity do not seem the best way to convince an ambivalent American public of the moral necessity of joining the war. In "Coming Home," Wharton allows herself to examine the moral ambiguities of war that she would not address in propaganda, such as *Fighting France*.

This story also illustrates a problem that would plague Wharton's *A Son at the Front*, her later novels such as *Twilight Sleep*, and the writing of many other modernists: the terrible isolation of the individual. Elaine Scarry's work on the body in pain explains how physical agony separates one human being from another:

> Physical pain happens, of course, not several miles below our feet or many miles above our heads but within the bodies of persons who inhabit the world through which we each day make our way, and who may at any moment be separated from us by only a space of several inches. The very temptation to invoke analogies to remote cosmologies (and there is a long tradition of such analogies) is itself a sign of pain's triumph, for it achieves its aversiveness in part by bringing about, even within the radius of several feet, this absolute split between one's sense of one's own reality and the reality of other persons. (4)

The self-contained, encapsulated nature of the body and the mind that receives the body's signals of pain prevent any understanding of that pain from being communicated to another mind. In a passage from "Coming Home," for example, Greer examines the wounded German officer (not yet identified as the monstrous Scharlach):

> In the shaky lantern gleam I caught a glimpse of a livid face and a torn uniform, and saw that he was an officer, and nearly done for. Réchamp had climbed to the box, and seemed not to be noticing what was going on at the back of the motor. I understood that he loathed the job, and wanted not to see the face of the man we were carrying;.... The man lay motionless on his back, conscious, but desperately weak. Once I turned my pocket lamp on him and saw that he was young—about thirty—with damp dark hair and a thin face. He had received a flesh wound above the eyes, and his forehead was bandaged, but the rest of the face uncovered. As the light fell on him he lifted his eyelids and looked at me: his look was inscrutable. (92)

Here two men stand within inches or feet of a man in mortal agony from a stomach wound. Jean prefers not even to look, perhaps because he is already plotting the German's murder. Greer, however, examines the man twice. The first time he clearly identifies the man's pain through his "livid face" and his assessment of the man as "nearly done for." The second time Greer observes attributes about the man that are irrelevant to his pain (his age, his hair color, his face). Neither time does or can Greer fully comprehend the pain the wounded man must be feeling, and the man himself can only hint at his agony through his "inscrutable" look. Greer can "see that the man was suffering atrociously," but he cannot feel it. The visual exchange between the two men (Greer can "see" the suffering, the officer conveys it through a "look") indicates how far beyond the verbal the one man's agony is. The German officer is, to use Scarry's phrase, in a "remote cosmology" a long way away from the other two men.

This remoteness highlights the deep gulfs of experience that separate the other characters from each other, as well as the frame narrator from Greer and the reader from all of them. Jean and Yvonne are not in physical pain but rather emotional agony, which prevents them from finding a way to communicate their suffering to each other. During Yvonne and Greer's private talk, Greer wonders, "What was it the girl's silence was crying out to me?" (84). On the way back to the lines, Greer and Jean sit largely without speaking, pondering the mystery of the events at Réchamp, and this time the silence covers a pain

Greer hopes will not be expressed: "all the while I sat at his side I kept hearing the echo of the question he was inwardly asking himself, and hoping to God he wouldn't put it to me...." (91 ellipses in original). These characters have all discovered that their suffering cannot be communicated, and hence each one has been brutally reminded of the isolation experience has created for them. This gulf between individuals is emphasized at the end of the story by the absence of the frame narrator's voice. Readers must make their own conclusions and judgments through the gaps literally inscribed on the page as ellipses.

A Son at the Front and the Modern War Novel

In her other war writing, Wharton does not address or even pose the difficult moral questions that "Coming Home" raises, but she does return to the problem of pain and its link to the separate worlds characters inhabit. *A Son at the Front* continues to raise these issues as well as picks up some of the foundational questions of "Coming Home": what is "civilization," and what does it mean to live in a civilized society? These questions are crucial for writers and characters scarred by the war and facing life beyond it. At the end of Willa Cather's *One of Ours*, for example, Claude Wheeler's mother regards the war as only a pause in the "flood of meanness and greed" (370) and feels grateful her son has not lived to feel postwar disillusionment. Nick Carraway, the narrator of F. Scott Fitzgerald's *The Great Gatsby* (1925), finds himself longing for "the world to be in uniform and at a sort of moral attention forever" (19–20); instead, he must face a society that values pretty surfaces and good times but rejects the obligations of responsible human conduct. For Ernest Hemingway's Frederic Henry in *A Farewell to Arms* (1929), the war sweeps away the fragments of the past and leaves him facing an empty, uncertain future, void of love and meaning. For Wharton, however, although the war was transformative, it did not mark a complete break in history. In *A Son at the Front*, characters face the threat of such a loss of meaning and of civilization, but John Campton, although devastated by the death of his son, recovers enough to participate in and continue artistic traditions. For Campton, the real horror is that despite the devastation of war, life does go on.

A Son at the Front is a behind-the-lines novel about life in Paris during the early years of World War I. As the novel begins, John Campton, an American painter living abroad, eagerly awaits the arrival of his son George, whose portrait brought his father fame a few years before. Campton and his wife Julia divorced when George was young, and George was raised by his mother and his stepfather, Anderson Brant. Campton now hopes to take a long journey with his son and get to know him better, but his plans are interrupted by the outbreak of war. George, born in France, is a member of the French army and is mobilized. His father and step-parents scheme to keep him at a "safe" desk job on the grounds of a bout of tuberculosis he had the previous year, but George transfers to the front without informing his parents, although he does confide in family friend Adele Anthony and his friend Boylston. Adele and Boylston jump headlong into charity work, and even the hapless and inert Campton participates. Gradually Campton becomes uncomfortable with the thought of his son shirking his duty while so many other young men are dying, but at this point he gets word that George is wounded. Campton and Brant join forces to care for George, who recovers—but also insists on returning to the front lines. George is wounded a second time, and although he seems to be recovering, he dies on the day the United States declares war on Germany. His father struggles to resume his life and return to his art.

Evidence shows that Wharton based her soldier characters on soldiers she knew: her friend Ronald Simmons, her cousin Newbold Rhinelander, and the many young American men she came across in Paris. She dedicated *A Son at the Front* (as well as the earlier *The Marne*) to Ronald Simmons, who worked in military intelligence. Although Wharton valued her relationship with Simmons—and she certainly knew him better than Newbold Rhinelander, whom she seems to have met just once—Simmons is not a model for the soldiers George or his firebrand cousin Benny Upsher. Wharton's notes for the novel include the comment: "Upsher is not Simmons—but 'Boylston' may be—" (Beinecke). Even still, Simmons' letters suggest a much more discontented and insecure young man than any of Wharton's soldiers. On July 7, 1918, Simmons wrote Wharton: "I have had so very little experience in life...that I constantly doubt whether I am of any use to anyone in the work which I am trying to do. From time to time I get encouraged by actual results achieved but what a selfish *madhouse* it all is! Even you can never know how I envy those men who have the nerves, health and qualities to go to the Front—get away from these below-stairs intrigues and achieve glory or peace like normal, clean human beings" (Beinecke, emphasis in original). Simmons' lack of confidence in himself appears in neither George nor Boylston. His frustration with the world of military intelligence, war charities, and other behind-the-lines work—the "selfish madhouse" that makes the battlefront seem the place of morality and humanity—may, however, be quietly lurking in George, who feels strongly that behind-the-lines work is not "his" work.

Both Newbold Rhinelander and George Campton have the "nerves, health and qualities to go to the Front." George repeatedly and in different forms reiterates Newbold Rhinelander's comment in a September 4, 1918 letter to his mother: "have you reflected on how you and I would feel if I didn't get a good crack at the Hun?" (Beinecke). Newbold's eagerness for battle is a sharp contrast from the war-weary soldiers of Ernest Hemingway and John Dos Passos, for example—a contrast of which Wharton was well aware. As Olin-Ammentorp notes, "she had met a number of young American soldiers, and her impressions were almost exclusively positive; in none of them did she encounter the demoralization recorded by numerous English authors, as well as American authors like Hemingway, Dos Passos, and e.e. cummings" (123). Wharton's soldiers are probably more historically accurate. Even Hemingway, for example, enjoyed the war experience until he was injured, and only ten years afterward did he create Frederic Henry. As historian David Kennedy points out, most American soldiers who wrote about the war did not discuss what we would call modernist disillusionment. Instead, Kennedy shows, the diaries and letters of many American soldiers read like travel writing (*Over Here* 205–6) and reflect the propaganda and ideology heard at home (212). The disillusion and alienation felt by Frederic Henry are not unrelated to the war but grew out of the disaffection felt by his author during the 1920s.

Wharton does not describe battle scenes in *A Son at the Front*. As Olin-Ammentorp indicates, Wharton was extremely conscious of her exclusion from the "real business" of war (34–35). Yet she manages to convey the horror and chaos of mechanized warfare. She portrays the betrayal of technology, a standard tope of World War I literature, through Campton's reaction to the opening salvos of the war: "Aeroplanes throwing bombs? Aeroplanes as engines of destruction? He had always thought of them as a kind of giant kite that fools went up in when they were tired of breaking their necks in other ways. But aeroplane bombardment as a cause for declaring war? The bad faith of it was so manifest that he threw down the papers half relieved" (81). The "bad faith" overtly referred to is Germany's accusation of France's bombing, but the text also suggests that Campton regards bombing to be a betrayal committed by the planes themselves. This horror and shock at mechanized warfare can be found in most World War I novels; in *Three Soldiers* (1925), for example, John Dos Passos insists on the inhumanity of war by organizing the text with section headings describing the war and the military as a machine.

Although she saw little actual fighting, Wharton did have direct experience at the front lines, bringing medical supplies and other relief on several visits. In a letter to Henry James, dated February 28, 1915, Wharton describes some of what she saw:

> We went first to Châlons s/ Marne, & it was extraordinary, not more than 4 hours from Paris, to find ourselves to all appearance completely in the war-zone. It is the big base of the Eastern army, & the streets swarm with soldiers & with military motors & ambulances. We went to see a hospital with 900 cases of typhoid, where *everything* was lacking—a depressing beginning, for even if I had emptied my motor-load into their laps it would have been a goutte d'eau in a desert. (Lewis and Lewis *Letters* 348 emphasis in original)

A few days later she wrote James about

> a hamlet plunged to the eaves in mud, where beds had been rigged up in two or three little houses, a primitive operating-room installed, &c. Picture this all under a white winter sky, driving great flurries of snow across the mud-&-cinder-coloured landscape, with the steel-cold Meuse winding between beaten poplars—Cook standing with Her in a knot of mud-coated military motors & artillery horses, soldiers coming & going, cavalrymen riding up with messages, poor bandaged creatures in rag-bag clothes leaning in doorways, & always, over & above us, the boom, boom, boom, of the guns on the grey heights to the east. (Lewis and Lewis *Letters* 351)

Wharton drew on these visits to the front lines to describe Campton's horror at the military hospital: "Below him lay the court. A line of stretchers was being carried across it, not empty this time, but each one with a bloody burden. Doctors, nurses, orderlies hurried to and fro. Drub, drub, drub, went the guns, shaking the windows, rolling their fierce din along the cloudy sky, down the corridors of the hospital and the pavement of the streets, like huge bowls crashing through story above story of a kind of sky-scraping bowling alley" (285). Like many authors of World War I novels, Wharton conveys the ironic mundaneness of the front. Despite the endless line of wounded bodies and the pounding of the guns, so pervasive that Campton hears it later in the beating of the ocean waves, people adapt. When Campton and Brant arrive at George's hospital, Campton spots a "young doctor in a cotton blouse...lighting a cigarette and laughing with a nurse—laughing!" (276). Wharton even hints at the boredom of the trenches. George (supposedly at his desk job but actually on the front lines) writes to his father that "war makes a lot of things look differently, especially this sedentary kind of war: it's rather like going over all the old odds-and-ends in one's cupboards" (196). The portrayal of mechanized warfare, the confusion of the hospital, and the juxtaposition of horror with the everyday are classic elements of war novels.

The most modernist and least understood part of *A Son at the Front* is the structure of its narration. The story focuses on Campton, and the reader has access to the events and characters of the novel only through Campton's understanding and interpretation of those events and characters. We may even be tempted to trust Campton's interpretations more than we otherwise would because he is a successful artist who perceives the world through his eyes; after all, we tend to trust vision as the final arbiter of truth. But Campton is not the narrator. Over and over, we are reminded that Campton does not know everything he thinks he does, whether because he is lied to (for example, by George about his whereabouts) or, more often, because he cannot or will not fully comprehend what he sees. For example, the narrator tells us that "It was clear that the boy hated what was ahead of him" (72), but we come to understand that "it is clear" to Campton only, and to the reader, George's attitude toward the war is far more ambiguous. Other examples show Campton's limited vision. He regards Adele Anthony "as an eternal schoolgirl; now she had grown into a woman" (175). But just because Campton "had always thought" of Adele as a "schoolgirl" and now sees her as "a woman" does not make his judgment correct. Were Adele to portray herself she might not delineate or define her life as Campton does. George's faith in her—she is the only one of his four parental figures that he trusts with the secret of his transferring to the front—indicates that he, at any rate, sees something steadfast in her. He actually puts her in a position to "parent" Campton, Julia, and Brant. She reassures Campton of his son's safety by showing him her own letter from George, a fake letter George has sent her for this purpose. Adele is a complex character with motivations beyond Campton's comprehension.

Similarly, just because Campton chooses to attribute gallant motives to George does not mean those motives exist. George is a puzzle, to both his father and his readers. Campton's idealistic vision of his son can be mediated by a comparison of George with other literary soldiers. After the reality of violence shocks George out of his blasé insistence that the war will never happen, he reacts with high-minded idealism and anger. His subsequent actions, however, suggest that he is driven less by ideology than by the more mundane reasons common to many soldiers. He never fully explains why he switches from his desk job to the front. Campton assumes George's reasons are noble and George lets him, but George may have felt guilt at watching other young men head off to war or he may have been drawn by an interest in battle itself. According to Boylston, George was initially "intellectually" indifferent to the war, "but he told me that when he saw the first men on their way back from the front—with the first mud on them—he knew he belonged where they'd come from" (391). Literature is full of young men who can find no place except on the front lines.[3] Before the war, Campton has already acknowledged his son's desultory approach to life: "He had hoped that George would develop some marked talent, some irresistible tendency which would decide his future too definitely for interference; but George was twenty-five, and no call had come.... Campton knew that this absence of a special bent...gave the boy his peculiar charm. The trouble was that it made him the prey of other people's plans for him" (31). Indeed, George becomes "prey" to the French government's plans for him, but only to a point: George himself chooses the front lines, and he is happy there. He tells Campton, "You don't know how I thank my stars that there weren't any 'problems' for me, but just a plain job that picked me up by the collar, and dropped me down where I belonged" (324). When his father suggests, on learning that George wants to return to the front after being wounded, that he has already done his duty and can now help the war effort in another way, George replies, "But if I happen to have only one line?" (359). George is driven less by the idea of noble sacrifice than by the feeling that front-line work is the only work—"a plain job"—he is suited for. His decision is about his abilities, not his ideals.

George rarely articulates his reasons for wanting to fight, but when he does, they prove to be complex. He explains his desire to return to the front in both idealistic and pragmatic ways: "When we're all in it you wouldn't have me looking on, would you? And then there are my men—I've got to get back to my men" (359). It is the appearance of his orderly that immediately precedes George's decision to return to the front. When Campton observes their meeting, he sees "the look the two exchanged: it lasted only for the taking of a breath; a moment later officer and soldier were laughing like boys.... But again the glance was an illumination; it came straight from that far country, the Benny Upsher country, which Campton so feared to see in his son's eyes" (377). "Benny Upsher country" has been read as the realm of idealism, yet Benny Upsher has little to say for himself, other than that he wants to be "in this" (105), that "all [he] sees is that hulking bully trying to do Belgium in" (107), and, most emphatically, that he wants to join George's regiment specifically. Benny is driven by a desire for the adventure of war and for comradeship. Through George, we see that that comradeship has forged ties that cannot be broken; the soldiers have bonded over their experience of war, an experience that excludes anyone who has not also lived through battle.

Campton sees his son "living his real life in some inconceivable region" (310), which Campton attributes to the moral modeling of the fire of war. However, George's silences and faraway look may be due to trauma and the isolating experience of war. Madge Talkett, George's married mistress, reports to Campton that George insists on marrying her: "He says he wants only things that last—that are permanent—things that hold a man fast. That sometimes he feels as if he were being swept away on a flood, and were trying to catch at things—at anything—as he's rushed along under the waves..." (343). Mrs. Talkett and Campton interpret George's words and demands as resulting from a new, higher order of morality. But these words also suggest desperation, and George later tells his father that he does not actually want Mrs. Talkett to divorce her husband because he knows he does not have a right to his own future. Charges of sentimentalism in the novel seem based largely on the last pages of the novel, when Campton feels he can finally paint George and capture his "glow" (397), and he believes that he "[understands]—at last" (399). It is much easier to understand George when he is dead and can offer no words or actions that conflict with the father's interpretation. The dead George can become a fixed symbol of "force and youth and hope" (399) even if the living George was far more complicated.

Campton is not the only one to misunderstand George. Boylston, attempting to explain George's desire to be at the front, suggests the motive of "*Dulce et decorum*," but he adds a "perhaps" right afterward (391). And just before this explanation, Boylston admits that he does not understand a soldier's motivation: "We don't really know—do we, sir?—exactly how any of them feel? Any more than if they were—" (390). Campton supplies the ending of the question: "dead." The crucible of battle separates soldiers from noncombatants.

Wharton structures her narrative through ambiguity, and she leaves room for the reader to see gaps or failures in Campton's interpretation of George. My point is not that George's or Boylston's worldview outweighs or is more right than Campton's but rather that each character has his or her own biases and interpretations, and the reader is allowed access only to Campton's. Knowledge of the literary tradition of soldiers forces the reader to reevaluate Campton's interpretation of his son. *A Son at the Front* recalls *The Reef* in its emphasis on subjectivity, but here we have no contrasting voice to remind us of the perils of knowing only one point of view. Campton is trapped in his own limited worldview, and we are trapped with him.

As in "Coming Home," pain functions as both a cause of the isolation of individuals and a reminder that that isolation already exists. At George's bedside the first time he is injured, Campton feels that his son belongs to another world completely: "It was in the moment of identifying his son that he felt the son he had known to be lost to him forever" (280). In these scenes, we see how incapable Campton is of imagining the interior life of another human being. He shows no signs of awareness of the pain George must be suffering but focuses instead on his "utter alienation from that dark delirious man who for brief intervals suddenly became his son, and then as suddenly wandered off into strangeness" (288). As George recovers, "Campton found his son as difficult to get at as a baby; he looked at his father with eyes as void of experience, or at least as of any means of conveying it" (292). Like Campton, we cannot feel George's pain or even imagine it. Further, we cannot understand George's feelings and motivations in regard to the war. Scarry's argument about the incommunicableness of pain can be a tool for understanding Wharton's text; that is, some of the isolation Campton feels from George, and George from Campton, comes from the entirely individual experience of George's bodily wounding. Campton even feels that, as Scarry points out about the language used to describe pain (that of "remote cosmologies"), George is in his own "secret world" (295), "rising from the depths of the sea" (296).

But physical pain also becomes a metaphor for all experience that cannot be conveyed in words and that consequently become reminders of the isolation of the individual. As Campton and Brant rush to the hospital at the front where George lies wounded, Campton knows that sitting next to him is a man worrying as much as himself, but he does not care:

> He said to himself that the man was no doubt suffering horribly; but he was not conscious of any impulse of compassion. He and Mr. Brant were like two strangers pinned down together in a railway-smash: the shared agony did not bring them nearer. On the contrary, Campton, as the hours passed, felt himself more and more exasperated by the mute anguish at his side. (273)

Campton's, and especially the reader's, increasing awareness of this isolation makes Campton's subsequent feelings that he and George are unified in thought highly suspect. Campton is "sure that George always knew what was passing through his mind" (291), yet, situated as we are in Campton's point of view, no evidence appears that father and son's "incessant silent communion" (312) exists other than in Campton's head. The suspicion persists: what if Campton is wrong, and the two men are not thinking the same thing? What then binds one human being to another?

Homosocial Bonds and the Continuity of Power

As critics have noted, homoeroticism strongly marks the relationships between men in *A Son at the Front*, and I suggest that it is through this desire that Wharton exposes the structures of "civilization" and how those structures are and will be perpetuated. In *Between Men*, Eve Kosofsky Sedgwick theorizes "male homosocial desire" as a continuum that encompasses all relations among men. She defines "desire" as not necessarily or inherently sexual but rather as "the affective or social force, the glue, even when its manifestation is hostility or hatred or something less emotively charged, that shapes an important relationship" (2). In our insistently heterosexual society, it is useful to see, as Judith Sensibar points out, the ways in which homosocial or homosexual desire disrupts traditional notions of male sexuality and male relationships ("Behind the Lines"). Yet, as Sedgwick demonstrates, while male homosocial activities are linked to homosexuality, they also are part of heterosexual systems of meaning and identity. That is, while male homosocial desire can be subversive, it can—and usually does—support the status quo, particularly in the case of wealthy white men. In *A Son at the Front*, male homosocial desire both subverts and reinforces patriarchal systems of authority and meaning.

The increasing strength of the relationship between John Campton and Anderson Brant, in which the two men function better as a couple than either seems to with Julia, recalls the traffic in women that serves to bond men. In chapter 3, I focused on "unmediated male bonding" between men in Wharton's short stories—stories that are narrow windows into the world. In *A Son at the Front*, Wharton's men have less opportunity to evade women, although Campton makes a good effort. Campton and Brant seem to bond through the exchange of Julia. For Campton's part, however, it is actually George, who has supplanted all women in his father's life, who serves to make the tie between both men stronger. It is less clear that Brant understands the bone of contention and source of their bond to be George. Brant seems to consider it to be Julia, as suggested by his repeated evasions when he needs to refer to her in conversation with Campton. He catches himself each time before he is about to say "my wife" and instead substitutes "Mrs. Brant" or "George's mother" (248, 249).

This elision of "my wife," however, also leaves open the spot by Brant's side, and Campton and Brant's relationship questions the definition of "couple." Is it possible, in that time and place, for two men to be a "couple"? At first, it seems so; they have similar views and work well together. Early in the novel, when Campton discovers that he and Brant agree that they must prevent George's knowing that they are trying to keep him out of combat, he feels "a sense of their possessing a common ground of understanding that Campton had never found in his wife" (25). The feeling is accompanied by an "almost brotherly" look between the two: "'We men know...' the look said" (26 ellipses in original). The moment is rooted in common experience and in a common outlook unique to gender. Further, the men bond over the work that must be done to take care of George when he is wounded. In an emotional moment, Campton makes one of his snide remarks about Brant's "ways" (290) of using money and influence, but he quickly apologizes, saying, "I know—I know how you feel" (293). Afterward, the two men develop a routine and interdependence as they care for George, and Brant becomes free to use his "ways" to George's benefit. They even seem to alternate in moments of effeminacy: Brant cedes Campton's masculine right as the "father" to be at George's bedside, itself a feminine place, while Campton acknowledges Brant's greater resources and power in the world of finance and politics. Together they suggest an ideal, postfeminist "couple": two people who complement and acknowledge each other's strengths and who gain power through their combined resources.

Their power, however, becomes precisely the reason why they cannot last and why they ultimately do not define a "couple" in their time. Their very effeminacies serve as reminders that they are not women, and women cannot be shut out forever. Campton becomes so dependent, emotionally as well as practically, on Brant that he begins to fear that Julia will "unsettle things, break the spell, agitate, and unnerve them all" (295). Julia does not unsettle things in the way Campton predicts (George's fever does not go back up), but her arrival does break up the working system between men because her presence requires Brant to leave. Social orthodoxy prevents the three of them from staying at George's bedside in the Catholic hospital; as Julia vaguely explains, "we can't very well...all three of us...especially with these nuns..." (299 ellipses in original). Campton's desire for Brant to stay is also a desire not to be left alone with his former wife. Brant becomes a shield that protects Campton from, if not heterosexuality, at least heterosexual relationships. He fears Julia because he does not understand her. For one thing, "her manner of loving their son was too different" (298), and, for another, "he could never tell what form her thoughts about George might be taking" (299). Again, we run into the problem of Campton's assumptions: as with George, Campton feels that he and Brant "were thinking of things in the same way" (298). We do not see into Brant's head, so we do not know if Campton is right. But with his frank acknowledgment that he does not know what Julia is thinking, Campton again comes up against the wide gap between one human being and another. This time, however, the gap is inscribed as gender difference. Campton and Brant's relationship presents the illusion of communion; Campton and Julia's exposes that illusion. In this case, male homosocial desire, or life without Julia, supports the comforting belief that one human being can fully understand another.

The most commented upon homoerotic bond in the novel is that between father and son. Campton's sexual longing for his son is discussed by me elsewhere[4] and by Sensibar, among others. Sensibar links the passage in which Campton observes and draws the body of his sleeping son (53–54) to "the frankly homoerotic poetry and fiction of the war—the religio-erotic motif of the knight-effigy" ("Behind the Lines" 250) identified by Paul Fussell in the work of British soldier-poets such as Sigfried Sassoon, Wilfrid Gibson, and Wilfred Owen.[5] Sensibar is right to see that the novel is a radical critique of "masculinist, homophobic gender classifications" (253)— that Campton's gaze commodifies and eroticizes his son and thus challenges the glorification of male battlefront relationships. On the other hand, that same gaze, by producing the drawing of George's body that will be used to sculpt his memorial, ultimately makes George into an image of sacrifice and nobility that will in turn inspire other young men to charge into battle. Whether or not Wharton's description of the father's gaze disrupts the valorization of the "brother in arms" motif, Campton's art will perpetuate that motif.

Campton's longing for companionship with his son also foreshadows, and is preempted by, George's future relationships with his comrades. At the opening of the novel, Campton wants to travel with

George in order to forge bonds of comradeship: "this was to be their last chance, as it was almost their first, of being together quietly, confidentially, uninterruptedly" (11). Instead, George travels to the front, and, although the novel does not record what happens there, George clearly bonds with his fellow-soldiers. On her trips to the front, Wharton visited with soldiers and might have sensed their camaderie, as Percy Lubbock suggests in his biography of Wharton (122). More definitely, she had access to the letters Newbold Rhinelander wrote to his mother. These letters reveal a young man proud to be fighting, longing for the adventure of battle, and enjoying the company of his comrades. On September 18, 1918, he wrote:

> I am truly ashamed to say that since I have been here I haven't been over the lines yet. Two of the teams have been over on reconnaissance and I'm hoping my turn will come very soon. It's such fun being here more like a small happy family than a post [*sic*]. I have made two 220 mile flights carrying precious photos (of the lines) between one French headquarters and another, and upon the first occasion my observer and I had a wonderful time dining with the General Staff of the French Aviation! Wow![6]

Newbold Rhinelander's plane disappeared in a gunfight shortly after he sent this letter, and his friend W. Clarkson Potter wrote to Newbold's father Thomas Rhinelander on September 29, 1918, describing himself as "Newbold's best friend over here" and noting how they "had lived together, bunked together, been on every party together, shared all our possessions, inseparable in every way and finally fought together." Potter continues: "Bo's loss to this squadron is irretrievable, he was the very life and soul of it, always cheerful and perpetually singing rag-time and playing the mandolin day in and day out: besides being a 'finished pilot' one of the *very best* the Air Service had. I am absolutely lost and 'down and out' without him" (Beinecke emphasis in original). The letters from these two soldiers speak of an enthusiasm for military life and bonds that could be forged only in the specific circumstances of war. In *A Son at the Front*, the brief glimpse of George with his orderly evokes those ties and, as discussed earlier, the relationship between those two men turns out to outweigh George's relationships with everyone else, including his parents and his mistress. "It's the thought of their men that pulls them all back," Boylston says (391). These bonds between men (that, at that point in history, could exist *only* between men) allow the war to continue.

War and Western Civilization

The structures of civilization—art, patriotism, family relationships, language, the constructed personal identity, and even the "civilized" body—are emblazoned throughout the novel. *A Son at the Front* is entirely about the notion of civilization, and Wharton directly engages with modernist concerns about what civilization is, what use its rules serve, and what its artifacts mean. The first lines of the novel bear close investigation: "John Campton, the American portrait-painter, stood in his bare studio in Montmartre at the end of a summer afternoon contemplating a battered calendar that hung against the wall" (3). The main character is given a name, which situates him as a specific member of a particular family, and a description, which identifies both his nationality and his work. He is further placed in space, his studio in Montmartre, and time, a certain time of day in a certain season within a larger framework of time as indicated by the calendar. All of these descriptors are cultural identifiers that distinguish this man from an ancient Greek statesman or an African tribeswoman or a twenty-first century Russian.[7] One might argue that such details are inherently necessary to a novel and thus become so minor as to become meaningless; after all, novelists almost always must locate their characters in time, space, profession, nationality, and so on. As this novel continues, however, and proves itself to be a story about World War I, the war to "protect" Western civilization, it becomes increasingly necessary to understand what that civilization is. Just a little farther on the page, Campton underscores the constructed nature of time when he tears off the current page of the calendar to reveal the next day, "to bring the moment nearer" (3). "July 30, 1914" is a cultural construct, using a system of names for months and another system for the number of days in a month and a fairly arbitrary system of counting and identifying years. A date is not a fixed value, and by tearing off the current day, even as a self-indulgent amusement, Campton reminds us of the long history of human beliefs and cultures (the combination of the early, erroneous Christian belief in the year of Christ's birth with the Gregorian calendar of months) that make a date.

As Scarry argues, war is intricately related to civilization: "War is in the massive fact of itself a huge structure for the derealization of cultural constructs and, simultaneously, for their eventual reconstitution" (137). The body, Scarry argues, is the locus of civilization, which may be extended to rooms and buildings, artifacts that are extensions of the body. She explains that "the human animal is in its early years 'civilized,' learns to stand upright, to walk, to wave and signal, to listen, to speak, and the general 'civilizing' process takes place within particular 'civil' realms, a particular hemisphere, a particular nation, a particular state, a particular region" (109). When Campton hugs the young George on his return from school, he does so to make sure "he was the same Geordie, only bigger, browner, with thicker curlier hair, and tougher muscles under his jacket" (283). Campton needs this physical connection, as if he is searching for an essential George that does not change despite the months and years apart from his father. Yet even the "tougher muscles" belie Campton's attempt, for George's body demonstrates changes, probably very specific changes as his body learns rugby or polo or whatever sports he played while being schooled in England and later as he performed military service in France. The adult George participates in what Scarry calls the "unmaking" of the world by allowing the French government to assume authority over his body and to recondition that body to behave in "uncivilized" ways, such as killing the enemy and presenting itself as a target for the enemy to try to kill.

Before he is "unmade," George is "made" into a "civilized" human being by one of the most powerful constructs of Western civilization: the family. It is the nature of the family to generate and regenerate itself, and the novel gestures at the psychological development of two generations of Campton men. At the beginning of the novel, while awaiting the arrival of his son, John Campton recollects his own Oedipal drama. When he first came to Paris, Campton greatly admired an established painter and hoped for that painter's approval: "If he could get near enough to Beausite, the ruling light of the galaxy, he thought he might do things not unworthy of that great master" (4). Campton was unable to get Beausite to acknowledge him, a trauma in itself, but Campton also comes to realize that the "great master" is no longer the artistic force he had once held in such esteem; Beausite's work is "only the light from a dead star." The "son" usurps the "father": "Beausite had vanished from the heavens, and the youth he had sneered at throned there in his stead" (5). Campton's Oedipal struggle has been transferred out of childhood into adulthood and is not over the mother figure but rather over art. Still, the experience teaches Campton that the father's authority is transient at best.

The novel provides less information on George's psychological development, but he has four parents (Julia, Campton, Anderson Brant, Adele Anthony) to contend with instead of two. He apparently never openly challenges either father—except by transferring out of his desk job to a front-line position against what he knows are his parents' wishes. By making this switch in secret, George points out his father's (or fathers') lack of knowledge and his (their) lack of power in a parallel to Campton's discovery of Beausite's hollow talent. George also finds that he cannot talk with his father about his desire to return to the front. He tries once, but Campton's violent reaction forces him to back away from the subject (358–62). Campton fails not only his son but also another young man, his son's friend Boylston, when Boylston comes to ask Campton to chair a charity organization: "It was as though the modest youth, taking his host's measure, had reluctantly found him wanting, and from that moment had felt less in awe of his genius" (132). The war places Campton in a position to father, and therefore to be exposed as lacking the full authority the child imagines he has, not only his biological offspring but all soldiers. Indeed, at the end of the novel Campton imagines all the American soldiers as "George's brothers" (418) and hence his sons.

The war redraws the lines of established and expected family relationships. When war looms, Julia Brant reluctantly expresses her regret that her son has recovered from tuberculosis: "that was the view that war made mothers take of the chief blessing they could ask for their children!" (18). The unnaturalness of this wish, shared by Campton, is magnified infinitely by the experience of Dr. Fortin-Lescluze, who must operate on his own son only to find that it is too late: "I took off both legs, but gangrene had set in" (121). The father, who had a part in creating the body of his son, must now participate in the destruction of that body. Dr. Fortin-Lescluze's position is then reflected back to Campton, who finds himself starting to wish that his son were in danger on the front lines. He wonders about his son's "moral balance" (133) at not apparently responding more violently to Germany's crimes and about his "indifference" (134) to the war. Campton "nervously" offers arguments against his right to encourage George to join the fight: "What right have useless old men like me, sitting here with my cigar by this good fire, to preach blood and butchery to boys like George and your nephew?" (186). Eventually he realizes that his desire for George to take part in the war outweighs his need to keep his son safe, and this conviction puts him at odds with George's mother, who believes a parent should protect his child at all costs. War transforms the "fathers" into "useless old men" who must use whatever remaining authority they have to encourage the young men to make sacrifices they themselves cannot. It is not a comfortable—or "civilized"—position.

As has often been observed, war changes language. The immediate threat of destruction forces people to reexamine their relationship to each other, to their country, and to death, and this reexamination is necessarily mediated by words. In *A Son at the Front*, Wharton continues the tradition of the war novel by revealing the weak points in language. Campton is stymied by the phrase: "A son in the war—." He thinks: "What did it mean, and what must it feel like, for parents in this safe denationalized modern world to be suddenly saying to each other with white lips: A son in the war?" (70). The word "son" evokes the problems of family relationship suggested earlier, of how a "father" suddenly must allow, perhaps even encourage, a male child to risk his life. The word "war" is another problem, for, as I showed above, characters not at the front are permanently barred from truly knowing what "war" means. Language takes on a life of its own, as Campton acknowledges when he reflects on the word "front": "how that word had insinuated itself into the language!" (123). That is, the tools by which characters identify themselves and their world have suddenly become unstable; words seem to have an active life of their own and thus possess power to reimagine what things and events are possible. Anticipating Hemingway's Frederic Henry by several years,[8] Wharton's Dastrey observes, "I was considering how the meaning had evaporated out of lots of our old words, as if the general smash-up had broken their stoppers" (187). Dastrey suggests that words are like Pandora's box, and with their "stoppers" removed, they twist out of control. Even the name "George" becomes empty as Campton feels shut out of his son's life by "an impenetrable veil" (402). For civilization to exist, words must at least appear to be pinned down; they are the means by which one human can express an idea to another.

Campton ultimately comes to accept the war as necessary in order to preserve a way of life and a set of values. He comes remarkably close to framing the need for war in Scarry's terms. Scarry argues that "war is a contest between two states who are attempting to assert conflicting ideas of themselves: objects of damage in war are bodies, material culture, and ultimately immaterial culture" (114), the last of which is the real target of the enemy. That is, a combatant force seeks to destroy its enemy's conception of itself: "The dispute that leads to the war involves a process by which each side calls into question the legitimacy and thereby erodes the reality of the other country's issues, beliefs, ideas, self-conception" (128). Early in *A Son at the Front*, Campton admits that on occasion he needs "some substitute for the background of domestic sympathy," which he finds in his friend Paul Dastrey (9). He later acknowledges that such everyday culture is worth defending:

> The last four months had shown him man as a defenceless animal suddenly torn from his shell, stripped of all the interwoven tendrils of association, habit, background, daily ways and words, daily sights and sounds, and flung out of the human habitable world into naked ether, where nothing breathes or lives. That was what war did; that was why those who best understood it in all its farthest-reaching abomination willingly gave their lives to put an end to it. (183–84)

Human rituals order life; they make it "habitable." With this realization, Campton begins to feel that serving in the war is necessary and that no "civilized man could afford to stand aside from such a conflict" (188). A "civilized man" must choose to decivilize himself to protect and maintain his civilization. When Dastrey declares that without the young men lost in battle the only thing worth fighting for is "France, an Idea," he identifies exactly what is at stake: France's conception of itself, an immaterial part of culture in which Campton and the others have a vital interest.

A Son at the Front points out that the "Idea" of France does continue after World War I, and the novel, unlike much of modern fiction, insists on the continuity of Western civilization rather than on its disruption. Campton's art makes this continuity clear. The night before George is mobilized, Campton spies him sleeping:

> "Like a statue of a young knight I've seen somewhere," he said to himself, vexed and surprised that he, whose plastic memories were always so precise, should not remember where; and then his pencil stopped. What he had really thought was: "Like the *effigy* of a young knight"—though he had instinctively changed the word as it formed itself. [...] It was the clinging sheet, no doubt, that gave him that look...and the white glare of the electric burner. (53–54 emphasis in original)

I discussed the homoerotics of this scene earlier; here I wish to consider another connection Campton makes. He sees his son as an effigy, in this case a statue on a sarcophagus, a tradition dating back to the Crusades. The knight-effigy commemorated the knight's glory in battle, loyalty to the king, and religious piety in his sacrifice. The knight-effigy reinforced the principles underlying the society for which the knight fought. The language Campton uses to think about the war suggests a crusade as he mourns the soldiers who leave "not even a child..., to carry on the faith they had died for" (365).[9] In death, George continues the knight-effigy tradition as he is memorialized by his father to meet the needs of his mother, Brant, and Adele as well as of the larger community. Campton must go back to pre-war drawings of George to make his sculpture; this is partly a matter of practical necessity, since Campton has few wartime drawings of George. Still, the George that will result from Campton's sculpture is not the George transformed by war, the George who has seen horror and violence. Campton memorializes his son by resurrecting the pre-war George, and the untouched George will figure in art to valorize war and to inspire future generations of young men to enter into battle. In this way, the war, rather than becoming a violent and incontrovertible break from the past, perpetuates the values of the past.

For Campton, the war is not a catalyst of shocking change. Civilization is neither improved nor destroyed by the war, and the main evidence for this is Campton's own failure to change. The war instigates minor alterations in him, such as his increased respect for Brant, and he learns more about the war and discovers his own feelings of responsibility to it. His personality, however, remains basically the same: he continues to resist the demands made on him by other people. He jangles his coins in his pocket at the end of the novel, when Boylston comes to his studio to discuss a monument for George, just as he did during an earlier visit, when Boylston asks him to join the board of the charity "Friends of French Art." Campton also sees that the people around him have stayed the same: "He grinned at the thought that he had once believed in the regenerative power of war—that salutary shock of great moral and social upheavals" (334). Instead, Campton recognizes that the petty people around him have remained petty. This lack of change is comforting to Campton, since it is exactly what he believes George fought for ("the interwoven tendrils of association, habit, background, daily ways and words, daily sights and sounds").

Anthropology, Civilization, and War

Wharton's interest in anthropology has been explored by critics particularly in relation to novels such as *The Custom of the Country* and *The Age of Innocence*, with their investigations into the "tribal" rituals of old New York. Cecelia Tichi argues that Wharton uses Darwinian theories to portray the decline of Ralph Marvell's society and Ralph himself, and Dale Bauer points out that "Wharton had, in *The Age of Innocence*, only a few years before Margaret Mead's *Coming of Age in Samoa* and Bronislaw Malinowski's *Sex and Repression in Savage Society*, already dismantled the binary opposition between primitive and civilized cultures" (11). Wharton wrote much of *A Son at the Front* in between work on those two novels, and an examination of the influence of Wharton's interest in anthropology on the novel is particularly relevant. As I have established, many people, including Wharton, understood World War I to be a struggle for the survival of a treasured civilization, and as that struggle took place, Wharton could not help reflecting on the foundations and future of that civilization.

Campton believes that his society, in a Darwinian fashion, will not last forever: "All civilizations had their orbit; all societies rose and fell. Some day, no doubt, by the action of that law, everything that made the world livable to Campton and his kind would crumble in the new ruins above the old" (194). But Campton does not believe that the rise and fall of civilizations happen entirely without willful human intervention:

> The Powers of Darkness were always watching and seeking their hour; but the past was a record of their failures as well as of their triumphs. Campton, brushing up on his history, remembered the great turning-points of progress, saw how the liberties of England had been born of the ruthless discipline of the Norman conquest, and how even out of the hideous welter of the French Revolution and the Napoleonic wars had come more freedom and a wiser order. (194)

The evolution of civilization can be directed by the actions of those within it and even by their beliefs: "the efficacy of the sacrifice was always in proportion to the worth of the victims" (194). For Campton, France and its allies are engaged in a battle to prove their fitness to survive.

In addition to the influence of Darwin, *A Son at the Front* reflects other developments in anthropology, including the work of Franz Boas. Boas's *The Mind of Primitive Man* was published in 1911, and this book, which significantly altered how anthropologists thought about race,[10] also posited the theory that all societies, given enough time, will "advance": "What, then, is the difference between the civilization of the Old World and that of the New World? It is essentially a difference in time. The one reached a certain stage three thousand or four thousand years sooner than the other" (23).[11] Boas carefully qualifies that the progression of civilization is limited to certain parts of civilization: "It is obvious that the history of industrial development is almost throughout that of increasing complexity. On the other hand, human activities that do not depend upon reasoning do not show a similar type of evolution" (159). Boas points to a universal complexity of language, sophistication in art and music, structures of social relationships, and religion as examples (160). Ultimately, however, Boas accepts the idea of "advance of culture": "the increasing intellectual achievements as expressed in thought, in inventions, in devices for gaining greater security of existence and in relief from the ever-pressing necessity of obtaining food and shelter, bring about differentiations in the activities of the community that give to life a more varied, richer tone" (180). Progress is not "absolute," but rather it must be judged according to "the special ideal we have in mind" (187). *A Son at the Front* engages the progressive theory of civilization (the "advance of culture") in two divergent ways.

Early in the novel, George Campton expresses the belief, also held by his father, that civilization exists on a line of progress. In the days before war is declared, George refuses to take the possibility of violent hostilities seriously: "the tone he took was that the whole affair, from the point of view of twentieth-century civilization, was too monstrous an incongruity for something not to put a stop to it at the eleventh hour" (32). When war comes, it threatens the continuation of that line. As young Louis Dastrey says, "war's rot; but to get rid of war forever we've got to fight this one first" (76), alluding to the Wilsonian rhetoric of "making the world safe for democracy" and "making war to end war." The line of civilized progression, however, does not proceed in only one direction. At the beginning of the war, George declares, "this kind of thing has got to stop. We shall go straight back to cannibalism if it doesn't" (91). The line of forward "progress" can not only be halted but also can be thrust into reverse, and backward stages are clearly undesirable, violent, and terrifying. War itself is a step back: "Germany was conducting [the war] on methods that civilization had made men forget" (133). Nevertheless, both Camptons believe that passing through this reverse stage can result in ultimate advancement.

Although John Campton believes in the rhetoric of the "advance of culture," he himself often disproves the theory. He consistently behaves with disregard for the niceties of cultured life, from bluntly telling his wife that she is "not paintable" (46) to his inability to order his own studio (57). He frequently "sneers" at his ex-wife (17) and her second husband (249, 290, 425). Campton's most difficult characteristic, though, is his "savagery," which appears throughout the novel and signifies the lack of "progress" in human and cultural development. George even asks his father in a letter not to "be too savage to Uncle Andy" (197); immediately after receiving this letter, Campton visits the charity headquarters where refugees are "bringing fresh tales of death, fresh details of savagery" (198). Thus Wharton links Campton's behavior with that of the Germans. Campton's savagery and the German atrocities dispel the belief in the "advance of culture," for the savagery in both cases lies continually beneath the surface. Campton even knows this: he acknowledges that he himself has "senseless violence" within him and that he often acts "like a brute" (293). He believes that the animal instincts in humans are the problem. He reflects that "the average person is always just obeying impulses stored up thousands of years ago, and never re-examined since" (201), and he considers war to be "an ancestral blood-madness" (226). Even George exhibits contradictory understandings of the idea of civilization. His comment that the invading Germans are "not fit to live with white people" (92) is racist in the way we think of racism today, but it is also racist in the underlying assumption that the Germans are not as far along in the process of civilization. Ironically, just after George makes that statement, he walks out of the room "whistling the waltz from the Rosenkavalier" (93), an opera by the German Richard Strauss first performed in Dresden in 1911. Determining who is "civilized" and who is not turns out to be not so simple.

The only counterbalance to this savagery, *A Son at the Front* suggests, is art. The novel's insistence on the need for beauty, even in war, leaves it open to charges of sentimentalism. Mrs. Talkett, easily dismissed as a flighty woman with petty concerns, identifies this desire: "after all, ugliness is the only *real* death, isn't it?" (224 emphasis in original). Yet here she expresses what Campton comes to feel at the end: that people need beauty even in the midst of war. Wharton's idea of beauty, which she articulated early in her career in *The Decoration of Houses* (1897) and just two years after *A Son at the Front* in *The Writing of Fiction*, depended on order and harmony, to which war and its chaos are direct threats. But war can be ordered through art, through Campton's painterly eye on the streets and rail stations of Paris, his paintings of George and the American soldiers, and Wharton's own writing—even though the process of making art may take awhile and the final ordering must take place after the war is over. During the early days of the chaos and fear of war, Campton believes that "'art' had lost its meaning" (128). One of the things that binds father and son, however, is the belief that the transformation of reality into art is a vital part of living: "Initiation had come to them in different ways, but their ardour for beauty had the same root. The visible world, and its transposition in terms of one art or another, were thereafter the subject of their interminable talks" (30). Near the end of the novel Campton "seemed to understand for the first time—he who had served Beauty all his days—how profoundly, at certain hours, it may become the symbol of things hoped for and things died for" (410–11). Such a symbol is necessary to hold together France's "immaterial culture" and actually becomes part of the war effort.

Yet there is no escaping that, to Wharton, the artist is a devouring creature, terrible in his own way. Campton abandoned his wife and young son on a quest for his art, and he comes to the conclusion that the decision was necessary. Adele Anthony agrees: "I see perfectly that if you'd let everything else go to keep George you'd never have become the great John Campton: the *real* John Campton you were meant to be. And it wouldn't have been half as satisfactory for you—or for George either" (117 emphasis in original). Campton is, in fact, a kind of modern cannibal, devouring his son, Adele, and others for the sake of his painting. He does the work of "transposition" automatically. Even at George's bedside, he reorders his son's face: "As he sat there, trying to picture the gradual resurrection of George's pre-war face out of the delicately penciled white mask on the pillow, he noted the curious change of planes produced by suffering and emaciation, and the altered relation of lights and shadows" (296). Adele recognizes this tendency in Campton (317), but she does not condemn him for it. Campton's brutal side does not mean that his art is a negative force; rather, Wharton suggests that civilization requires artists to make beauty out of violence.

Conclusion

In *A Son at the Front*, Wharton engages in modernist conversations about the isolation and alienation of the self, the trauma of war, and the nature of civilization, and she does so using an ironic narrative voice that leaves the reader questioning perceptions and authority. The isolation of bodily pain becomes a metaphor for the alienation of individuals brought about by unique experiences and the limitations of language. The horror of war forever separates those who have experienced it from those who have not, but even so, the emotional journeys undertaken by those behind the lines are not negligible. Unlike many other writers of the time, Wharton demonstrates that established forms of art can and do continue to order life. For Wharton, "the broken bones of history... rising from the battlefields" will reknit themselves, not perfectly renewed but not helplessly destroyed either. Art such as Campton's, the idealized vision that erases the changes in his son and instead memorializes the pre-war George, smoothes over history and lets stand values that will permit, even encourage, war to happen again. Wharton's art, on the other hand, presents itself to the reader with all its ambiguities and uncertainties. While Campton chooses to memorialize George, Wharton memorializes experience.

CHAPTER 5

"The Readjustment of Personal Relations": Marriage, Modernism, and the Alienated Self

In literature, the prospect of marriage frequently offers the illusion that the individual can become complete in that he or she will be part of a unified whole. This illusion is especially pervasive for female characters, as men usually have other opportunities for fulfillment through their jobs and other social contact. Feminist critics have aptly demonstrated that marriage tends to be offered to women as the ultimate goal of life and selfhood.[1] The myth of unity is easily shattered as individual desires rise to the surface. In *Save Me the Waltz*, Zelda Fitzgerald's 1932 novel, for example, husband and wife find themselves at odds over their personal goals, among other things, and "the weight of their individual reasons separated them like a barrage" (153). The marital unit contains two distinct personalities, each with his or her own perceptions, experiences, and desires, and these differences can create discord that belies unity. Divorce, the private and public acknowledgment that the unified whole does not exist, signifies those differences and gaps between individuals, and within the context of the modernist movement, it also represents the lack of unity within the individual herself. Edith Wharton's *Twilight Sleep* (1927) shows that the disintegration of marriage both reflects and causes this breakdown; that is, in the novel, divorce decenters individuals and represents this decentering. Divorce, as event and as symbol, illuminates the fragility of the way characters view themselves and their relationships.

In chapter 1, I demonstrated how an increasing emphasis on a subjective worldview leaves individuals without a solid system for making decisions in relationships. In this chapter, I investigate Wharton's depictions of marriage not as social or economic critiques but rather as her interest in how marriage and divorce affect the individual. Courtship and marriage are frequently at the center of Wharton's novels, and critics have acknowledged this focus. In *The House of Mirth* (1905), Wharton examines the pressures on women to marry and the sacrifices they must make to forge an alliance that will ultimately be their sole means of economic support. As Elizabeth Ammons puts it, "The modern world may be in its twentieth century, Wharton seems to say, but the issues of marriage and work for women are far from solved; Lily, for all her new yearnings, has no new ideas or alternatives" (38). In *The Custom of the Country* (1913), Wharton portrays marriage strictly as a business, "stripping it," as Ammons writes, "of all sentiment and sentimentality" (97). Debra Ann MacComb argues that this novel "proves that divorce is the logical mechanism for market expansion, providing women with the means to forge nuptial careers based not on a single liaison but on successive—and ever more successful—unions" (765). Divorce in *Twilight Sleep*, however, is not only about financial or social gain but also about an impossible quest for self-fulfillment. My concern in this chapter is not with a character like Undine, who, as MacComb puts it, is "never touched by an emotion larger than the desire for position or possession" (767), but rather with characters who do feel the effects of marriage and divorce profoundly. With few exceptions, Wharton's women are not free of sentiment and sentimentality; Charity Royall, Anna Leath, Sophy Viner, Ellen Olenska, Susy Lansing, Kate and Anne Clephane, Nona Manford—these women do feel passion and desire, pain and disappointment, and these emotions need to be accounted for in their understanding and experience of marriage and divorce. This chapter starts with a discussion of Wharton's early portrayals of marriage and divorce and how they affect individual identity and culminates in her late novel *Twilight Sleep*.

Wharton's Early Critiques of Marriage

In 1904, Wharton published the short story collection *The Descent of Man*. Two stories in particular, "The Other Two" and "The Reckoning," suggest that the self is fluid and that marriage affects people to the very core. Taken together, these propositions make marriage a slippery and even dangerous undertaking: if the self can change and if marriage is a powerful force, married characters find their lives altering beyond their control. In *The Fiction of Relationship*, Arnold Weinstein suggests that "relationship may be a fiction, something made rather than given, built of our belief, not fact" (3). For Wharton's characters, the discovery that relationships are a fiction can be devastating and frequently leads to revelations about themselves, their marriages, and even reality itself that characters find themselves unequal to understanding or coping with. And even if they can cope with the new reality, that ability in itself becomes disturbing.

In "The Other Two," Mr. and Mrs. Waythorn have just returned from their honeymoon, having been called home because Mrs. Waythorn's daughter from her first marriage has fallen ill. Mrs. Waythorn has been married twice before; her first husband was apparently an uncultured "brute" and the second one unfaithful. Although Waythorn previously knew the second husband, he gets to know both men much better through the course of the story. The first husband, Haskett, comes to visit his sick daughter and turns out not to be a brute but rather a quiet, unimposing man. The second husband, Varick, who is brash but at least a "gentleman," asks Waythorn for help with a business deal. Waythorn accepts that he will be running into these men regularly, but as he comes to know them better, he becomes increasingly perplexed about his wife's character: how could she adapt herself to living with three such different men? He concludes that she is " 'as easy as an old shoe'—a shoe that too many feet had worn.... Alice Haskett—Alice Varick—Alice Waythorn—she had been each in turn, and had left hanging to each name a little of her privacy, a little of her personality, a little of the inmost self where the unknown god abides" (98). The story ends with Alice finding her three husbands in the library and, in an odd tableau, gracefully serving them all tea.

The story indicts a society in which wives are expected to be ornamental and submissive to their husbands. As Cynthia Griffin Wolff points out, through her third husband's eyes, Alice is "a grotesque, a specialized form of monster" (109). Waythorn is "sickened" by Alice's "pliancy" (98), yet in ordering her to obey the terms of her custody arrangement with Haskett, he demonstrates that he himself demands that his wife adapt to his desires. He expects her to "divine" his wishes in regard to her seeing her previous husbands (93). Even as he observes that with each marriage comes the "obliteration of the self which had been his wife" (91), Waythorn perpetuates the cycle. It never occurs to him to talk to her about her feelings about each former relationship because, going into the marriage "with [his] ears shut" against gossip (74), he would prefer not to know. He wants his wife to be an independent being, literally and figuratively divorced from her past, while readers recognize that Alice's "pliancy" is necessary to her social and economic existence.

Yet what happens to Alice with each marriage is described in contradictory terms. On the one hand, Waythorn believes that his wife is an accumulation of the personalities imposed on her with each union: "Waythorn compared himself to a member of a syndicate. He held so many shares in his wife's personality and his predecessors were his partners in the business" (99). On the other hand, he thinks each marriage has failed to touch Alice's inner soul: "Alice took her change of husbands like a change of weather" (99). Told from Waythorn's point of view, the story does not reveal what Alice herself thinks. Is Alice essentially untouched by each marriage, or is she so used to the vagaries of life that she habitually adapts her very self to each situation? How much suppression of her "unknown god" is necessitated by her social and economic need for marriage? How much is imposed by the specific personalities to whom she finds herself joined? The story hints that there is more to Alice than Waythorn sees; after all, she disposes of one unsatisfactory husband after another, with each remarriage moving up the economic and social ladder as a prototype for Undine Spragg. Unlike Undine, however, Alice appears to retain a capacity for human feeling in her relationships, and it is the mystery of this humanity that haunts her husband and the reader. Although the story is a social critique that paves the way for *The House of Mirth* and *The Custom of the Country*, it also poses questions about relationships and identity that I will address in my discussion of *Twilight Sleep*.

In "The Reckoning," Julia Westall watches her marriage, built on "The New Ethics," fall apart. As the story opens, she listens to her husband deliver a public talk about the new morality of marriage: "The marriage law of the new dispensation will be: *Thou shalt not be unfaithful—to thyself*" (161 emphasis in original). This principle was Julia's own idea. Ten years earlier, she divorced her "impossible" first husband because she was not happy and entered her second marriage on the grounds that either partner should be free to leave whenever he or she chose. Now she is uneasy with articulating the principle in front of others because, she discovers, over the years her "theoretical attitude toward marriage" has reverted into a traditional one. Her husband, however, insists on holding her to their original agreement, and he has decided to claim his freedom and marry someone else. Although devastated by the news, Julia agrees to his request for a divorce. Suffering, she wanders around the city until she finds herself at her first husband's door. She confesses to him that her theories of marriage have the potential to do great damage, and she asks him to forgive her for the pain she caused him.

"The Reckoning" investigates how or whether marriage can accommodate two living, changing human beings. Julia's theoretical view of marriage supposedly addresses the problems of individuals living under an institution: "People grew at varying rates, and the yoke that was an easy fit for the one might soon become galling to the other. That was what divorce was for: the readjustment of personal relations" (176). This philosophy allows her to leave her first husband without considering his feelings or even whether he understands what her reasons are. Only after she is blindsided by her second husband's request for a divorce does she realize the pain and confusion of the one who is left. She also discovers, too late, that a marriage does not consist of two people:

> It was unconsciously, insidiously, that her ten years of happiness with Westall had developed another conception of the [marriage] tie; a reversion, rather, to the old instinct of passionate dependency and possessorship that now made her blood revolt at the mere hint of change. Change? Renewal? Was that what they had called it, in their foolish jargon? Destruction, extermination rather—this rending of a myriad fibres interwoven with another's being! He and she were one, one in the mystic sense which alone gave marriage its significance. (178)

In an ironic inversion of the marriage myth, Julia comes to believe that two individuals can and do unify. The story does not make clear the reason for the changes in her attitude, but it seems that time has integrated their lives. After Westall announces his desire for a divorce, Julia has trouble understanding words that once seemed basic, such as "husband" (184) and "her" (185). These words are signifiers of relationship and identity, and with the destruction of her marriage, Julia finds she no longer understands herself or the man to whom she is married. She has subjected her marriage to individual whims without realizing that with her marriage stands or falls her sense of herself.

Wharton indicates that Julia's recourses for structuring her world are few. The story does not mention religion as an arbiter for behavior, and Julia admits that the law offers no protection. She would feel herself a hypocrite for seeking legal recourse when she has so often spoken out against laws that perpetuate unhappy marriages. More important, she realizes that the law cannot give her what she wants: "The law she had despised was still there, might still be invoked... invoked, but to what end? Could she ask it to chain Westall to her side?" (186 ellipses in original). Legally she could refuse to give her husband a divorce, but the law cannot force him to love her. Even social opinion cannot keep Westall from leaving her since her own early ideas have been instrumental in relaxing public attitudes toward divorce. Marriage and divorce have become solely private, personal choices. Ironically, the only solution she can think of is also based on individual choice rather than on an external structure: "If we don't recognize an inner law...the obligation that love creates...being loved as well as loving...there is nothing to prevent our spreading ruin unhindered" (195 ellipses in original). Without this individual commitment to an "inner law," new divorce laws and new attitudes toward marriage almost ensure that Julia will end up being left alone. As Wharton makes clear, particularly in *Twilight Sleep*, without external structures to encourage marriage, the individual has little incentive to adhere to an "inner law." It is even more difficult to ensure that two people will make such a commitment.

In *The House of Mirth*, published the year after *The Descent of Man*, marriage functions mainly as a business contract: women receive social status and financial backing in exchange for their ornamental use in their husband's home and the social power they bring to the marital unit. Critics have widely commented on Wharton's portrayal of this structure and noted that Lily Bart resists participating in such a system and ultimately refuses to be merely a decorative object of exchange. Ammons, for example, lays out clearly the specialized role Lily would perform as a high society wife, and she suggests that "the terrible image of helplessness" (35) of a married woman's life prevents Lily from closing the deal with Percy Gryce, Simon Rosedale, or even, perhaps, Lawrence Selden. Wai-Chee Dimock, in her fascinating article about exchange in the novel, describes how "the power of the marketplace...resides...in its ability to reproduce itself, in its ability to assimilate everything else into its domain" (783). In her view, Lily does not marry because she refuses to participate in a society in which monetary exchange subsumes all other forms of relationship.

Although both of these explanations for Lily's failure to marry are convincing, another interpretation bears investigation. The language of exchange in relation to marriage appears largely in regard to Lily's potential marriages (what she can get from Percy Gryce [64], how she might make a "return" on Rosedale's offer to make her society's ruling queen [237], Selden's reluctance to "invest" in Lily) rather than to the marriages that actually exist. An examination of actual, not merely potential, marriages in the novel reveals that despite the language of the marketplace, foundations of marriage are more than financial and not based simply on the concept of exchange. Or, to put it another way, describing marriage in solely financial terms disregards the emotions—or the implications of the lack of emotion—that may exist within the marriages in *The House of Mirth*. The Trenor and Dorset marriages are abusive and even sadistic, and ultimately Lily, consciously or not, fears not only the loss of herself in marriage but also the monster that she sees marriage will make her.

The Trenors best illustrate the idea of marriage as contract: Gus Trenor provides the financial backing for his wife's social activities, activities that in turn support Gus's business interests. The most explicit example of this system is Gus's plan to exchange a dinner invitation from his wife for one of Simon Rosedale's stock market "tips." Judy Trenor remains largely indifferent to Gus's activities, even his attentions to other women; early in the novel she states that "I know [Carry Fisher] borrows money of Gus—but then I'd *pay* her to keep him in a good humour, so I can't complain, after all" (54 emphasis in original). Still, Lily realizes, too late, that "if [Judy] was careless of his affections she was plainly jealous of his pocket" (307). According to the model of marriage as an economic contract, Judy resents other women receiving part of her side of the marital bargain.

Judy does not cut Lily when Lily first starts borrowing money from Gus, however. In fact, Lily is relieved to see that "the complacency with which her hostess regarded these attentions freed them of the least hint of ambiguity. Mrs. Trenor evidently assumed that Lily's growing intimacy with her husband was simply an indirect way of returning her own kindness" (113). Just as Judy says she would pay Carry Fisher to keep Gus amused, she seems happy for Lily to participate in the same arrangement. Judy turns against Lily only after Gus lures Lily to his house alone, Lily is turned off the Dorset boat by Bertha, and Lily is disinherited. Judy rejects Lily not only because of Lily's financial borrowing from Gus but also because of the sexual scandal surrounding her. There are several possible explanations for Judy's behavior: she resents Lily's betrayal of the women's friendship; she objects to being replaced sexually; she must cut Lily in order to maintain her own social standing; or she is, in fact, jealous of Gus's affections. The most likely answer is all of the above, but it is a mistake to forget the last reason and to eliminate the possibility that Judy does care for Gus. Simon Rosedale once observes to Lily about her apparent relationship to Gus: "Well, I wasn't thinking of Mrs. Trenor at the moment—they say Gus doesn't always, you know" (151). This comment is particularly revealing: to be "thinking of" one's spouse suggests that one would refrain from certain behavior to prevent hurting that spouse. The Trenor marriage demonstrates that living a marriage according to the contract model is impossible, for people, unlike businesses or institutions, have feelings. Even if all Judy resents is the appearance that her husband is unfaithful or his giving away of money she considers hers, her reaction—whether of anger or of pain—is emotional; it is personal rather than indifferently contractual.

The Dorsets offer another, even more powerful lesson in the dangers of marriage. Lily assumes Bertha Dorset clings to her husband in order to maintain her social standing. As Lily knows, "the code of Lily's world decreed that a woman's husband should be the only judge of her conduct: she was technically above suspicion while she had the shelter of his approval, or even of his indifference" (138). This description of marriage supports the model of the relationship as a social and economic contract. Yet Bertha gets more out of the marriage than status and shelter for her love affairs; she gets an in-house object for her sadistic power games. Bertha, described as "sinuous" with "a pair of dark exaggerated eyes," becomes the snake that "was like a disembodied spirit who took up a great deal of room" (30). In taking up this room, Bertha continually and necessarily shoves others out of the way. One of the first things readers learn about the Dorsets as a couple is that "she delights in making people miserable, and especially poor George" (58). At Monte Carlo, George finally confronts Bertha about her relationship with Ned Silverton and threatens divorce, and he then consults Lawrence Selden, who makes George wait overnight to make any decisions. In the morning, Selden notes a significant change in George's attitude: "Five minutes' talk sufficed to show that some alien influence had been at work, and that it had not so much subdued his resentment as weakened his will, so that he moved under it in a state of apathy, like a dangerous lunatic who has been drugged" (283). The influence is Bertha's, and here she is described as "alien"—foreign, unknown, and beyond the realm of normal comprehension. She has made her husband into a "dangerous lunatic" and then has succeeded in "drugging" him, becoming, in effect, both the cause and the treatment of her husband's madness.

George Dorset's appeal to Lily to give him the key to set him free further illustrates to Lily the extent to which Bertha enjoys tormenting her husband. When they meet months after the scandal in Europe, Lily sees George with "his head hanging" and recognizes in him "the chief of Bertha's victims" (326). Trading on Bertha's letters as a means of punishing Bertha and reestablishing herself, through marriage to either George Dorset or Simon Rosedale, becomes both more seductive and more distasteful to Lily the more she sees of the ravages Bertha has left. Candace Waid points out Bertha's centrality to the novel, for it is her compromising letters on which the crucial moral questions turn. Waid also notes that Bertha serves as Lily's double: "From the moment Bertha Dorset first appears in the second chapter of *The House of Mirth*, walking into a railway car and wondering aloud whether she can have Lily Bart's place, questions concerning place, displacement, poses, and positions are at issue between the two women" (21). Waid speculates that Bertha fears Lily's displacing her (22), but to extend Waid's argument in another direction, I suggest that Lily fears displacing Bertha. If Bertha is the reigning queen of New York society, a position she holds only through George's backing, then to Lily's eyes marriage becomes equivalent to sadism—not only, as so often noted, in the husband's patriarchal abuse of his wife but also through the wife's manipulation and control of her husband. Becoming a wife means simultaneously losing power over oneself and gaining an unhealthy amount of power over someone else. Lily recognizes this paradox as early as her attempt to marry Percy Gryce. She understands that his instinctive frugality will not accord with the life she wants to lead, but she maps out a strategy to control him after they are married, so that "she felt sure that in a short time she would be able to play the game in her own way" (64). This notion of marriage as a "game" is only a short step from the cat-and-mouse torment that is the Dorsets' relationship.

The Dorsets seem to have a lot in common with another married couple of Lily's experience: her parents. Lily remembers Mr. and Mrs. Bart in this way:

> Ruling the turbulent element called home was the vigorous and determined figure of a mother still young enough to dance her ball-dresses to rags, while the hazy outline of a neutral-tinted father filled an intermediate space between the butler and the man who came to wind the clocks. Even to the eyes of infancy, Mrs. Hudson Bart had appeared young; but Lily could not recall the time when her father had not been bald and slightly stooping, with streaks of grey in his hair, and a tired walk. (37)

Lily's father is the prototype for George Dorset—a man beaten down by his wife, unable to cope with her demands or resist her expenditures. He dies in the Sisyphean attempt to keep his wife and daughter happy. The novel's consistent portrayal of spouses, and especially wives, as careless abusers suggests that Lily's failure to marry is the result of her reluctance to become an abuser herself.

Wharton offers an alternative marriage structure in Nettie Struther and her husband, who accepts her despite her unfortunate past and provides her with the emotional strength to be happy. In the Struther marriage, each partner respects and forgives the other rather than exploits the other's weaknesses; the key is that Nettie's husband "cared for [her] enough" (426). In no other marriage in the novel do partners "care for" each other. The Struthers' "caring" is powerful enough to spill over to their child and even to Lily. Critic Hildegard Hoeller, in her discussion of the economy of sentiment in Wharton's work, argues that in Nettie's kitchen "Wharton's narrative voice also transcends its usual economy of control and irony.... In this scene, the narrator 'mothers' us with unexpected warmth and sentiment, just as Nettie mothers her baby.... Wharton gives to us, as readers, almost as abundantly as Nettie does to Lily" (117). Nettie and her husband are the exception rather than the rule, and Selden's delay in deciding whether he "cares for" Lily "enough" has tragic consequences.

Marriage and Modernism in *Twilight Sleep*

More than twenty years after *The House of Mirth*, Wharton continued to examine the effects of marriage on the individual. She went through her own divorce, and she observed changes in broader cultural attitudes toward marriage. The birth control movement and the corresponding push for greater female independence helped alter the nature of matrimony. As Judge Ben Lindsey and Wainwright Evans demonstrated in *The Companionate Marriage*, a 1927 study of new trends in marriage, more and more unions were based on sexual desire. Historian Linda Gordon notes that in the Bohemian free love movement of the early twentieth century, people came to define love in terms of their sexual experiences; that is, they "were making sex the very center of love. As love became more sexualized, its imagery divorced from the ideal of purity, it also became more transient—or, more accurately, its transience became acceptable" (133). Love, sex, and marriage became more entangled and simultaneously more separable, as marital unions were more easily dissolved by less stringent divorce laws and social attitudes toward divorce. The idea of love, now so closely related to sexual attraction, became more fragile.

Wharton's 1927 novel *Twilight Sleep* suggests that the increasing incidence of and more tolerant attitudes toward divorce add to the pervasive feelings of fractured identity and emptiness in human relationships that characterize modernist writing. *Twilight Sleep*, a long neglected and generally disparaged[2] novel, explores the possibilities and limitations of human relationships. I find useful a comparison with another, more famous modernist novel, Virginia Woolf's *To the*

Lighthouse.³ Published in the same year, the two novels address similar questions about people's ability to establish a sense of self and to communicate and connect, suggesting that human relationships—whether between husbands and wives, parents and children, or even friends—are a central concern to modernist writers. Like other modernist works, including *To the Lighthouse*, *Twilight Sleep* relies on shifting narrators and contradictory interpretations of events, forcing the reader to interpret and engage with the text on his or her own. While the remainder of this chapter focuses on *Twilight Sleep*, *To the Lighthouse* provides a comparison point through which connections between marriage and the modernist sense of self can be illuminated in Wharton's work.

Twilight Sleep follows members of a wealthy New York family and their attempts to create satisfactory, meaningful relationships. Pauline Manford manages an active social life for herself and her second husband, Dexter, while her first husband Arthur Wyant, a member of the old New York aristocracy, remains on the fringes of her family's life. Jim Wyant, Pauline and Arthur's son, has married the beautiful but shallow Lita Cliffe. Nona Manford, daughter of Pauline and Dexter, seems the solid center of the family, taking upon herself the troubles of the others. Nona sees, for example, both that Lita is bored with her husband and looking for excitement, whether in the film industry or with another man, and also that the man in question is Nona's father Dexter. The novel comes to a climax at the Manfords' country house when Arthur Wyant interrupts a tryst between his son's wife Lita and his former wife's husband Dexter and accidentally shoots and wounds Nona. The affair between Lita and Dexter is concealed from Pauline, and the novel ends with the family dispersing to vacations at various parts of the globe, retreating, in consistent fashion, from their problems.

In telling the story, Wharton uses the technique of changing and inconsistent points of view to show the conflicts and mysteries in human relationships. Wharton's characters reveal the "fiction of relationship," as we see their relationships assessed and imagined from several perspectives. Weinstein argues that "authorial choices made in...fictions—point-of view narrative, first-person lyricism, *style indirect libre*, delayed discourses, stream of consciousness, surreal environment, even word play—both form and inform the story of relationship" (25–26). Wharton's trio of more or less unreliable points of view (those of Pauline, Dexter, and Nona Manford) reveals the limited extent to which characters are capable of understanding each other. Pauline Manford's point of view, for example, reflects her reliance on language as a defense mechanism and thus only suggests the ominous undercurrents of Lita's restlessness and Dexter's wandering eye. Late in the novel, for instance, Pauline writes to her son that all is well, and the letter "had reassured her merely to write it: given her the feeling, to which she had always secretly inclined, that a thing was so if one said it was, and doubly so if one wrote it down" (257). At almost that same moment, however, Dexter and Lita begin their affair, revealing Pauline's shocking inability to see what is happening in her own house. Dexter's point of view also reflects, at first, a willful blindness to his increasing attraction to Lita, as he imagines that he visits Lita and Jim's home only to visit with the baby. His vanity, revealed by his frequent checking of his reflection after his young secretary leaves his office and by his belief that he can pass for Lita's "elder brother" (216), suggests that he is too absorbed in himself to pay much attention to others. Nona appears to be the most reliable narrator, yet an external narrative voice occasionally points to her age as an excuse for her naïve yearning to do the right thing: "Her precocious half-knowledge of the human dilemma was combined with a youthful belief that the duration of pain was proportioned to its intensity" (186). Weinstein suggests that "the novel form also teaches us that subjectivity and blindness go hand in hand, that the single vision is every bit as cyclopic as it is delicious" (24). The "delicious-ness" of one character's narration is also seductive, and Wharton's strategy requires that the reader resist the "single vision" and be willing to balance one viewpoint against another. In *Twilight Sleep*, narrative choices emphasize the subjectivity of interpretation and the resulting distance between characters.

The varying narrative interpretations and accompanying misunderstandings within relationships are made most apparent during the Manfords' dinner party. The dinner scene, reminiscent of the Ramsays' dinner party in *To the Lighthouse*, epitomizes the disjunction among the characters. In Woolf's novel, Mrs. Ramsay succeeds in reading the emotions of her dinner companions, from her husband's frustration at the prolonging of the soup course to Charles Tansley's need to assert himself. Pauline Manford, in contrast, views her table with a less penetrating eye. She prides herself at having seated her husband next to Mrs. Gladys Toy, a woman she believes he is "taken" with, and generously giving him the chance for a harmless flirtation. Nona perceives this move as her mother's idea of a "reward" for her father and at the same time notes that Mrs. Toy's "obvious charms were no more to him...than those of the florid Bathsheba in the tapestry behind his chair" (68). The narrative shift to Dexter confirms his daughter's intuition: he finds Mrs. Toy's conversation tedious and insipid. Later, when Dexter does pursue a relationship with Mrs. Toy, it is not a harmless flirtation but a consummated sexual affair. The stark disjunction between Pauline's and Dexter's views of each other forces the reader to acknowledge gaps that the characters themselves only half-recognize. Pauline's failure to read her husband is indicative of a modernist sense of isolation—of an inability to understand or know another individual.

In *Twilight Sleep*, the relationship of marriage, dependent on communication, falters and fails. Weinstein argues that the novel as a genre is peculiarly suited for the depiction of relationships because the form both portrays relationships among characters over time and allows for the possibility that relationships are themselves "fiction." To Weinstein, a "relationship" "entails an opening, an extension of the individual." He suggests that a relationship is the fusion of time with passion—a willful decision to make "something stick" (25), as Wharton's Julia Westall envisions in "The Reckoning." Both "extending the individual" and willfulness, however, can become problematic, as Wharton shows. The characters in *Twilight Sleep*, perpetually dissatisfied with themselves, lack the ability to remain interested in an activity, a spiritual system, or a decorating scheme, much less in another person.

In Wharton's stories about old New York, marriage, satisfactory or not, is treated by characters as a permanent condition; despite adultery, financial impropriety, or boredom, one remained married to one's spouse. In Wharton's writing about the 1920s, divorce is no longer scandalous but rather has an established place in society. This change is apparent in *The Mother's Recompense* (1925): a disgraced Kate Clephane fled New York with her lover but is welcomed back twenty years later, with scarcely anyone mentioning her divorce. Kate herself, however, seems to feel that she deserves to be punished; as Dale Bauer argues, "the feeling that the new society may pardon her past indiscretions scares her as much as the symbolic incest.... Kate's guilt at least confirms her sense of identity over and against the blankness and terror of the undifferentiated mass of people who now populate her old New York social scene, a world where a smooth indifference reigns and renunciation has no meaning" (70). *Twilight Sleep* too shows the difference twenty years make in New York attitudes toward divorce and remarriage, but the later novel examines the social scene from a view opposing Kate's. Pauline is a pioneer in these changing attitudes; she divorced her first husband Arthur Wyant "in the early days of the new century [when] divorce had not become a social institution in New York" (26). Pauline, coming from "new" money, did not feel the shame of divorce as did Arthur, of an old New York family. By the time the novel is set, divorce is widely accepted. As Nona asks her mother: "Don't they almost all get tired of each other? And when they do, will anything ever stop their having another try? Think of your big dinners! Doesn't Maisie always have to make out a list of previous marriages as long as a cross-word puzzle, to prevent your calling people by the wrong names?" (30). Lita's drawing room symbolizes "the modern marriage state" in that it looks "more like the waiting-room of a glorified railway station than the setting of an established way of life" (31). Pauline embraces this kind of society; she "could conceive of nothing more shocking than a social organization which did not recognize divorce, and let all kinds of domestic evils fester undisturbed, instead of having people's lives disinfected and whitewashed at regular intervals, like the cellar" (21–22). But the acts of "disinfecting" and "whitewashing" become easy substitutes for developing a real relationship. Instead of working through marital problems, Pauline and her society endorse walking away from them.

One of the dark sides of this attitude, the novel suggests, is that characters fail to develop a strong sense of identity. One of Wharton's primary complaints about modern society was its tendency, in her view, to discourage the development of the "inner life" that to her was so precious. In a June 9, 1925 letter to Daisy Chandler, Wharton commented on her reading of *The Life of Pasteur*: "He *did* feel life to be a vale of soul-making! I wonder who does in the day we live in?" (Beinecke). In *Twilight Sleep*, by "disinfecting" their lives, characters choose not to look within themselves but rather to blame external factors. Although Lita Wyant, wife of Jim and daughter-in-law of Pauline, declares she wants a divorce in order to assert her right to "self-expression" (111),[4] Wharton portrays most of the characters and Lita in particular as lacking a secure sense of self. The title of the novel refers to the drug-induced state in which women avoid the pain of childbirth, but Wharton also uses the term to refer to the mechanisms through which all characters, women and men, avoid the harsh realties of life: new spiritual gurus, shopping, dancing, golf, tarpon-fishing. Lita, viewed by others as a "baleful siren," a "misguided child" (163), a "poor little girl" (216), and a "brittle plaything" (242) and as having a "queer little half-formed mind" (14), embodies the "fastness" of the times; she is the symbol of all that is shallow and lazy in the postwar generation. Disparaging the decoration scheme of her drawing room, Lita asks Nona: "Do you mean to say you like anything you liked two years ago?" Nona responds, "Yes—you!" (33). Lita, however, goes in for fads in people as well as in décor. To other characters, she reflects no inner life: "Lita's face was what it always was: something so complete and accomplished that one could not imagine its being altered by any interior disturbance" (281). In Nona's view particularly, Lita has no self to express:

> That was all life meant to Lita—would ever mean. Good floors to practise new dance-steps on, men—any men—to dance with and be flattered by, women—any women—to stare and envy one, dull people to startle, stupid people to shock—but never any one, Nona questioned, whom one wanted neither to startle nor shock, neither to be envied nor flattered by, but just to lose one's self in for good and all? Lita lose herself—? Why, all she wanted was to keep on finding herself, immeasurably magnified, in every pair of eyes she met! (242)

Nona believes Lita has no essential interiority and needs others to define her, and becoming a film star would provide Lita with the largest possible audience in which she would be "magnified."

Seeing Lita only from the vantage point of the other characters, the reader may also be tempted to interpret her as empty and superficial. Yet when we consider Lita in the context of other Wharton novels, she becomes a more complicated character. Lita wants to be free of her marriage because she feels stifled—just like Newland Archer and Kate Clephane, characters that Wharton does portray sympathetically. Newland chooses to stay married to May, and he pays a high emotional price for it. Kate leaves both husband and daughter, also at great expense. When Lita states that in her marriage she feels "I'm a sort of all-round fake" (195), she encapsulates the problem that most Wharton women experience in their marriages. In contrast to these other characters, however, Lita lives in a time when she has an acceptable way out. Unlike Newland or Kate, Lita does not risk her reputation or even financial hardship since her devoted husband Jim says if she left he would support her and their baby. Lita's desire for a divorce is disturbing because Wharton presents her, unlike Newland or Kate, unsympathetically, as if wanting a divorce when it is easy to obtain makes Lita callous. Wharton's social critique in the novel reveals her belief that divorce should be difficult out of respect for the institution that it dissolves and the individual pain that it causes.

Lita also threatens the family structure with her directness and her refusal to ignore her own desires. Unlike Pauline, Lita uses words to reveal truth rather than create it. In one brief speech to Dexter, she exposes his affair with Mrs. Toy, rejects his idealism of her as "sacred," and explicitly states that she came to the country to be with him: "I thought that was why you were here...Do you suppose I'd have come all this way just to be taught to love fresh air and family life? The hypocrisy—!" (255 ellipses in original). Lita not only has desires but also acts on them. Because her society is still so afraid of a woman acting on her own desire, however, others around her tend to refract that desire into something else. While Lita's temptations frequently involve Hollywood and dancing, several characters, usually the men, tend to worry about Lita running off with someone else (Dexter fears her link with the potential film star Michelangelo [166], while Arthur eventually figures out the man is Dexter). At one point, Dexter mistakes Lita herself for a man because she is wearing his own overcoat, and he reacts with "a furious stab of jealousy" (254). This moment reveals that the menace of "someone else" actually is terror of her desires and individuality—Lita *is* the "other man" who jeopardizes her relationships.[5] In this way, Lita critiques the "hypocrisy" of a society that proselytizes self-expression and individuality while actually expecting, even if no longer requiring, a woman to remain subservient to her husband's desires.

Despite the hints of her complexity as a character, Lita remains shallow in the eyes of the others, and the problems of identity that she represents pose difficulties when characters attempt to interact on an intimate level. Characters seem to lack depth, partly because of their problems with language. The novel, like other modernist works such as *To the Lighthouse*, Faulkner's *The Sound and the Fury*, and Hemingway's *Farewell to Arms*, indicates that words have a hollowness to them that prevents characters from communicating. R. W. B. Lewis criticizes *Twilight Sleep* because "issues of genuine moral gravity are, in fact, at stake in the novel, but they remain blurred amid the comings and goings" (474). The comings and goings, on the contrary, are essential to the meaning of the novel. Although continual movement is part of the characters' futile attempts to add significance to their lives, most often characters dash about to find others with whom to discuss crises (the revelation that Pauline's spiritual guide has led dance classes for scantily clad young women, Lita's desire to divorce Jim, and Arthur Wyant's drinking) and possible courses of action—though little action is ever taken. The prevalence of talking in *Twilight Sleep* points to the frailty of words in creating reality. For Pauline, the promise of a word is a ghost worth chasing, and the word "Immediacy," a touch phrase of one of her new spiritual cures, gives her a sense of comfort in itself (271). In another example, at an early dinner party the narrator describes Pauline's guests in terms of what is said about them:

> Manford [who] *was said* to be "taken" by [Mrs. Toy].... the brilliant Alfred Cosby, who *was known to have said* [Nona] was the cleverest girl in New York.... Aggie Heuston, whose coldness certainly made her look distinguished, though *people complained* she was dull.... Dear good old Stan...! People who knew him well *said* he wasn't as sardonic as he looked. (64–65)

Pauline's knowledge rests not on her own developed relationships with the people at her table but on what an indeterminate and undefined "they" say. In the world of the novel, what is said is highly valued even if void of meaning or authority. The lack of meaning in words, then, eliminates an essential means by which characters might come to know one another.

Twilight Sleep delves more deeply into the problems of relationships with the marriage of Pauline and Dexter Manford and gives marital failure a distinctly modernist cause as well as result. Weinstein's definition of a relationship as "an extension of the individual" requires that a character have an inner sense of self, resources that can reach out to another person and create a connection. The Manfords show the difficulty of creating and maintaining a marriage when individuals are not only unwilling but actually unable to open up. Pauline's mind, for example, always looks outward, toward activities, events, and problems. Having an unexpected free hour to herself, "she didn't in the least know what to do with it. That was something which no one had ever thought of teaching her; and the sense of being surrounded by a sudden void, into which she could reach out on all sides without touching an engagement or an obligation, produced in her a sort of mental dizziness" (116). Wharton suggests that a sense of self is something learned and, as she does in *The Custom of the Country*, blames an American society that does not cultivate inner resources in women for Pauline's "mental dizziness." When Pauline speaks to her husband Dexter, she genuinely desires connection with him, but she does not know how to get it. She relies on stereotypes of the "good wife" in her interactions with her husband. She "heroically" submits to his desire to cancel an important dinner invitation and dine alone (160), and when he commits her money without consulting her first, she protests inwardly but submits outwardly. She views herself as stronger for these submissions, but in hiding her true feelings, she reveals little of herself to her husband. Even if she were to attempt to communicate, however, she has limited ability to do so: "Intimacy, to her, meant the tireless discussion of facts, not necessarily of a domestic order, but definite and palpable facts.... In confidential moments she preferred the homelier themes, and would have enjoyed best of all being tender and gay about the coal cellar, or reticent and brave about the leak in the boiler" (169). She knows that Dexter is not interested in and is actually frustrated by such conversations about "facts," but she does not have anything else to say.

In many ways, the Manfords' marriage and the Ramsays' marriage in *To the Lighthouse* can be seen as distorted refractions of each other. Mrs. Ramsay is a master of silent communication (Weinstein calls her the "high priestess of relationship" [47]); she cannot say she loves her husband but "triumphs" anyway: "She had not said it: yet he knew" (124). Dexter Manford's image of the perfect marriage matches the marriage that Mr. Ramsay seems to have. Dexter has a vision of a satisfactory intellectual and professional life, with time in the country and lots of children, all built on the image of "a woman lifting a calm face from her book": "there would somehow, underneath it all, be a great pool of silence, a reservoir on which one could always draw and flood one's soul with peace. This vision was vague and contradictory, but it all seemed to meet and mingle in the woman's eyes..." (72 ellipses in original). Mrs. Ramsay is such a woman, whose silence does reveal depths of meaning. In *Twilight Sleep*, Dexter envisions his stepdaughter-in-law Lita as the perfect woman, mistaking her beauty and "deep silences" (215) for the reservoir of peace. For Dexter, this idyllic dream of marriage is an escape, just like tarpon-fishing and golf, and it relies on an ideal of a woman rather than her reality.

Wharton's earlier novel *The Age of Innocence* undercuts this ideal of the "great pool of silence." As Dallas Archer says to his father, "You just sat and watched each other, and guessed at what was going on underneath. A deaf-and-dumb asylum, in fact!" (357). The Archer marriage is not a model of conjugal happiness or companionship, and its beginnings, if not its entirety, are founded on intrigue and entrapment. This kind of silence blocks relationships; it prevents Weinstein's "extension of the individual." Wharton's disillusionment with silent communication goes back further, however. In her unpublished "love diary," titled "The Life Apart," she recounts her own feelings of unspoken communion with Morton Fullerton: "the other day, when you were reproaching me for never giving you any sign of my love for you, I felt like answering: 'But there is a contact of thoughts that seems so much closer than a kiss.'" Fullerton, apparently, did not agree; otherwise he would not have been "reproaching her." In the next paragraph, she acknowledges that "there are other days, tormented days—this is one of them—when that sense of mystic nearness fails me."[6] However much Wharton may have desired and valued the "contact of thoughts," she did not achieve it in her romantic relationship, and her characters do not find it either.

In *Twilight Sleep*, Pauline, like Mrs. Ramsay, is known for her "famous tact" (60), yet she cannot find the means to communicate her love and desire for her husband. Even at moments when she believes they are united in their goals, she finds herself unexpectedly blocked by "one of those invisible barriers against which she had so often bruised her perceptions" (134). In one of their rare private conversations, she fails to find a way to reach him: "If only she had known how to reveal the secret tremors that were rippling through her! There were women not half as clever and tactful—not younger, either, nor even as good-looking—who would have known at once what to say, or how to spell the mute syllables of soul-telegraphy" (169). The Ramsays' moment of silent bonding fails to occur for the Manfords, and Pauline is left feeling "inexistent": "He did not remember to say goodnight to her: how should he have, when she was no longer there for him?" (176). Pauline blames herself for their failure to connect with each other, but it is likely that at this point Dexter is thinking of Lita. Wharton interrogates the social expectation that the woman should always know how to reach the man. This scene reveals a dark side of marriage: the wife feels herself responsible for the "housekeeping" aspects of the relationship—the daily connections, the emotional life—and ends up invisible when she cannot achieve the impossible. This eradication of her sense of self continues to diminish her, as Pauline's fears about the loss of her marriage prevent her from too closely questioning events on the night Nona is shot.

That Woolf and Wharton were creating female characters who attempt "soul-telegraphy" in novels that appeared in the same year suggests that women modernists were deeply engaged in questions about identity, relationships, and the literary representation of both. Unlike most male writers, Woolf and Wharton explored heterosexual relationships from the woman's point of view and sought to expose the problems created by gender expectations in such relationships. That Pauline Manford fails where Mrs. Ramsay succeeds suggests that Wharton's outlook was bleaker than Woolf's, yet Mrs. Ramsay's silent communication is also problematic. For a woman writer, a female character who cannot express herself in words is a double bind, boding ill for the author herself. The striking similarities between Wharton's and Woolf's 1927 novels reveal two different treatments of the same anxieties.

Nona Manford and the "Plain Human Tangle"

The narrative of *Twilight Sleep* most overtly addresses the problems of relationships through the viewpoint of Nona Manford, daughter of Pauline and Dexter. Nona, a privileged and insightful witness to the fragile marriages of her parents and her brother, regards heterosexual relationships with trepidation. She herself loves Stanley Heuston, an unhappily married man whose strongly religious wife Aggie will not consider divorce. Nona refuses to have an affair with Stanley, yet, on the surface, their relationship has strengths that other relationships in the novel do not. Nona feels that "no one understood her as well as Stanley" (47), and she believes that they have an unspoken connection: "[she] knew by his silence that he was thinking her thoughts. That was the final touch of magic" (144). Nona's belief in these silent moments of communion, however, is undermined by her mother's failure to achieve them later in the novel. Wharton shows, with Pauline and Dexter's relationship, that silent "knowing" is impossible, and Nona and Stanley's relationship bears this out as well. Two days after an argument with Stanley, Nona regrets her angry words, and when she hears the phone ring, she feels sure that Stanley "must have felt the same need that she had!" Answering the phone with the presumptuous "It's you, darling?" (180), Nona instead hears her brother, who wants to meet with her to discuss Lita's desire for a divorce. As her mother discovers, the feeling of "knowing" another person through silent communion is ultimately self-created and almost inevitably fallible.

Nona is the character in *Twilight Sleep* most consciously concerned with the nature of relationships, both the distances and the simultaneous interconnectedness between individuals. Her father Dexter realizes the inescapable links of familial and social ties, embodied literally in the physicality of his house:

> It was not the splendour of his house that oppressed him but the sense of the corporative bond it imposed. It seemed part of an elaborate social and domestic structure, put together with the baffling ingenuity of certain bird's-nests of which he had seen the pictures. His own career, Pauline's multiple activities, the problem of poor Arthur Wyant, Nona, Jim, Lita Wyant, the Mahatma, the tiresome Grant Lindons, the perennial and inevitable Amalasuntha, for whom the house was being illuminated tonight—all were strands woven into the very pile of carpet he trod on his way up the stairs. (62)

For Nona, though, people are not bound so much by "corporative ties" as by emotional ones. "What troubles me," she tells her mother, "is the plain human tangle" (276). Nona sees that, although individuals may feel isolated, they have intense and far-reaching effects on each other; the actions of one person ripple outward in both space and time. Her mother's divorce from Arthur Wyant, Lita's desire to divorce Jim, Nona's own love for Stanley—all of these things have affected or have the potential to affect other people profoundly. Nona feels that, as a result, no person is truly individual. Julia Westall comes to a similar conclusion in "The Reckoning"—that married people are not two but actually one—although Nona's revelation is broader than Julia's. None believes that all people become bits of the pieces around them. After a conversation with Jim about Lita's desire for divorce, Nona suffers for her brother's situation: "Where, for instance, did one's own self end and one's neighbour begin?" (186). The pain she feels for Jim prevents her from sending a telegram to Stanley because she refuses to be responsible for hurting Stanley's wife. Nona wonders "if her personality didn't even include certain shreds and fibres of Aggie" (201).

In this way, *Twilight Sleep* shows how divorce becomes the domino that sets off a downward spiral of emptiness, a point most apparent to Nona. The dissolving of marriage vows threatens to undermine not just morality and decency but also selfhood; in the novel, divorce rips pieces of people away, leaving behind something that is less than honest and complete and consequently that cannot reach out to another individual. Nona observes how Pauline and Arthur Wyant's divorce, for example, has made Arthur reclusive and has shattered his idea of what his life should be. Of an older generation and restrictive society, Arthur has failed to move forward after Pauline's defection, and the divorce has affected his very sense of self. He becomes confused when he visits the Manfords' country house, which he once shared with Pauline, and he wonders, "am I in my own house or another man's?" (293), recalling Nona's similar questioning of where oneself ends and the next person begins. The idea that his son's marriage may be failing further destabilizes him mentally, as Jim's potential divorce reminds Arthur of his own stalemated life. Arthur encourages Jim to fight, literally, for Lita, and when Jim refuses, Arthur himself arrives at Lita's room to shoot her intended lover in obedience to an older, disavowed code of honor. Arthur's actions do not fit his current world, although it turns out that there are no actions that fit this modern situation of divorce.

When Lita announces that she wishes to divorce Jim, almost everyone around the couple tries to stop her. Only Jim, despite the pain he feels, does not. Nona, Pauline, Dexter, and Arthur insist that there must be a way to save the marriage. Except for Arthur, who wants Jim to act like a "Knight of the Round Table" and "[hit] some other fellow over the head" (182), none of the people who want to prevent the divorce behaves out of loyalty to the sanctity of marriage. Rather, they simply do not want Jim to be hurt (although both Pauline and Nona separately wonder if keeping the selfish Lita is really in Jim's best interests [197, 242]). They act out of respect for an individual's feelings, but this reasoning soon runs them into trouble. Pauline asks Lita to consider that divorcing Jim would "nearly kill him," to which Lita responds, "But oughtn't he to take into account that he doesn't interest me any longer?" (196). Pauline, who argues for both birth control and motherhood on the grounds of every person's right to "personality" (97), is forced to admit that Lita has a point. In a culture that values the individual over everything else, conflicting desires must result in someone not getting what he or she wants.

The novel as a whole does not condemn divorce. Wharton herself, of course, was freed from a difficult marriage by divorce, and it seems likely that part of Pauline's horror at societies that do not allow divorce is also Wharton's. In *The Custom of the Country*, Ammons suggests, Wharton worked out her frustrations as her own divorce was finalized: "personally, divorce was repugnant to Wharton; but so was marriage in many respects, and *The Custom of the Country* gave her the opportunity to attack both with a vengeance" (99). This conflicted attitude toward divorce appears in several of Wharton's novels. While *The Custom of the Country* shows Undine Spragg's multiple marriages as destructive to herself and the people around her and *The Children* (1928) demonstrates the damage marital instability can do to children, Wharton's 1923 novel *A Son at the Front*, as well as *Twilight Sleep*, suggests that divorce, rather than traumatizing the children, has created a loving and supportive extended family. In *A Son at the Front*, George Campton benefits from the worshipful love of four parental figures, while in *Twilight Sleep* Nona and Jim have their mother's two husbands as father figures. This extended family is not entirely pain-free, however, and the recognition of the pain underlying the affectionate words is important. Underneath the apparently friendly relations between the Manfords and Arthur Wyant lies the unspoken knowledge that the extended family is built on Arthur's suffering.

Twilight Sleep emphasizes that despite the social acceptance and even necessity of divorce, the breaking up of marriage is not a simple act. Wharton wrote to John Hugh Smith on February 12, 1909, as her marriage to Teddy Wharton continued to disintegrate, "I wonder, among all the tangles of this mortal coil which one contains tighter knots to undo, and consequently suggests more tugging, and pain, and diversified elements of misery, than the marriage tie—and which, consequently, is more 'made to the hand' of the psychologist and the dramatist?" (Lewis and Lewis *Letters* 175). Although the context of Wharton's remark is a discussion of literature (she and Teddy did not divorce until 1913), she was at that point probably seriously considering divorce. She was in the midst of the affair with Fullerton, and news from Teddy's doctors was not good. That summer, a doctor wrote Wharton that her husband would do better living with her at the Mount, and Shari Benstock notes that "that diagnosis handed Edith an impossible choice: return to America and face illness and unhappiness herself, or remain in Paris with an ill and irritable husband" (*No Gifts* 220). Wharton's letter reveals the intensely personal pain that marital failure causes, pain that cannot be easily put into words or shared with someone else. In *Twilight Sleep*, Pauline recognizes that "human nature had not changed as fast as social usage, and if Jim's wife left him nothing could prevent his suffering in the same old way" (198). Similarly, Nona thinks that "it was one thing to theorize on the detachability of human beings, another to watch them torn apart by the bleeding roots. This botanist who had recently discovered that plants were susceptible to pain, and that transplanting was a major operation—might he not, if he turned his attention to modern men and women, find the same thing to be still true of a few of them?" (184). Wharton recognizes that human pain has not disappeared, despite the shallowness she accuses her characters of. This pain, in fact, is one of the few true feelings that these characters have.

Nona's desire to prevent people's being hurt has been read as self-sacrificial—as Nona does in fact feel—and morally conservative. Carol Singley sees Nona as Wharton's response to Pauline's spiritual irresponsibility: "To counteract [Pauline's] recklessness, Wharton reinstates Calvinism, expressed through Nona, a 'little Puritan,' who assumes the family burdens and forgoes her own happiness" (35). Similarly, Bauer calls Nona "the holdout for traditional values" (104). These interpretations, however, seem to signify a conservatism in Nona that does not exist. She does try to prevent her father's affair with Lita, yet she never claims to act from a sense of morality. Similarly, her refusal to run off with Stanley comes not from traditional morality but rather from her recognition of the spiral of instability divorce both represents and reproduces. She wishes she "knew the best new way of being decent" (206)—her "conservatism" is an attempt to visualize a new system of morality. Having seen the pain of divorce as well as the pointlessness of forcing Lita to stay with Jim, Nona searches for a way to walk a fine line between the old ways—of requiring people to stay in restricting or damaging relationships—and the new—of viewing marriage as something easily shed. This is a balancing act that the novel implies cannot be achieved, as *Twilight Sleep* ends with Nona's wish to join a convent.

Perhaps because of the fragility of marriage and heterosexual relationships, *Twilight Sleep* suggests that the enduring bond between people is not between spouses or lovers but between mothers and daughters. *Twilight Sleep* and *To the Lighthouse* both rely primarily on women of two generations as narrators: Pauline and Nona Manford; Mrs. Ramsay and Lily Briscoe. Both novels shift viewpoints to other characters as well, but the narrative binary of the two women is the most significant. Understanding the combined narration of Pauline and Nona in *Twilight Sleep* is essential to working through the complexities of the novel; to depend on one as more reliable than the other is to do them both and the novel itself an injustice. The shifting viewpoints and intertwined narrators inscribe in the text the modernist interdependency of selves that the novel portrays. The discrepancies between the two women's stories reveal each woman's individual interpretive powers and limitations and the shifting narrative terrain of modernist fiction.

While the differing perspectives among characters show the limitations of an individual's perspective—especially so of Pauline, who shies away from unpleasantness—Pauline's and Nona's points of view do sometimes coincide. They differ in their response to the events of the dinner party, for example, but mother's and daughter's perspectives dovetail in looking at the mess the party leaves behind. Nona sees "empty cocktail glasses and ravaged cigar-boxes..., wisps of torn tulle and trampled orchids" (79) while her mother notes that "the glamour of balls never did last: they so quickly became a matter for those domestic undertakers, the charwomen, housemaids, and electricians" (82). Both women, with the female eye for household irregularities, see the glory of the evening transformed into garbage that must be cleared away. That it is the mess of the party that mother's and daughter's narratives agree on is significant. While the two women disagree on "cures" for modern society, they both recognize, at some level, the flaws of the system in which they live and which they themselves reproduce. Furthermore, this agreement on a view of domesticity suggests that gender creates connections between mother and daughter that a heterosexual relationship cannot provide.[7]

Ironically, the primary conflict between Pauline and Nona is the mother's wish to see the daughter married—just as Mrs. Ramsay encourages Lily to marry. Yet in both cases the younger woman's horror of marriage comes from the mother figure's experience as a wife. Lily Briscoe, watching the Ramsays' marriage, sees the immense toll maintaining a relationship takes on the woman, and Lily would rather direct that energy toward art. Nona Manford sees her mother's first husband hurt and alone following their divorce and her second husband, Nona's father, caught in infidelity. Unlike Lily, Nona has no artistic ambition and hence nothing with which to substitute the desire for a place in the heterosexual economy. The absence of redemption at the end of *Twilight Sleep* places the novel in the frustrated modernist position of a loss of faith, summed up by Nona's desire to join "a convent where nobody believes in anything" (315).

Still, mother and daughter desire a connection with each other that is prevented by marriage itself. Marriage standing in the way of mother/daughter relationships is not a new theme for Wharton in this novel; she explores it also in *The Mother's Recompense*, when Kate Clephane removes herself from her daughter's life rather than hurt her with the knowledge of her affair with Chris Fenno. Susan Woods suggests that Kate finds "solace in separation" (42) and in her daughter's ignorance of what might harm her. Goodman argues that "Kate cannot conceive of unbarring her secret, naming her daughter..., but in truth she cannot actually name Anne because the child has always been more a concept, a dream, a part of the romance and tragedy of her own narrative than a reality" (*Friends and Rivals* 110). Although some similarities exist between Kate and Anne Clephane and Pauline and Nona Manford (both daughters, for example, often end up mothering their mothers), in *Twilight Sleep*, mother/daughter relationships have evolved: while Anne Clephane never knows the reason for her mother's departure, Nona Manford does understand her mother's position, and Pauline and Nona see each other as separate beings, not merely as players in "the romance and tragedy of her own narrative." Critics argue whether Pauline is a good mother,[8] but the view that Pauline is a bad mother is contradicted explicitly by other characters in the novel. Both Pauline's husbands and both her children acknowledge that despite her faults, Pauline is an excellent mother. Dexter acknowledges that Nona's being "firm as a rock" and "naturally straight" (in contrast to Lita, the orphan with the flighty aunt) are to Pauline's credit (109). While Pauline's point of view often shows her to be oblivious to the desires of those around her, her vision of Nona as a "teething child" is revealing: "Perhaps that was what [Nona] was, morally; perhaps some new experience was forcing its way through the tender flesh of her soul" (275). Nona is, we know, pondering "the new best way of being decent." In Pauline, a character both blind and aware, Wharton demonstrates a common predicament for women: she subconsciously knows the truth about her husband's attraction to Lita but out of self-interest refuses to acknowledge what she knows (235).

A moment at the end of *Twilight Sleep* signals a complicity between mother and daughter. Recovering in bed and looking at Pauline, Nona sees "the flicker of anxiety pass back and forward, like a light moving from window to window in a long-uninhabited house. The glimpse startled the girl and caught her by the heart" (314). It is unclear what Pauline knows about the night Arthur Wyant accidentally shoots Nona when both rush to Lita's room to stop her affair with Dexter. Pauline seems to have chosen to blind herself to the implications of the situation in order to preserve her own failing marriage. She, who once "whitewashed" and "disinfected" her life by getting rid of her first unfaithful husband, now seems incapable of doing the same with her second. Pauline's loyalties are first to herself and her husband, and the flickering light Nona sees in her mother's eyes may be guilt at the sacrifice she is asking, perhaps unconsciously, her daughter to make. Pauline chooses to insist on her place in a heterosexual system, even though before her, in her daughter's wounded body, is the cost that system exacts. Nona, seeing the "flicker" behind her mother's eyes, is touched; between mother and daughter occurs a moment of communication that could never be spoken but can be experienced. It is a moment that, while it will never be discussed, perhaps will be incorporated into their relationship, and the possibility of a sympathetic communication between women rather than between heterosexual spouses further erodes the myth that marriage completes a woman's life.

Conclusion

For Wharton, marriage provided a focused forum for investigating the nature of the individual and of relationships. By the 1900s, religion no longer had the power to dictate the permanence of wedlock; the state facilitated easy divorce; and by the 1920s, social opinion, at least in urban areas, did not care. Only the individual, then, could decide whether to remain in an unhappy marriage—and the individual also was the only one who determined what "unhappy" meant. Marriage thus no longer provided any boundaries for defining the self, and divorce, or the possibility of divorce, threatened the individual with increasing fluidity. In her last two completed novels, *Hudson River Bracketed* and *The Gods Arrive*, discussed in the final chapter, Wharton continued to explore the impact of marriage, divorce, and romantic relationships on the individual. She adds in her portrait of the artist, thus combining struggles of art, identity, and love to produce her last—though I do not suggest definitive—statement about her life and work.

Twilight Sleep conveys the sense of modernist isolation that the characters feel, and, like other modernist writers, Wharton suggests that relief from this isolation occurs not in words but in a different realm, where meaning is construed from experience and interpretation, although not from hope and ideals. The similarities of women's experiences—Pauline's and Nona's—provide a building ground for a relationship in a way that the disparate lives of Pauline and Dexter cannot. None of the characters in *Twilight Sleep* is a truly reliable interpreter, yet their failures remind the reader of the pitfalls of his or her own act of reading and interpretation. Weinstein's argument that the novel form is uniquely suited to the portrayal of relationships because "it encompasses the central tension at hand: the play between individual vision/desire and the opaqueness of the other" (24) illuminates as well the reader's relationship with the text; the reader becomes the individual desiring knowledge of the novel, while the novel itself becomes the opaque form the reader seeks to know. Novels always contain gaps, and modernist fiction like *Twilight Sleep* that emphasizes and enforces those gaps in their very structure make the reader's quest for knowledge of the text both more tantalizing and more elusive. Desire is fundamental to the reading experience, made so by the conflicting narrators and left so by the lack of resolution. Thus divorce—the breaking of a perceived permanent relationship—becomes a metaphor for modernist anxieties. The characters are divided from each other and, with the prevalence of divorce, perceive that divisibility as simple. In *Twilight Sleep*, Wharton presents the reader with a text that represents both the "ease" of separation and the simultaneous impossibility of teasing out relationships, and she forces the reader into a compromised position, desiring knowledge and union with the text but always prevented, ever deferred, from sorting it all out. *Twilight Sleep*, in both form and content, proves to have more in common with modern fiction than her outspokenness against modernism would suggest.

CHAPTER 6

Antimodernism and Looking Pretty: Wharton's Artistic Practice

In James Joyce's *Portrait of the Artist as a Young Man* (1916), Stephen Dedalus declares that "I will not serve that in which I no longer believe whether it call itself my home, my fatherland or my church: and I will try to express myself in some mode of life or art as freely as I can and as wholly as I can, using for my defence the only arms I allow myself to use—silence, exile, and cunning" (247). A few years later, in *This Side of Paradise* (1920), F. Scott Fitzgerald's alter ego Amory Blaine finds "no God in his heart...yet the waters of disillusion had left a deposit on his soul, responsibility and a love of life, the faint stirring of old ambitions and unrealized dreams" (282). He states, "I know myself..., but that is all." With the rise of the modernists came the figure of the isolated artist, young, tormented, and disillusioned but blessed with a mystical insight into life and a superhuman ability to create. He was undoubtedly male. By definition, a writer such as Edith Wharton was excluded from the elite club of artists. She herself did not define an artist in this way, however, and her stridency against modernism no doubt comes in part from her anger at what she saw as an idealistic, misogynist, misanthropic, and extremely narrow definition of "the artist." In her last two completed novels, *Hudson River Bracketed* (1929) and *The Gods Arrive* (1932), Wharton explicitly tackles the nature of the writer in the literary world of the 1920s, using these texts simultaneously as a way to look back on her own career, to critique the contemporary view of the writer and the literary marketplace, and to articulate her own definition of the artist. Her definition, while insisting on the need for order in art, allows for the vagaries of genius while placing a clearly feminine stamp on creativity: the desire to make art pretty.

After writing *Twilight Sleep*, Wharton suffered a series of debilitating personal and professional difficulties. Walter Berry, her good friend since they met in 1893 and the principle supporter of her writing, died in 1927. She had relied on his criticism in her professional life and on his companionship and support in her personal affairs. She was with him in his last days, the only person he would see, and his death struck her hard. After he died on October 12, 1927, Wharton wrote in her diary, "The love of all my life died today, & I with him" (Beinecke). She herself fell severely ill in the winter of 1929 after catching an infection that brought on heart palpitations, forcing her to face her own mortality. The severe cold weather of that winter also destroyed her beloved gardens at Ste. Claire, her winter home on the Riviera, and this devastation was a blow that hit no less hard than her own ill health. Professionally, she still commanded top prices, but she faced editors who were less accommodating than she was used to and critics who found her out of touch. As early as 1922, reviews for *The Glimpses of the Moon* suggested that the expatriate Wharton had been away too long to portray American speech and customs convincingly. Edmund Wilson criticized her command over spoken English, and Wharton took his comments to heart (Lewis 446). Still, *The Glimpses of the Moon* sold well, as did *Twilight Sleep* and her next novel, *The Children* (1928). By the time she wrote *Hudson River Bracketed*, Wharton found herself a little put out at the disparity between her sales record and the critics' regard for her work. One critic asserted that *The Mother's Recompense* (1925) made Wharton the equal of young Fitzgerald (Lewis 465), while another critic compared the novel unfavorably with Virginia Woolf's *Mrs. Dalloway* (Benstock 385). Biographer R. W. B. Lewis points out that Wharton's last novels reveal "her sense of deepening hurt at being critically underrated or disregarded in favor of younger writers, even while she remained one of the best-selling novelists in the country" (492). More personally, Wharton would later claim that *Hudson River Bracketed* and *The Gods Arrive* were among her top five favorite novels (the other three that made the list were *Summer, The Custom of the Country*, and *The Children*).

Since before World War I, Wharton had been interested in writing the story of an artist. She had begun a novel called *Literature*, which was to be about the literary growth of a young man named Dicky Thaxter. She abandoned the project when the war broke out, intending to take it up again, but she never finished the planned novel. In the Vance Weston/Halo Spear novels, she finally returned to the subject. On January 1, 1930, she wrote Elisina Tyler, thanking her for her praise of *Hudson River Bracketed* and adding, "It is a theme that I have carried in my mind for years, & that Walter was always urging me to use; indeed I had begun it before the war, but in our own milieu, & the setting of my own youth. After the war it took me long to re-think it & transpose it into the crude terms of modern America" (Lewis and Lewis *Letters* 525). In the story of the artist Vance Weston, she incorporated some of her personal experiences, which Shari Benstock identifies as "her own ambitions and insights and inner loneliness" (*No Gifts* 422). Lewis connects Vance's struggle with old literary forms in the modern marketplace as Wharton's own, and he also argues that through Vance we can recognize her "impulse...to attach herself to the former age" (492). Yet, as I shall show, these two novels complicate a reading that identifies Wharton with Vance Weston, and instead, like many other critics, I see a stronger connection between Wharton and Halo Spear. Unlike these critics, however, I believe Wharton's artistic statement rests less in Halo's creative power as a mother than in her domestic instincts and abilities.

Hudson River Bracketed follows Vance Weston as he travels from his home in the Midwest to New York City, where he circles from its outskirts to the center of its literary world on his way to developing his ability and career as a writer. Along the way he meets the upper-class but free-spirited Halo Spear, who allows him access to the library of an empty family home, called the Willows, and who tutors him in the delights of English literature. Vance also meets the provincial Laura Lou Tracy and falls for her beauty; they marry, despite having little in common. Halo, in order to relieve the debts her parents have incurred, marries the wealthy Lewis Tarrant, who has aspirations to be a literary editor. Nevertheless, Halo becomes Vance's muse and literary collaborator, working with him on his first novel *Instead*, a meditative exploration of the previous owner of the Willows. Held to a low-paying contract by his editor, none other than Halo's husband Lewis Tarrant, Vance is unable to support his wife financially, and Laura Lou dies of tuberculosis. Almost simultaneously, Halo's husband asks her for a divorce, and *Hudson River Bracketed* ends with Halo and Vance meeting with the promise of a future.

The Gods Arrive picks up a few months later. Halo and Vance are on their way to Europe, even though Halo's divorce has not yet been finalized. The two resolve to live together bound only by their love, with the understanding that they will marry when Halo is divorced. Lewis Tarrant, however, stubbornly refuses to grant the divorce now that Halo has moved on to another man. Halo and Vance wander through Europe, encountering various literary types and then retreating to solitude so Vance can write, first in Spain, later in France. Halo becomes not Vance's collaborator and best editor but rather his domestic support staff, and although she is disappointed in this role, she continues to provide Vance with the surroundings he needs in order to write. Halo tolerates his periodic unannounced disappearances without recrimination, and when he abandons her for the girl who betrayed him years ago, the selfish Floss Delaney, Halo returns to the house of their early collaboration to bear his child. Vance stumbles upon her there, contrite and ashamed, and she welcomes him back with literally open arms.

Critics generally regard these final novels as failures and have little to say about them. Cynthia Griffin Wolff calls them "deplorable" (192). Elizabeth Ammons finds the novels "not very successful" because Wharton's criticism of the United States combined with her interest in motherhood and women's independence "is achieved at the cost of the heroine's integrity as a believable character" (189). More recently, Penelope Vita-Finzi has examined the novels for clues to Wharton's artistic practice, and Stephanie Lewis Thompson believes the novels articulate Wharton's reasons for finding modernism "inherently corrupt" (114). *Hudson River Bracketed* and *The Gods Arrive* are generally treated together in critical studies because they follow the same characters and maintain the same structure (shifting between Halo's and Vance's viewpoint). I will also discuss the two works together, but I believe it is important to note the differences between the novels: *Hudson River Bracketed* focuses on Vance's early struggles to become a writer, with Halo serving a largely peripheral function; *The Gods Arrive* chronicles Vance's literary development but Halo becomes a much more involved character, and the *kunstlerroman* and romance plots receive equal attention.[1] These novels, along with Wharton's critical writing, demonstrate Wharton's well-known dislike of modernist aesthetics and the modern conception of the artist even as they show her engagement with other modern issues and concerns, such as the importance of the past in life and art, the isolated individual, the possibilities of relationships, and the independent woman.

Wharton's Orderly Artistic Practice

In 1924, Wharton started a diary with "My Motto": "Order the beauty even of Beauty is" (Beinecke).[2] She felt strongly that a novel should have form and structure that organized the writer's ideas and that held them together; Wharton regarded novels much as she regarded houses, with an emphasis on the architectural design. Indeed,

"Hudson River Bracketed" is a type of early nineteenth-century architecture. Wharton's interest in architectural structure as a method of literary order can be seen in her response to her editor William Cary Brownell when he praised *The House of Mirth* in 1905:

> I am so surprised & pleased, & altogether taken aback, that I can't decently compose my countenance about it. I was pleased with bits, myself; but as I go over the proofs the whole thing strikes me as so loosely built, with so many dangling threads, & cul-de-sacs, & long dusty stretches, that I had reached the point of wondering how I had ever dared to try my hand at a long thing—So your seeing a certain amount of architecture in it rejoices me above everything. (Lewis and Lewis *Letters* 94)

In her unfinished and unpublished first attempt at an autobiography, *Life and I*, written in 1932, Wharton offers an even earlier picture of her insistence on order. Her need "to order my thoughts, & get things into some kind of logical relation to each other" grew out of "my whole childhood—the sense of bewilderment, of the need of guidance, the longing to understand *what it was all about*" (Beinecke 27–28 emphasis in original). In *The Writing of Fiction*, published in 1925, four years before *Hudson River Bracketed*, Wharton most consistently emphasizes "the need of selection" (11) in order to transform life into art. To select, one needs a principle of selection, a reason for one's choice of subject. Wharton held that "a good subject...must contain in itself something that sheds a light on our moral experience"; otherwise it "remains...a mere irrelevant happening" (24). In other words, fiction should help us "understand *what it was all about*."

According to Wharton, selecting and ordering material necessitate intense, time-consuming work. In *The Writing of Fiction*, she dismisses the myth of "Inspiration" on which the artist can rest—the illusion that the artist "has only to let that sovereign impulse carry him where it will" (18). On the contrary, Wharton insists, a writer needs training in order to make the best, or possibly any, use of inspiration. Even once a writer has achieved some skill, he or she still must put in time to transform inspiration into a form that can convey meaning to others. In an undated letter sent to Morton Fullerton, Wharton comments that "prose, like chocolate, must be 'worked' *twelve times* to reach a proper consistency" (Ransom Center emphasis in original). In *Hudson River Bracketed*, Halo Tarrant, studying Vance Weston's hands, compares them to her husband Lewis's delicate hands, which resemble those stereotypically belonging to a poet: "The boy's hands were different: sturdier, less diaphanous, with blunter fingertips, though the fingers were long and flexible. A worker's hand, she thought; a maker's hand. She wondered what he would make" (215). As a "maker," Vance will perform the labor necessary to creativity. In *The Gods Arrive*, Wharton shows her scorn for the "writer" who does not write in the character Alders, a young man who talks a thin game and who can never remember what subject he is supposed to be writing about. She also shows her sympathy for the genius Chris Churley, who fails to find the motivation to write and who kills himself rather than succumb to a mundane existence. These writers are not "makers" because they lack the discipline to perform the labor of art.

But order and labor are not all. Wharton admits that writing requires an extra element not easily accounted for. In *Life and I*, she recalls her early attempts at writing verse. She began to recognize poetic forms and could use them: "I was proud of this knowledge, & zealous to conform to the 'rules of English versification'; and yet—and yet—I couldn't see that Shakespeare or Milton had! This was almost as dark a problem as the Atonement—life & art seemed equally beset with difficulties for a little girl! And whenever I took to poetry myself, I found the lawless 'redundant syllables' slipping in—& I generally let them stay" (Beinecke 42). Something about art, she found, would not submit itself entirely to rules. In *The Writing of Fiction*, Wharton identifies "inspiration" or "genius" as the motivating creative force. With this ability, the writer creates a new world: "To the artist his world is as solidly real as the world of experience, or even more so, but in a way entirely different; it is a world to and from which he passes without any sense of effort, but always *with an uninterrupted awareness of the passing*. In this world are begotten and born the creatures of his imagination, more living to him than his own flesh-and-blood" (85 emphasis in original). The "lawless" extra syllables in poetry, the vision of the self-created world: these things stem from the personal energy and insight that are vitally necessary to the creation of art.

For Wharton, art comes from selection, work, and imagination, stewed together over a period of time during which the subject "grow[s] slowly in [the writer's] mind" (43). During this time and with the help of imagination and work, the "magic transposition" occurs that "is the image of life transposed in the brain of the artist, a world wherein the creative breath has made all things new" (59). Genius or talent is not enough to make art: "To its making go patience, meditation, concentration, all the quiet habits of the mind now so little practised [*sic*], so seldom inculcated; and to these must be added the final imponderable, genius, without which the rest is useless, and which, conversely, would be unusable without the rest" (71). In *Edith Wharton and the Art of Fiction*, Vita-Finzi articulates Wharton's balanced conception of the writer:

> Edith Wharton's conscious conviction that order underlay all that was best in society and art meant that, when it came to describing and formulating a theory of fiction, the classical principles of proportion, decorum, harmony, and form, achieved through conscious intention and selection, were inescapable. But her intellectual wish for rules and formulae to guide the writer could not override her intuitive knowledge of an inexplicable, subjective quality coming from an unknowable source within the individual artist. (2)

Vita-Finzi explains that these combined beliefs placed Wharton "between the two stools of dogmatic assertion and vague speculation" when it came to articulating a theory of fiction. Frederick Wegener similarly suggests that "at the heart of the creative process, Wharton thus places a liminal, indefinite experience radically at odds, to say the least, with the ideal of conscious, wide-awake, deliberate craftsmanship generally promoted in her critical work" ("Enthusiasm" 29). Wegener concludes that Wharton's apparently oppositional thinking on the nature of writing remained "fruitfully unresolved" (31). Wharton believed that the artist was neither a simple laborer who put pen to paper nor an ethereal otherworldly being but rather a combination of both.

The Problem with "Making It New"

Wharton's explicit antimodernism has made it easy for critics to accept her writing and her literary placement at her own valuation. In her critical writings, she is shrill and unrelenting in her rejection of the new methods in literature. In "Permanent Values in Fiction," Wharton attacks the younger writers for valuing "theory" over character: "Whatever ideas or views [the modern writer] deals in, he barely troubles to manufacture mouthpieces for them, even of the most rudimentary sort; and the characters in modern fiction are often (as, for instance, in the novels of D. H. Lawrence) no more differentiated than a set of megaphones, through all of which the same voice interminably reiterates the same ideas" (*Uncollected Critical Writings* 175). Yet, as Wegener points out, one of the disappointments of her critical essays is their failure to reveal Wharton's full range of response to her contemporaries: "a writer capable of appreciating Colette and Rilke, Yeats and *Spoon River Anthology*, Gide and Huxley, Cocteau and *Vile Bodies* and *The Great Gatsby*, seems far from wholly or indiscriminately unresponsive to the work of newer poets and novelists of the time" ("Enthusiasm" 33). Wharton's dismissal of the modernists, whom she usually does not name in the published critical essays, is profoundly unsatisfactory. (She is more explicit in her letters, throwing barbs at Joyce, Woolf, Faulkner, and Eliot.) In "Tendencies in Modern Fiction," Wharton suggests that by insisting on "the rejection of the past," the war-devastated generation of new writers has "definitely impoverished the present" (*Uncollected Critical Writings* 170). T. S. Eliot, after all, announced in "A Preface to Modern Literature," an essay published in *Vanity Fair* in 1923, that "This is an exceptional [literary] period, in its being so little the offspring of the preceding" (118). To Wharton, for whom "the accumulated leaf-mould of tradition is essential to the nurture of new growths in art" (170), such a lack of interest in the past is untenable, and in *Hudson River Bracketed* and *The Gods Arrive*, she portrays an artist with as an intense reliance on the past as her own.

Vance's writing style is rendered fresh through his use of old techniques. Lewis Tarrant describes his first short story: "this boy has had the nerve to go back to a quiet, almost old-fashioned style: no jerks, no paradoxes—not even afraid of lingering over his transitions" (*Hudson River Bracketed* 225). Thus Vance's writing contrasts directly with that of Gertrude Stein, Ezra Pound, Ernest Hemingway, T.S. Eliot (out of whose poem *The Waste Land* Ezra Pound edited the transitions), and John Dos Passos. Through Vance's opinions about contemporary literature, we see Wharton's: "These brilliant verbal gymnastics—or the staccato enumeration of the series of physical aspects and sensations—they all left him with the sense of an immense emptiness underneath, just where, in his own vision of the world, the deep forces stirred and wove men's fate." He thinks, "No, life's not like that, people are not like that. The real stuff is way down, not on the surface" (320). Vance reflects Wharton's belief that writing should make vivid the character's conscious inner life. In *The Writing of Fiction*, she says, "Modern fiction really began when the 'action' of the novel was transferred from the street to the soul" (7)—that is, when fiction began to focus on character and the interior self rather than on external events.

In the face of Ezra Pound's mantra to "make it new," *Hudson River Bracketed* emphasizes the importance of the past in art and in living.

In the first sentence of the novel, Wharton establishes that by the age of nineteen, Vance Weston invented a new religion. He soon gives it up, however, and as the novel progresses, he articulates why. Responding to his grandmother's faddish proselytizing of a "new" faith, he argues that "the greatest proof of the validity of a religion was its age, its duration, its having stood through centuries of change" (444). He wonders, "Who wanted a new religion, anyhow, when the old one was there, so little exhausted or ever understood, in all its age-long beauty?" (445). Vance's growth in understanding religion corresponds to his increasing understanding of the source of his writing. Coming east from the midwestern town where he was raised, Vance is amazed at the old houses that have been in families for generations, and these houses offer him a new view of the world as a "many-vistaed universe reaching away on all sides" (91). Old things—religions, houses—provide a structure that supports the artist and offers opportunities to see and build new ideas.

Vance has his second literary success with the short novel *Instead*, a story inspired by a house called the Willows. The Willows is owned by a relative of Halo's, though no one currently lives in it. Vance initially gains access to the house when staying with his cousins, the Tracys, who serve as its caretakers. After marrying the Tracy daughter Laura Lou, Vance too is called upon to check up on the house, and on one of his visits, he is inspired both by the portrait of its last resident, Elinor Lorburn, and by the long history the house has seen: "Under the high ceilings of the bedrooms, with their carved bedsteads and beruffled dressing tables, he had now and then an elusive sense of life, of someone slipping through doors just ahead, of a whisper of sandals across flowered carpets, as if his approach had dispersed a lingering congress of memories" (*Hudson River Bracketed* 316). He imagines the past coming to life, or rather, imagines back to when the past was the present. "This is the Past—if only I could get back into it," he thinks (318). He remembers that he has once "gotten back into it" when he was young:

> He had recalled, then, waking in the night years before at Euphoria, as a little boy, and hearing the bell of the Roman Catholic church toll the hour. That solemn reverberation, like the note of Joshua's trumpet, had made the walls of the present fall, and the little boy had reached back for the first time into the past. His first sight of the Willows had renewed that far-off impression; he had felt that the old house was full of muffled reverberations which his hand might set going if he could find the rope. (323)

Explaining his project to Halo, Vance says, "What interests me would be to get back into the minds of the people who lived in these places—to try and see what we came out of. Til I do I'll never understand why we are what we are" (325). Art, for Vance, is a quest for individual and communal identity that can only occur in full awareness of the past.

Here Wharton articulates most clearly her objection to Pound's "make it new": she insists that the past shapes not merely individuals but also the world in which individuals exist and which shapes them. In *The Writing of Fiction*, Wharton describes the individual as centered in his or her environment, and the writer "draw[s] his dramatic action as much from the relation of his characters to their houses, streets, towns, professions, inherited habits and opinions, as from their fortuitous contacts with each other" (8). This "relation" grows out of long-established social and political structures. Coming out of a new town in the Midwest, Vance feels unanchored. His task in "reaching back" to the past is hindered by "the meagerness of his inherited experience" (*Hudson River Bracketed* 323). He feels his midwestern background has failed to provide him with a sense of personal or cultural history; "the pioneers" who settled the wilderness "had left the rarest [qualities] of all behind" (323). That the Spears have lived for generations in the same houses shocks and amazes him. At the Willows, he finds he is able to appropriate someone else's past: "Suddenly lifted out of a boundless contiguity of Euphorias, his mind struck root deep down in accumulated layers of experience, in centuries of struggle, passion, and aspiration—so that this absurd house, the joke of Halo's childhood, was to him the very emblem of man's long effort, was Chartres, the Parthenon, the Pyramids" (338). In *The Writing of Fiction*, Wharton maintains that "original vision is never much afraid of using accepted forms" (109). She did not cling to old forms for old forms' sake, but rather she saw a connection between the form of fiction and the way people live. Vita-Finzi explains this philosophy: "[Wharton's] idea of order was founded in traditional society and the art of the past. To her, the past provided precepts and models for living and for art. For the artist, personal and technical difficulties could be solved by adopting traditional solutions. Traditional society provided the structure that people—the artist at least as much as others—needed in order to function fully and progress" (1–2). Vance finds the very wellspring of creativity, both form and subject, in things that are handed down.

The Modern Writer: Portrait of the Male Artist as a Young Ass

One of the difficulties for readers of this pair of novels is Vance Weston as a writer. That is, one wonders why Wharton, an established artist writing a semiautobiographical tale, would create such an unlikeable character as the hero of a *kunstlerroman*. Vance foolishly marries young, neglects his wife Laura Lou, and fails to care for her adequately when she is ill; he throws temper tantrums in his editor's office and tends to sulk when he feels thwarted. He later takes Halo for granted and rejects her as an intellectual equal, and then he leaves her for the obviously selfish, social-climbing Floss Delaney. Altogether, he is an unsympathetic character. Critic Abby Werlock argues that Wharton exacted "subtle revenge" against her former lover Morton Fullerton in the creation of Vance Weston. Werlock astutely points out that Vance resembles Fullerton, "self-centered and pompous," a man who "would not change" (185)—an intriguing interpretation of Vance Weston's obtuseness in his relationship with Halo and Halo's own struggle to assert her independence (182). Still, given that twenty years passed between the end of the affair and the writing of the novel, one feels there is more at stake for Wharton than revenge against a former lover.

In *Hudson River Bracketed* and *The Gods Arrive*, Wharton rejects not only a form of writing but a social construction of the idea of the artist. Dale Bauer argues that *The Gods Arrive* shows Wharton's "scorn" of "the misguided and distorting idealization of male genius" (142). Carol Singley similarly blames the culture of the era for Vance's focus on himself: "Popular creeds encourage Vance to function as his own god" (198). Judith Sensibar, in an essay on Wharton's earlier novel *The Children*, argues that "*The Children*...is Edith Wharton's revision, from a woman's view, of one of mainstream Modernism's central and most compelling tropes; its romanticization of the erotic immaturity of the perennial bachelor and its insistence that this figure was the age's new Representative Man, whose acutely self-conscious sensibility, won by the sacrifice of adult sexuality, was 'the very type of the great creative artist'" ("Bachelor Type" 159). Sensibar points to characters created by Eliot and James—and I would add Joyce and Hemingway—as a source of frustration to Wharton; that is, she objected to the idealization of J. Alfred Prufrock as the artistic man. Sensibar bases her analysis on Martin Boyne of *The Children*; with a few variations, I argue,

Wharton extended this critique in *Hudson River Bracketed* and *The Gods Arrive*.

The artist of the 1920s was envisioned as self-centered and unable to—and hence, not expected to—meet conventional social expectations, such as consideration for others. In *Hudson River Bracketed*, the Tarrants throw a party for Vance, and people surround him asking questions about writing, including "whether he didn't think a real artist must always be a law unto himself (this from the two or three of the younger women)" (278). The nature of the artist is both gendered and sexualized, as the young women serve as Vance's groupies. Even the prominent Mrs. Jet Pulsifer caters to him, suggesting that she will secure him the coveted Pulsifer Prize if he will be her "great great friend" (302). Vance refuses to accommodate her (not out of moral prudery but rather because he naively misses her meaning), and she punishes him by having the prize awarded elsewhere. Yet as his career progresses, Vance becomes less immune to the flattery of women who are attracted by his literary fame. In *The Gods Arrive*, Floss Delaney tells Vance that she came to a party specifically to see him, and Vance thinks, "Who else in the world would have known exactly what he longed to have said to him at that particular moment? Ah, this was what women were for" (293). Although Halo's motives for submitting to Vance are presented as more noble than those of these other women, she also participates in the cult of artist worship, as I discuss below.

These novels demonstrate Wharton's deep scorn for the model of the artist as male and as requiring female nurturing in order to create. Although she might have seen herself as "nurtured" by her male friends Walter Berry, Henry James, Bernard Berenson, Morton Fullerton, and a host of others, as I discussed in chapter 3, her relationships with these men were not inversions of Vance and Halo's. Female nurturing of male talent is not the same as male nurturing of female talent. Berry, James, Berenson, and Fullerton did not wait patiently at home while Wharton wandered off for days at a time without notice; they did not see to the finding of new domiciles and the setting up of domestic spaces whenever she wished to change location to feed her writing; they did not bear her children in meek silence without bothering her about the very existence of those children. The social and biological construction of gender roles would never allow such an inversion, and in these two novels, especially *The Gods Arrive*, such an impossibility is precisely Wharton's point.

Further, Wharton's very writing of these two novels undermines, even destroys, the validity of the life Vance Weston leads. He needs female nurturing, but his author does not, or at least not in the sexualized and all-consuming way of the male artist. (After all, Wharton's extreme dependence on her housekeeper Catherine Gross and her maid Elise demonstrate her own need for female, even maternal attention.) The most striking example of the male writer feeding on his female muse may be the relationship of F. Scott and Zelda Fitzgerald, a marriage of two artists. Zelda Sayre Fitzgerald had mental illness in her family, but biographers speculate that her anxiety over her failing marriage, Scott's need to control her and their life, and her feeling that her creative instincts were being thwarted all contributed to her breakdowns. Biographer Linda Wagner-Martin, for example, shows that at the beginning of her first treatment for mental illness, Zelda presented "classic anxiety symptoms, the relentless need to control her uncontrollable life" (129). Wagner-Martin also suspects that "had Zelda's talent in ballet been nurtured rather than ridiculed, if her interests in writing and painting had been supported," she might have recovered from her first breakdown more fully (139). In writing her pair of novels about Vance Weston and Halo Spear, Wharton points out that an alternative model of "the artist" existed: Wharton herself. Although one might argue that Wharton's writing career did have a human casualty—Teddy Wharton, who suffered from manic depression and whom Wharton knew she sacrificed in order to preserve her own artistic life—the difference between Wharton and the male writers who divorced wives or whose wives went insane in the service of male creativity is the public perception that it is acceptable for men's creativity to eat up their women.

Vance's marriage to Laura Lou in *Hudson River Bracketed* illustrates the sacrifice of a woman to the male artist. Vance insists on marrying Laura Lou even though he hardly knows her and she is engaged to someone else, rushing her into the marriage although he has no home to give her and without her mother's knowledge. Their first day of marriage foretells their future: Vance stuffs Laura Lou so full of rich food that she becomes ill, and he imagines her sleeping body as a dead one. He wonders, "What do I know about her? What does she know about me?" (237). He becomes frightened at how soon and how easily she submits her entire self to him: "He had not imagined that one human life could be so swiftly and completely absorbed into another" (253). But much of the time Vance forgets

Laura Lou and only rarely does he recognize that she has her own interior self—and even then he considers that her interiority must be less than his:

> Vance, as he looked up at her, was obscurely troubled by the thought that behind that low round forehead with its straying curls there lurked a whole hidden world. This little creature, who seemed as transparent as a crystal cup...–this Laura Lou, like all her kind, was a painted veil over the unknown. And no doubt to her he was the same; and she knew infinitely less of him than he of her, *if only because there was so much more to know.* (288)

This condescension toward Laura Lou's inner self demonstrates Wharton's suspicion of the artist who sacrifices others to his art. Vance does not blame himself when Laura Lou dies and in fact actually forgives *her* at her funeral—for what, it is not clear, except perhaps for the burden she placed on him simply by existing and requiring the food and shelter that he had committed himself to provide. As in *Twilight Sleep*, marriage becomes the microcosm through which Vance experiences alienation from all human beings and comes to understand himself as essentially alone. He experiences his aloneness, however, as something unique to the artist; in the closing lines of *Hudson River Bracketed*, "he wondered if at crucial moments the same veil of unreality would always fall between himself and the soul nearest him, if the creator of imaginary beings must always feel alone among the real ones" (536). Vance comes to value his egotism as essential to his creativity.

The pattern repeats itself in Vance and Halo's relationship in *The Gods Arrive*. Early in the novel, Vance announces that he is "as hungry as a cannibal" (24). Indeed he feeds on Halo, gaining confidence in himself as a writer at the expense of Halo's confidence in herself as a person. Halo schools herself in the rules of living with a male genius, hiding her disappointments and annoyances and ever maintaining a cheerful countenance: "Women who cast in their lot with great men, with geniuses, even with brilliant dreamers whose dreams never take shape, should be armed against emotional storms and terrors" (152). After their first fight, Halo decides not to let her own feelings or thoughts contradict Vance's for fear of disturbing his artistic impulses, and they do not quarrel again. As a result, their relationship becomes an "artifice": "There were times when the effort to be careless and buoyant made her feel old and wary; others when the perfection of the present filled her with a new dread of the future" (61–62). In

Paris, when Vance goes away for a weekend with little notice to Halo, she realizes "that everything she had done for the last year—from choosing her hats and dresses to replenishing the fire, getting the right lamp shades, the right *menu* for dinner, the right flowers for the brown jar on Vance's table—everything had been done not for herself but for Vance" (104). Instead of rousing her from her submission, this revelation brushes past her, and in the next paragraph, she decides Vance was right to go away without consulting her: "probably she deserved it; she had always been too critical, had made her likes and dislikes too evident. As if they mattered, or anything did, except that she should go on serving and inspiring this child of genius with whom a whim of the gods had entrusted her" (105). As with Laura Lou, Vance seldom thinks about Halo's interior self: "'Funny...' he reflected... 'when I go away anywhere I always shut up the idea of her in a box, as if she were a toy; or turn her to the wall, like an unfinished picture...'" (122 ellipses in original). During the two years after their first quarrel, communication between them diminishes until at one point Vance must ask Halo if she is even there: "I can't sleep till I know if it's really you here, or only a ghost of you, who's sorry for me" (336). Although Vance worries that pity has removed the real Halo, it is her submission to him and his "genius" that has actually dispersed her. She has so disciplined herself that she rarely reveals to him her true thoughts.

Ultimately, Vance Weston never does grow up. He never becomes much more than a self-centered artist, and *The Gods Arrive* ends with Halo welcoming him home after his infidelities as her second child. Some critics see development in Vance: Wolff, for example, argues that Vance's trials have made him "ready to undertake the burdens of manhood" (393). Julie Olin-Ammentorp makes an interesting case for Vance's growth, using Julia Kristeva's "Stabat Mater" to interpret the end of the novel as Vance's achievement of humility: "Part and parcel of his achievement of adulthood is his recognition that he is dependent upon others, particularly Halo, for his life as for the continuing of his work" ("Maternality" 306). Werlock is less convinced of Vance's maturity: "Vance has returned—but he has returned before. Perhaps he may become a better writer; perhaps, now that he acknowledges his weakness, a positive value inheres in his new humility. However, like the real-life Morton Fullerton, he falls short of being the sort of man Halo or Wharton had envisioned" ("Revenge" 192). Indeed, a close look at the novel undermines confidence in Vance's maturity. He takes to heart his grandmother's dying words: "Maybe we haven't made enough of pain—been too afraid of it. Don't be afraid of it" (*The Gods Arrive* 409). Reading St. Augustine while recovering from pneumonia, he discovers the need to eat "the food of the full-grown" (418). Both moments of revelation suggest that he is on his way to maturity, but "his legs still rambled away from him like a baby's when he attempted his daily walk" (419). Although he understands it is "time to eat of that food" (421), he also immediately sees that "the food of the full-grown seemed too strong a fare for him" (422). Wandering about the Willows, "it came over him that he was seeking the solace of these old memories as a frightened child runs to hide its face in its nurse's lap" (427). He does not even realize Halo is at Paul's Landing, so it is difficult to imagine that he is returning to her, responsibly or otherwise. When he discovers that she is there, he says goodbye—it is Halo who convinces him to stay.

A Modern Woman: Halo, Marriage, and Art

In *The Gods Arrive*, Wharton pairs the themes of the progress of the writer with the structure of adult heterosexual relationships. By depicting the failure of Vance and Halo's unconventional relationship, Wharton argues for marriage and the female experience as foundations of creativity. That is, through Halo, Wharton demonstrates what effective and healthy creativity is. Other critics have made this point: Werlock, for example, posits Halo as "the real hero of the novel" (182) whose pregnancy becomes "a metaphor for the creative process" (194). Thompson also sees maternity, "metaphorical as well as literal," as Halo's creative function (120), though she admits that locating female power in pregnancy "reminds us of Wharton's uneasiness about the position of the woman in the modern world" (121). I believe that it is less Halo's pregnancy that signifies her creativity than her gift with domesticity and her ability to establish and live happily within routines. She creates life—her own. She is a modern woman who avoids the showiness of modernity; she takes risks by living with a man to whom she is not married, but she does not flaunt the fact. She also appreciates the past and knows what it is to be rooted. *The Gods Arrive* is the portrait of two artists struggling to find their ground in their two different mediums.

Understanding marriage is essential to both Vance's and Halo's creative quests, for both characters must negotiate bad marriages and face a potential marriage with each other. In *Hudson River Bracketed*, Vance and Halo find themselves rushed or pushed into marriages they might not have chosen, had they felt less the pressures of passion, in Vance's case, or indebtedness, in Halo's. Both marriages become traps or cages. Laura Lou does not fit into Vance's life, and he thinks of her rarely; when he does, he feels heavily the burden of caring materially for another person. Halo finds Lewis Tarrant moody and whimsical and often in need of her attention. For their own personal growth, both Vance and Halo must shed their first marriages but retain their faith in the institution itself.

In *The Gods Arrive*, Halo and Vance believe they can live without marriage—that their love and passion for each other will bind them in the same way the social legitimacy and legality of marriage would. In *Hudson River Bracketed*, Vance first declares his love to Halo, calling her "the whole earth to me!" Halo quietly replies, "That's too much to be to anyone" (419). Yet in *The Gods Arrive*, Halo makes the opposite error: she admits, more and more, that she is not the "whole earth" to Vance. By relinquishing her claim to Vance's attention, she grants him permission not to think of her. She also fails to recognize that she has made him *her* "whole earth." Without the bonds of marriage, they have no incentive to make their relationship work, and Halo's submission to Vance's "artistic" whims comes from a fear of the loss of the relationship as well as from her belief in sustaining Vance's creativity. Vance, on the other hand, wants to be married in order not to have to worry about the relationship. After an argument, he returns with a gift for Halo and asks, "Can't we get married pretty soon now?" (61), as if marriage would prevent their quarreling again. In *The Gods Arrive*, both Vance and Halo must reevaluate their conception of what marriage does. During a visit to Halo in France while Vance is away in London, Halo's friend and literary critic George Frenside comments, "We most of us need a frame-work, a support—the maddest lovers do. Marriage may be too tight a fit—may dislocate and deform. But it shapes life too; prevents growing lopsided, or drifting" (317). That these words are spoken by a confirmed bachelor, a character created by a divorcée, makes them no less true in the world of the novel. As I have shown in chapter 5, Wharton was not unaware of the problems of marriage, yet she continued to believe in it as a structure that shaped society and that could, as Frenside says, "prevent drifting."

Marriage, Wharton believed, is like architecture; like the novel form, it provides structure. When Halo explains to Frenside that "the only thing I care for is *his* freedom. I want him to feel as free as air," he responds: "H'm—free as air. The untrammelled artist. Well, I don't believe it's the ideal state for the artist, any more than it is for the retail grocer. We all of us seem to need chains—and wings"

(*The Gods Arrive* 318 emphasis in original). Frenside shatters the myth of the artist—unquestionably male—who rises above, around, and beyond the rules that govern "everyday people." Although the artist may have special insight, Frenside and Wharton refuse to subscribe to the idea that artists' needs are much different and especially more sacred than those of the rest of us. By comparing a writer to a "retail grocer," Frenside suggests that writing is an occupation like any other—and writers are workers like other humans. And their relationships need conventional structure, just as everyone else's do.

Ironically, Vance recognizes the problem with "free love" and acknowledges the need for marriage relatively early in *The Gods Arrive*, almost before Halo does. After leaving Halo without a thought for two days, he lies on his bed and wonders: "How did two people who had once filled each other's universe manage to hold together as the tide receded? Why, by the world-old compulsion of marriage, he supposed. Marriage was a trick, a sham, if you looked at it in one way; but it was the only means man had yet devised for defending himself from his own frivolity" (120). He is struck by marriage as "an emanation of the will of man" (120); that is, he finds marriage to be powerful because it represents two people's ability, especially in an age of easy divorce, to choose to stay together. *The Gods Arrive* thus harkens back almost thirty years to Wharton's story "The Reckoning," when Julia Westall discovers the need "to recognize an inner law...the obligation that love creates...being loved as well as loving" (195 ellipses in original). Later, Vance connects the marriage bond to his work as a writer:

> If, after a life-time with Grandpa Scrimser, [his grandmother] could still believe in the sanctifying influence of wedlock, then the real unbreakable tie between bodies and soul must have its origin in the depths of which the average man and woman were hardly conscious, but which the poet groped for and fed on with all his hungry tentacles. (390)

Marriage, then, has the same source as art. But both Vance and Halo fail to communicate to each other their recognition of this need. Instead, they each remain silent out of inordinate respect for the other's privacy and freedom.

Halo is finally roused to express her true self by what she sees as Vance's artistic betrayal. His third novel, *Colossus*, is imitative of the modern fad and lacks substance. Before Halo offers her opinion on *Colossus*, she wonders, "Was it worth while to put his literary achievement above her private happiness—and perhaps his? She was not sure;

but she had to speak as her mind moved her" (*The Gods Arrive* 342). Halo prevents herself from criticizing Vance's impulsive disappearances, his whimsical desires to move, his long absence in London, and his association with Floss Delaney, but she refuses to hold her tongue about his art. She tells Vance that the book is "drawn away from your own immediate vision" (343), a truth he reacts badly to. Her open criticism leads to their "intellectual divorce" (345) and ultimately drives him away. After he leaves, Halo begins to regenerate, a growth symbolized by both her pregnancy and her desire to resume her maiden name (368). Speaking her true opinion about art releases Halo from the haze of submission to a genius not her own.

Part of Halo's growth as an artist comes from her impending motherhood. Wharton's late fiction demonstrates her interest in mothering and motherhood—a "near obsession," according to Ammons (168)—from *Summer*'s Charity Royall, the motherless mother-to-be, to *The Glimpses of the Moon*'s Susy Lansing, who finds redemption in motherhood, to *The Mother's Recompense*'s Kate Clephane, the disenfranchised mother. This last pair of novels is no exception. Olin-Ammentorp sees in Halo a woman who can handle motherhood on her own: "Unlike earlier pregnant women in Wharton novels, Halo neither uses her pregnancy to 'get' or 'keep' a man (like May Welland in *The Age of Innocence*), nor needs a man for financial support (like Charity Royall in *Summer*). In Halo, Wharton creates a woman who can manage on her own—who, to return to the Virgin Mary, seems almost to conceive apart from any mortal male help" (307–8). Although this argument has its merits—it illuminates Halo's strength and independence—it fails to take note of several complicating elements of Halo's pregnancy that limit its ability to be purely redemptive. In *Hudson River Bracketed*, we learn that Halo has been pregnant before and bore a son who died young (184); this second child, whom Halo is convinced is also a son, seems under no such threat. Hence fatherhood does appear to be a powerful factor: the first child was Lewis Tarrant's, and his early death suggests the sterility of Lewis's mind and energy. Vance's creativity seems to join with Halo's strength to create a new child, a child of the future. In "Wharton and Epiphany," Sharon Kim suggests that Wharton rewrites the modern epiphany so that such moments become more about connection: "By figuring this epiphany as a child, a synthesis of two parents, Wharton creates a place within Anglo-American modernism for an older, perhaps more female, source of creative production than that of the emerging modernists" (150). The creative powers of both Vance and Halo are necessary for this epiphany and for the possible future represented by their child.

Further complicating motherhood, pregnancy becomes confused with death in *Hudson River Bracketed*. When Vance catches Laura Lou stuffing bloody rags into the stove and looking dark around the eyes, he thinks she must be pregnant. The reader may suspect, from Laura Lou's physical weakness and continual bloody rags, that if she is pregnant, she has miscarried or had an abortion. Yet this is not the answer either: rather than preparing to bring life into the world, Laura Lou is nearing her own death, and the rags she burns are the evidence of the tuberculosis that will kill her. Halo hides her pregnancy from Vance so as not to bother him; Laura Lou, far more horribly, feels she must hide her fatal illness from him. Childbirth and death, then, are the two things that must be hidden from the artist to protect his work—if this is true, how feeble must that artist's genius and abilities be? A true artist has the strength to face life and death, as Vance discovers when he struggles to live through a bout of pneumonia. Halo has this strength, and she quietly demands that the rest of the world develop it too when she refuses to hide herself and her child away as objects of shame.

Finally, Halo can rest assured in her ability to mother a child on her own only because an elderly relative has left her the Willows and a significant sum of money. It is not enough simply to imagine childbirth and motherhood as forms of creativity; such a link ignores the financial dependency so many women face when they become pregnant, in or out of wedlock. Unlike the penniless Charity Royall, Halo does not need to marry to support her child, a difference of which Wharton would not have been unaware. To be a mother—a creator—a woman needs, in Virginia Woolf's famous terms, a room of one's own and an independent income. Halo has them; Charity does not. Motherhood alone is not the key to artistic power.

Halo lives through tradition and order without losing her individuality or vitality, and she exercises her creativity through her domesticity and her ties to tradition. She is practiced in the "art of securing 'amusing' lodgings at famine prices" (*The Gods Arrive* 30), a skill she learned from her parents. When she moves into an apartment, she adds her own domestic touches and runs the household in an orderly way. Halo and Vance's rented house on the coast of France is "full of a friendly shabby gaiety" largely because of Halo's work: "she had hidden the dingy papering of the hall under a gay striped cotton, and had herself repainted and cushioned the tumble-down chairs in the verandah" (175). Her domestic skill contrasts with Laura Lou's slovenliness in *Hudson River Bracketed* and with Floss Delaney's carelessness in *The Gods Arrive*. Floss's room "looked untidy yet unlived in" and to Vance seems "squalid" after living with Halo. Vance connects the two women's domestic habits with their personalities: "Floss had none of Halo Tarrant's gift for making a room seem a part of herself—unless indeed this cold disorder did reflect something akin to itself in her own character" (403). Just after this thought, Vance discovers Floss has put through a real-estate deal by blackmailing a wealthy family with their son's love letters to her, and he is horrified by her amorality. Her lack of domestic order corresponds directly to her lack of ethics. Halo's domestic abilities signify her strength of character and provide an outlet for her artistic energies. Suffering from the loss of Vance, Halo discovers "how far pots and pans could go toward filling an empty heart" (431). Halo's ability to be comforted by "pots and pans" indicates that the structure of domestic routine is part of the link to continuity that gives people peace and inspiration. Thus in *The Gods Arrive*, Wharton joins the desires for tradition, domesticity, and art into a continuum of basic human necessity.

Conclusion

The most convincing argument for Halo as the creative center of the novels comes from Wharton's analysis of creativity in her own life. In *Life and I*, she links creativity and the order she believed it required with femininity. She claims her first memory is of being kissed by a cousin while both children are out walking with their fathers, and she particularly remembers that she had on her best bonnet: "Thus I may truly say that my first conscious sensations were produced by the two deepest-seated instincts of my nature—the desire to love & to look pretty." She carefully defines looking pretty as "an aesthetic desire, rather than a form of vanity" (Beinecke 1). She continues: "I always saw the visible world as a series of pictures, more or less harmoniously composed, and the wish *to make the picture prettier* was, as nearly as I can define it, the form my feminine instinct of pleasing took" (1–2 emphasis in original). In this way, Wharton challenges the masculine grip on artistic creativity and asserts a distinctly feminine source of artistry. She draws on what she defines as "the feminine instinct of pleasing" as a way to acknowledge, confront, and use femininity as a source of power. In *Sexchanges*, Volume 2 of *No Man's Land*, Sandra M. Gilbert and Susan Gubar suggest that many women writers of the era responded to artistic and sexual pressures by feeling that "the transformation or annihilation of gender [was] theologically necessary" (347). Wharton, although sometimes helped by feeling herself masculine, did not. We may be suspicious of the essentialism Wharton seems to give to "the feminine instinct of pleasing," but whether such an instinct is innate or, as is more probable, especially given the society in which Wharton was raised, nurtured is beside the point. Wharton made hay out of what was inculcated in her from birth: she transformed the training that should have been a source of oppression into a deep well on which she could draw to shape her art.

Afterword

At the end of *The Age of Innocence*, Newland Archer declines to walk up to Ellen Olenska's Paris apartment on the grounds that he is "old-fashioned." He is often understood to mean that he prefers the beauty and coherence of old New York ways, the New York of the 1870s in which the novel begins and in which Edith Wharton grew up. Yet Newland has spent the intervening years adapting to and even leading the social changes of his society, becoming active in politics and welcoming the marriage of his son to the daughter of a social outcast. He has negotiated the beginnings of the fragmented world that led to T. S. Eliot's *The Waste Land* and James Joyce's *Ulysses* (1922), and his refusal to visit Ellen Olenska speaks not only of a reverence for the past but also of an understanding that seeing her will not heal old wounds. The world has not changed as much as his son Dallas believes, and the past is still connected to the present.

For Edith Wharton, literary modernism was distasteful because it affronted her aesthetic sensibilities, seemed to celebrate amorality, and insulted her impressive career. Yet she could not deny her own interest in "the new," whether "the new" was automobiles, Anita Loos' *Gentlemen Prefer Blondes*, or changing patterns in family structures. Her curiosity kept her engaged with the changing world, and even though she often looked back, she did so with an eye also on the present. At the end of *A Backward Glance*, she wrote: "The world is a welter and has always been one; but though all the cranks and the theorists cannot master the old floundering monster, or force it for long into any of their neat plans of readjustment, here and there a saint or a genius suddenly sends a little ray through the fog, and helps humanity to stumble on, and perhaps up" (379). If she could offer "a ray through the fog," we should examine that ray, if for no better reason than to understand the fog. But Wharton's writing offers much better reasons than that: her work illuminates the issues and concerns of Americans during the first part of the twentieth century. *The Reef* demonstrates Wharton's interest in and concern with the celebration of the subjective interpretation of the world. The novel insists on a need for structure and order in human life, as do *Twilight Sleep, Hudson River Bracketed,* and *The Gods Arrive.* Charity Royall's journey can be understood through the history of the birth control movement in the United States and through Progressive Era attitudes toward prostitution. At the same time, Wharton's short stories show, through form and content, a concern with masculinity and the nature of male social and political power. World War I presented another reason and angle for Wharton's ongoing interest in the nature of civilization and the role of art in sustaining culture and values. *Twilight Sleep* demonstrates her continued interest in marriage and divorce, particularly in the age of the roaring twenties. Above all, the changing nature of the artist—or perceived nature of the artist—captured her attention, at the same time drawing her greatest wrath.

What, then, can we conclude about Wharton as a modernist? By approaching modernism as a series of conversations, and one could include far more topics of debate than I have here, we see that Wharton participated in the literary, social, and political questions of the modernist era without necessarily agreeing with other modernist writers. Modernism then becomes a less monolithic movement, less an exclusive club. Scholars have been moving in this direction in the discussion of modernism for some time now; my study is one more step. We enjoy modernism for its "newness," the heart of which is a burst of creative energy facilitated by and interrogating late nineteenth- and early twentieth-century life. The voices engaged with social, political, and artistic change were not unanimous, but that does not mean that they do not belong in the same field of study. Unlike the love triangles of F. Scott Fitzgerald's *The Great Gatsby,* infidelity kills no one in Wharton's *Twilight Sleep,* but the despair of Nona Manford need not be dismissed in favor of that of Nick Carraway. Both characters believe the carefree United States, or at least New York, of the 1920s suffers from a lack of ethical behavior. Ernest Hemingway's Catherine Barkley dies giving birth to a stillborn son, while Wharton's Halo Spear seems poised to enjoy the future with her child, but Hemingway's disillusionment must not be privileged over Wharton's cautious optimism.

Although Wharton did not identify as a modernist, she did believe herself to be an important voice in contemporary affairs. By not being limited by Wharton's own placement of her work outside the now-dominant arena of modernism and not insisting on a label, we enlarge the era's range and scope. Vexing questions of what women's new sexual freedom meant, for example, benefit from male and female, conservative and liberal, and intergenerational perspectives. Understanding the cultural impact of World War I can be enlarged by understanding the stories of those who had a mature view of the world before, during, and after it. In the process, we acknowledge the artist's freedom to express her ideas without critically punishing her if we find those ideas too conservative. After all, as Wharton wrote in *A Backward Glance*, one of the great joys in life is "discovering the newest and most worth while books, and the talking them over together" (118).

Notes

Introduction

1. In a letter to Robert Grant, dated November 19, 1907, Wharton analyzes her writing method: "I am beginning to see exactly where my weakest point is. I conceive my subjects like a man—that is, rather more architectonically & dramatically than most women—& then execute them like a woman; or rather, I sacrifice, to my desire for construction & breadth, the small incidental effects that women have always excelled in, the episodical characterisation, I mean. The worst of it is that this fault is congenital, not the result of an ambition to do big things" (Lewis and Lewis *Letters* 124).
2. The manuscript of *Life and I* is available in the Edith Wharton Collection, Yale Collection of American Literature, Beinecke Rare Book and Manuscript Library.
3. Even after her literary success, Wharton found that professional authorship remained a taboo topic: "None of my relations ever spoke to me of my books, either to praise or blame—they simply ignored them; and among the immense tribe of my New York cousins, though it included many with whom I was on terms of affectionate intimacy, the subject was avoided as though it were a kind of family disgrace, which might be condoned but could not be forgotten" (*A Backward Glance* 144).
4. In his Pulitzer-Prize winning biography of Wharton, R. W. B. Lewis guesses at the intimacy of the relationship, although in 1975 Wharton's letters to Fullerton had not yet been discovered. Shari Benstock's biography *No Gifts from Chance: A Biography of Edith Wharton* (1994) and Hermione Lee's *Edith Wharton* (2007) have the benefit of the letters, and Gloria Erlich's *The Sexual Education of Edith Wharton* (1992) examines the role Fullerton played in Wharton's psychological and literary life.
5. Edith Wharton's letters to Morton Fullerton are housed at the Harry Ransom Humanities Research Center at the University of Texas at Austin. Some of the letters are collected in R. W. B. and Nancy Lewis's volume *The Letters of Edith Wharton*. The letters from Fullerton to Wharton apparently do not survive.

6. Yale University granted Wharton an honorary doctorate in 1923, and she was pleased to accept. She later made arrangements for her papers to be donated to Yale, where they are currently housed at the Beinecke Rare Book and Manuscript Library in the Yale Collection of American Literature.
7. *Literature* is housed at the Beinecke Library, but this and other unpublished works will soon be available in *The Unpublished Works of Edith Wharton*, edited by Laura Rattray and scheduled for publication in 2009 by Pickering and Chatto Publishers.
8. Recently, however, Hildegard Hoeller, in her study *Edith Wharton's Dialogue with Realism and Sentimental Fiction* (2000), has found intriguing and convincing connections between Wharton's work and an earlier generation of female sentimental writers.
9. Lewis describes the violent reaction the performance provoked: "after the opening soft sounds, the first crashing chords had scarcely been struck before the entire theater was in an uproar. Most of the audience erupted in a storm of booing, shouting, and whistling; but there were also immediate adherents to what became recognized as a landmark of modern music, and opponents and enthusiasts literally spat at one another" (346).
10. DeKoven, however, is another critic who does not include Wharton in her list of women modernists ("Woolf, Richardson, Mansfield, West, Rhys, Gilman, Chopin, Stein, Cather, H. D., Moore, Larsen, Hursten, and Barnes" [192]).

Chapter 1 Troubling the Subjective: The Problem of Impressionism in *The Reef*

1. Wharton's letters to Fullerton were acquired by the Harry Ransom Humanities Research Center at the University of Texas at Austin in 1980, the same year Ammons' book was published. Previous to the discovery of the letters, Wharton biographer R. W. B. Lewis speculated that Wharton and Fullerton had engaged in an affair, but there was no evidence of the nature of the relationship.
2. See Meyer Schapiro, *Impressionism: Reflections and Perceptions*, Chapter 1, for background and discussion of the terms "impression" and "sensation." Norma Broude, in Part II of her *Impressionism: A Feminist Reading*, also explains the scientific principles behind Impressionist art.
3. See Clark's chapter "Olympia's Choice" in *The Painting of Modern Life*.
4. See the Introduction to Clark's *The Painting of Modern Life*.
5. See Helen Killoran's *Edith Wharton: Art and Allusion* (1996), Eleanor Dwight's essay "Wharton and Art" in *A Historical Guide to*

Edith Wharton (2003), and Emily Orlando's *Edith Wharton and the Visual Arts* (2007).
6. Many people associated actresses with prostitutes in the nineteenth and early twentieth centuries. Wharton demonstrates this connection in *The Reef* through Anna's mother-in-law, Madame de Chantelle, who reacts with horror at learning that her grandson wishes to marry a woman who once intended to go on the stage, and in the form of Sophy's sister, who claims to "sing" but is generally regarded as a prostitute.
7. This passage comes from a letter dated June 10; no year is given, but it must have been written in 1912 as Wharton was finishing the manuscript of *The Reef* (Ransom Center).
8. Miss Painter's Christianity does not reflect Wharton's own position on morality. Lewis, writing about a period during Wharton's life a few years before she wrote *The Reef*, during the affair with Morton Fullerton, suggests that "Edith was now a declared agnostic and put no stock in the notion that certain acts were evil and prohibited 'per se.' Her religious sense at this stage was a combination of a private mystical streak and a belief in the sanctity of other persons" (221).
9. Wharton asked this question of herself in a letter to Fullerton, probably in 1909: "If I could lean on *some feeling* in you—a good & loyal friendship, if there's nothing else!—then I could go on, bear things, write, & arrange my life.... I don't know what you want, or what I am! You write to me like a lover, you treat me like a casual acquaintance!" (Ransom Center emphasis in original). The problem of not knowing "what I am" in both Wharton's and Anna's cases comes from confusing signals from the male lover.
10. Jennie Kassanoff points out another horror: by experiencing "passion" as both Anna and Wharton have done, they are also experiencing "democracy" (99). The sexual experience that makes them "like other women" destroys illusions of class boundaries.
11. Her other objections to stream of consciousness will be discussed in chapter 6.

Chapter 2 "Any Change May Mean Something": *Summer*, Sexuality, and Single Women

1. In a compelling reading, Veronica Makowsky and Lynn Z. Bloom argue that Harney's imperialist and romantic vision impairs his ability to see Charity as an individual and that he views her on par with the books in the library (224–25).
2. In "*Summer* and Its Critics' Discomfort," Kathleen Pfeiffer argues that Charity is complicit in her own submission to Harney and ultimately to Mr. Royall: "Through such abandonment of personal taste, financial security, and faith in her own individuality, Charity allows

herself to be taken in by the ideology of male superiority" (150). This submission is part of Wharton's critique of America, Pfeiffer suggests, as Charity and the United States are closely linked.
3. Many thanks to Dakin Dalpoas for first pointing out this connection to me.
4. See, for example, Bauer, 29–30 and Candace Waid, Chapter 3.
5. In his biography of Margaret Sanger, David Kennedy notes that she was not above exaggerating her claims about the lack of birth control information in the United States. Furthermore, although many people flocked to Sanger's lectures and wrote her pleading for information, evidence also suggests that most Americans were well informed about contraception. According to Kennedy, Sanger's most important contribution to the birth control movement was making the issue public (70).
6. In 1913, journalist Hutchins Hapgood interviewed women who became prostitutes and describes one conversation in particular: "This girl feels…that at the root of prostitution is the spiritual demand for a better life than our industrial and social conditions make possible for great numbers of women. They do not go into prostitution for prostitution's sake, but from boredom, from restlessness, from spiritual stagnation and despair. They do not go into it because they are naturally base, nor because they cannot get enough to eat to keep them alive, but because they ignorantly hope that any change may mean something, or because they have lost hope. It is in reality a blind seeking for a better life, or the effect of despair because they have not been able to secure a better life—more amusement, more joy, more love, more pleasure" (quoted in Connelly 34).
7. Historian Mark Thomas Connelly points out that the "wages-and-sin" theory for why women became prostitutes was not a simple answer to the question because many poor women did *not* become prostitutes (33).
8. See Connelly, Chapter 6; Stange, Chapters 4 and 5.
9. Critics have consistently found Mr. Royall ambiguous, but here I am looking specifically at the meaning of his behavior in the context of the white slavery literature.
10. See Stange, 79–80.

Chapter 3 "Unmediated Bonding Between Men": The Accumulation of Men in the Short Stories

1. Mary Cadwalader married Wharton's brother Frederic Jones in 1870; Beatrix was born in 1872 (only ten years after her aunt, Edith Newbold Jones). Minnie and Frederic separated in 1882 and divorced in 1896, but Wharton, who was significantly younger than her

brothers and not close with any of her immediate family, maintained a devoted relationship with Minnie and Beatrix.
2. Lubbock, for his part, felt the break was less necessary, but his unflattering biography, *A Portrait of Edith Wharton*, suggests that he did not forgive her either.
3. Benstock suggests that Lenman is "a grotesque version of Teddy, whose joints and big toes were swollen with gout, his face now a mask of pain and his eyelids heavy and pouchy" (*No Gifts* 244). Wharton may have also felt that husband and character had in common the way they held others hostage to their whims.

CHAPTER 4   "A SIGN OF PAIN'S TRIUMPH": WAR, ART, AND CIVILIZATION

1. Simmons died in a hospital of double pneumonia; Rhinelander was shot down and for a few weeks was believed to be missing. Wharton wrote several letters to his father, Thomas Rhinelander, detailing her search for information about Newbold, before the young man was declared dead.
2. Claire M. Tylee, among others, investigates the journalism, diaries, fictions, and memoirs by women who witnessed and participated as nurses, V. A. D.s, and other occupations in World War I.
3. Willa Cather's Claude Wheeler, of *One of Ours* (1922), fails in educating himself, farming, and marriage before he finds his identity as a soldier in World War I. In William Faulkner's *Soldiers' Pay* (1926), Donald Mahon lacks motivation to recover from his injuries and fades away, while other returning soldiers drift through postwar life.
4. See Haytock, *At Home, At War: Domesticity and World War I in American Literature*.
5. See Fussell, Chapter 8 "Soldier Boys," for an extended discussion of homoeroticism in British war poetry.
6. Typescripts of these letters are among Wharton's papers at the Beinecke Library at Yale University.
7. These markers would not have been insignificant to Wharton. She was well educated and traveled widely, including a family sojourn in Europe that began when she was four years old and taught her the nuances of different cultures, particularly languages, customs, and architecture. Wharton wrote insightfully about her travels and her experiences of various countries, including Italy (*Italian Villas and Their Gardens* [1904] and *Italian Backgrounds* [1905]), France (*French Ways and their Meaning* [1919]), and Morocco (*In Morocco* [1920]).
8. During the retreat from Caporetto, Frederic Henry's disillusionment with the war comes to a head: "Abstract words such as glory, honor, courage, or hallow were obscene besides the concrete names of villages, the numbers of roads, the names of rivers, the numbers of regiments, and the dates" (185).

9. Although Campton sees the war as a kind of crusade, it is less clear that Wharton does. In "Edith Wharton as Propagandist and Novelist: Competing Visions of 'The Great War,'" Judith Sensibar finds a mix of complacency and unease toward French imperialism in Wharton's *In Morocco* and *A Son at the Front*. There are, of course, limits to how far World War I, French imperialism in Morocco, and Western European imperialism during the Crusades can be said to be similar; nevertheless, the reference to the knight-effigy and its roots in the Crusades of the Middle Ages support Sensibar's claim that Wharton's texts addressed "the complicated psychology of male homosexual panic and the ways in which social disruptions caused by World War I exposed and affected socially constructed notions of state, family, and masculinity and femininity" (165).
10. For example, Boas rejects the idea that white Europeans are inherently superior to other races and insists that any perceived superiorities in cultural or psychological development are themselves socially created: "The judgment of the mental status of a people is generally guided by the difference between its social status and our own, and the greater the difference between their intellectual, emotional and moral processes and those which are found in our civilization, the harsher our judgment" (21).
11. Boas's theory of cultural development is actually more complex. He rejects the "theory of a unilinear cultural development" (164)—that is, the theory that all civilizations start at the same point and pass through the same phases in the same order. He demonstrates that some societies might experience developments in their systems of agriculture or hunting and herding at different points (165–66); he also postulates that some peoples might start cultural development at different points and end up in the same place (169–70).

Chapter 5 "The Readjustment of Personal Relations": Marriage, Modernism, and the Alienated Self

1. For a discussion of literary responses to the myth of marriage as the epitome of fulfillment for women, see Rachel Blau DuPlessis's *Writing Beyond the Ending: Narrative Strategies of Twentieth-Century Women Writers*.
2. Biographer R. W. B. Lewis, for instance, calls the novel "overplotted," "melodramatic" (474), and "seriously and variously marred" (523). Cynthia Griffin Wolff also criticizes the novel for being overly dramatic and adds that it is flawed by "sloppy management of the social criticism" (376). More recently, critics have found the novel interesting for that social criticism of 1920s New York. Hermione Lee offers the historical basis for some characters, such as the Mahatma

(639–40). Dale Bauer examines the novel for its treatment of eugenics, and Jean C. Griffith notes the threatening relationship of Lita to jazz culture and racial otherness.
3. Anne MacMaster provides an interesting comparison of Woolf and Wharton in "Beginning with the Same Ending: Virginia Woolf and Edith Wharton." MacMaster argues that Woolf was influenced by Wharton's "killing the angel in the house" in *The House of Mirth*, thus allowing Woolf to kill her own angel and find space in which to write.
4. Bauer shows that in the 1920s the phrase "self-expression" "also means a commitment to creativity that is a transgression against the church, the law, and even social custom" (139). In this light, Lita's desire for "self-expression" takes on overtones more threatening to Pauline's world.
5. Jean C. Griffith points to another threat Lita poses—that of miscegenation. As a woman who frequents cabarets, dances to jazz, and relies on the racially ambiguous Mahatma, Lita allows her whiteness to be questioned, and "in leaving her white family, Lita would be leaving whiteness" (87).
6. The "love diary" is housed at the Lilly Library at Indiana University.
7. Susan Goodman points out a similar theme in *The Mother's Recompense*: Kate Clephane, after being reunited with her daughter, discovers that though she previously had viewed herself only in relation to men, motherhood causes her to define herself in relation to women (*Friends and Rivals* 114). Goodman suggests that this shift is indicative of Kate's coming to maturity and requires Kate to recognize some hard truths about herself as she begins to identify, sometimes unflatteringly, with the women around her.
8. Ammons, for example, views Pauline as an example of poor mothering; Bauer, on the other hand, recognizes that Wharton herself does not judge Pauline by the standards of mothering that she describes: "By reading *Twilight Sleep* as a fiction about Pauline's failure as a mother, we reinforce the essentialist notion of femininity, of motherhood as erasing otherness" (102).

Chapter 6   Antimodernism and Looking Pretty: Wharton's Artistic Practice

1. Critical discussions of Halo draw almost entirely on *The Gods Arrive*; see Julie Olin-Ammentorp, "Wharton through a Kristevan Lens: The Maternity of *The Gods Arrive*" and Abby Werlock, "Edith Wharton's Subtle Revenge?: Morton Fullerton and the Female Artist in *Hudson River Bracketed* and *The Gods Arrive*."
2. This line comes from Thomas Traherne's poem "The Vision."

Bibliography

Ammons, Elizabeth. *Edith Wharton's Argument with America*. Athens, GA: University of Georgia Press, 1980.

Ashton, James. *The Book of Nature: Containing Information for Young People Who Think of Getting Married*. 1865. Reprinted in *Birth Control and Family Planning in Nineteenth-Century America*. Ed. Charles Rosenberg and Carroll Smith-Rosenberg. New York: Arno Press, 1974.

Baudelaire, Charles. *The Painter of Modern Life and Other Essays*. Trans. Jonathan Mayne. London: Phaidon Press, 1964.

Bauer, Dale. *Edith Wharton's Brave New Politics*. Madison, WI: University of Wisconsin Press, 1994.

Benstock, Shari. *No Gifts from Chance: A Biography of Edith Wharton*. New York: Charles Scribner's Sons, 1994.

———. *Women of the Left Bank: Paris, 1900–1940*. Austin: University of Texas Press, 1986.

Broude, Norma. *Impressionism: A Feminist Reading: The Gendering of Art, Science, and Nature in the Nineteenth Century*. New York: Rizzoli, 1991.

Campbell, Donna. *Resisting Regionalism: Gender and Naturalism in American Fiction, 1885–1915*. Athens, OH: Ohio University Press, 1997.

Capo, Beth Widmaier. "'How Shall We Change the Law?': Birth Control Rhetoric and the Modern American Narrative." *Literature and Law*. Ed. Michael Meyer. New York: Rodopi, 2004. 119–44.

Carney, Mary. "Wharton's Short Fiction of War: The Politics of 'Coming Home.'" *Postmodern Approaches to the Short Story*. Ed. Farhat Iftekharrudin, Joseph Boyden, Joseph Longo, and Mary Rohrberger. Westport, CT: Praeger, 2003. 109–20.

Cather, Willa. *Not Under Forty*. New York: Knopf, 1936.

———. *One of Ours*. New York: Vintage, 1922.

Clark, T. J. *The Painting of Modern Life: Paris in the Art of Manet and His Followers*. Princeton: Princeton University Press, 1999.

Clayson, Hollis. *Painted Love: Prostitution in French Art of the Impressionist Era*. New Haven: Yale University Press, 1991.

Colquitt, Clare. "Unpacking Her Treasures: Edith Wharton's 'Mysterious Correspondence' with Morton Fullerton." *Library Chronicle of the University of Texas at Austin* 31 (1995): 73–108.

Condé, Mary. "Payments and Face Values: Edith Wharton's *A Son at the Front*." *Women's Fiction and the Great War*. Ed. Suzanne Raitt and Trudi Tate. Oxford: Clarendon Press, 1997. 47–64.

Connelly, Mark Thomas. *The Response to Prostitution in the Progressive Era*. Chapel Hill: University of North Carolina Press, 1980.

Cooperman, Stanley. *World War I and the American Novel*. Baltimore: Johns Hopkins Press, 1967.

Dawson, Melanie. "'Too Young for the Part:' Narrative Closure and Feminine Evolution in Wharton's '20s Fiction." *Arizona Quarterly* 47.4 (2001): 89–119.

DeKoven, Marianne. "Modernism and Gender." *The Cambridge Companion to Modernism*. Ed. Michael Levenson. Cambridge: Cambridge University Press, 1999. 174–93.

Dimock, Wai-Chee. "Debasing Exchange: Edith Wharton's *The House of Mirth*." *PMLA* 100.5 (1985): 783–92.

DuPlessis, Rachel Blau. *Writing Beyond the Ending: Narrative Strategies of Twentieth-Century Women Writers*. Bloomington: Indiana University Press, 1985.

Dwight, Eleanor. "Wharton and Art." *A Historical Guide to Edith Wharton*. Ed. Carol J. Singley. New York: Oxford University Press, 2003. 181–210.

Dyman, Jenni. *Lurking Feminism: The Ghost Stories of Edith Wharton*. New York: Peter Lang, 1996.

Eliot, T. S. "A Preface to Modern Literature." *Vanity Fair* November 1923: 44, 118.

———. *The Waste Land*. New York: Norton, 2000.

Erlich, Gloria. *The Sexual Education of Edith Wharton*. Berkeley: University of California Press, 1992.

Faery, Rebecca Blevins. "Wharton's *Reef*: The Inscription of Female Sexuality." *Edith Wharton: New Critical Essays*. Ed. Alfred Bendixen and Annette Zilversmit. New York: Garland Publishing, Inc., 1992. 79–96.

Faulkner, William. *Soldiers' Pay*. New York: Liveright, 1997.

Fedorko, Kathy A. *Gender and the Gothic in the Fiction of Edith Wharton*. Tuscaloosa, AL: University of Alabama Press, 1995.

Fitzgerald, F. Scott. *The Great Gatsby*. New York: Scribner, 1925.

———. *This Side of Paradise*. New York: A. L. Burt Company, 1920.

Fitzgerald, Zelda. *Save Me the Waltz*. *The Collected Writings of Zelda Fitzgerald*. Ed. Matthew J. Bruccoli. Tuscaloosa: University of Alabama Press, 1991.

Fracasso, Evelyn. *Edith Wharton's Prisoners of Consciousness: A Study of Theme and Technique in the Tales*. Westport, CT: Greenwood Press, 1994.

Fussell, Paul. *The Great War and Modern Memory*. New York: Oxford University Press, 1975.

Gallagher, Jean. *The World Wars Through the Female Gaze*. Carbondale, IL: Southern Illinois University Press, 1998.

Gilbert, Sandra M. and Susan Gubar. *No Man's Land: The Place of the Woman Writer in the Twentieth Century: Vol. 1: The War of the Words*. New Haven: Yale University Press, 1988.

———. *No Man's Land: The Place of the Woman Writer in the Twentieth Century: Vol. 2: Sexchanges*. New Haven: Yale University Press, 1988.

Goodman, Susan. *Edith Wharton's Inner Circle*. Austin: University of Texas Press, 1994.

———. *Edith Wharton's Women: Friends and Rivals*. Hanover, NH: University Press of New England, 1990.

Gordon, Linda. *The Moral Property of Women: A History of Birth Control Politics in America*. Urbana, IL: University of Illinois Press, 2002.

Gribben, Alan. "'The Heart is Insatiable:' A Selection from Edith Wharton's Letters to Morton Fullerton, 1907–1915." *Library Chronicle of the University of Texas at Austin* 31 (1995): 7–71.

Griffith, Jean C. "'Lita Is-Jazz': The Harlem Renaissance, Cabaret Culture, and Racial Amalgamation in Edith Wharton's *Twilight Sleep*." *Studies in the Novel* 38.1 (2006): 74–94.

Hadley, Kathy Miller. *In the Interstices of the Tale: Edith Wharton's Narrative Strategies*. New York: Peter Lang, 1993.

Hapke, Laura. *Girls Who Went Wrong: Prostitutes in American Fiction, 1885–1917*. Bowling Green, OH: Bowling Green University Popular Press, 1989.

Hemingway, Ernest. *A Farewell to Arms*. New York: Macmillan, 1957.

Herbert, Robert L. *Impressionism: Art, Leisure, and Parisian Society*. New Haven: Yale University Press, 1988.

Hobson, Barbara Meil. *Uneasy Virtue: The Politics of Prostitution and the American Reform Tradition*. New York: Basic Books, 1987.

Hoeller, Hildegard. *Edith Wharton's Dialogue with Realism and Sentimental Fiction*. Gainesville: University of Florida Press, 2000.

Jirousek, Lori. "Haunting Hysteria: Wharton, Freeman, and the Ghosts of Masculinity." *American Literary Realism* 32.1 (1999): 51–69.

Johnson, Laura K. "Edith Wharton and the Fiction of Marital Unity." *Modern Fiction Studies* 47.4 (2001): 947–77.

Joyce, James. *A Portrait of the Artist as a Young Man*. New York: Penguin, 1964.

———. *Ulysses*. New York: Vintage, 1961.

Kaplan, Amy. *The Social Construction of American Realism*. Chicago: University of Chicago Press, 1988.

Kassanoff, Jennie. *Edith Wharton and the Politics of Race*. New York: Cambridge University Press, 2004.

Kennedy, David M. *Birth Control in America: The Career of Margaret Sanger*. New Haven: Yale University Press, 1970.

———. *Over Here: The First World War and American Society*. New York: Oxford University Press, 1980.

Killoran, Helen. *Edith Wharton: Art and Allusion*. Tuscaloosa: University of Alabama Press, 1996.

Kim, Sharon. "Edith Wharton and Epiphany." *Journal of Modern Literature* 29.3 (2006): 150–75.

Lee, Hermione. *Edith Wharton*. New York: Knopf, 2007.
Lewis, R. W. B. *Edith Wharton: A Biography*. New York: Harper and Row, Publishers, 1975.
Lewis, R. W. B. and Nancy Lewis. *The Letters of Edith Wharton*. New York: Collier, 1988.
Lubbock, Percy. *Portrait of Edith Wharton*. New York: Appleton, 1947.
MacComb, Debra Ann. "New Wives for Old: Divorce and the Leisure-Class Marriage Market in Edith Wharton's *The Custom of the Country*." *American Literature* 68.5 (1996): 765–97.
MacMaster, Anne. "Beginning with the Same Ending: Virginia Woolf and Edith Wharton." *Virginia Woolf: Texts and Contexts*. Ed. Beth Rigel Daugherty and Eileen Barrett. New York: Pace University Press, 1996. 216–22.
Mainwaring, Marion. *Mysteries of Paris: The Quest for Morton Fullerton*. Hanover, NH: University Press of New England, 2001.
Makowsky, Veronica and Lynn Z. Bloom. "Edith Wharton's Tentative Embrace of Charity: Class and Character in *Summer*." *American Literary Realism* 32.3 (2000): 220–33.
Manzulli, Mia. "'Garden Talks:' The Correspondence of Edith Wharton and Beatrix Farrand." *A Forward Glance: New Essays on Edith Wharton*. Ed. Clare Colquitt, Susan Goodman, and Candace Waid. Newark: University of Delaware Press, 1999. 35–48.
McDowell, Margaret B. "Edith Wharton's Ghost Tales Reconsidered." *Edith Wharton: New Critical Essays*. Ed. Alfred Bendixen and Annette Zilversmit. New York: Garland Publishing, 1992. 291–314.
Nettels, Elsa. "Gender and First-Person Narration in Edith Wharton's Short Fiction." *Edith Wharton: New Critical Essays*. Ed. Alfred Bendixen and Annette Zilversmit. New York: Garland Publishing, 1992. 245–60.
Ohler, Paul J. *Edith Wharton's "Evolutionary Conception": Darwinian Allegory in Her Major Novels*. New York: Routledge, 2006.
Olin-Ammentorp, Julie. *Edith Wharton's Writings from the Great War*. Gainesville: University Press of Florida, 2004.
———. "Wharton through a Kristevan Lens: The Maternality of *The Gods Arrive*." *Wretched Exotic: Essays on Edith Wharton in Europe*. Ed. Katherine Joslin and Alan Price. New York: Peter Lang, 1993. 295–312.
Orlando, Emily. *Edith Wharton and the Visual Arts*. Tuscaloosa: University of Alabama Press, 2007.
Peel, Robin. *Apart from Modernism: Edith Wharton, Politics, and Fiction Before World War I*. Madison, NJ: Fairleigh Dickinson University Press, 2005.
Pfeiffer, Kathleen. "*Summer* and Its Critics' Discomfort." *Women's Studies* 20 (1991): 141–52.
Price, Alan. *The End of the Age of Innocence: Edith Wharton and the First World War*. New York: St. Martin's, 1996.

Rado, Lisa, editor. *Modernism, Gender, and Culture: A Cultural Studies Approach*. New York: Garland Publishing, 1997.

Ramsden, George, comp. *Edith Wharton's Library*. Settrington, NY: Stone Trough Books, 1999.

Renfroe, Alicia. "Prior Claims and Sovereign Rights: The Sexual Contract in Edith Wharton's *Summer*." *Literature and Law*. Ed. Michael Meyer. New York: Rodopi, 2004. 193–206.

Rich, Charlotte. "Fictions of Colonial Anxiety: Edith Wharton's 'The Seed of the Faith' and 'A Bottle of Perrier.'" *Journal of the Short Story in English* 43 (2004): 59–74.

Riddle, John M. *Eve's Herbs: A History of Contraception and Birth Control in the West*. Cambridge, MA: Harvard University Press, 1997.

Rubin, Gayle. "The Traffic in Women: Notes on the 'Political Economy' of Sex." *Toward an Anthropology of Women*. Ed. Rayna R. Reiter. New York: Monthly Review Press, 1975. 157–210.

Sanger, Margaret. *Margaret Sanger: An Autobiography*. New York: W.W. Norton & Company, 1938.

———. *My Fight for Birth Control*. New York: Maxwell Reprint Company, 1969.

———. "What Every Girl Should Know: Sexual Impulses—Part II." *New York Call* December 29, 1912. Reprinted in *The Selected Works of Margaret Sanger: Vol. 1: The Woman Rebel, 1900–1928*. Ed. Esther Katz. Urbana: University of Illinois Press, 2003. 41–46.

Scarry, Elaine. *The Body in Pain: The Making and Unmaking of the World*. New York: Oxford University Press, 1985.

Schapiro, Meyer. *Impressionism: Reflections and Perceptions*. New York: George Braziller, 1997.

Scott, Bonnie Kime, ed. *The Gender of Modernism: A Critical Anthology*. Bloomington: Indiana University Press, 1990.

Sedgwick, Eve Kosofsky. *Between Men: English Literature and Male Homosocial Desire*. New York: Columbia University Press, 1985.

Sensibar, Judith L. "'Behind the Lines' in Edith Wharton's *A Son at the Front*: Re-writing a Masculinist Tradition." *Wretched Exotic: Essays on Edith Wharton in Europe*. Ed. Katherine Joslin and Alan Price. New York: Peter Lang, 1993. 241–58.

———. "Edith Wharton as Propagandist and Novelist: Competing Visions of 'The Great War.'" *A Forward Glance: New Essays on Edith Wharton*. Ed. Clare Colquitt, Susan Goodman, and Candace Waid. Newark: University of Delaware Press, 1999. 149–71.

———. "Edith Wharton Reads the Bachelor Type: Her Critique of Modernism's Representative Man." *Edith Wharton: New Critical Essays*. Ed. Alfred Bendixen and Annette Zilversmit. New York: Garland Publishing, 1992. 159–80.

Singley, Carol J. *Edith Wharton: Matters of Mind and Spirit*. New York: Cambridge University Press, 1995.

Singley, Carol J. "Gothic Borrowings and Innovations in Edith Wharton's 'A Bottle of Perrier.'" *Edith Wharton: New Critical Essays.* Ed. Alfred Bendixen and Annette Zilversmit. New York: Garland Publishing, 1992. 271–90.

Skillern, Rhonda. "Becoming a 'Good Girl:' Law, Language, and Ritual in Edith Wharton's *Summer.*" *The Cambridge Companion to Edith Wharton.* Ed. Millicent Bell. Cambridge: Cambridge University Press, 1995. 117–36.

Smith, Paul. *Impressionism: Beneath the Surface.* New York: Harry N. Abrams, 1995.

Stange, Margit. *Personal Property: Wives, White Slaves, and the Market in Women.* Baltimore: Johns Hopkins University Press, 1998.

Stevenson, Pascha Antrece. "Ethan Frome and Charity Royall: Edith Wharton's Noble Savages." *Women's Studies: An Interdisciplinary Journal* 32.4 (2003): 411–29.

Strychacz, Thomas. *Modernism, Mass Culture, and Professionalism.* New York: Cambridge University Press, 1993.

Thomas, William I. *The Unadjusted Girl.* 1923. Montclair, NJ: Patterson Smith, 1969.

Thompson, Stephanie Lewis. *Influencing America's Tastes: Realism in the Works of Wharton, Cather, & Hurst.* Gainesville: University of Florida Press, 2002.

Tichi, Cecelia. "Emerson, Darwin, and *The Custom of the Country.*" *A Historical Guide to Edith Wharton.* Ed. Carol J. Singley. New York: Oxford University Press, 2003. 89–114.

Tintner, Adeline R. *Edith Wharton in Context: Essays on Intertextuality.* Tuscaloosa: University of Alabama Press, 1999.

Tone, Andrea. *Devices and Desires: A History of Contraceptives in America.* New York: Hill and Wang, 2001.

Tonkovich, Nicole. "An Excess of Recompense: The Feminine Economy of *The Mother's Recompense.*" *American Literary Realism* 26.3 (1994): 12–32.

Tylee, Claire M. *The Great War and Women's Consciousness: Images of Militarism and Womanhood in Women's Writings, 1914–64.* Iowa City: University of Iowa Press, 1990.

Vita-Finzi, Penelope. *Edith Wharton and the Art of Fiction.* New York: St. Martin's Press, 1990.

Wagner-Martin, Linda. *The Modern American Novel, 1914–1945: A Critical History.* Boston: Twayne Publishers, 1990.

———. *Zelda Sayre Fitzgerald: An American Woman's Life.* New York: Palgrave Macmillan, 2004.

Wagner-Martin, Linda and Robert A. Martin. "The Salons of Wharton's Fiction." *Wretched Exotic: Essays on Edith Wharton in Europe.* Ed. Katherine Joslin and Alan Price. New York: Peter Lang, 1993. 97–110.

Waid, Candace. *Edith Wharton's Letters from the Underworld: Fictions of Women and Writing.* Chapel Hill: University of North Carolina Press, 1990.

Wegener, Frederick. "'Enthusiasm Guided by Acumen': Edith Wharton as a Critical Writer." *Edith Wharton: Uncollected Critical Writings*. Ed. Frederick Wegener. Princeton: University of Princeton Press, 1996. 3–52.

———. "Form, 'Selection,' and Ideology in Edith Wharton's Antimodernist Aesthetic." *A Forward Glance: New Essays on Edith Wharton*. Ed. Clare Colquitt, Susan Goodman, and Candance Waid. Newark: University of Delaware Press, 1999. 116–38.

Weinstein, Arnold. *The Fiction of Relationship*. Princeton: Princeton University Press, 1988.

Werlock, Abby H. P. "Edith Wharton's Subtle Revenge?: Morton Fullerton and the Female Artist in *Hudson River Bracketed* and *The Gods Arrive*." *Edith Wharton: New Critical Essays*. Ed. Alfred Bendixen and Annette Zilversmit. New York: Garland Publishing, 1992. 181–200.

———. "Whitman, Wharton, and the Sexuality in *Summer*." *Speaking the Other Self: American Women Writers*. Ed. Jeanne Campbell Reesman. Athens, GA: University of Georgia Press, 1997. 246–62.

Wershoven, Carol. *The Female Intruder in the Novels of Edith Wharton*. Rutherford, NJ: Fairleigh Dickinson University Press, 1982.

Wharton, Edith. *The Age of Innocence*. New York: Collier Books, 1987.

———. *A Backward Glance*. New York: Charles Scribner's Sons, 1964.

———. *The Children*. New York: Collier Books, 1992.

———. *Crucial Instances*. New York: AMS Press, 1969.

———. *The Custom of the Country*. New York: Charles Scribner's Sons, 1913.

———. *The Descent of Man*. Freeport, NY: Books for Libraries Press, 1970 [reprint].

———. *Edith Wharton: Uncollected Critical Writings*. Ed. Frederick Wegener. Princeton: University of Princeton Press, 1996.

———. *Fighting France, from Dunkerque to Belfort*. New York: Charles Scribner's Sons, 1915.

———. *The Glimpses of the Moon*. New York: Appleton, 1922.

———. *The Gods Arrive*. New York: Charles Scribner's Sons, 1932.

———. *The House of Mirth*. New York: Collier Books, 1987.

———. *Hudson River Bracketed*. New York: Charles Scribner's Sons, 1929.

———. *The Marne*. London: Macmillan, 1918.

———. *The Mother's Recompense*. New York: Charles Scribner's Sons, 1986.

———. *The Reef*. New York: Scribner's, 1912.

———. *The Selected Stories of Edith Wharton*. Ed. R. W. B. Lewis. New York: Charles Scribner's Sons, 1991.

———. *A Son at the Front*. New York: Charles Scribner's Sons, 1923.

———. *Summer*. New York: Collier Books, 1981.

———. *Tales of Men and Ghosts*. New York: Charles Scribner's Sons, 1910.

———. *Twilight Sleep*. New York: Simon and Schuster, 1997.

———. *The Writing of Fiction*. New York: Touchstone, 1997.

———. *Xingu and Other Stories*. New York: Charles Scribner's Sons, 1916.

White, Barbara A. *Edith Wharton: A Study of the Short Fiction*. New York: Twayne Publishers, 1991.

Witzig, Denise. "The Writer's Wardrobe: Wharton Cross-Dressed." *A Forward Glance: New Essays on Edith Wharton*. Ed. Clare Colquitt, Susan Goodman, and Candace Waid. Newark: University of Delaware Press, 1999. 49–61.
Wolff, Cynthia Griffin. *A Feast of Words: The Triumph of Edith Wharton*. New York: Oxford University Press, 1977.
Woods, Susan L. "The Solace of Separation: Feminist Theory, Autobiography, Edith Wharton and Me." *Creating Safe Space: Violence and Women's Writing*. Ed. Tomoko Kuribayashi and Julie Tharp. Albany: SUNY Press, 1998. 27–46.
Woolf, Virginia. "Mr. Bennett and Mrs. Brown." *The Captain's Death Bed and Other Essays*. New York: Harcourt, Brace, and Co., 1950. 94–120.
———. *To the Lighthouse*. New York: Harcourt Brace Jovanovich, Publishers, 1981.
Zilversmit, Annette, ed. *Reading the Letters of Edith Wharton*. Special Edition of *Women's Studies* 2 (1991): 93–207.

Index

abortion, 54, 56, 57
  see also Summer
Age of Innocence, The, 2–3, 12, 13, 16, 75, 125, 132, 145, 148, 177, 181
  film of, 14
"All Souls," 84
Ammons, Elizabeth, 11–22, 13, 22, 33, 47, 60, 132, 136, 152, 162, 177, 186 n. 1, 191 n. 8
anthropology, 125
Ashton, James, 55
Atlantic Monthly, 10, 85

Backward Glance, A, 3, 76, 181, 183, 185 n. 3
Bahlmann, Anna, 102
Barnes, Djuna, 8
Baudelaire, Charles, 24, 30
Bauer, Dale, 14, 48, 50, 53, 73, 126, 143, 169, 188 n. 4, 191 n. 2, 191 n. 4, 191 n. 8
  on eugenics, 55
Benstock, Shari, 4, 6, 7, 65, 153, 161, 185 n. 4, 189 n. 3
  Women of the Left Bank, 13, 16
Berenson, Bernard, 43, 76, 77, 78, 79–80, 170
Berenson, Mary, 77
Berry, Walter, 10, 76, 78, 79, 159–60, 170
birth control, 18, 54, 56–7
  Comstock law, 54
  male knowledge of, 57
  in the nineteenth century, 54, 56–7
  and prostitution, 55, 57, 58
  in the twentieth century, 57–8
  and voluntary motherhood, 54–5
  Wharton's critique of the lack of knowledge of, 56–7
  and World War I, 58
  see also eugenics
birth control movement, 46, 58, 140, 182
  and *Summer*, 54–8
  see also Sanger, Margaret
Blanche, Jacque Emile, 23
Bloom, Lynn Z., 187 n. 1
Boas, Franz, 126–9, 190 n. 10, 190 n. 11
"Bolted Door, The," 88–92
Book of the Homeless, The, 43, 102
"Bottle of Perrier, A," 18, 78, 79–84, 89, 94, 97
Bowen, Elizabeth, 9
Broude, Norma, 28, 38, 186 n. 2
Brownell, William Cary, 163
Burlingame, Edward, 4

Campbell, Donna, 11
Capo, Beth Widmaier, 57
Carney, Mary, 105
Cassatt, Mary, 27
Cather, Willa, 11
  A Lost Lady, 11
  One of Ours, 108, 189 n. 3
Certain People, 80
Cézanne, Paul, 8, 21, 25
Chandler, Margaret "Daisy" Terry, 77, 78, 144
Chesnutt, Charles, 11

Children, The, 152, 160, 169
Chopin, Kate, 11
Civil War, 3
Clark, T. J., 27, 37, 39, 186 n. 3, 186 n. 4
Clayson, Hollis, 37
Colquitt, Clare, 4
"Coming Home," 88, 101, 103–8
Companionate Marriage, The, 140
"Confessional, The," 88
Connelly, Mark Thomas, 46, 62, 64, 65, 67, 188 n. 6, 188 n. 7, 188 n. 8
Conrad, Joseph, 9
contraception, *see* birth control
Cooperman, Stanley, 19
Couture, Thomas, 24
Crane, Stephen, 10, 11, 59
    Maggie: A Girl of the Streets, 10, 59
Crucial Instances, 88
Cubism, 44
cummings, e. e., 110
Custom of the Country, The, 12, 23, 46, 99, 125, 147, 160
    marriage in, 19, 132, 152
    Spragg, Undine, 132, 134
Cutting, Sybil, 78

Dadaism, 44
Darwin, Charles, 126
"Daunt Diana, The," 88
Dawson, Melanie, 69
Decoration of Houses, The, 128
Degas, Edgar, 27, 40
DeKoven, Marianne, 15, 186 n. 10
Descent of Man, The, 132, 136
Dimock, Wai-Chee, 136
divorce, 131–2, 156–7
    the Whartons', 5–7, 140, 152, 153
    see also Twilight Sleep
Dos Passos, John, 44, 110, 111, 166
Dreiser, Theodore, 11, 57

DuPlessis, Rachel Blau, 190 n. 1
Dwight, Eleanor, 186–7 n. 5
Dyman, Jenni, 83, 95

Eliot, T. S., 14, 16, 21, 41, 45, 166, 169, 181
    "Preface to Modern Fiction, A," 166
    Waste Land, The, 14, 21, 45, 181
Erlich, Gloria, 12, 185 n. 4
Ethan Frome, 11, 12
eugenics, 14, 55
Evans, Wainwright, 140
"Eyes, The," 94–7

Faery, Rebecca Blevins, 38
Farrand, Beatrix Jones, 77, 189 n. 1
Faulkner, William, 16, 21, 43, 45, 146, 166, 189 n. 3
Fedorko, Kathy A., 12, 94–5
feminist literary criticism, 12, 131
Fénéon, Félix, 32
Fighting France, from Dunkerque to Belfort, 7, 102, 106
Fitzgerald, F. Scott, 8, 16, 160, 171
    Great Gatsby, The, 63, 108, 182
    Side of Paradise, This, 159
Fitzgerald, Zelda Sayre, 63, 171
    Save Me the Waltz, 63, 131
flapper, 68, 69, 73
Fracasso, Evelyn, 88–9
Frederic, Harold, 59
Freeman, Mary Wilkins, 11
French Ways and their Meaning, 43, 102, 189 n. 7
Fruit of the Tree, The, 99
"Full Circle," 92–3
Fullerton, William Morton, 4–5, 6, 76, 79, 148–9, 163, 170, 173, 185 n. 4, 185 n. 5, 186 n. 1, 187 n. 9
    influence on Wharton's writing, 5, 55, 169

introduction of Wharton to
    Impressionism, 23
  as model for Culwin, 95
  and *The Reef,* 22–3, 36
  and *Summer,* 52–3
Fussell, Paul, 19, 118, 189 n. 5

Gibson, Wilfrid, 118
Gilbert, Sandra M., 15, 79, 179
Glimpses of the Moon, The, 132, 160, 177
Gods Arrive, The, 19–20, 157, 159, 160–2, 164, 166, 170, 182
  autobiographical elements of, 161, 169
  marriage in, 175–6
  motherhood in, 174, 177–8, 182
  Spear, Halo, 66, 72, 73, 161, 170, 172–3, 174–9, 191 n. 1
  Weston, Vance, 161, 169, 172–4, 175, 176
  Wharton's alternative artistic vision in, 174–9
Goodman, Susan, 76–8, 155, 191 n. 7
Gordon, Linda, 54–5, 57, 58, 61–2, 63, 67, 73, 140
Great Depression, 3, 55
Grant, Robert, 185 n. 1
Greater Inclination, The, 4
Gribben, Alan, 5
Griffith, Jean C., 191 n. 2, 191 n. 5
Gross, Catherine, 171
Gubar, Susan, 15, 79, 179

Hadley, Kathy Miller, 14
Hapgood, Hutchins, 188 n. 6
Hapke, Laura, 59
Hardy, Thomas: *Tess of the D'Urbervilles,* 59
Hawthorne, Nathaniel, 86
Hemingway, Ernest, 8, 16, 41, 44, 45, 110, 166, 169
  Farewell to Arms, A, 108, 110, 123, 146, 182, 189 n. 8

"Her Son," 102
Herbert, Robert L., 40
Hermit and the Wild Woman, The, 88
"His Father's Son," 93–4
Hobson, Barbara Meil, 59–60, 61, 62–3
Hoeller, Hildegard, 140, 186 n. 8
homosexuality
  in "The Eyes," 95
  in "The Long Run," 86–7
House of Mirth, The, 5, 9, 11, 12, 67, 163
  Bart, Lily, 59, 66, 67–8, 69, 73
  film of, 14
  marriage in, 19, 67, 132, 134, 136–40
  Struther, Nettie, 66, 68, 73, 139–40
Howells, William Dean, 10–11, 71
Hudson River Bracketed, 19–20, 157, 159, 160–2, 163–4, 166, 170, 174–5, 178, 182
  autobiographical elements of, 161, 169
  importance of the past in, 166–8
  pregnancy in, 178
  Spear, Halo, 66, 72, 73, 161, 174–5, 177
  Weston, Vance, 161, 163–4, 166–8, 169, 170, 171–2, 175
Huxley, Aldous, 9

Impressionism, French, 1, 17, 22, 23–8, 38
  flâneur, 30, 31
  individualism of, 25–6
  as influence on modernism, 17, 21, 43
  as narrative form in *The Reef,* 22, 28–35, 42
  and rise of middle class, 27, 37
  and prostitutes, 27, 37
  see also neo-Impressionism
In Morocco, 80, 189 n. 7, 190 n. 9
Italian Backgrounds, 189 n. 7

Italian Villas and their Gardens, 189 n. 7

James, Henry, 7, 21, 102, 111, 169
   friendship with Wharton, 6, 9, 76, 77, 79, 170
   literary relationship with Wharton, 11
   realism, 10–11
James, William, 43–4
Jewett, Sarah Orne, 11
Jirousek, Lori, 79
Jones, Frederic, 188 n. 1
Jones, Lucretia, 12, 71
Jones, Mary "Minnie" Cadwalader, 77, 188–9 n. 1
Joyce, James, 7, 8, 16, 21, 41, 43, 166, 169
   Portrait of the Artist as a Young Man, A, 159
   Ulysses, 14, 45, 181

Kaplan, Amy, 2
Kassanoff, Jennie, 15, 187 n. 10
Kennedy, David, 110, 188 n. 5
Killoran, Helen, 28, 186 n. 5
Kim, Sharon, 177
Kristeva, Julia, 173

"Lady's Maid's Bell, The," 84
Lapsley, Gaillard, 6, 9, 10, 11, 76, 78
Lawrence, D. H., 7, 165
Lee, Hermione, 9, 15, 23, 185 n. 4, 190–1 n. 2
Levin, Jonathan, 43–4
Lewis, R. W. B., 7, 23, 86, 95, 146, 160, 185 n. 4, 186 n. 1, 190 n. 2
Life and I, 3, 4, 71, 163, 164, 179, 185 n. 2
"Life Apart, The," 148–9, 191 n. 6
Lindsey, Judge Ben, 140
Literature, 7, 160, 186 n. 7
local color, 11
Lodge, Bay, 76
London, Jack, 11
"Long Run, The," 85–8
"Looking Glass, The," 84
Loos, Anita
   Gentleman Prefer Blondes, 9, 181
Lubbock, Percy, 76, 78, 119, 189 n. 2

MacComb, Debra Ann, 132
MacMaster, Anne, 191 n. 3
Makowsky, Veronica, 187 n. 1
Manet, Édouard, 24–5, 27, 39, 40
Mansfield, Katherine, 9
Manzulli, Mia, 77
Marne, The, 102, 109
marriage, 19, 72, 140
   in literature, 131–3, 190 n. 1
   the Whartons', 4, 5–6, 22, 153
   see also House of Mirth, The; "Other Two, The;" "Reckoning, The;" Twilight Sleep
Martin, Robert A., 9
masculinity, 18, 45
   accumulation of, 81, 83–4, 85, 99
   as competition, 82–3
   and homosocial desire, 75–6, 116
   in pairs, 85–8, 90–3, 97–8
   and power, 75–6, 79, 87–8, 92, 94, 97, 99, 182
   see under individual titles
Matisse, Henri, 21, 44
Maugham, Somerset, 9
Milton, John, 164
modernism
   alienation of individual in, 21–2, 41, 101, 106–8, 129, 131, 140, 157
   and the artist, 159, 169–74, 176
   and civilization, 120–5
   influence of Impressionism on, 21
   interest in the individual, 21, 144
   male bias of, 15–16, 78–9, 159
   and mass culture, 15

study of, 1, 2, 16–17
Wharton's engagement with, 1, 2, 8, 14, 181–3
Wharton's exclusion from, 1, 9, 13
and women, 2, 16–17, 45–6, 79, 179–80
and World War I, 19, 101, 108–16
Monet, Claude, 25, 26, 27, 29, 38, 43
Morisot, Berthe, 25, 27
Mother's Recompense, The, 5, 69, 102, 143, 155, 160
  Clephane, Anne, 66, 69, 70–2, 73, 132
  Clephane, Kate, 69, 70–2, 73, 132, 145, 191 n. 7
  Gates, Lilla, 66, 69–70, 73
  motherhood in, 71–2, 177–8
Mount, The, 4, 54, 76, 153
movies, 46

National Birth Control League, 58
naturalism, 10–11
neo-Impressionism, 28, 32, 39
Nettels, Elsa, 85
New Woman, 16, 46, 54, 73
New York Armory Show, 14
Norris, Frank, 11
Norton, Charles Eliot, 77
Norton, Robert, 76
Norton, Sara "Sally," 65, 77

Ohler, Paul J., 15
old New York, 3–4, 41, 125, 143–4, 181, 183 n. 3
Old New York, 16
Olin-Ammentorp, Julie, 19, 102, 110, 173, 177, 191 n. 1
Orlando, Emily, 15, 187 n. 5
"Other Two, The," 132–4
Owen, Wilfrid, 118

"Painter of Modern Life, The," 24
Paris, 4, 6, 8–10, 21, 39, 65, 76, 109
  in *The Reef*, 30, 39–40
Peel, Robin, 15

"Permanent Values in Fiction," 165
Perry, Lilla Cabot, 26
Pershing, General John J., 58
Pfeiffer, Kathleen, 187–8 n. 2
Phillips, David Graham, 59, 60
Picasso, Pablo, 8, 21, 44
Pissaro, Camille, 25, 27
Positivist philosophy, 25, 41
Pound, Ezra, 16, 21, 166
Price, Alan, 7, 8, 102
prostitution, 18, 59–63, 187 n. 6, 188 n. 6
  and birth control, 55, 58
  economic advantages of, 59–61
  in Impressionist art, 27, 37
  in literature, 59, 69–70
  in the Progressive Era, 18, 46, 62–3, 182
  in *Summer*, 59–63
  white slavery scare, 64–6
  and World War I, 62–3

Rado, Lisa, 13
Rattray, Laura, 186 n. 7
realism, 10–11
"Reckoning, The," 132, 134–6, 143, 151, 176
Reef, The, 5, 18, 21–2, 23, 46, 70, 181, 187 n. 7, 187 n. 8
  artists in, 36–42
  autobiographical aspects of, 23
  Darrow, George, 28, 29–33, 35
  female sexuality in, 33, 37, 38, 42
  impressionistic narration of, 22, 28–35, 42
  individualism in, 28, 41
  interpretation in, 34–6, 41
  Leath, Anna, 28, 31, 32–4, 35, 40, 62, 132
  morality in, 22, 32, 39, 41–2, 43
  and social class, 39–40, 42, 187 n. 6
  subjectivity in, 43, 115
  Viner, Sophy, 28, 29, 31, 36, 38–40, 41–2, 46, 62, 73, 132

Reef—continued
　writing of, 22, 23, 36, 43
　see also Impressionism, French
　　and Paris
Renoir, Pierre-Auguste, 25, 27
Rhinelander, Newbold, 102,
　109–10, 119, 189 n. 1
Rhinelander, Thomas, 119, 189 n. 1
Rich, Charlotte, 80, 81, 82, 84
Riddle, John M., 57
Rite of Spring, The, 14
Rood, Ogden, 28
Rowson, Susanna: *Charlotte
　Temple,* 59
Rubin, Gayle, 75
Russell, Bertrand, 9

Sanger, Margaret, 18, 46, 58,
　188 n. 5
　in France, 56
　"What Every Girl Should
　　Know," 58
Sassoon, Sigfried, 118
Scarry, Elaine, 103, 106–7, 115,
　120–1, 123
Schapiro, Meyer, 25, 26, 43,
　186 n. 2
Scott, Bonnie Kime, 13
Scott, Geoffrey, 78
Sedgwick, Eve Kosofsky, 18, 75–6,
　116
"Seed of the Faith, The," 80
Sensibar, Judith, 80, 116, 118, 169,
　190 n. 9
sentimentalism, 114, 128, 140
Seurat, Georges, 28, 32
sexuality, women's, 45, 52–3, 55,
　67, 140
　effect on women's friendships, 63
　in Impressionist art, 27, 46–7
　in *The Mother's Recompense,* 72
　in *The Reef,* 23, 42
　in *Summer,* 47–9, 51–4, 61–2
Shakespeare, William, 164
Simmons, Ronald, 102, 109–10,
　189 n. 1

Sinclair, May, 9
Singley, Carol, 48, 83, 169
Skillern, Rhonda, 47
Smith, John Hugh, 6, 9, 76, 78,
　153
Smith, Paul, 26, 30, 41
Son at the Front, A, 99, 101, 102,
　106, 108–30, 152, 190 n. 9
　anthropology in, 125–9
　family relationships in, 121–2,
　　152
　and homosocial power, 113–14,
　　116–19
　ideas about civilization in, 108,
　　116, 120–9
　isolation in, 115–16, 129
　modernist narration of, 112–16
　real-life inspirations for, 109–10,
　　119
　role of art in, 118, 124–5, 128–30
Stange, Margit, 65–6, 188 n. 8,
　188 n. 10
Ste. Claire, 160
Stein, Gertrude, 8–9, 21, 43, 44,
　166
Stevens, Wallace, 44
Strauss, Richard, 128
Stravinsky, Igor, 14, 186 n. 9
stream of consciousness, 43–4
Strychacz, Thomas, 16
Sturgis, Howard, 76, 79
Summer, 5, 9, 18, 46, 102, 160
　and abortion, 48, 53, 56
　and contraception, 56, 58
　Hawes, Julia, 48–9, 53–4, 58, 59,
　　60, 62, 70
　historical v. literary readings of,
　　56, 57–8, 59–63
　Merkle, Dr., 53, 56, 65, 66
　pregnancy in, 49, 53, 59, 63, 177,
　　178
　prostitution in, 48–9, 59–63
　Royall, Charity, 42, 47–52,
　　58, 59, 60–1, 62, 63,
　　64–6, 68, 73, 132, 182,
　　187–8 n. 2

Royall, Mr., 49, 50, 51, 53–4, 61, 62, 63, 64, 66
 sexuality in, 47–9, 51–4, 61–2
 and white slavery, 64–6
Susan Lenox, 60

Tales of Men and Ghosts, 88, 92, 93
technology, 2–3, 10, 181
 and World War I, 101, 110–11
"Tendencies in Modern Fiction," 166
Thomas, I. A., 68–9
Thompson, Stephanie Lewis, 15, 162, 164
Tichi, Cecelia, 125–6
Traherne, Thomas, 191 n. 2
"Triumph of Night, The," 94, 97–9
Twain, Mark, 10–11
Twilight Sleep, 10, 19, 72, 99, 102, 106, 131, 136, 140–57, 159, 160, 172, 182
 in comparison to *To the Lighthouse*, 140–1, 142, 146, 148, 149, 154, 155
 divorce in, 143–4, 150, 151–4, 157
 individualism in, 152, 191 n. 4
 Manford, Nona, 66, 73, 132, 142, 150–1, 153–6
 Manford, Pauline, 141–2, 143–4, 147–8, 149, 152, 154–6, 191 n. 8
 marriage in, 143–4, 147–8, 154, 156–7
 narration of, 141–3, 154
 Wyant, Lita, 73, 144–6, 152
Tylee, Claire M., 189 n. 2
Tyler, Elisina, 9, 77, 160
Tyler, Royall, 9

Unadjusted Girl, The, 68–9
urbanization, 45–6

Valley of Decision, The, 10
Velázquez, Diego, 25

"Verdict, The," 88
Victorianism, 1, 39, 45, 51, 54, 57, 61, 62, 68–9
Vita-Finzi, Penelope, 13, 162, 165, 168
voluntary motherhood, 54–5

Wagner-Martin, Linda, 9, 16, 171
Waid, Candace, 12, 138–9, 188 n. 4
Waugh, Evelyn, 9
Wegener, Frederick, 13, 165, 165–6
Weinstein, Arnold, 132–3, 141, 142, 143, 148, 157
Wells, H. G., 9
Werlock, Abby, 169, 173, 174, 191 n. 1
Wershoven, Carol, 12
Wharton, Edith
 aesthetics of, 13, 21–2, 44, 128, 162–5, 166–8, 179–80
 affair with Fullerton, William Morton, 4–5, 22–3, 52–3, 148–9, 153, 185 n. 4, 185 n. 5, 186 n. 1, 187 n. 9
 antimodernism of, 2, 13, 19–20, 21–22, 44, 144, 159, 165–74, 181
 anxiety about male power, 76, 78–9, 83–4, 99
 attitude toward United States, 3, 9–10
 attitude toward World War I, 7–8, 101–3
 charity work during World War I, 7, 77, 102
 decoration of houses, 6
 dismissal of local colorists, 11
 divorce from Wharton, Teddy, 5–7, 140, 152, 153
 early life, 3
 education of, 4
 female friends of, 76–7
 friendships with modernists, 9
 and gardens, 77, 160
 interest in anthropology, 125–6

Wharton, Edith—*continued*
  interest in modernism, 1, 2, 8, 14, 181–3
  interest in motherhood, 13, 177
  interest in popular culture, 10, 181
  male friends of, 18, 76, 77–8, 85
  marriage of to Edward Wharton, 4, 5–6, 22, 153
  as professional writer, 11–2, 76, 77, 160, 183 n. 3
  as realist writer, 11–12
  relationship with mother, 12, 71
  on single women, 66–7
  travels in Europe of, 3, 189 n. 7
  trips to the front during World War I, 7, 104, 111
  trips to North Africa, 79–80
  use of male narrators, 84–5, 93
  works: see *under individual titles*
Wharton, Edward "Teddy", 153, 171
  extramarital affair of, 6
  marriage of to Edith Newbold Jones, 4, 5–6, 22, 153
  mental illness of, 6, 22, 153
  as model for Lenman, 189 n. 3
White, Barbara, 84, 95
white slavery scare, 64–6
Wilder, Thornton, 8
Williams, William Carlos, 44
Wilson, Edmund, 160
Winthrop, Edgerton, 79, 102
Wolff, Cynthia Griffin, 7, 11, 13, 94, 133, 162, 173, 190 n. 2
women, 17, 45–6, 132
  changes in lives of, 54, 57–8
  in the city, 45–6, 64, 67, 72
  and economics, 47, 55, 67–8, 133, 188 n. 7
  and heterosexuality, 63, 67
  in *The Reef*, 41
  "traffic in," 75, 116–17
  Wharton's interest in, 2, 12, 60, 73
Woods, Susan, 155
Woolf, Virginia, 8, 14, 43, 140, 149, 166, 178, 191 n. 3
  "Mr. Bennett and Mrs. Brown," 14
  Mrs. Dalloway, 160
  To the Lighthouse, 140–1, 142, 146, 148, 149, 154, 155
World War I, 3, 7–8, 14, 19, 46, 101–2, 182
  atrocity stories about, 65
  moral problems raised by, 106
  rhetoric of, 127
  as war of culture, 8, 19, 127–8
  Wharton's propaganda for, 7, 102, 106
  and white slavery scare, 65
  see also "Coming Home;" A Son at the Front
World War II, 3, 55
Writing of Fiction, The, 19–20, 128, 163–5, 166, 168

Xingu and Other Stories, 85, 88, 97, 103

Yale University, 186 n. 6

Previously Published Works

*At Home, At War: Domesticity and World War I
in American Literature*